The BUTTERFLY CAFÉ

DIANE HAWLEY NAGATOMO

Black Rose Writing | Texas

ISBN: 978-1-68513-225-5
PUBLISHED BY BLACK ROSE WRITING
www.blackrosewriting.com

Printed in the United States of America
Suggested Retail Price (SRP) $22.95

The Butterfly Café is printed in Baskerville

*As a planet-friendly publisher, Black Rose Writing does its best to eliminate unnecessary waste to reduce paper usage and energy costs, while never compromising the reading experience. As a result, the final word count vs. page count may not meet common expectations.

For my family

Praise for
The Butterfly Café

"In Nagatomo's riveting debut, the newly widowed, yet ever resilient American Jessie Yamada navigates secrets and scandals in her Japanese husband's past, as she struggles to reconstruct her life. *The Butterfly Café* presents a fully contemporary view of Japan, with vividly drawn complicated characters, while imparting fascinating glimpses of the country's history. But most of all, it's a celebration of second chances and found families. Also, there are cookies. This is the novel I've been waiting for."

–Suzanne Kamata,
author of award winning *The Baseball Widow*

"*The Butterfly Café* is a compulsive page-turner that radiates a warm humanity. Its heroine is wonderfully fallible but also inspiringly decent, looking for and often finding the best in those around her. In despair on finding herself in the most challenging of circumstances after her Japanese husband's death in a car accident, Jessie Yamada forges a new path in life with the assistance of kind friends, developing her own resilience and strength in the process and unexpectedly finding happiness and fulfilment. It's a tale that just may go some way towards restoring your faith in your fellow human beings in these troubled times."

–Lea O'Harra,
author of *Dead Reckoning*

"'It takes a village to raise a child...' and Jessica finds one when her husband dies unexpectedly and she inherits a cafe from his grandmother. With engaging characters, and more than a sprinkling of Japanese history, customs, and family relations, this is a great read."

–Rebecca Otowa,
author of *The Mad Kyoto Shoe Swapper and Other Stories*

"Diane Nagatomo immerses the reader in Japanese culture in this page-turner about an American woman whose Japanese husband is killed, leaving her with his gambling debts and sordid secrets. It's a story of loss, finding oneself, true friendship, and second-chance romance."

–Muriel Ellis Pritchett,
author of *Sour Grapes and Balmy Knight*

"Diane Hawley Nagatomo's *The Butterfly Café* is a lovely, engaging romance full of twists, turns and surprises, as sweet as its title. Five stars!"

–Patti Liszkay,
author of *The Equal and Opposite Reactions Trilogy*

The BUTTERFLY CAFÉ

CHAPTER ONE

"Jimmy!" Jessie shouted into the phone for the third time.

"Mghhhmh? Hmmzz?"

"Wake up!"

"Jessie?" Jimmy said groggily, "Wha-whasa time?"

"Sorry for calling this late. But I didn't know what else to do. The cop said I had to hurry. But how can I hurry when it's the middle of the night and the trains aren't running?"

"Cop?" Jimmy was beginning to shake the sleep out of his voice. "What cop?"

"The cop that called to tell me that Kiyoshi's been in an accident."

"Oh, fuck!" Jimmy exclaimed, now fully awake. "How serious is it?"

"I don't know. I was sound asleep and could barely understand the guy's Japanese. The only thing I know for sure is that I have to hurry. I have to be there to sign for an operation or procedure or something."

"Be where?"

"Somewhere in Nagano. Kiyoshi went there with Chinese clients to play golf yesterday. Oh, god, Jimmy. What am I supposed to do? The guy said to come immediately, but it's the middle of the night, and the trains aren't running and—"

"Jessie! Stop! Calm down! You go by car."

"Drive?"

"Look, I know Kiyoshi's got his rules and all about you not driving his precious car. But surely even he'd make an exception for something like this."

"But—"

"You didn't do anything stupid and let your license expire, did you?"

"No. But I haven't driven since we were teaching in Gumma. And never in Tokyo."

"Well, there's no way I can take you because I was out last night, and I'm pretty sure I smell like the bottom of a whisky bottle. Yuya can't either because he and Kizuna are visiting his parents this weekend. He's got our car."

"Oh, shit. I'm going to have to drive."

"Look, I'll come with you. I'll navigate."

"I can't ask you to do that. You're probably busy tomorrow and—"

"Do you want to go all by yourself or not?"

Jessie choked out a sob of relief. "You're the best friend ever."

"Aren't I, though? Listen, make some coffee and give me half an hour. It shouldn't be hard to get a taxi from here even though it's so late."

Jessie shivered as she tugged on a pair of jeans and slipped a navy wool sweater over her head. She splashed water on her face, ran the brush through her shoulder-length brown hair, and tied it back into a ponytail. She packed pajamas, underwear, and toiletries for Kiyoshi, hoping that if she showed up with his stuff, he would be less upset with her for using the car. Then, feeling a bit like a thief, she unlocked the bottom drawer in the desk. An ace of hearts fluttered to the floor as it opened, making her wonder if he had rigged it to see if it was opened when he wasn't around. While rummaging for the keys, her eyes fell on his registered seal in its handmade case, and she put it in her purse in case he needed it.

Jessie prayed that the accident was nothing serious. Because if Kiyoshi had to recuperate at home, it wouldn't be just a simple matter of having him underfoot day and night in their cramped sixty-eight-square-meter company apartment. She would have to cancel all her private English conversation lessons. She couldn't risk him finding out that she had been teaching on the sly, no matter how badly she needed the money.

She tiptoed into Miya's room and looked down at her daughter, her dark brown hair splayed across the pillow. Miya had inherited Kiyoshi's good looks—his creamy complexion, full lips, and delicately structured chin. But thank God, not his nasty temper. The way Miya scrunched up her pointy little nose and flashed her hazel eyes when she was mad over something—like not being allowed on Thunder Mountain at Tokyo Disneyland for being too short—was more like Jessie's dad when he got going on some topic of social injustice. Not like Kiyoshi, who could hold a grudge for days. Miya had kicked her quilt to the floor and was mumbling something about the kindergarten's pet rabbit. As Jessie pulled it back over her, she wondered for the millionth time how she had created this perfect little human with a man she had hardly known.

It was all a blur now, but Kiyoshi had been as charismatic as a cult leader when she first met him. He pursued her in a manner that would shame every Harlequin romance hero. He lavished her with expensive dinners. He hung on her every word and made her feel beautiful, important, and smart. In bed, he was nothing short of a magician. And, perhaps even most importantly, he provided a good reason for staying in Japan after her teaching contract with the JET program had ended. Just a month after meeting him in a quaint café in Shimokitazawa (where he had literally charmed the pants right off her three hours later), she was hopping on an airplane bound for Guam to go get married. Without telling a single soul, not even Jimmy. Under her new husband's spell, she didn't have a single coherent thought running through her head when he suggested making a baby in their honeymoon suite. By the time she had come to her senses and realized that she had married a walking firecracker, she was stuck with him. But even if a time machine magically appeared and offered the chance to go back and change everything, she knew she wouldn't take it. Not if it meant there would be no Miya.

It was funny how the housewives in Fujimi Corporation Housing Complex were always teasing Jessie for having landed a husband as handsome as an anime hero. She was pretty sure they wondered among themselves how someone like her had managed to do that, but she wasn't always this dowdy. It wasn't just that extra pregnancy weight. There was a time her hair was highlighted and layered, and she never left the house without, as her grandmother liked to say, putting on her face. But new clothes, fancy haircuts, and nice makeup to accentuate her pale blue eyes cost money. It was hard enough to manage their household on what Kiyoshi gave her every month, let alone use any of it on herself. Yeah, the neighbors thought Jessie was lucky, all right. But honestly? She was more than a little envious of her next-door neighbor for her short, bespectacled, and half-bald husband, who always wore suits a tad too large. Through their walls, nothing but laughter was heard.

There was a quiet rap on the door, and Jessie hurried to let Jimmy in.

"Any news?" he asked.

"Not since that phone call from the cops." Jessie handed him a thermos of coffee and got a whiff of his breath. "I guess it's good that I'm driving because you do stink."

He flashed an apologetic smile, exposing teeth that looked like the result of extensive orthodontic work but were from growing up on a Nebraska dairy farm where he and his siblings guzzled milk as if it had been pumped from a fountain. He popped a mint into his mouth and asked, "Did you talk to Kiyoshi yet?"

Jessie shook her head.

"Maybe there isn't a good signal. You know what the countryside can be like."

They managed to get Miya down three flights of stairs, over to the parking lot, and into the car without waking her. While the engine was warming up, Jessie typed the address the cop had given her into the navigation system. The expressway was practically empty, and they made excellent time, stopping only twice to go to the bathroom and refuel on coffee. It hadn't occurred to either of them that it would be this icy in November, so the final stretch of the trip on the dark, twisty, mountainous roads was harrowing. If she hadn't been clutching the steering wheel and driving like an old lady going to church when she came around one hairpin curve, she never would have seen that family of monkeys crossing the road. When they finally arrived at the hospital, a pale wintry sun was rising over the mountains, and Jessie was a nervous wreck. Her arms and shoulders ached with tension and her eyes burned from lack of sleep. As she parked the car, the whole purpose of the trip came back to her: somewhere in that building was her injured husband.

"Mommy, are we running away from home with Uncle Jimmy?" came Miya's sleepy voice from the back seat after Jessie switched off the engine.

"Of course not, sweetie," Jessie said, wondering how much Miya understood about her parents' rocky relationship. "Daddy's been in an accident, and we've come to get him. Uncle Jimmy came along to give directions so I wouldn't get lost."

The night clerk in the emergency room froze when they approached her, gaping at them as if they were aliens from the future.

"We're here about Kiyoshi Yamada," said Jimmy in fluent Japanese.

The woman gathered herself and pointed toward the swinging doors. "Dr. Miyagawa is expecting you in his office."

Jimmy nodded at Jessie and then turned to Miya. "Hey, Kiddo. Let's go check out what's in those vending machines over there."

Jessie rapped on the doctor's door and stuck her head in. A white-haired man with a lined forehead stubbed out a cigarette into an overflowing ashtray and beckoned her to come in. He moved a towering stack of files to make space for Jessie to sit. Giving no indication of surprise that she was a foreigner, he asked if she preferred speaking in English or Japanese. She answered English. Something about his manner scared her, and she wasn't sure if her brain would operate in Japanese.

"Where's my husband? When can I see him?"

The doctor knitted his bushy white eyebrows together. "I'm afraid the accident was quite serious." His accent suggested that he had spent a significant amount of time in the UK.

"But there's an operation or something you can do, right?"

The doctor slid a box of tissues across his desk with his nicotine-stained fingers. "I'm terribly sorry."

Five minutes later, Jessie returned to the waiting room, her eyes red and swollen. Blinking back tears, she shook her head at Jimmy. "Miya," she whispered hoarsely, "I need you to stay here with the nurses for a few minutes. Jimmy and I have to do something. But we'll be right back."

As soon as they were out of Miya's sight, Jessie burst into tears. "Oh, Jimmy! It's far worse than I'd imagined. Kiyoshi's neck is broken and—"

"Oh, Jessie, I'm so—"

"He's paralyzed, Jimmy. Paralyzed! And brain dead!"

Jimmy wound his arm around her shoulder and supported her as they followed the nurse down a long passage reeking of disinfectant. From the way the lighting was, it was impossible to tell if it was night or day.

"I told them you were my brother. Just in case they wouldn't let you come in with me, I told them that. I can't do this by myself. I just can't!"

"Shh. You don't have to. I'm here. I won't leave you."

When they entered the ICU, Jessie thought that the person hooked up to the beeping and flashing machines was someone else and that the cops had been wrong. But when she came closer to the bed, she saw that there had been no mistake. She leaned over and gently shook Kiyoshi's shoulder. "Wake up! It's me."

The nurse laid her hand on Jessie's arm, empathy all over her face, before slipping out of the room to give them privacy. It had been many years since Jessie last prayed, but she knelt by the bed. While the prayers came easily, the miracle did not.

"And there's more bad news, I'm afraid," the doctor said a little while later in a small windowless conference room outside the ICU. He paused when a nurse carried in cups of steaming hot green tea. He waited for Jessie and Jimmy to pick up theirs before continuing. "Mrs. Yamada, we need to talk about the other passen—"

"Oh, I didn't even think about them! Are they okay? I need to call the company. They need to know, right? And what about the embassy? Do we have to contact the Chinese embassy?" Jessie's stomach heaved. She set the teacup down, wondering if she would make it to the wastepaper basket in the corner.

The doctor opened the file in front of him again and glanced through it. "There was only one other passenger in the car," he said. "I'm very sorry to tell you this, but she was killed in the accident. And I don't think she was Chinese."

"Kiyoshi was with a *woman*?"

"A much older woman," he added quickly. "His grandmother, I believe. According to the insurance card in her wallet, her name was Sachiko Yamada, and she was eighty-three years old. This is your husband's grandmother, correct? Or perhaps," he said with some uncertainty, "an aunt?"

"B-but my husband didn't have any relatives. They all died years ago. It must be a mistake."

"I will ask the police to check again." The doctor closed the file, leaned forward slightly, and cleared his throat. "The EKG shows no neurological activity. It's merely the respirator that is keeping Mr. Yamada alive."

Jessie's teeth began to chatter. "Are you sure? Absolutely sure that there's no hope?"

"I'm sorry," he said. "I know this is difficult for you. But a strict procedure must be followed in cases like this."

"But my daughter…she needs to…we need to…"

"You'll have a chance to say a proper goodbye. But is there anyone else you'd like to call? Someone who also needs to come?"

Jessie shook her head.

The doctor placed the papers on the table and pointed to each place she needed to make an imprint of the Yamada seal. Jessie knew she was essentially signing Kiyoshi's death warrant, and when the document was completed, it was spotted with tears.

"I do not mean to sound insensitive," the doctor said quietly, "but you should be aware that once I file the death report, your husband's bank accounts will be frozen. That is the law. If my daughter was in the same situation, I'd advise her to make sure she had enough funds to last for at least a month."

"But I don't have the cash cards. Kiyoshi keeps them."

The doctor coughed a little into his hand. "As his wife, you have every right to go through his pockets."

At the ATM in the hospital lobby, Jessie stared at the screen. She tried again, thinking she must have somehow punched in the wrong PINs. Same as before: insufficient funds. She couldn't even withdraw ten thousand yen.

Standing a few feet behind, Jimmy came forward when he heard Jessie swearing under her breath. "Is everything all right, Jess?"

"I don't know. It looks like there's no money in the accounts. In any of them."

"Maybe Kiyoshi moved it somewhere else."

That sounded exactly like something Kiyoshi would do without telling her, but remembering he was on his deathbed, she pushed those thoughts aside and removed her own bank card from a hidden pocket in her wallet. When the balance flashed on the screen, she knew the problem wasn't with the ATM.

"It has to be a mistake," Jimmy said after she made the withdrawal. "You'll straighten it out when the banks open."

"But what about what the doctor said? About the bank accounts becoming frozen after—"

"Don't worry about that right now."

Jessie went to get Miya, and as they walked back to the ICU, she did a very poor job telling her that she would have to say goodbye to her father. When they entered the room, Kiyoshi was no longer hooked up to the machines.

"Is that Daddy?"

"Yes."

"Did he get a big ouchy?"

"Yes. A very big ouchy."

"Does it hurt?"

"No. The doctor gave him a lot of medicine. He's sleeping right now."

Jessie sat down and pulled Miya onto her lap. Unsure whether Kiyoshi could hear her, she picked up his hand and began to talk. About the day they had met. Their honeymoon in Guam. The day that Miya was born. The trip they had taken to the beach in Chiba last summer. Jessie's voice wavered, and she realized that their marriage hadn't been all bad. There *had* been some good moments.

When Kiyoshi took his last breath, Jessie's eyes were so full of tears she could hardly see.

"Where is Daddy now?" Miya asked.

"With the angels," Jessie said, swallowing hard. And even though Kiyoshi was an atheist, she added, "He'll be watching you from heaven."

"Will he be back in time for Christmas?"

Jessie pulled her daughter close.

CHAPTER TWO

Two uniformed police officers opened the door to the conference room where Jessie, Jimmy, and Miya were sitting in stunned silence. "Mrs. Yamada?" said the older of the two in polite Japanese. "We'd like to speak with you now if that's all right,"

Jimmy tugged Miya's hand. "Let's go find something to eat."

The police moved aside for them to leave before stepping into the tiny room. They bowed, offered formulaic condolences, and sat across from Jessie with their backs ramrod straight and their hands placed formally on their knees.

The younger one started speaking. "We believe the driver swerved to avoid hitting an animal—possibly a deer. He lost control and hit a tree. The female passenger was thrown from the rented car and killed immediately. We're not sure how long it was before a delivery truck driver came across the accident—we estimate about ten or fifteen minutes. An ambulance was called, and as you know…"

To Jessie, his words sounded as if they were being spoken underwater.

"As difficult as this must be," he continued, "we need to ask you to identify the body and sign the appropriate papers for your husband's grandmother."

"Excuse me?"

"Unless there's someone else in the family who could do it. A blood relative? A Japanese person?"

"My husband told me that his grandmother was dead."

"Maybe that was the other grandmother."

Jessie hadn't considered that. But she knew nothing about either side of Kiyoshi's family. She had simply believed him when he said he was completely alone, that his family was all gone.

"Dr. Miyagawa informed us that you were unsure," said the older one. "So, we checked. The woman is on the Yamada family register. As are you and your daughter."

"The family register?"

"When the priests arrive," he continued, "you can ask them. They will know more."

"Priests?" How in the world did the Catholics figure into all of this?

"Yes. We learned from Mr. Kanemitsu, the proprietor at the inn where Mr. Yamada and the elderly Mrs. Yamada were staying, that they were here for a memorial service at the temple."

"Oh," Jessie said, realizing they were talking about Buddhist priests and some sort of Buddhist ceremony. She twisted a length of hair around her finger and tugged it until a patch of pain on her scalp became unbearable.

The police insisted she was the next of kin, and with no strength to argue, she followed them to the hospital morgue. There, she declared that to the best of her knowledge the woman killed in the accident (a person she had never laid eyes on before) was eighty-three-year-old Sachiko Yamada, a resident of Omori, Tokyo. For the second time that day, the Yamada seal was stamped on an official death certificate. And with that action, the remains of her husband and his alleged grandmother were now her responsibility.

Jimmy and Miya were in the waiting room when she got back. Her entire body felt numb, and when she sat down, Miya climbed into her lap and put her thumb in her mouth. Jessie didn't reprimand her, even though it had been more than a year since she had broken that habit.

There was another knock on the door, and a different stranger poked his head in. "Mrs. Yamada?" he said, speaking in rapid but heavily accented English. "I'm from Mizumori Temple."

Wearing gray sweatpants and a hoodie and sporting a buzz haircut, Jessie thought the man seemed more like a high school gym teacher than a Buddhist priest. It turned out she wasn't totally wrong.

"I'm Taka Matsumura," he said. "My father is head priest at the temple, and he'll be here soon. I teach math in junior high school, but I am priest, too. And I speak English a little because of working holiday in Australia when I was a student. So, my father asked me to come and explain. And help with decisions. About funerals and stuff. The doctor called to say that the younger Mrs. Yamada is gaijin. Oh, excuse me. I should say foreigner, not gaijin. I know some people don't like that. Sorry! Anyway, here I am, straight from school to help you. I will do my best, so please excuse my broken English."

"Thank you for coming, Mr. Matsumura. Your English is great." Jessie answered, her voice hoarse with tears. "But I'm sorry to take you away from work."

"Call me Taka," he said, shaking their hands in a very un-Japanese manner. "No worries about work. I often have to leave school to do temple business. But let me say, I'm very sorry about Mr. Kiyoshi Yamada and Mrs. Sachiko Yamada."

"Thank you for your kind words. I'm so glad you're here," Jessie said truthfully. "Did you know them?"

"Well, I know Sachiko. Everyone calls her that, and so do I. She comes every year for anniversary ceremony. Sometimes I'm busy, so I don't see her, but sometimes I do."

"Anniversary ceremony?" asked Jessie.

"The ceremony of the day her daughter died. My father always prays for it. This year Mr. Yamada was here, too. We were all quite surprised about that. So, by the way, do you know Japanese funerals? Foreign funerals are most different, I believe."

Jessie hadn't even thought that far ahead, but, of course, Kiyoshi needed a funeral. His grandmother, too. She didn't have a clue what to expect because the only funeral she had ever been to in her life was Grandma Frances's. And considering the way her father and his hippie friends had conducted the service themselves, that was hardly anything to go by.

While Taka explained what it took to get a Japanese person properly sent off into the afterlife, it was becoming evident that the money she withdrew earlier wouldn't go far at all.

"Um, maybe we could have a simple service." Jessie didn't want to sound like she was asking for the bargain plan, but it was best to be upfront with the fact that she didn't have any money.

"But Sachiko's funeral is paid up," Taka said. "Didn't you know?"

Jessie shook her head.

"Yes, she arranged that a long time ago. But not Mr. Yamada. He did not. But then, why would he? He was still a young man."

Jessie reached for the box of tissues and wiped her eyes again.

"Of course, the Yamada grave is ready because Mr. Okada planned ahead."

"I'm sorry," Jessie said. "But who's Mr. Okada?"

"Mr. Yamada's grandfather, of course," Taka answered. "He bought the space next to Okada family graves for Sachiko. Considering the circumstances, it was most unusual."

Jessie glanced over at Jimmy, who seemed just as confused as she was. "What do you mean the circumstances were unusual?" she asked.

"Because Sachiko was mistress, of course," Taka replied. Not noticing their surprise at how the conversation had veered from making funeral arrangements for Jessie's family to what seemed to be local gossip, he continued. "It was very unusual to buy a grave. Everyone was shocked. My grandfather was shocked. But," he added hastily as if there was some need to apologize, "not in bad way, of course. Just shocked way. But Okada family people felt insulted, especially with such a big headstone. A very expensive headstone, so grandfather was happy for long time. But now all that story is old. It's forgotten. And besides, everybody is dead anyway."

"Oh, I see," Jessie said, not seeing anything much at all.

"Now it's all about the love story," said Taka. "Who cares about the scandal now?"

"Scandal?" Jessie was pretty sure that Taka wouldn't be this forthcoming with such details if he were speaking to them in Japanese.

"Well," he continued. "Back then, it was a scandal. Especially for the Okada family. After all, Sachiko wasn't even twenty when Mr. Yamada fell in love and bought her geisha contract. But you know what they say: love is love. And you can't do anything about that."

Just as that was sinking in, an older man entered the room looking exactly like you'd expect a Buddhist priest to look: round, bald, and in a dark kimono. Right behind him was another man wearing a black suit and a somber expression. Taka's father and the Fuji Sunrise Memorial Enterprises representative expressed their condolences and produced business cards. Jessie pushed aside her embarrassment and asked Taka to make it perfectly clear that she really did not have any money. They had probably never been asked for a funeral discount before, but after some discussion, they compromised and agreed to allow some of the money earmarked for the grandmother's funeral to go toward her grandson's.

Unfortunately, that could not apply to the post-life Buddhist name the grandmother had ordered from the temple. Maybe it was a big deal for Japanese people, but unless Jessie was willing to sell a kidney to pay for it, Kiyoshi would have to make do with the earthly name he already had. There was no way Jessie had an extra million yen lying around to get him a new one. The Dharma name was supposed to prevent the return of the deceased, but she was just going to have to take her chances with that.

A little while later, Jessie realized she hadn't contacted her mother since she had sent her a brief text before leaving the house. Her phone battery had died somewhere halfway to Nagano, and when she plugged it in to recharge, dozens of concerned messages popped up.

"Jessie!" her mother exclaimed, picking up on the first ring. "We've been praying nonstop for Kiyoshi's speedy recovery."

Jessie wanted to cry again, but she had no more tears left. "He's gone, Mom. There wasn't anything the doctors could do."

"Oh, dear sweet Jesus in heaven! The good Lord must have had a plan to call that young man home."

It took a moment for Jessie to understand that her mother was acting on autopilot. Because she, of all people, would never be able to forget the fact that Kiyoshi was an atheist and wouldn't be dining with Jesus any time soon.

"I'm not sure if Tom and I can get away for the funeral," her mother said. "And you know your sister's wedding plans are taking—"

"It's okay," Jessie said before she got ideas in her head about coming. "It's just going to be a small ceremony here. Tomorrow. There isn't enough time for you to come." The last thing she needed was her mother and Bible-thumping stepfather at a Buddhist funeral behaving as if they were in the midst of some kind of devil-worshiping sacrifice. She said nothing about Kiyoshi's grandmother because how could she even begin explaining what she herself didn't understand?

"What about John?" her mother asked. "Did you call him yet?"

"No, but I'll call Daddy next." Jessie would have given anything to have him hold her in one of his great big bear hugs. But the other last thing in the world she needed was for him to try to come to Japan. He would never get past the drug-sniffing dogs at the airport.

"Oh, Jessie. You're so young to be a widow. Too young. Such a tragedy." Her mother's voice was velvet with concern.

Jessie sniffed. Until that precise moment, she hadn't thought of herself as such. Widows were old—like those ladies from the church who always sat together in the front pew at Sunday services.

"How will you ever manage, dear?"

Jessie reached for the tissues again and blew her nose. "I don't know, Mom, but—"

"It'll be a tight squeeze. You'll have to double up, just like in the old days. Until after your sister's wedding. Until Bethany moves in with Justin. Only this time, Miya will be with you."

"Huh?"

"When you come back."

"I don't think—"

"What better place to be than with your own kind at a time like this?"

Jessie discovered that old cliché was true. A person's life could flash before their very eyes. Her entire future was being laid out for her.

"I'll talk to Reverend Bob's wife and make sure she knows that Miya will enroll in the school soon." Her mom added, "Honey, the Lord works in mysterious ways. You never know what his divine plan is, but sometimes things turn out for—"

"The doctor's just come in," Jessie lied. "Sorry, but I've got to go sign some papers." She switched off her phone and stared blankly at the wall.

Several hours later, Jessie and Miya huddled in the back seat while Jimmy drove to the inn where Kiyoshi and his grandmother had been staying. Jimmy caught Jessie's eye at a traffic light in the rearview mirror. "I'm really sorry," he said quietly. "About everything. I didn't mean…"

Unable to speak, Jessie nodded and swallowed hard. A tear slid down her cheek when she remembered all the times she thought things far worse than what Jimmy ever said. All he did was state the truth: Kiyoshi was controlling, domineering, and volatile. All he ever said was that she would be better off if she left him. That he hated seeing her orchestrate her every move by anticipating Kiyoshi's unpredictable reactions. The only thing Jimmy was guilty of was urging her to take her life back.

But how many times had she wished that Kiyoshi were dead? How many times did she think that would make things so much easier for her? She wouldn't have to worry about some old fart of a judge giving him custody of Miya because he worked for a big whoopty-do Japanese trading company, and she had no steady job and a meager bank account. What a fool she had been for pooling all her savings with his when they got married, for not knowing that joint bank accounts didn't exist in Japan. It didn't matter how much money had been put aside toward their dream house— because she had absolutely no intention of moving anywhere with him. Forget the dream house—what she dreamed about now was having a fresh start. With Miya.

Driving away from the hospital where her husband's body lay, Jessie told herself that she never actually wanted Kiyoshi to *die*. That thinking those thoughts didn't *cause* his death. Her stomach churned like she had polished off a container full of battery acid, and the weight of Miya leaning against her was the only thing preventing her from screaming at the top of her lungs. She squeezed her eyes shut and wished she could take every last one of those thoughts back.

As soon as the three arrived at the inn, the proprietor rushed out to greet them. Mr. Kanemitsu ushered them to a Western-style reception room that was quite warm, thanks to a kerosene stove giving off noxious fumes in the corner. It looked like a dozen old ladies had banded together in a mad frenzy to crochet enough doilies to cover everything in sight. Jessie bent to pick up an antimacassar she had knocked off the arm of the sofa and sat down. Miya climbed into her lap and didn't even point at the Barbie in a crocheted hoop skirt sitting astride a tissue box on the table in front of them.

A woman in a plaid woolen kimono came in with a tray of tea, and while she poured, Mr. Kanemitsu spoke to them in a country dialect that was hard to follow. But they immediately understood when he suggested they might like to refresh themselves in the inn's hot springs. A therapeutic soak was precisely what they all needed.

CHAPTER THREE

Jessie and Miya got undressed and stored their clothes in pink plastic baskets. They stepped into the steaming bathroom, and squatting on two wooden stools next to the spigots against the wall, they scrubbed themselves from head to toe and rinsed off. They stuck their toes into the nearest bath, but it was too hot. Another tub was filled with cooler, milky white water. They eased in, and when Jessie saw the sign above the tub saying that this water was good for rejuvenating skin cells, she took a deep breath and submerged her entire body. Feeling a hundred years old, she needed all the rejuvenating help she could get. Jessie was relieved that they had the place to themselves and that there'd be no need to make small talk with some naked granny who was brave enough to strike up a conversation with a foreigner.

"Mommy! Look!" Miya climbed out of the tub and headed toward the door leading to the outdoor baths.

The wintry air felt good against their heated skin when they stepped naked into the garden and into the pond-like bath that smelled faintly of sulfur. They positioned themselves under the steaming waterfall, letting it cascade down onto their heads and shoulders. Snowflakes floated down from the sky, and Miya giggled as she caught them with her hands.

For a moment, Jessie forgot why they were there.

After the bath, the innkeeper's wife brought trays of soba noodles, but Jessie had no appetite. "Jimmy," she said after the woman had left the room, "I can manage things from tomorrow. You don't have to stay."

"Listen, I don't have classes on Mondays, and I already canceled Tuesday. I can stay until after the funerals."

"But you don't have to—"

"Nonsense," said Jimmy. "Don't forget what you did for me that time."

"What time?"

"The time when Spencer told me he had tested positive for HIV."

"Oh, that. But—"

"No buts. You were the one who went with me all the way to Tokyo to the testing center when we had only been in Japan for about a month and barely knew ten Japanese words between the two of us. And if it weren't for you telling everyone at work that I had the stomach flu when I was drunk the whole time waiting for the results, I would've gotten fired."

"Yeah," said Jessie, a disgusted look on her face. "I remember all that. Especially the part where the whole thing turned out to be a sick joke that creep cooked up."

"And don't forget," continued Jimmy, "I was responsible for your hangover from hell. The one that took you a week to recover from."

Jessie laughed despite everything. "Well, I suppose you do owe me for that." Over grilled chicken on sticks and copious amounts of sake from a local yakitori bar near their house, they cemented their friendship by conjuring up a multitude of ways to mutilate and maim the evil ex. Spencer, Jessie had slurred right before she threw up in the gutter on the way home, was her enemy for life.

Jimmy reached for her hand. "We help each other out. That's what we do. What we've always done."

Jessie nodded and blinked back another wave of tears. If Jimmy hadn't been her next-door neighbor, she wouldn't have lasted a year in Japan. She probably would have headed straight back to West Covina and reunited with her cheating ex-fiancé. Even though Gumma was way out in the Japanese boondocks, with her fundamentalist upbringing, it was about as exciting as could be. But still, besides a chain-smoking Australian who had been teaching English out of his kitchen for decades, Jimmy and Jessie were the only foreigners in town. They immediately bonded over their mutual hatred for their boss, a misogynistic homophobe whose singular goal in life seemed to be to make everyone miserable.

"Anyway, the point is this," said Jimmy. "I called Yuya. He's going to send my suit and one of Kizuna's dresses for Miya. They'll arrive tomorrow morning."

Jessie was touched by her friends' thoughtfulness. "You're one lucky man, you know that? Yuya is a keeper."

"That's why I married him. At least I did in America." Jimmy was always rankled that Japan still didn't recognize same-sex marriage. "So now, the only thing you'll need to do is get something for yourself."

"Huh?"

"Are you planning to go to the funerals in your jeans?"

After lunch, they got in the car and headed to the only supermarket in town with a clothing section on the second floor. While there was quite an assortment of funeral dresses—the cheapest of which was more than twenty-thousand yen—none of them fit Jessie. The one that covered her hips couldn't be buttoned up in the front. The resourceful saleslady returned with a black sweater, but even that didn't help.

"I'm going to have to wear my jeans," she said. "There's no way I can squeeze into anything here."

Jimmy mentioned Jessie's clothing crisis to Taka when they arrived at the temple, and Taka told his mother. She left the room and returned a few minutes later with an armful of black dresses.

"My mother-in-law was quite fat," the woman said cheerfully. "So I think her clothes would fit you perfectly."

Size-ten beggars couldn't afford to be choosers, so Jessie went to try one on. If only the mother-in-law had been tall as well as fat. But still, proper length was a minor issue. At least her boobs weren't hanging out.

After dinner, Taka came to see them at the inn. Mr. Kanemitsu's wife brought beer and dried squid snacks to the reception room with all the crocheted doilies. Taka and Mr. Kanemitsu, who were old friends, drank deeply and then had a refill. Jessie didn't touch her glass, afraid she would fall asleep instantly. All she wanted to do was stretch out and turn her brain off, but she didn't want to miss the chance to learn more about Kiyoshi's family. It was hard to follow Mr. Kanemitsu's dialect, even with Taka's translation. The more they drank, the more garbled the story became, but what she got out of them was this:

Kiyoshi's grandmother had been an Akasaka geisha and was given the name Cho-Cho. Jessie had always thought that was a made-up name, strictly from *Madame Butterfly* and Hollywood movies. But Cho-cho had been a popular geisha name in that house since the 1910s and one reserved for the most promising girls. Neither Taka nor Mr. Kanemitsu could remember precisely what Saburo Okada's father or grandfather had done, but a memorial stone in the city park with the family name engraved on it attested to the fact they had been significant. Saburo had worked for the government, but they couldn't remember the details of that either. What they did know was that he broke the rules men generally followed in those days when it came to maintaining a mistress. It was one thing to buy her geisha contract, but it was another to move right in with her and take her everywhere.

Jessie listened to their stories in stunned silence. How was it she knew nothing about any of this? How did Kiyoshi manage to keep it secret? And why? None of it made any sense. Had he been so ashamed of his gaijin wife that he couldn't introduce her to his grandmother? Or was it the other way around? Had he been ashamed of his grandmother for being a geisha?

"Do you happen to know," Jimmy asked Taka, "how Sachiko became a geisha in the first place?"

"Oh, yes," said Taka. "Foreigners like to know that. That movie— what was it called? Something about remembering the geisha? I know that movie was very popular with foreigners. Anyway, the story of Sachiko is quite different from movie."

Taka and Mr. Kanemitsu went back and forth in Japanese for a few minutes. Jessie looked at Jimmy, who was shaking his head. It seemed he couldn't catch what they were saying either.

"So," said Taka, downing his beer and pouring everyone another round, whether they wanted it or not. "They say Sachiko joined geisha house very young. Maybe first as maid. Then as apprentice. But after war, she became real geisha."

"Was her mother a geisha, too?" asked Jimmy.

"Oh, no. Parents had a shop. But they were killed in Tokyo firebombing. Her brothers and sisters, too," said Taka. "By the way, do you know about the firebombing?

Jessie shook her head, but before Taka had a chance to start explaining, Jimmy spoke up. "Yes, I do know about that. In fact, I was just reading about it the other day. The most destructive bombing raid in history. About a hundred thousand people— mostly civilians—were killed because of American incendiary bombs. More people than in Hiroshima or Nagasaki."

"Yes," said Taka. "We Japanese call it the 'Night of the Black Snow.' In just one night, so many people died. Almost all of Tokyo was burned down. Sachiko's whole family died in that. But she did not. For some reason, she was a lucky one. I think she escaped to a river or something and didn't get burned up. Somehow, she started working at geisha house. That was good for her, I guess. There were worse places for a child to end up. You can imagine. But the geisha house had food. And she was smart girl, they say. A pretty one, too. She learned the arts there. Singing, dancing, and lots of old-fashioned stuff like that. And, of course, she met Mr. Okada, and the love story began. Too bad he had heart attack. Poor Sachiko, with baby on the way and everything."

"But how did she manage then? After her..." Jessie wasn't sure what to call the guy. "Um, after Kiyoshi's grandfather died?"

"Mr. Okada bought a building in Akasaka. It was small, but Akasaka land always very expensive. And the building was in Sachiko's name. Family wanted it back, but it was hers, all legal, fair and square. She opened bar on first floor of building. It was called Sachiko's. I guess she wanted everyone to know for sure that it was hers. And the bar was very expensive kind. You know, company presidents and politicians drinking place. She was rich, but they say she lost much money when bubble economy burst in 1990s."

Mr. Kanemitsu got up, pulled a bottle of Johnny Walker from the cupboard, and yelled for his wife to bring ice. Jessie was too frazzled to think straight, and when Mr. Kanemitsu started to pour triple shots, she gave Jimmy a look. He put his hand over his glass, and they both stood. Miya had fallen asleep in front of the television in the corner, so Jimmy picked her up and carried her to their Japanese-style room, where futons were laid out for Jessie, Miya, and the fake brother.

Jessie fell asleep instantly but woke at three a.m. with her pillow soaked with tears. It hit her with a jolt. Her husband was dead. Gone forever. He would never see his daughter again. Never watch her grow up. Never walk her down the aisle when she gets married. Never be a grandfather. She shivered under the down covers and eventually dozed off as the sky was brightening.

Taka, who seemed remarkably perky considering all the alcohol he had consumed the night before, took them to the temple graveyard the following afternoon. The enormous Yamada headstone still had the chrysanthemums laid in front of it from Kiyoshi's mother's memorial service, but the purple and gold petals had been damaged by frost. Just a few meters away was the Okada headstone. No wonder the Okada family had been upset. If someone wanted to install his mistress right next door for all eternity, it probably should have been done with a bit less flash: their headstones were nearly identical in size. Jessie imagined the Okada spirits were having conniptions right about now over the pending arrival of their new neighbors.

They hurried back to the temple when snow began falling—not the big fluffy flakes that fall gently into your hair. It was the nasty kind that was mixed with rain and wind and knew its way under an umbrella.

"Taka," Jessie asked while warming her hands in front of a kerosene heater in a reception room in the temple. "Can you tell me anything about Kiyoshi's mother?" During last night's reminiscing, they hadn't said a thing about her. "What kind of cancer did she have? When did she die? Do you know?"

"Cancer?" he said, looking at her with surprise. "No, it wasn't cancer." With a hushed voice, he added, "I don't know if it good for me to tell you or not, but she did suicide. It was terrible thing. Hanging in front of child like that."

"W-what?"

"Kiyoshi was very small. Little guy. He found her after nap and crying so much, he went to look for neighbor." He lowered his voice even more. "They say there never was father. And that was probably suicide problem."

"Suicide," whispered Jessie in disbelief. Was that why Kiyoshi never talked about his mother? Maybe it was too painful. Or perhaps, shameful.

Just then, Taka's father came into the room with a yellowed manila folder containing the paperwork Sachiko had completed in 1999. "I've been trying to call this person," he said, pointing to the business card stapled at the top of one of the papers. "But the number's been discontinued. I googled the company's name, but it looks like it's no longer in existence. You will need to decide whether or not…"

As the ceremonial plans were finalized, Jessie grew sorry for Sachiko. It was beginning to look like her well-planned and pre-paid funeral was going to proceed with just Jessie, Jimmy, and Miya in attendance. Two and a half foreigners.

Jessie bet she never saw that one coming.

CHAPTER FOUR

Jessie was numb with exhaustion when the two funerals were finally over. She expected Miya to be up half the night since she had slept most of the way home in the car, but she crawled into bed and listlessly flipped through her picture books until falling asleep in a surprisingly short amount of time. Jessie removed Miya's thumb from her mouth and went to fix a cup of tea. Remembering Kiyoshi's bottle of whisky under the sink, she added a healthy splash to the tea. She read over her notes on the Buddhist care and feeding of the newly deceased and thought how horrified her parents would have been if they had seen her engaging in what they would call pagan rituals. Despite all the time and money expended, the funerals turned out to be sad little affairs in grand surroundings. For Sachiko's funeral, Taka's father was decked out in a gorgeous embroidered robe. His deep voice echoed throughout the temple as he performed the necessary chants for her spirit to make its way to the other side. Jessie, Miya, and Jimmy stood, sat, bowed, and lit incense by mimicking Taka and Mr. Kanemitsu—the only other people at her funeral.

Kiyoshi's section chief and general manager from Fujimi Corporation arrived the afternoon of Sachiko's funeral—just in time for Kiyoshi's wake. They got rip-roaring drunk in front of

Kiyoshi's casket and stumbled around bleary-eyed the next day at the funeral. It was a good thing that no one else from the company had come because the bar bill alone would have put Jessie in the poorhouse.

And then, there were the ceremonies at the crematorium, which were for family members only. The whole process had been a huge shock. While Taka's father chanted, a uniformed crematorium employee bowed deeply to the three mourners and then to the deceased before closing the coffin. Then he pushed a button. A door was raised, and Sachiko's coffin slid through it on a conveyer belt to the incinerator. The next day it was the same all over again for Kiyoshi's services. The chanting, the bowing. And moving the still-sizzling bones from the incinerator tray into the urns with extraordinarily long chopsticks. Jessie got up and added another splash of whisky to her cup, this time without the tea. She never imagined she would have to do anything like that with human bones even once in her life, let alone twice in two days.

She looked over at the urns housing her husband and his grandmother. They couldn't stay where they were on the sofa, and they needed the dining room table to eat. She brought a small foldable table in from the balcony, wiped it down, and covered it with a dark green tablecloth. It didn't look right as their temporary resting place, but that was the best she could do—all the other tablecloths had Disney characters on them. She arranged the candles and incense Taka had given her and rechecked her notes. Food offerings. That's what was missing.

A search through the cupboards for something that wouldn't involve cooking uncovered a box of Godiva chocolates from a student. But before putting them on a nice plate in front of the urns, she ate the entire package, washing it down with the rest of the whisky. Wondering what it would take to become an alcoholic, she set the empty whisky bottle in the trash.

Taka had said it was perfectly acceptable for them to eat the food offerings later, so she made ham and cheese sandwiches, covered them with plastic wrap, and set them in front of the urns. It was getting late, and she knew she should go to bed. Her body was exhausted, but her mind was racing around like it was training for the Olympics. Caring for her husband's and his grandmother's remains until their interment ceremony in forty-nine days was the least of her worries. She called Kiyoshi's banks on Monday, but they said they couldn't tell her anything over the phone. The snarky receptionist said she would have to go to the branch where the accounts were opened. It was a hassle, but she needed to track down their money. And that meant going all the way to Yokohama.

It occurred to her that nothing was stopping her from going through every single drawer in Kiyoshi's desk, even the locked one. Maybe the new bankbooks would be in it—but no such luck. Just the old ones that hadn't been updated for several years. She noticed the folder with copies of the documents she submitted when she had changed her visa status from spouse to permanent resident and pulled that out. Studying those papers for the first time, she found her and Miya's names as Kiyoshi's wife and child on the official family register. His mother was listed, with her dates of birth and death. But there was no mention of a father. The date of his grandmother's birth was recorded, but not her death. Well, obviously not, thought Jessie. Six months ago, she had been alive and kicking.

"At least now that I've got permanent residency," she mumbled, "they can't kick me out of the country. Husband or no husband!" A large belch came out of nowhere, and she set the papers down. It would be better to wait until after the whisky was out of her system before looking at anything else. But while shutting the drawer, she noticed some cash sticking out of an envelope. At least she could pay the utility bills tomorrow without having to go to the bank.

She turned on the laptop that Kiyoshi bought last year after he threw hers across the room. All contrite, he set everything up for her, passwords and all. She used it to correspond with her parents and people from her church back home. She googled Japanese recipes and Japanese language study sites on it. She read the news in English and in Japanese. Her thirty-three Facebook friends were mainly her relatives, with whom she sometimes shared videos of cute cats. Then she retrieved Jimmy's old iPad that she kept hidden in her bag of sanitary supplies in the bathroom. This was where her real digital life happened.

No longer needing to worry about her browser history, she logged into her alternate Gmail account on the laptop and answered a few emails from her students. She opened her secret Facebook account and scrolled through the posts in the foreign women's group. After chewing on her thumbnail for a moment, she took the plunge. *Hi, everyone*, she wrote. *My name is Jessie Yamada. I've been a member of this group for five years now. As you can see from my profile picture, I've been using an alias. This is my first posting here. My husband died in a car accident last week and…* She stopped, wondering how much she should write. But she decided to just say it all. *Now I'm alone with a five-year-old daughter. I'm having so many mixed feelings about this. My marriage wasn't happy, and I was planning to leave. I'm overwhelmed by everything and feeling terribly guilty. I don't really know why I'm writing or what I want to ask here. But if you all could send positive thoughts my way so that I can get through all this, I'd really appreciate it.*

She probably wouldn't have sent the message if it hadn't been for all that whisky. Within seconds, there were three likes and four supportive comments.

CHAPTER FIVE

On Monday morning, Miya went back to kindergarten, and Jessie went to Yokohama to clear things up with the banks. It turned out there had been no mistake. Kiyoshi's accounts were significantly in the red—something Jessie hadn't even known to be possible. The branch manager's irritating and condescending tone suggested that this predicament was somehow of her own making, and she escaped as quickly as she could. Feeling numb, she returned to Tokyo for her meeting at Kiyoshi's company. As she entered the office, a dozen of his coworkers jumped up from their desks to offer condolences. Jessie bowed and murmured back before Mr. Kato, the guy who had gotten as drunk as a skunk at Kiyoshi's wake, escorted her into a small conference room. Mr. Banno, an English speaker from the legal department, was there waiting. As soon as a uniformed office lady brought in cups of tea, they got down to business.

Mr. Banno slid a small, clear plastic box across the table containing the personal items from Kiyoshi's desk. Jessie nearly fainted with relief when he also handed her an envelope containing his December salary and winter bonus. They could survive on that for months. "Unfortunately," he said, "your husband borrowed against his retirement fund to buy a new car, so I'm sorry to say that money is no longer available."

Jessie didn't know how to respond. Their car was five years old.

"I'm also sorry," he added, "that he had defaulted on his life insurance payments, so, unfortunately, that means—"

Mr. Kato, drumming his fingers impatiently on the table, finally blurted out in Japanese, "Mrs. Yamada. Were you aware that your husband gambled online during working hours?"

Jessie knew that Kiyoshi liked to play pachinko, but this was the first she had heard of anything like that.

"There will be no censure because of the current circumstances. Therefore, the Yamada name will not be disgraced," said Mr. Kato.

Jessie stared at him. The way he spoke implied Kiyoshi had dodged a bullet by getting himself killed.

"You will go back to America soon, is that correct? We need your apartment for your husband's replacement. This is all very inconvenient for the company, you know. It's very irregular to have to make changes like this in the middle of the fiscal year, and we all will have to make sacrifices."

"Excuse me?"

"What Mr. Kato means," said Mr. Banno in English, "is that we know you'll be happier when you go home. When you return to your own family."

Jessie swallowed her anger. They didn't know a damn thing about her or her family. "Am I hearing this right? You're kicking us out? But Kiyoshi only died last week!"

"I'm so sorry." At least Mr. Banno had the decency to look embarrassed.

"And how much time do I have before you throw my daughter and me out into the streets?"

"Two weeks," said Mr. Kato, jumping in, this time in English. "We not hard people. We have heart. That's Japanese spirit. That's plenty of time for packing and going to America."

"Mrs. Yamada," Mr. Banno called out as Jessie hurried out of the room before she vomited on the table. "Please feel free to use our company's health insurance until the end of the year."

. . .

When Jessie got home, she was fuming. She yanked Kiyoshi's suits off the hangers and dumped them onto the straw tatami mats in their tiny Japanese-style room. Then his shirts, socks, and underwear. His shampoo, moisturizer, and hair tonic. His tennis racket, golf shoes, and wet suit. She swept his precious comic books from the bookshelf. The only thing that stopped her from taking a hammer to his J-pop CD collection was the fact that she would have to be the one to clean it all up.

Her phone rang, and she answered, thinking it was Jimmy calling to check how things went at Kiyoshi's company.

"Jessie! Why haven't you been answering your phone? I don't know how many times I've called."

Oh, crap. This was all she needed. "Sorry, Mom. I've been so busy. It's been so overwhelming."

Her mother's voice softened. "Of course, dear. I know you have so much on your plate right now. Now, tell me. How are you coping? How's Miya?"

"We're fine."

"Are you sure? Your voice sounds shaky."

Because she seemed so concerned, Jessie almost blurted everything out. Instead, she said she was taking it one day at a time.

"Honey, why don't you come home for Christmas? It's been such a long time since we spent the holidays together. We miss you."

"I miss you, too, Mom," she answered and realized it was true.

"I've been praying that you'll make it home in time for the celebrations. And you remember Noah Stevens, right? He's the one with the two little girls whose wife died last year of cancer. Well, he…"

And with that, the moment was killed. Jessie stopped her mother before she got too far into singing the praises of one of the most boring people on the planet as a potential replacement for Kiyoshi. "Look, Mom. Miya's kindergarten bus is due, and I've got to go pick her up."

"But honey—"

"I'll call after things get settled. I promise."

Jessie reached for the wine on the counter, poured the last inch into a mug, and took a swig. "Oh, shit," she muttered as she poured the wine-laced coffee down the drain. "I should've drunk it straight from the bottle." She put her head on the table and closed her eyes. What else was there to do but go home and live with her mother and Tom? They would welcome the prodigal daughter with open arms, pretending her wayward Japan years hadn't happened (despite the existence of Miya). But they would also get down to reprogramming her back into the Church of the Loving Christ. She would have to sit through Pastor Joe's bigoted sermons week after week. Ranting and raving about people like Jimmy and Yuya. About how most of the population was heading straight to hell, but members of their congregation were not. And Wednesday night services would be on top of that. She would have to follow their rules if she was under their roof, and church attendance would be one of them.

But that wouldn't be the worst of it. Miya would end up going to that half-baked school Jessie's dad had gotten her out of when he took her mom back to court when she was ten. The judge agreed Jessie would be better off in public school, and her three-month stint in the church's basement came to a screeching halt. She didn't understand the big deal it was at the time because the only thing she cared about was having access to all the books in the school library. But her half-sister Bethany hadn't been so lucky. That church school had narrowed her outlook on the world, making it practically impossible for her to go to college or get a regular job. Thanks to her drug-addled dad, Jessie was employable. She didn't care if Miya went to UCLA like she did, but she had higher aspirations for her daughter than for her to end up with a questionable high school diploma.

But what other option was there? Jessie was essentially broke. Possibly in colossal debt. All that money Kiyoshi swore they had been saving to buy a house turned out to be nothing but a big fat lie. She might have been able to manage for a while on the income from her private students if they weren't being kicked out of the cheap company housing. If she had more time, she could look for a regular job with a steady paycheck. Tears of hopelessness streamed down Jessie's face. Going back to California wouldn't be *that* bad, she told herself while ignoring the incoming calls from her mother.

.   .   .

Jessie grabbed Miya's arm before she could dash to the playground with the other children. She felt she would rather run around Tokyo Station stark naked than stand around and have the other mothers looking at her out of the corner of their eyes. Was she the last person in the Fujimi Corporate Housing Complex to know what a fuckup Kiyoshi had been at work?

"We've got to go straight home, Miya."

"But, Mommy. I want to—"

"Not today."

Miya looked up into Jessie's red-rimmed eyes, slipped her hand into her mother's, and they walked quietly home.

"Why's Daddy's stuff all over the floor?" Miya asked.

"I- I'm just organizing everything. Look," Jessie added with false cheerfulness. "Netflix is showing that princess movie you've wanted to see." She switched on the TV and opened the cupboard to get some cookies. Her breath hitched a little when she turned around and saw her daughter lying on the floor, rubbing the cashmere sweater that Kiyoshi always wore on the weekends against her face.

Jessie was back at the desk later that night, studying the calendar. Where would she go if she had to leave in just two weeks? And what the hell was she supposed to do with the urns? Would it be possible to move the interment ceremony ahead of the standard forty-nine-day period? She certainly couldn't be dragging human remains back to California just because of a technicality.

She should have smacked that bastard boss of Kiyoshi's right in the nose when he said the company was being generous in letting them live there for two weeks. Shit, if she could afford it, she would move out tomorrow. Kiyoshi's workplace gambling was almost up there with that guy in the accounting department who got caught with an under-aged hooker in a meeting room at seven in the morning. Everyone was *still* talking about that.

It was stupid to open the bankbooks again. All the negative balances that appeared when updating them at the bank had become permanently engraved in Jessie's brain. Just like the overdue statement from a loan company that came by special delivery a few days back. A fucking million yen! She was terrified to open the two envelopes that came in the mail that afternoon—one from Visa and the other from a loan company with the deceptive name of Promise. How much more debt did Kiyoshi have? How much was she going to be personally responsible for? And that didn't even include the money she had borrowed from Jimmy as a down payment toward Kiyoshi's funeral. Even with the double discount deal the temple had given her, she was still up to her eyeballs in funeral debt.

Breathe, she ordered herself, trying to keep her chest from exploding. Take deep breaths. In. Out. In. Out. But what little calm she managed to muster up evaporated when Jimmy texted to see how things had gone at the company.

Oh, just fucking terrific, she texted back, stabbing the keyboard on her phone with her index finger as if it was murdering baby cockroaches.

Within seconds, the phone rang. "They're kicking us out, Jimmy," Jessie whisper-yelled into the phone. As mad as she was, she didn't want to wake up Miya. "As soon as they possibly fucking can, they're kicking us out. We've got to move out of this fucking apartment. And I'm going to have to fucking move back to fucking California and send Miya to that fucking school."

"Are you drunk?"

"I wish I was drunk. In fact, I wish Kiyoshi was alive, so I could kill him again."

"What the hell happened, Jess? Oh! Never mind. Hang on a sec." A moment later, he was back on the line. "Listen. We're coming right over."

Less than fifteen minutes later, Jimmy and Yuya were at the door.

"How did you get here so fast?" Jessie asked.

"How could we not drop everything and come?" said Jimmy.

"But we did grab some emergency supplies first," added Yuya. Having lived in Sydney as a child with his parents, his voice still had an Australian twang. He set bottles of wine and some cheese, crackers, and chocolate on the table. Saying nothing about her mismatched wine glasses from the hundred-yen shop, he deftly twisted the cork with his own fancy corkscrew and released it from a 2012 Bordeaux. He looked like a Japanese version of a 1930s movie star: tall, dark, and handsome. He was about the same height as Jimmy but much more muscular. His build, he liked to boast, was not because of a gym membership but because of hard physical labor. Tonight, he wasn't wearing *tobi*-trousers, the uniform of construction workers. It was Armani jeans and a jacket that probably cost more than Jessie earned from several months of private teaching. Entirely befitting for a guy who owned his own company.

"This is exactly what I needed," Jessie said, taking a long sip of the wine. She took comfort in how indignant they were on her behalf when she told them about her visit to Kiyoshi's company. By the time she was on her second glass, she felt better but, at the same time, worse. "I have no idea how much debt there is," she sighed. "But I do know it's a hell of a lot more than my savings." She spread a slice of Camembert cheese on a cracker and ate it. Then, she said, attempting to be matter-of-fact, "I suppose I have no choice but to go back to California." Her eyes filled with tears, sad ones this time, when she added, "There's no other solution."

"Can't you stay and teach English?" asked Yuya.

"Maybe I could if I had more time before they throw us out of the apartment. I called all the schools, and no one is hiring in December. Not even that dispatch company with a terrible reputation. I even called them."

"Have you tried any of the international schools?" asked Jimmy. "I know it wouldn't be the right timing, but maybe there's an opening. You do have a teaching credential. And you used to be an actual high school English teacher. That's got to count for something."

"Yeah, I called them all, but it turns out licensed English teachers are a dime a dozen. One did ask me if I'd be able to teach chemistry. Not even in my wildest imagination," she added with a laugh. Then she sighed and said, "Why wasn't I smart like you, Jimmy? Why didn't I get my master's degree when we had all that free time at the board of education? Why was I such an idiot?"

Jimmy nodded sympathetically but didn't bring up the fact that he had repeatedly told her she should do something more useful back then than sit around reading racy romance novels.

"Oh," Jessie said. "I *did* get one offer, though."

"Really?" said Yuya.

"Yeah, it was for a Skype lesson. A private session. The guy explicitly asked for a female teacher under the age of thirty. Preferably blond. After midnight."

"And?" asked Jimmy.

"Well, it turns out I'm not ready to settle for just any job. Not yet."

"Jessie," said Yuya, changing the subject. "Did you ever find anyone who knew Kiyoshi's grandmother?"

"No, but I was thinking I should go over to her place to see if she had any neighbors or friends. It'd be pretty terrible if they filed a missing person's report and found out what happened that way."

"Where did she live?" asked Yuya.

"In Omori somewhere. Let me check on Google Maps." Jessie got the laptop and typed in the address. They watched as the camera zoomed in on a shabby three-story building. "That's it," she said. "She must have lived in one of the apartments."

"What's that on the first floor?" asked Jimmy.

"It looks like a coffee shop."

"I bet the owner knew her," said Yuya. "Maybe he's the landlord. You could get a key and go through her stuff."

"I've got enough to do with Kiyoshi's stuff here, let alone go poking around through hers."

"What if," Yuya said, "you can find out what happened between her and her grandson?"

"I never thought of that."

"And besides," Yuya added, "there might be some money."

"But that has nothing to do with me. She's not my grandmother."

"No. But she is Miya's great-grandmother. And that might count for something."

CHAPTER SIX

Jessie got off the train at Omori Station. Google Maps led her past pachinko parlors, hostess clubs, bars, and restaurants. She turned left at a Denny's and walked along a residential side street. On the other side of a park was a shopping arcade resembling the one in her neighborhood, but the shoppers here seemed quite elderly. She passed Piggy Piggy Pork Cutlet Restaurant, Hair and Make-Do Salon, and Watanabe Stationery before Google Maps announced that she had arrived at her destination. The blinds were drawn on the café and a closed sign was hung on the door. Jessie craned her neck for signs of someone living in one of the apartments above the café and wondered if she should go knock on the doors.

"Can I help you?"

Jessie jumped and turned to find a tiny woman, splay-legged, hands on her hips, and glaring up at her as if she were the ringleader of a gaijin crime syndicate. Jessie felt like she had been caught doing something illegal. "I-I'm looking for someone who knows Mrs. Yamada. Mrs. Sachiko Yamada."

"Why? You want to sell some English lessons?"

Jessie suppressed a nervous giggle. "No, I need to talk to someone who knows her. About something important."

"Well, go ahead. What is it?"

This wasn't how the visit to the grandmother's neighborhood was supposed to go. "So, you're her friend?"

"That's right. What do you want?"

Jessie mustered up as much polite language as possible and informed her that Sachiko Yamada had died in a car accident.

"And exactly how do you know that?"

"My husband was her grandson," Jessie said quietly. "Kiyoshi Yamada. And he was killed in the same accident."

The woman's face crumbled, and under her black hair and heavy make-up, Jessie could see that she was quite a bit older than she had first appeared. She unlocked the door to the café, flipped on the lights, and motioned Jessie to follow. Jessie gave a polite little cough the moment she stepped inside and started breathing through her mouth.

Cats emerged from behind the counter, under the table, and on top of the bookcase. They swarmed to the woman, rubbing against her and wrapping their tails around her legs. She nudged them back with her foot, grabbed a bag of kibble from a cupboard, and poured some into plastic margarine containers by the door. As she filled the water bowls up, Jessie took in the surroundings. The grimy tables, counter, and barstools were stacked with possibly every newspaper printed in the last decade. The walls were adorned with dusty pictures of butterflies, and a calendar from 2003 (also of butterflies) was taped on the wall. Next to the cash register was a ledger anchored by an abacus.

"You want something to drink?"

"Um...no, thank you."

"Just as well, I suppose. I don't know where anything is," the woman said as she went to crack a window.

Jessie's phone buzzed. It was Jimmy wanting to know how things were going. She messaged a quick response: *Bizarre!*

The woman sat down, produced some individually wrapped lozenges from her pocket, and held one out. Jessie took it, hoping the menthol would counteract the acrid smell penetrating her nostrils.

"How come I never heard anything about you?"

"I don't know," replied Jessie. "To be perfectly honest, I didn't know anything about Mrs. Yamada, either."

"How come Mr. Suzuki didn't come to tell me about this?"

"Who?"

"Sachiko's lawyer. He takes care of all her financial affairs."

"If he's the person whose business card the temple people had in Nagano, we couldn't get ahold of him. The number on his business card was disconnected."

"Well, of course, it was. Mr. Suzuki retired a long time ago." The woman looked at Jessie as if she were simply too foolish to figure that one out on her own. "He lives with his daughter by the river."

"Oh."

"Maybe I should give him a call," she said, attempting a threatening tone.

"Please do," Jessie insisted. Maybe he would know what the hell she was supposed to do next.

The woman pulled out a flip-open phone and made several loud calls to track him down. Then she snapped it shut and announced, "He'll be here soon."

"I'm really sorry that I was the one to bring you this bad news," Jessie said when she realized the woman was blinking back tears. "I'm sorry that you've lost your friend, Mrs.—"

"Watanabe." She reached into the sleeve of her sweater, pulled out a paper napkin, and dabbed at her eyes. "And you say Kiyoshi was also killed?"

"Yes. In the same accident." Jessie's eyes filled with tears, temporarily forgetting the financial fix he had left her in. "Did you know my husband, too?"

"Sure, I did. Ever since they moved here in…let me think back. Kiyoshi was in elementary school, and that was the year my son Taro…"

While the woman spoke, Jessie realized that growing up in Yokohama was another one of Kiyoshi's lies.

"Sachiko never said anything about Kiyoshi marrying a gaijin," continued Mrs. Watanabe. "But then, Sachiko never talked much about him after they had that big fight. Until recently, I thought he had moved to New York, Hong Kong, or somewhere."

"What big fight?"

"When Sachiko accused him of—" She stopped short and pursed her lips as if she had remembered she was supposed to be suspicious of Jessie.

"So, they lived above your shop all this time?" Jessie asked.

"Above my shop? No. I live there." She indicated the stationery shop next door. "With Taro. Sachiko lives here."

Jessie stared blankly at her before figuring that the owner of the café must be away—perhaps, from the look of things—on an extended trip. That would explain why the woman had the keys to the place. "Well, I suppose the landlord will want me to clear out her things, so they can rent the apartment to someone else."

"Huh?"

Jessie remembered that Taka had said everyone called Kiyoshi's grandmother by her first name, so she said, "Surely the landlord will want to rent out Sachiko's apartment."

"What landlord?"

It took a few seconds to get it. The butterflies everywhere began to make sense. "This is *Sachiko's* café?"

"Why, sure it is." Mrs. Watanabe swept off the mangy cat that had jumped on the table between them and added with a guffaw, "Whose café did you think it was? Mine?"

"I didn't realize Kiyoshi's grandmother had a café. I thought it was a bar."

"That was before she bought this building and moved here."

Just then, an elderly gentleman dashed through the door in a beautifully cut suit that smelled faintly of mothballs. The two old people talked about and pointed at Jessie for a good five minutes.

Finally, he turned to Jessie, bowed formally, and presented her with a business card.

Jessie responded by bowing in return. Then she handed him a copy of the family register that had been in Kiyoshi's desk and the hospital's death certificates. He studied the documents (with Mrs. Watanabe peering over his shoulder), making her glad that she had brought them to prove she was who she said she was.

"I'm very sorry for your loss," he said, bowing again. "And I'm sorry that you were unable to reach me last week. I had no idea. We weren't expecting Sachiko to come back until early December. She was planning to go to Kyoto after her trip to Nagano."

Then he took a handkerchief out of his pocket, thoroughly wiped down a chair, and sat next to Mrs. Watanabe. Jessie described Sachiko's wake and funeral, omitting that it had been somewhat watered down to accommodate Kiyoshi's. Mr. Suzuki and Mrs. Watanabe interrupted her every few sentences, and while they repeated everything back to each other, Jessie watched two cats hissing in the corner. She wondered if this was how Alice felt when she fell down that rabbit hole.

An hour later, Mrs. Watanabe said she had to go to feed her son, and Mr. Suzuki suggested they also get a bite to eat. He steered her past the restaurants on the street, saying that some things might be better said in more private surroundings.

They ended up at Denny's near the station, and after ordering the seafood pasta set of the day, he turned to her. "I'm sure you have many questions. But I need to be absolutely clear about the chain of events." He paused when the waitress set down mugs of corn soup. "Of course, I'll contact the doctor and the police to confirm, but you can fill me in for now."

Jessie repeated everything she had already said several times, but this time, he scribbled in the notebook he had taken from his breast pocket.

"So, Sachiko passed away at the accident. And Kiyoshi was later. You're certain?"

"Yes. My daughter and I were with him when he d-died."

"Good."

"Good?"

"Let me explain. You may be aware that Kiyoshi and his grandmother were not on good terms."

"I figured that was the case. But why—"

"I'll explain later. But the important thing is this. Sachiko never changed her will. Kiyoshi was her heir. Unless he were to die first. Then the bulk of her estate was to go to the child of a very distant cousin. You're legally married, aren't you?" After Jessie nodded, he added, "That means, according to the law, you've inherited your husband's estate."

"But he doesn't have anything. He's in terrible debt."

He simplified his Japanese and explained, "Your husband inherited Sachiko's money and had it for about six or seven hours. After he passed away, you, as his wife, are entitled to his inheritance from Sachiko. Well, you and Miya-chan, that is."

Jessie stiffened. "How do you know my daughter's name?"

"Your husband visited last month—for the first time in years— and tried to mend the broken fences with his grandmother. Kiyoshi told Sachiko all about you and your daughter. She already knew, of course, because she made it her business to know."

"What happened between them?" Jessie asked.

Mr. Suzuki took a noisy sip of the soup. "Maybe now is not the time to go into everything, but simply speaking, Kiyoshi had a habit of getting into financial difficulties. Sachiko became tired of bailing him out, and she refused to give him more money."

"So, he was gambling even then."

"But the real problem was the missing jewelry. And that was— how should I put it? The straw that broke the camel's back. Sachiko had had enough."

"Missing jewelry?" Despite everything, Jessie never imagined Kiyoshi to be a thief.

"Sachiko might have forgiven him if he had apologized. If he had confessed that he had been desperate and didn't know what else to do. But he wouldn't do that. He said he didn't take it. But," he added quietly, "Kiyoshi had a problem telling the truth."

Jessie was becoming more and more aware of that.

"And there were some other things that happened at that time, as well. It's not important now, but I believe both parties were at fault. The two of them needed to ask for forgiveness, to apologize. But they were just too stubborn."

Then he returned to the issue of the will. "After Kiyoshi visited last week—well, I suppose it was two weeks ago now, it looked like they were going to make things right. The thirtieth anniversary of Kiyoshi's mother's death was coming up. They'd decided to attend the memorial service together. It was going to be a healing trip— to put the past behind them."

The waitress set their pasta in front of them. Mr. Suzuki sprinkled his with a liberal amount of Tabasco and tackled the squid spaghetti with a pair of chopsticks like it was a bowl of Chinese noodles. After a minute, he looked up and said, "The chain of events is of utmost importance for you and your daughter. Otherwise, Sachiko's estate could go to that fourth cousin in Aomori. Needless to say, any debts incurred by your husband would have to be paid first. That's the law. But Miya's money is separate."

"What money?"

"Sachiko started an education account when she was born. I believe it has about two million yen in it."

Jessie wasn't sure if the tears in her eyes were from relief or anger. Her daughter's future had a head start, but because of two people's stubbornness, Miya never had the chance to meet her great-grandmother.

"I have something I have to do this afternoon. But if you come back tomorrow, I will give you the keys, and you can have a look around."

"Thank you. I'd really like to do that."

"Would you like me to handle this for you? To represent you? Or do you have another lawyer in mind?"

Him thinking that she had another lawyer lurking in the background almost caused Jessie to choke with laughter. "I'd be extremely grateful if you could continue to represent me like you did my husband's grandmother."

"I'm happy to hear that." His grin suggested he must have been quite a handsome guy back in his day. "I can devote myself to you, as you are currently my only client."

"How long have you represented Sachiko?"

"Since the 1970s."

If anyone knew her business, it would undoubtedly be him.

. . .

"So, tell us! How'd it go today?" asked Jimmy. "The only message from you was that it was bizarre."

"I need some wine. Immediately. Then I'll tell you," Jessie said. "And lower your voice. Miya just went to sleep, and she'd be up in a flash if she knew you guys were here."

Ignoring the cheaper bottle that Jessie had picked up on the way home, Yuya opened their Shiraz.

"First of all," Jessie said when they got settled, holding up her glass and clinking it with theirs, "it *was* bizarre. Unbelievably so. Here's the thing, guys. I think I might have inherited a café. Unless I dreamed up the whole thing. But I've been pinching myself black and blue all afternoon, and I haven't woken up yet. So, it must be true. Can you believe it? A café. But you should've seen—"

"What on god's green earth are you rambling on about?" asked Jimmy.

"I'm trying to tell you. When Kiyoshi's grandmother sold her bar, she bought a building in Omori with a café on the first floor. And she and Kiyoshi lived above it when he was growing up. When she died, Kiyoshi inherited the building. And it seems I inherited it from Kiyoshi."

Jimmy whistled when she got to the part about the missing jewelry. "Well, that explains a lot of things. I know I'd be pretty pissed off if my grandson turned out to be a thief."

"The thing is, I can see Kiyoshi doing something compulsive, like taking the jewelry," said Jessie. "And maybe even selling it. But you know what he was like when he lost his temper." She swirled her wine around in her glass just like the guys were doing. "He usually tried to make up for it afterward. I can't see him holding a grudge all these years. That's not like him at all. It doesn't make sense."

"Not to speak ill of the dead," said Jimmy, "but Kiyoshi was, you know, Kiyoshi. If you remember correctly, there wasn't a whole lot of logic for half of the stuff he did."

"I guess the important thing is that they made up," said Jessie. "At least, that's what I learned today. And now I know why he was in such a good mood the night before he went on that trip."

"Because his grandmother was going to bail him out of debt?" asked Jimmy.

Before Jessie had a chance to answer, Yuya interjected. "Does it really matter? The end result is the same." When he noticed Jessie's glass was empty, he offered a refill.

"I'd better not. I'm totally exhausted."

"Well, I guess that's not surprising," said Yuya, "considering that you left home today a pauper and returned an heiress."

"I'm not so sure I'd put it like that," Jessie said, remembering the funky state of the building. "For one thing, there isn't any money. It seems that most of it disappeared when the economy tanked. And before I can inherit Kiyoshi's estate, his gambling debts will have to be paid off. Mr. Suzuki—that's the lawyer— wasn't sure, but he thinks they may be about the same."

"What about the building?" asked Yuya. "That must be worth quite a lot."

"Yes, but Sachiko didn't own the land—it's rented from a temple. That's the case with all the shops on that street. But if she did own the land, I'd have to sell it to cover the inheritance taxes."

Yuya nodded. "Yeah, that's a big problem with inherited property. I see that all the time with my clients."

"But," Jessie said, "there's a house in Chiba that Sachiko bought years ago as an investment. It's paid for, and the tenants' rent covers taxes and repairs. My lawyer says if I sell it, it'd probably cover the taxes I do have to pay."

Jimmy raised his eyebrows. "Your lawyer?"

"That's right, Jimmy. My lawyer. Don't you just love how that sounds?"

"Does this mean you're going to stay in Japan?" asked Jimmy.

"I guess it does. For now, anyway. At least I've got a place to live. But to be honest, it was pretty awful." As Jessie described the smell, the clutter, the torn wallpaper, the broken furniture—the reality of the dilapidated state of the Butterfly Café set in. Could she and Miya really live in such a place? Maybe she should just cut her losses and go back to California.

"All of that's fixable," said Yuya as if he had read her mind. "Tell us about the neighborhood."

"It was all right, I suppose. It was a little run down. Mostly local shops."

"You didn't get to see the apartment?" asked Jimmy. "The place where presumably you'd live?"

"There wasn't enough time because Mr. Suzuki had to go to his dancing lessons. Today was tango day, and he was in a big hurry to get there on time." When the guys laughed, she laughed, too. "Seriously, I can see him whirling his dance partners around the floor, doing a dip, or whatever it's called. I'm not kidding. He's quite a dapper old gentleman. In fact," she said, looking at Yuya, "he reminds me of you."

"Me?"

"Well, you in thirty or forty years. Still strutting his stuff. Although, in his case, it's for the ladies. You should've seen how that Mrs. Watanabe got all girlish around him. And she's really old, too!"

"So, when are you going back?" asked Jimmy.

"And more importantly, when can we see it?" added Yuya.

"Tomorrow. Can you come?" She clearly needed someone else's objective opinion before going down the entirely new career path of being the barista of a rundown café.

"I could meet you there after my first-period class," Jimmy said.

"I've got to oversee a wallpapering job in Yokohama," said Yuya, "but I could get there around four."

"Okay. I'll see if I can have Miya go to her friend's house again, like today. I don't want to take her there until I decide for sure what I'm going to do. And I've got to figure out what to do with the cats. Otherwise, she'll beg to keep them. Grandma may have been a crazy cat lady, but I have no intention of turning into one."

CHAPTER SEVEN

Jimmy, Jessie, and Mr. Suzuki hadn't been in the Butterfly Café for more than a minute and a half before Mrs. Watanabe came sailing in. She scooped kibble into the cats' bowls and plopped down at a table. Mr. Suzuki dusted off the chair across from her and sat down as well. Today, he was dressed a bit more casually. Instead of a suit, it was a gray sports jacket with dark gray slacks. And, somewhat surprisingly, considering how chilly it was outside, a floral aloha shirt. "The kitchen is over there," he said, pointing toward the curtain at the end of the counter. "And here are the keys for the two apartments upstairs."

"Man, you weren't kidding about the smell," whispered Jimmy when they were behind the counter.

The soles of their shoes squished unpleasantly on the sticky linoleum floor. Jessie pushed aside the curtain, and they stepped into the kitchen, about half the size of the restaurant area. She gasped. "Oh, my god! Look at that!" The enormous six-burner stovetop was covered with greasy dust, but the oven looked like it had only been used to store pans. "I've never seen an oven this big in Japan," said Jessie, an image of homemade cakes, brownies, cookies, and pies flashing before her eyes.

"And the fridge! It's humongous and—oh, holy fuck!" Jimmy slammed the door shut. Whatever was rotting away in it smelled far worse than the cats.

A cockroach the size of a hamster scuttled across the floor, and Jessie shrieked. She grabbed a newspaper, but it escaped under the fridge before she could kill it. She crouched down and put her hands over her face. "Oh, god, Jimmy. This place is *terrible*. I don't know what I was thinking. We can't possibly live here."

Jimmy squatted in front of her and put his hands on her shoulders. "Think of what it can be, not what it is now. It just needs some tidying up, that's all." He stood and moved a pile of newspapers on the counter but pushed them right back. "You don't want to see what's behind that. Let's go upstairs."

"Shit," muttered Jessie. "Just what I need. More cats." The squeaky newborn mews had been a dead giveaway.

They walked past the old couple laughing together about something and climbed the steep staircase in the shop's back corner. At the top of the stairs were two doors, one to the apartment and one to the outside stairwell. Jessie unlocked the apartment, and they stepped into a mess that would have shocked the producers of *Hoarders*.

"It seems she never had the cats up here. It doesn't stink. At least," Jimmy said, scrunching his nose because the apartment did smell funky, "not of cats."

Jessie pointed at all the packages of toilet paper stacked up behind the dining table. "Do you think she might've had some kind of inside information on a new world order where toilet paper would be the currency?"

"If that's the case, you'll be set. For life, maybe." Jimmy circled around several plastic boxes containing shoes and headed to the dining table, piled high with papers, magazines, prescription and nonprescription drugs, and snacks. He dug around in a large wooden bowl and found an unopened box of Country Ma'am chocolate chip cookies.

"What?" he said when Jessie gave him a look as he ripped it open. "I didn't have breakfast."

Against her better judgment, she reached for a cookie, too.

"Well, I thought my grandma was bad," said Jimmy, surveying the wardrobes, chests, and plastic storage boxes in the bedroom next to the living room. "She was buying up everything in sight at the thrift shops and stuffing her closets with it."

"I don't think any of this came from thrift shops." Jessie stroked a full-length mink coat that was hanging on the curtain rod. The other bedroom was pretty much the same, except that the fur coat hanging on that curtain rod was a silver fox.

In the equally cluttered Japanese-style room, a futon was laid on the tatami mats under towering bookshelves crammed with all sorts of odds and ends, including a few books.

"Jesus," said Jimmy. "Can you imagine sleeping in here during an earthquake?"

There was a small Buddhist altar—a butsudan—in the corner. Jessie pushed aside the bowl of molding tangerines, picked up a framed photo, and saw a woman with Miya's face staring right up at her. "Look at this, Jimmy," Jessie whispered. "This has to be Kiyoshi's mother."

"How come he never mentioned how much Miya looks like her?"

Jessie's feelings toward her husband had been swinging wildly back and forth between anger and pity. Today, pity was winning out. "I don't know," she said quietly, putting the photo back in its spot. She slid open the paper door to the closet to find a large commercial safe below the shelf holding more bedding.

"Maybe it's full of money," said Jimmy with a hopeful voice.

She pressed down on the lever, and the door swung open easily. Other than a few appliance warranties, it was practically empty. "I guess, considering everything else, we're lucky it isn't stuffed with dirty underwear or something."

Jimmy laughed. "I bet it's from when she had her bar. She must've been dealing with lots of cash back then. It looks like it's fifty years old, at least."

Jessie's eyes fell on several enlarged snapshots of her and Miya in Shinjuku Park propped up in the bookcase. "What the hell is this? Was she *spying* on us?"

"She probably just wanted to see her granddaughter."

"But that's no excuse! She—"

"Don't forget the money she had been saving for Miya."

That made Jessie pause but not feel any less violated.

"Don't worry about it now. Let's go see what's on the third floor."

They climbed the outside stairwell and unlocked the door to the upstairs apartment, which was dark and dank. After seeing how dirty the floor was, they decided to be very un-Japanese about it and keep their shoes on. Jessie opened the window and drew the dusty curtains, but all the sunlight did was accentuate the grime. The tatami mats were stained and tattered, and the sliding paper doors were faded and torn. It looked like nothing had been upgraded since the building was constructed in the 1980s. There were old appliances all over the place, including a couple of boom boxes and what must have been one of the original microwave ovens sold in Japan. Musty smells emanated from the boxes of books and papers stacked up along the wall.

"I guess I won't be renting out this place any time soon," said Jessie. "Unless it's to the homeless."

"The way it looks right now, I doubt even they'd want it," said Jimmy.

The outside stairwell led them into a rickety laundry shed with not one but three old-fashioned washing machines—the kind with a separate tub for spinning clothes. They pushed open the door and stepped out into the warm sunshine. To the left was the Shinagawa River, and off in the distance was Tokyo Tower. They sat on a splintered wooden bench next to a collection of withering plants and took in the view.

"This place is one hell of a mess," Jessie said after a long silence. "But at least it's *my* mess."

"Atta girl," said Jimmy.

Back downstairs, they found Mr. Suzuki and Mrs. Watanabe eating convenience store rice balls and drinking bottles of oolong tea, so they headed to Delhi Curry Palace down the road for lunch. Over mutton curry and nan nearly the size of the table, they made a to-do list.

When they returned to the café, it was unlocked but empty. Jessie grabbed the wheeled shopping cart from behind the counter, and at the supermarket, they loaded it up with disinfectant, work gloves, garbage bags, kitty litter, and cockroach poison. They got the litter box situation under control first, followed by the refrigerators. They set the double-bagged garbage outside the back door, hoping the neighbors wouldn't think there were decomposing body parts stashed in them and call the police. Mrs. Watanabe arrived just as they started to tie up bundles of newspapers.

"Where did Mr. Suzuki go?" Jessie asked.

"To his balalaika lessons," Mrs. Watanabe replied.

"The Russian musical instrument?" asked Jessie.

"Yes. He's a fan of *Dr. Zhivago*. Big fan," Mrs. Watanabe added with appreciative emphasis. Then, with a harrumph, she grabbed the scissors and twine out of their hands. "I'll do this. Go get the ones upstairs."

"Now that's a man of eclectic tastes," Jimmy said to Jessie as they climbed the staircase.

Yuya arrived a little while later wearing his paint-splattered construction worker clothes. Jessie couldn't help but smile. Today he was a guy people would give a wide berth to on the train—a day laborer. Tomorrow, if he wore one of his Paul Stewart ensembles, people would think he was a young, up-and-coming executive.

People found it hard to believe he was both. He pecked Jimmy on the cheek and got to work. He went around the building, tapping walls, examining floorboards, and checking under sinks. From the way he was frowning, Jessie was certain he was going to tell her that the place needed to be condemned.

"It looks like a solid enough building," he said twenty minutes later. "That's the good news. And I can get a crew in here to help you with the cosmetic stuff—you know, pretty it up a bit so it'll be nicer for you to live in. But there could be some problems with the roof. And I'm pretty sure you'll have to replace the pipes on the third floor."

"How much is all that going to cost?" asked Jessie.

"Plenty."

"No avoiding it?"

Yuya shook his head. "Not if anyone's going to live there."

"What about the plumbing in Sachiko's apartment?"

"That looks okay. I think they replaced those pipes fairly recently."

"So, Miya and I have a roof over our heads? A livable place?"

"Yes," he replied. "I believe you do."

"And a ready-made business," added Jimmy. "Of sorts."

"I guess I never imagined I'd end up owning a café. Even one full of cats." Remembering the cockroach, she added, "And other questionable creatures."

CHAPTER EIGHT

December was well underway, and Jessie had been going to the Butterfly Café almost every day. Thanks to Mr. Suzuki threatening Kiyoshi's company with a lawsuit, she was no longer in immediate danger of eviction. They could remain in their apartment until after the mourning period ended and keep their health insurance for six months. But the company had treated her so shabbily she was planning to move as soon as humanly possible.

With the help of Cat Network Japan, she found a vet who'd neuter the cats and, to the shock of Mrs. Watanabe, people who would adopt them.

"I can't keep them," Jessie tried to explain. "There are too many."

"But Sachiko loved her kitties." Mrs. Watanabe picked up a friendly tiger-striped one and cradled it to her breast.

"Well, why don't you take them? I bet Sachiko would want you to have them."

Mrs. Watanabe looked as if Jessie had suggested she might enjoy getting a tattoo. She set the kitten down on the floor, saying she needed to be getting back to the stationery shop. Jessie didn't hear much about the cats after that, but it wasn't long before she was back to pester her.

Mrs. Watanabe's fifty-year-old son Taro had been taking care of their store after getting laid off from a small manufacturing company five years ago. According to neighborhood gossip, he hadn't gone outside since. Few customers ventured in because they preferred the flashy newer one in the station building. The only thing he had to do was sell cigarettes to the occasional passerby who couldn't be bothered to enter the neighboring convenience store. Mostly he sat by the front window, read comic books, watched daytime variety shows, and ate whatever his mother put in front of him. Mrs. Watanabe, on the other hand, liked gallivanting about the neighborhood, and it soon became obvious that the Butterfly Café was her go-to place. It seemed to have been that way for years, and the woman wasn't about to make any lifestyle changes now.

At first, Jessie thought Mr. Suzuki dropped by to keep an eye on things. But she soon realized he had a thing going for Mrs. Watanabe. And vice versa. Whenever he showed up, Mrs. Watanabe dropped whatever she was doing, and the two of them set up camp at one of the tables where they talked, played cards, and ate convenience store snacks. That afternoon, Jessie arrived at the café an hour earlier than planned. Mr. Suzuki and Mrs. Watanabe were at the back table when she walked through the door. The way Mrs. Watanabe jumped when she saw Jessie made her think that they had been up to something clandestine. That, and the fact the old guy's slacks were draped over a chair.

"P-please take your time," Jessie stammered when she realized Mrs. Watanabe was simply giving him a haircut. She headed straight into the kitchen, trying to forget the image of Mr. Suzuki's bony legs sticking out from his pink and yellow geometrically patterned boxer shorts. Jessie was going to have to have a talk with Mrs. Watanabe. She was fairly certain that hair grooming and food service weren't supposed to be carried out at the same table.

That evening, Jimmy dropped by the apartment for beer and nachos.

"There you go," he said. "That's how you can support yourself. You make the café into a senior citizen-dating spot. Or better yet, how about a matchmaking service? Now that the cats are gone, the possibilities are endless. You could even rent space by the hour."

For a moment, Jessie thought he was suggesting she convert the third-floor apartment into a senior citizen's love hotel. "Are you serious? At their age?"

Jimmy hooted. "What a dirty little mind you've got! I meant as a place for seniors to hang out. You know, a place for them to go and be with each other."

"That's actually a good idea. But I can't do anything about the café until the upstairs is livable." Jessie scooped up the last of the refried beans with a tortilla chip. "Well, at least I solved the problem of Mrs. Watanabe putting back everything I throw away."

"What'd you do? Change the locks?"

"Better than that. I simply ask her if she wants it. Either she takes it, or I throw it away. That's how I got rid of all those expired cans of mackerel."

Jimmy laughed and shuddered at the same time.

.   .   .

Jessie needed to call her mother to tell her that she wouldn't be returning to California any time soon. Jimmy was right. They might have already enrolled Miya in the church school for the winter session. He wasn't that far off when he joked that Miya would end up thinking that humans and dinosaurs frolicked through the jungles together if she were to go to that school.

"Hey, Mom," Jessie said as soon as she answered. "How's everything going? How's everyone? Any news?" That usually launched her mom directly into the latest and juiciest congregational gossip. But not today.

"Well, dear, everything is just fine. Now, Tom and I have been talking. We think it's best for Bethany to move out to the extra room in the garage. Because for her, it'd be temporary. She'll have her own home after the wedding. We'll put you and Miya right next to our room."

"But—"

"Now, how much are you planning to bring back with you? There's that storage space above the rafters in the garage, but the closets in the room are—"

Jessie cut her off. "Look, Mom, there's been a change of plans."

"What do you mean, a change of plans? You'll be coming home, and we'll—."

"Um. The thing is, I'm—"

"I know it will be an adjustment for you. For all of us. But it's for the best, you know. To be home where you belong."

Jessie inhaled deeply and told herself that her mother did mean well. Most of the time. "Mom—"

"You've had your overseas experience, and it's time to come back. To get yourself pulled together. You could go back to teaching. They're always looking for teachers."

"Well, it's like this, Mom. Some things have been happening here. Things I didn't tell you."

"What do you mean, things you didn't tell me?"

"Things I'm going to tell you now. I need you to listen to the entire story and not say a word until I'm done. All right?"

"But Jessie dear, you know that—"

"Not a word, or I won't tell you. I'll hang up and call again tomorrow."

"But Jessie, you know—"

"I'm hanging up now, Mom. G'bye."

"Wait! Okay. Go ahead."

Jessie told her mother that Kiyoshi hadn't been alone in the accident that killed him. That he hadn't been a complete orphan. And she, as Kiyoshi's heir, had inherited the grandmother's estate. Jessie omitted the geisha part and the running the bar part. She didn't mention anything about how Kiyoshi's debts had eaten up the cash either. Instead, she said, "So, you can see, it's impossible to move home. At least for now. My lawyer advises me to stay here until all the paperwork is completed. Until I take physical control of the property. And because it's complicated, I'll need to be on hand to manage it."

"Your lawyer?" her mother said with a sudden appreciative tone.

"Yes. My lawyer."

"A building? A whole building?"

"Yeah. Three stories. With a roof patio."

"Well, now. Isn't that something? Nancy Johnson was in Japan last year on that Sing for Jesus Tour. And she said that land in Tokyo was sky high in value. It's worth millions and millions of dollars."

Jessie had no idea who Nancy Johnson was, but she figured the woman was referring to Ginza. "Well, in some neighborhoods, it might be worth that much. Other areas, probably not." Jessie didn't tell her that her building was sitting on land belonging to a five-hundred-year-old temple because she had a pretty good idea how her mother would react to *that*.

"You know, dear," said her mother, switching gears. "You'd think Kiyoshi would've provided for you better with that wealthy background."

"He did just fine, Mom." Why did she *ever* think it was a good idea to send her mother pictures of their tiny apartment back when she thought it was cute? "Anyway, I just wanted to tell you why Miya and I won't be coming back. At least, not anytime soon."

"But what about your sister's wedding?"

"We'll be there. Wouldn't miss it for the world."

.   .   .

A few days later, Jessie took Miya to have dinner at Jimmy and Yuya's place. Yuya's daughter, Kizuna, hovered over the coffee table with her art supplies.

"Stand up, Kizuna," said Yuya in Japanese. "Stand up and say hello to our company."

The girl's eyes shot daggers at her father, but she heaved herself up and greeted Jessie with as little enthusiasm as possible. Yuya shook his head in apology when Kizuna plopped back down to her drawing. Jessie just shrugged. "Kids," she mouthed at him.

"Who's that?" Miya was visibly impressed by Kizuna's picture of a girl with enormous blue eyes and flowing yellow hair.

"She's the dragon queen," Kizuna replied. "She's going to fight the King of the Oceans."

"Can I draw, too?"

"Suit yourself." Kizuna tore out a page from her sketchbook and shoved some colored pencils toward Miya.

Jessie sat down and noticed the absence of wine bottles on the sideboard and wine glasses on the table. "Smells good, Jimmy," she said as he came in and set a pan of lasagna down on a trivet.

Tossing the oven mitts back onto the kitchen counter, he gestured toward the water glasses. "We've decided to set a better example for the younger generation."

Jessie laughed. "Probably not such a bad idea."

"So, did you talk to your mom like you were supposed to?"

"I did."

"And how did it go?"

"I guess she thinks I've inherited a swanky building somewhere like Ginza."

"And why would she think that?"

Jessie looked away.

"What're you going to do if she wants to come and visit?" asked Jimmy.

"I guess I'll worry about that then," Jessie replied.

"Sounds like a very mature plan."

Jessie threw a napkin at him. "I can't tell her what the place is really like. She'd have me committed. This way, she'll be a lot more agreeable about me staying."

"And how old are you again?" Jimmy asked.

Yuya brought in the salad and the garlic bread and poured glasses of water for everyone. "Dinner! Come on!"

Kizuna switched on the TV, but Yuya immediately switched it off.

"But," she cried. "It's seven. It's time to watch—"

"It's dinnertime. You know we don't have the TV on at dinner."

"But, I always—"

"Jimmy made a yummy dinner for us. And we have company."

"But—"

"Enough buts, Kizuna. Come on."

Kizuna scowled impressively through the first part of dinner, but Yuya and Jimmy carried on as if they hadn't noticed. After the girl had a second helping of lasagna, her face relaxed a little. When dinner was over, she asked Miya if she wanted to play, and they headed to the room that doubled as Kizuna's weekend bedroom and Yuya's office.

"So, it looks like you guys got a pretty good handle on things. No wine, but plenty of whine." Jessie chuckled at her own joke.

"Unfortunately, that's true," said Yuya. "It's been difficult. More than we thought it would be."

"Sure, it's difficult. What did you guys expect?" Jessie had never met Yuya's ex, but she was pretty sure Jimmy was right. Hidemi probably had gotten pregnant on purpose because she saw Yuya as a convenient way to leave her job as one of the last remaining elevator girls in a fancy department store. Yuya couldn't remember much about a friend's party after everyone started doing tequila shots. It was an enormous shock for him to wake up naked in a love hotel next to a woman. But that wasn't nearly as shocking as when she announced four weeks later that he had made her pregnant. Yuya did the right thing and married her, but after a year, they both admitted it had been an enormous mistake. He agreed to all the divorce terms, which gave Hidemi financial security and Yuya very little access to his daughter. Jimmy was the one who advised him to go back to court to get his visiting rights straightened out, and as a result, he got to see his daughter one weekend a month. Technically. Half the time, Hidemi cooked up some lame excuse to cancel. But all that changed recently—after getting a boyfriend, she couldn't pawn her kid off on them enough.

Jessie spoke with the voice of a maternal expert. "Now that Kizuna is spending every weekend with you guys, you'll have to do more normal things. Life isn't all Disneyland, karaoke, or shopping, you know."

"It's actually going to be more than that," said Jimmy.

"What do you mean?" asked Jessie.

"More than just weekends," he said.

"Hidemi wants to get married," said Yuya.

Jessie was surprised by Yuya's bitter tone. "Isn't that a good thing? Won't she have to stop bugging you about money then?"

"Yeah, but the guy doesn't like the fact that she's got a kid and—"

"To make an exceedingly long story short," Jimmy said, cutting Yuya off, "she's decided to give Kizuna back."

"What do you mean, she's decided to give Kizuna back?"

"She wants to marry the fucker," answered Jimmy. "But he says he won't take on someone else's kid. So, she's giving up Kizuna."

"Are you kidding me?" said Jessie, shocked.

"Hidemi says she needs," Jimmy added with air quotes, "a fresh start."

"What exactly does that mean?" asked Jessie.

"That means Kizuna's going to come and live with us full-time." Yuya reached for Jimmy's hand.

"That's good for us," said Jimmy. "We *want* her to come and live with us."

"But," Yuya said with a concerned look, "how do you tell an eight-year-old that her mother doesn't want her anymore?"

Jessie thought it could possibly be much harder than telling a five-year-old that her father was about to die.

"But get this," said Jimmy. "The guy got transferred to Osaka, and Hidemi's moving there with him. And leaving Kizuna behind."

"She's moving without her daughter? What kind of mother would do that?" Jessie knew she would go to hell and back for hers. And sometimes, she felt like she already had.

"What kind of mother?" scoffed Jimmy. "A total selfish bitch. That's what kind."

"Shh," said Jessie. "Lower your voice. Kizuna may not understand English, but Miya certainly can."

"Well, that's exactly what she is," said Jimmy.

"But if you say those things, you're no better than Hidemi is when she badmouths Yuya. And besides, what if she wanted to take Kizuna with her? Wouldn't that be far worse?"

"Jessie's right," said Yuya. "On both counts. I'd rather Kizuna stay here with us."

"What does she think about all this?" asked Jessie.

"She doesn't know what's going on yet, but I'm pretty sure she suspects something's not right," said Yuya.

"Listen, you guys will be great parents. But it's going to have to be different. You can't just be the cool dads one weekend a month—you'll have to be parents every single day of the year. But I'll help out whenever I can."

"Don't forget, you're moving," said Yuya.

"Not to the moon," said Jessie.

"To the other end of Tokyo. And that's practically the same thing," said Jimmy.

CHAPTER NINE

Jessie didn't wake up until Miya shook her shoulder. The moment she saw the clock, she shot out of bed. With just half an hour before the kindergarten bus was due, breakfast was going to have to be cereal. Jessie hurriedly cut up some vegetables for Miya's lunchbox, defrosted the cooked rice she kept in the freezer for emergencies, and unscrewed the top off a jar of salmon flakes. The smell of the fish brought on a sudden wave of nausea. Gagging, with her hand over her mouth, Jessie made it to the toilet just in time. When she finished retching, she brushed her teeth and started counting backward.

"Impossible," she told her reflection in the bathroom mirror. "Absolutely impossible."

Her reflection seemed to be smirking right back at her. *Impossible? Of course, it's possible. Don't you remember?*

"Oh, fuck," Jessie whispered in horror, remembering what had happened a few days before the accident. That morning, Kiyoshi had been particularly nasty because she had forgotten to pick up his suit at the cleaners. But that night, he came home with a bottle of expensive wine, wanting to celebrate some deal he was about to pull off at the company. Over dinner, he turned on the charisma and entertained her and Miya just as if they were a happy family.

Kiyoshi's ability to gush charm at will had always been his superpower, and like an idiot, she fell for it.

That night, for the first time in months, they had sex.

Of course, now she knew there had been no deal. No Chinese clients. No golf trip. That had to have been the day that Kiyoshi went to see his grandmother—the day they decided to put their disagreements behind them. Whatever it was, Kiyoshi came home that night elated. And because of *that*, she was now in deep shit trouble.

"Oh, fuck," she said again.

Jessie managed to get Miya off to kindergarten on time and headed straight to the drugstore. Back home, the pregnancy test sat on the table for the longest time while she tried to convince herself that she was overreacting. That she was just stressed out. Tired. Overwhelmed. Her hormones were out of whack. Whose wouldn't be after everything she had been through? She finally summoned up the courage to pee on the stick, but it didn't even take a full minute for the two blue lines to appear.

She leaned forward with her pants still around her ankles, put her head in her hands, and cried.

"Look what you've done now," she said to Kiyoshi's urn a few minutes later, as if this were entirely his fault. The fact was, though, they never took any precautions. They had given up after a year of trying for a second baby. But just because nothing happened didn't mean it was impossible—it only takes once. Once! How many times did her high school gym teacher try to drive that pearl of wisdom home to all the girls in her class? Apparently, not often enough in Jessie's case.

The scrambled eggs she fixed made her feel better until she vomited them up minutes later. Exhausted from that effort, she curled up on Miya's bed. Two hours later, she jerked awake, threw on a jacket, and dashed to the bus stop, arriving just as the bus pulled up. Miya raced around with the other children while Jessie gulped down a lungful of air and felt sorry for herself. She watched two of the mothers parading their pregnant stomachs around like badges of honor. Their husbands probably weren't racking up tons of gambling debt. Their husbands probably weren't lying about the money they were supposed to be saving for a house. Their husbands probably weren't gallivanting about with ex-geisha grandmothers.

Their husbands probably weren't *dead*!

"Mrs. Jessie," said one of the moms, tapping her shoulder. "It's raining! We're going to take the kids to the play center. Would you like to come?"

Jessie's head swiveled toward Mrs. Tanaka. She saw empathy in her eyes and was mortified to realize that her own were filled with tears. She swallowed hard and said, "I don't think we can go today."

"Maybe some company would be good for you."

The woman's kindness made Jessie feel worse. "I'd love that, but there's just so much to do."

Jessie had promised Miya an afternoon of baking and decorating to get them into the Christmas spirit. Her panic grew exponentially while putting up their tree and baking five cookies at a time in her tiny oven. At least the music Miya had chosen centered on reindeer, snowmen, and Santas. She didn't think she could handle any about babies in mangers. It was a relief to start watching the Christmas movie because then she could stare at the screen, not caring in the least how Kevin McCallister got the best of burglars when his parents forgot to take him with them on their fancy vacation.

After Miya went to sleep, Jessie tried to calm herself by sipping chamomile tea. She didn't have to go through with it, she told herself. She could call up just about any clinic in Tokyo and go have it taken care of. No questions asked. No protesters screaming "baby killer" at her.

No one would even have to know.

She googled "abortion in Tokyo" and stared at the screen for the longest time before clicking on a link that stated it had an English-speaking staff. While visiting other clinics' sites, she was beginning to think that it was just about as easy to shop around for an abortion as it was to find a place to hold a party.

Before crawling into bed, Jessie jotted down several numbers to call in the morning. But under the quilts, her mind raced.

How long a recovery period would she need? How would she get home from the clinic after it was over? How could she pick up Miya the same afternoon and carry on as if nothing had happened? What if something went wrong, and she started hemorrhaging buckets of blood and had to be rushed to the hospital? What if no one knew where she was? What if she *died*?

Jessie told herself that this would not be some dingy back-street clinic run by a shady butcher who had lost his medical license because of an addiction to painkillers. There would be no dirty instruments covered with lethal bacteria. This was Japan. Nothing secretive or shameful. And definitely not illegal.

She got out of bed to pee and ended up back at the computer. After clicking on an obstetrics link, it was almost as if someone else had taken control of the keyboard, leading her to one maternity site after another. As she typed in the date of conception to calculate the due date, she was pretty sure she wouldn't be visiting an abortion clinic anytime soon.

When the date flashed across her screen, Jessie squawked out a sound between a laugh and a cry. As if things couldn't get any worse, the baby was due on her sister's wedding day.

. . .

Jessie stumbled through the next few days, going back and forth between her apartment and the Butterfly Café in a state of despair. Her brain was foggy, and her nerves thrummed so loudly that it felt like they were playing some sort of internal banjo. The illusion of holding everything together dissipated the minute Miya fell asleep at night. That was when panic joined its good friend nausea to party it up in her stomach. What was she going to do? Other than eating another package of cookies that wouldn't stay down anyway, she had no idea. She should tell Jimmy and Yuya, but by not telling anyone, the pregnancy didn't seem quite real. She still had that other option. And just thinking about *that* made her want to puke again.

After holding onto this secret for over a week, Jessie was in the Butterfly Café waiting for one of her private students. Tomomi Nishino's husband was being transferred to San Francisco at the beginning of the year, and Jessie would lose the closest thing she had to a Japanese girlfriend. They usually met at the Starbucks near Tomomi's house, but since a foreign guy was coming with a truck to take some of Sachiko's old furniture and appliances that afternoon, they decided to meet at the café instead. Jessie had just set the books for the lesson on the table when a wave of nausea hit. Breathing deeply and counting to ten, she prayed that the cheese sandwich eaten half an hour earlier would stay put.

"Hello? Jessie?" A woman with a warm smile and hair down to her waist stood at the café's entrance.

"Tomomi! You made it!" Jessie jumped up, relieved that she wouldn't have to rush to the toilet after all. At least, not that instant. "Well, what do you think?" Jessie gestured toward the stained and tattered wallpaper. The scratched legs on the tables and chairs. The piles of junk in the corner.

It took a few seconds for Tomomi to respond. "It's...um, quite large."

Jessie smiled. No wonder Tomomi was her favorite student. "Only you could manage to come up with a compliment!"

"But it *is* large."

"Well, you're right about that. But believe it or not, it was worse before. A lot worse. Next time you come, it'll be really different."

"It has…" Tomomi paused to think of the right English word. "Potential. That's it. Potential." Just then, two kittens skidded across the floor in a wrestling match. "Didn't you give away the pussy cats?"

"I decided to keep these two. I thought they'd be good for Miya. For both of us."

Tomomi nodded and smiled. "Pets are nice."

Knowing that Tomomi would pay for the lesson even if they sat around and chatted, Jessie said, "Let's study first, and I'll show you around afterward."

An hour later, they put away their books and headed upstairs. "Don't have a heart attack when you see the mess. It's bad," Jessie warned as she unlocked the apartment and ushered Tomomi in. "Now you know why I didn't want to miss my chance with the guy coming to take the stuff away this afternoon."

"Oh, my. There are very many things here," Tomomi said, her arms crossed over her chest as she surveyed the apartment. "It's a big job for you to clean everything. But I think it will be very nice after. There are nice windows, and there is a good view."

"The view from the roof is even better. I'll take you up there, but first, I wanted to ask your advice about something." Jessie opened the door to one of the bedrooms, which was now knee deep in clothing encased in dry cleaning bags. "My husband's grandmother never got rid of a thing. Tomomi, you know a lot about fashion. Do you think I can sell any of this? It seems a waste to get rid of it."

"May I look?"

"Go ahead."

Tomomi kneeled to examine the dresses on the top of the pile. "Oh, my! This is Dior. And that one there is Chanel." She stroked the fabric of a third dress and sighed. "Beautiful. It's a little outdated, but it's still beautiful. May I see more?" After Jessie nodded, Tomomi pulled open a drawer packed with sweaters. Then another one that was filled with silk scarves. A third one was overflowing with costume jewelry.

"What do you think? Do you think I could sell this stuff?"

"Yes, I think so," answered Tomomi. "I know there's a website where people sell and buy things. My friend's daughter engages in that. I heard she sold a suit for five thousand yen. Because it was vintable."

"What?"

"You know. Elderly stuff. Clothes from the eighties."

Jessie had to think for a moment. "Oh, vintage. Well, there's plenty of vintage stuff here, that's for sure." It was hard not to be obvious that she was calculating how much money Sachiko's things could bring in. "Do you think you could find out more about it?"

Tomomi messaged her friend. Ten minutes later, the friend sent the link to the website. "Would you like me to help you set up the account? You could get started now."

They went downstairs, and with their heads bent over Jessie's iPad, they input the necessary information and registered Jessie as a member. She ran back upstairs to grab the Dior suit, and they checked it carefully for wear and tear and searched online to determine its value.

"Well, let's just try five thousand yen," Jessie said when they couldn't find any helpful information concerning a twenty-year-old designer suit. They took a picture and uploaded it to the website. Within minutes, it sold.

"I believe it's possible that you might be sitting on—what is it? A gold mine." Tomomi smiled as she conjured up an expression she had learned a few weeks earlier. "Lucky you!"

Without warning, Jessie blurted out, "I'm pregnant."

"What!" Tomomi was one of the few people Jessie had confided in about her marriage. No wonder she looked surprised.

"I didn't plan it. It just happened." Jessie looked for signs of judgment on Tomomi's face but only found concern. "You knew that I was thinking about leaving my husband. If he were still alive,

I don't think I could have. Not now. Not with a baby. I feel so guilty for thinking—"

"That you don't have to make the choice to go or stay?"

Jessie's eyes welled up. "That's it exactly. I feel terrible,"

"But why? You didn't make him die."

That was true, but Tomomi had no idea how many times Jessie had wished that Kiyoshi *were* dead.

"Are you feeling guilty because you have—how can I put it? Profited from his death? Now you have this building. This café."

"Everything here," Jessie said. "This new life hinges on…well, on my husband being dead. To be perfectly honest, Tomomi, I can hardly remember what things were like before. And it's only been a little more than a month."

"His death was his…destination. You can't change it from that to something else."

While Jessie was mulling that over, Bilal Chadra called, asking where he could park his truck to load up the stuff he came for.

CHAPTER TEN

"Merry Christmas!" Jessie and Miya said together to Yuya when he opened the door. "Merry Christmas, Jimmy!" Jessie called toward the kitchen. Kizuna offered a hurried greeting before pulling Miya into the room that was now solely hers. "I have an idea for a game," the eight-year-old said in her typical bossy manner. "You can be the—"

"Well, that didn't take long at all," said Jessie after the door was firmly shut on the adults. She noticed that the table that used to hold a collection of antique ceramic cats now supported a Lego city, various art supplies, and a half-eaten jumbo package of gummy bears.

"How about something to drink?" Yuya's red cashmere sweater and black jeans were festive enough without crossing into the land of tacky. But there was a smudge of something on his shoulder—possibly chocolate. "Wine?" he asked.

"I'm fine for now." Jessie wondered how she was going to get through the day because Christmas without booze would not go unnoticed around here. "So, have I missed the big meltdown yet?"

"Nope. Lucky you. That's still to come. But I've got the medicinal wine on ice, all ready to go."

Jessie laughed. Jimmy always insisted on putting on a major Christmas production. Solo. Every single year, about halfway through the preparations, he would storm out of the kitchen and yell that he was giving up. That they were all going to be eating Kentucky Fried Chicken next year, just like everyone else in Japan. Two glasses of wine later, he would head back into the kitchen to finish putting together a gourmet feast for a dozen people.

"I hope he realizes that kids don't always like the rare and exotic. And besides, it's just us this time. Not your usual crowd."

"Well, you know Jimmy," said Yuya. "We'll get what we get. But I do hope you're hungry. Because judging from the shopping we did this week, he's cooking for an army."

An explosion of giggles came from behind the door, and Jessie and Yuya smiled at each other. "What do you think's going on in there?" asked Jessie.

"Before you got here, Kizuna took the mattress off the bed and draped the blankets around the chair and the dresser."

"I guess that means she likes her new furniture."

Yuya laughed. "I guess so."

"Does she know that she's moving in for good?"

"Not yet. I'm worried about how she's going to take it. And what if things don't work out or if Hidemi changes her mind? What if we all get settled, and she wants Kizuna back? If that happens, I don't know what I'd do."

"You really shouldn't worry about what might or might not happen," Jessie said, even though that was her own particular theme song.

"You're absolutely right. So, here's what I'm going to do. I'm going to pray for Hidemi's eternal happiness with this guy, so she never wants to go back to the way things were."

"Now that's what I call a smart plan."

The phone in Yuya's pocket buzzed. "Bloody hell. Calling on a holiday! I've got to take this—it's a big client."

He opened the door and stepped into what used to be Jimmy's study, giving Jessie a glimpse of how they had doubled up in there. Deciding to go bother Jimmy, she poked her head into the kitchen. "Need any help?"

"Out!" he ordered, his brow dusty with flour and his Christmas tree apron thoroughly stained. "Go play. Go have some apple cider. Go eat a cracker. Do anything. I don't care. But don't bother me."

"All right, all right. Don't be such a grump!" She snagged an olive off a platter and plopped down on the sofa. The smells from the kitchen did not make her feel nauseous, and she hadn't thrown up since yesterday morning. She put her hand on her stomach— just to check—but it was as soft as usual. No sign of a baby yet. It felt good to talk to Tomomi about her pregnancy, but she would wait until ten weeks before telling anyone else. Bethany would be awfully upset when she found out Jessie couldn't be her maid of honor, but there was no point in ruining her sister's Christmas as well.

She went to pee for the hundredth time that day, and when she sat on the toilet, she found her underwear stained with blood. Her heart pounded in her ears as she wiped herself. More blood.

She headed straight to the kitchen after getting her jeans pulled up and her hands washed. "Jimmy—"

"I told you not to bother me," he said with his back to her. "Get out. I'm in the middle of making this sauce, and I need to concentrate."

"Jimmy—"

"Out!"

"I-I think I might be having a miscarriage."

He spun around. "What?"

Several minutes later, Jessie was sitting on the sofa, and Jimmy and Yuya were hovering over her, whispering anxiously.

"Should we call an ambulance?" asked Jimmy.

"No." Jessie felt like her voice was coming from the other side of the room. No ambulance. But—"

"I'll drive," said Yuya. "Jimmy can stay here with the girls. Which hospital?"

"I haven't been to the doctor yet," said Jessie. "So, I guess where Miya was born. Red Cross."

After Yuya went to get their car from the parking lot, Jimmy held Jessie's hand. "Why didn't you tell me?"

"I've only known for two weeks."

"Two weeks!"

"I didn't want you to think I was an idiot. I didn't plan it, Jimmy. Please don't judge me. I know it's crazy. But it just happened."

"Oh, Jessie, I won't judge you. I promise." But they both knew what his reaction would have been if things looked different.

"At first, I thought I'd get an abortion. I wasn't going to tell anyone, and I had it all decided. But just a couple of hours later, I changed my mind. I knew I couldn't go through with one. And maybe I didn't tell you because I thought I could still…" Jessie sobbed. "And now look what's happening. I'm losing the baby!"

"Shh. Let's get you to the hospital and see what they say." Jimmy's phone buzzed. "Yuya's outside. I'll walk you to the car."

"Don't tell the girls. Just say I've got a stomachache. Miya thinks that's why I've been throwing up."

Even though it was the weekend and the hospital was understaffed, Jessie was ushered into the doctor's cubicle immediately. The young doctor, seriously myopic but with skin as beautiful as Snow White, peered at her through her thick-lensed glasses. She greeted them in fluent English, smeared Jessie's belly with cold jelly, and moved the transducer up and down. The doctor studied the screen with a frown but relaxed when the swoosh of a heartbeat was heard.

"Is the baby okay?" Jessie asked, clutching Yuya's hand. "Am I having a miscarriage?"

"It's probably spotting. It's normal." Then the doctor narrowed her eyes at Yuya. "This would be a good time for you to start helping out more."

Before Jessie had a chance to explain, Yuya spoke up. "I'll make sure she takes it easy."

They got back when dinner was about ready. Neither girl seemed to notice the new rule of the day: Jessie wasn't allowed off the sofa except to go to the bathroom. And when they told the girls that Jessie and Miya would be spending the night, they were thrilled by the prospect of an impromptu slumber party.

Much later that evening, Jimmy and Jessie talked quietly.

"I wasn't sure about having a baby until it looked like I was losing it. I know it'll be hard. Harder than anything. But I don't care. I want *this* baby."

Yuya came into the living room wearing pajamas that might have been ironed within an inch of their lives. "Anyone up for some Baileys? Kahlua?" He looked at Jessie. "Warm milk?"

Jessie laughed and shook her head. "Thanks, but no. You guys go ahead, though. It's Christmas."

He pulled a bottle of Amaretto from the cabinet and held it up. Jimmy nodded, so Yuya poured it into two small crystal glasses and sat down. The girls' chatter was becoming quieter and quieter until, finally, there was nothing but silence on the other side of the door. Jessie didn't realize that she had also drifted off until Jimmy turned out the lights and they moved into their bedroom. She stretched out on the sofa and fell back asleep to the comforting sound of their deep, muted voices.

· · ·

Jessie followed the doctor's orders and tried to rest as much as possible. But that was easier said than done. Most of Miya's friends had gone to their families' hometowns for the holidays, so nobody was around to play with. Jessie kept Miya entertained the best she could, but since they couldn't go anywhere, that involved too many movies and too much junk food. Both were getting grumpy from being stuck inside.

Toward the end of the year, the guy who had taken Sachiko's stuff came to collect Kiyoshi's. She knew it could bring in good money, but sorting through it would stir up too many memories—some good, but some not so good. Giving it away was much easier, even though she suspected it was heading straight to a second-hand shop. But that morning, when Bilal Chakra started piling up things to carry down the stairs, Miya threw herself on top of her father's snowboarding clothes and launched into a spectacular tantrum. Mortified, Jessie asked if Bilal could come back another time.

"No problem. I know this is hard for you and your daughter." He spoke with sympathy, but his eyes were on all the free stuff. "Let me know when you want me to come back. Any time is okay."

Jessie rested her head against the front door after he was gone and closed her eyes. The neighbors on both sides were away, so she didn't have to worry about disturbing them. But if Mrs. Ueda from downstairs was home, she would be running right up to see what the commotion was. Dealing with her was one more headache Jessie didn't need right now.

"Miya," Jessie ordered, trying to keep from screaming herself. "Stop it right this minute. You're too old to be acting like this. You're nearly six, not two."

"*Daikirai*! Don't talk to me!"

Jessie recoiled. Kids often yelled that they hated their mothers, but that was the first time for Miya. "You don't mean that."

"Yes, I do! I don't want to move away. I don't want that man to take Daddy's stuff. What if he wants it when he comes back?"

"Oh, sweetie," Jessie whispered, her anger dissipating. How traumatic it must be for Miya to see her father's things carted out the door by a stranger. The poor kid knew nothing about his gambling, his debts, or the mystery surrounding his family. Jessie hadn't wanted to show her how worried sick she was—over money, over the baby, and whether she was making a terrible mistake by staying in Japan. All Miya knew was that her father was gone. All she knew was that everything in her life had been turned upside down and inside out. Jessie put her hand on her daughter's back and whispered. "I'm sorry, but Daddy's not coming back. I know you're feeling—"

Without warning, Jessie's throat filled with bile. She only had time to make it to the sink, where she vomited the noodles she had eaten for lunch into a saucepan. Miya jumped up and threw her arms around her mother's waist. "Mommy! I'm sorry! I didn't mean it! I don't hate you!"

"I know you didn't mean it," Jessie said when she could stand up straight, her insides feeling like they had just been through the spin cycle of a washing machine. She rinsed her mouth and shakily lowered herself to the floor, pulling Miya into her lap. Jessie wiped her daughter's tear-streaked face with her shirttail and hugged her tight.

"Are you going to die?" Miya was sobbing quietly now that the tantrum was over.

"What? No!"

"But Daddy died."

Jessie took her daughter's face into both hands and looked into her eyes. "That was an accident. It was just…well, a terrible thing."

"But Mommy, you're sick all the time now."

"Oh, sweetie. I just have a tummy ache. That's all." Jessie didn't want to tell her about the baby, not with the possibility of a miscarriage. "I'll get better soon."

"But Daddy—"

"I wish I could tell you he's coming back," Jessie said gently. "But he isn't."

"Not even as a ghost?"

"What?"

"You told me that Daddy is always with me and watching over me. I wake up and look for him in my room, but I don't see him. Why?"

"He'll always be a part of you. Inside of you. In your memory. That's what I meant when I said he'd always be with you. He's not a ghost. There's no such thing as ghosts."

"How do you know for sure?"

"Well, no one has ever seen a ghost."

"But Grandpa Tom says we can't see God, but he exists." Before the discussion took a more theological turn, Miya added, "But I guess if Daddy were a ghost, he wouldn't need his stuff."

"No," agreed Jessie. "He probably wouldn't."

"Because if he really were a ghost, he'd be able to swim underwater. And if he could do that, he wouldn't need his scuba toys, right?"

Jessie nodded, unable to respond. That pile of so-called scuba toys in the corner represented one of the worst times in her marriage. Kiyoshi knew how much she had been looking forward to her mother's fiftieth birthday party. He knew she had been planning on buying the airplane tickets the day his bonus came in. He had promised she could go, but instead, he went out and spent all the money on himself. A bunch of toys! She lied to her parents, giving them lame excuses about why she had to cancel her trip. Because if they had heard the truth, they would have gone through some stand-by-your-man routine. And which was worse? Being reminded that she was stupid enough to marry a total jerk or that she was stuck with one forever?

Kiyoshi never went diving after that expensive solo trip to Okinawa to take a diving course. Just like he never went bowling after getting his own bowling ball and kangaroo leather bowling shoes. Or took artsy-fartsy photos with that SLR Nikon he just had to have.

"I know it's sad to say goodbye to Daddy's things," Jessie said, forcing herself to remember that was all in the past. "But somebody will be able to use them. Don't you think Daddy would like that?" Jessie stroked Miya's cheek, and her spirits lifted slightly when she thought about how much Kiyoshi hated people touching his stuff.

"I tell you what. You can take that big empty plastic container over there and put any of Daddy's stuff in it you want to keep. If it fits, you can keep it. I've already saved pictures and letters and other important things for you. But you can pick out whatever else you want. As long as it fits in that box."

Jessie washed the saucepan she had been sick in and settled back on the sofa to watch the process.

"What about this, Mommy?" Miya held up Kiyoshi's expensive Coach leather briefcase.

"Sure," Jessie said, turning away so Miya couldn't see her face. Some businessman Kiyoshi was. Gambling at work, running up debts, and stealing from his grandmother. Indulging himself like a little boy buying up all sorts of expensive crap. Jessie was terrified another credit card bill would be dropped in the mailbox, demanding immediate payment. If Kiyoshi had been just half as selfish, just half as self-centered, she wouldn't have to feel so terrified now. Wasn't that what men were supposed to do for their families? Make sure they were safe?

Jessie nibbled on a soda cracker and washed it down with ginger ale, and for the umpteenth time, she asked herself if she was doing the right thing by staying in Japan. Would it be better for them to return to California and get a fresh start? Was it crazy staying in Japan when things were just so uncertain? Every day she went back and forth on this, trying to think what would be the best for the two of them.

Then she remembered. There were three of them now.

·   ·   ·

While Jimmy and Yuya took the girls to the movies two days later, Bilal Chadra returned for the rest of Kiyoshi's things. Jessie was braced for another scene when they got home, but Miya didn't even seem to notice the change in the apartment.

"How was it?" Jessie asked the guys after the girls went straight into Miya's bedroom to play.

Jimmy shuddered. "Horrific."

"It wasn't that bad," said Yuya.

"It wasn't that bad? Are you crazy? It was worse than bad." Jimmy turned to Jessie. "I don't know how you can stand those kids' movies. I feel like I've just spent a month in hell. The pandemonium! I got caramel popcorn stuck in my hair! Some kid a couple of rows back was throwing it!"

"Oh, come on. You're exaggerating. It wasn't—" Yuya stopped short. "Actually, you're right. It was that bad."

Jimmy reached over and patted Yuya affectionately on the cheek. "So, the next time we're in Nebraska, and I want you to come out to the barn with me, there's to be no more complaining about getting cow manure on your shoes. Understood? I have been to hell and back for you today. A little barnyard poop is nothing in comparison."

A laugh bubbled in Jessie's throat. "You guys are a couple of regular idiots. But I agree with Jimmy. Those kids' movies are terrible."

"How come you didn't warn us?" said Jimmy.

"What? And ruin all your fun?" she said.

"Bitch," Jimmy grumbled good-naturedly, and Jessie punched him in the arm. "So, tell us," he said. "Have you been a good girl and getting plenty of rest? Like the doctor ordered?"

"Kind of," said Jessie.

"You didn't feel sorry and help that guy carry everything down three flights of stairs, did you?" asked Jimmy.

"Of course not. I was just trying to figure out my finances. You know. Deciding on priorities. Like how important electricity and gas are compared to groceries and shoes."

"Which brings us to what we want to talk to you about." Yuya exchanged a look with Jimmy.

"What is it? What's going on?" A dozen worse-case scenarios flashed through Jessie's brain in half a second.

"Nothing terrible," said Yuya quickly. "Quite the opposite. We've been thinking about Sachiko's apartment. What about renting it to us?"

"What do you mean?" asked Jessie.

"We're going to have to move somewhere," Yuya continued. "Our place obviously isn't going to be big enough. We like our neighborhood but don't have ties there."

"So, we thought," Jimmy said, "that moving to Omori could solve all our problems."

"You know, so many changes are coming up for Kizuna," said Yuya. "A new house, a new life, a new school. Maybe it'd be good if our girls could go to the same school."

"And look how well they get along," added Jimmy.

Jessie stared at them. "Are you serious?"

"Dead serious," said Jimmy. "We've given it a lot of consideration. We think it's a pretty good solution to both our problems."

"But the apartment is unlivable. You said so yourself, Yuya."

"Yeah, but have you forgotten I'm in the remodeling business?"

"There's no way I can afford to get the plumbing fixed right now," said Jessie. "Not on top of the repairs in the café."

"I was thinking," said Yuya, "that maybe we could front the costs—"

"I can't take charity."

"We'll work out a deal with the rent," said Yuya. "You want renters, right?"

"Yeah, but—"

"So, why not rent to us? I'll pay for the plumbing now, and you can pay me back by reducing the rent for a few years. Eventually, we'd pay the going rate, and you'd have an apartment where the toilet and sinks would actually work."

"It's not just about you," said Jimmy. "We need your help. I didn't tell you this, but I was thinking about taking a leave of absence from the Ph.D. program—"

"But you're almost finished!"

"I know. But we don't want Kizuna to come home to an empty house," said Jimmy. "And if you're there…"

"You want me to babysit?"

"And vice versa," said Yuya. "You help us, we'll help you. Don't you think you'll need more help when the baby comes?"

Jessie's eyes filled with tears. "You have no idea how much of a relief it would be to have you guys there."

"Then why are you crying?" Jimmy asked.

"Hormones, you idiot!"

CHAPTER ELEVEN

As soon as the New Year holidays were over, Jessie was given a cautious green light to resume ordinary activity. On January fifth, she drove Miya to the Butterfly Café, squeezing what was increasingly beginning to feel like her own car into the parking space in the alley. The two kittens sleeping in a basket next to the stove scrambled under the counter when Jessie switched on the lights. Miya whooped with excitement when she learned they were to be hers. She took the small bag of dried fish her mother had produced to coax them out, and within minutes, they were climbing all over her.

"What are their names?" asked Miya.

"You can name them anything you want."

"Anything?"

"Well, sure."

"How about Kiyoshi? After Daddy? Don't you think he looks like Daddy?" Miya pointed at the tiger-striped one with black paws. "And that could be you. Not Mommy. Jessie. Oh! Wait!" she exclaimed before Jessie had to come up with a reason to object. "How about Mickey and Minnie? Like at Disneyland?"

They wouldn't have been Jessie's first choices a minute ago, but Mickey and Minnie it was.

Jessie hurried Miya up the staircase, cats and all. You just never knew when Mrs. Watanabe would appear, and she wanted to show her daughter around alone, at least the first time.

"There aren't any beds," said Miya with a frown.

"Not yet. But next week, we'll go to Ikea and pick out a new big-girl bed and desk for you. But first, you have to make a decision. Which bedroom do you want?"

Both rooms were practically identical, but Miya ran back and forth between them a few times before deciding on the one nearest the bathroom. Jessie bypassed the third floor because it was too much of a mess and took Miya up to the roof. It was cold, but they ate ham sandwiches and drank hot chocolate from a thermos in the wintry sunshine.

"Just think of all the barbecues and tea parties we can have up here once we get it fixed up."

"Mommy," Miya said after finishing her sandwich. "Do we have to move because Daddy did bad things at the company?"

"What! Who told you that?"

"Minako."

Jessie groaned. That girl's mother was one of the biggest gossips in the company housing complex. She wagged her big old fat tongue all over the place, not considering for a moment if it was appropriate for children to hear. "Oh, sweetie. Minako's wrong. Don't listen to her. We have to move because Daddy died in a car accident. That's all it is. He doesn't work for the company anymore, so we can't stay in our apartment."

"I don't like her so much," said Miya.

Jessie didn't either, but she didn't tell her daughter that.

"I like my other friends, though. I'm going to miss them."

"I know you will, sweetie."

"Can we go back and visit?"

"Sure, we can. But you'll make lots of new friends here. You'll see."

Despite Miya's protests, Jessie insisted on leaving the cats behind, and they set off to explore the neighborhood. Jessie introduced her daughter to the various shopkeepers on the street before heading to the park. There, they sat on a bench and discussed how to decorate Miya's bedroom.

"Mrs. Jessie!" called a voice. Mrs. Kikuchi from the Hair and Make-Do Salon approached with her two granddaughters, Sumi and Wakako. She plopped down to tell her about an upcoming neighborhood event. But Jessie's attention was more on Miya, who was being quizzed by the girls about her name, age, and where she lived. Her favorite TV show, her favorite color, and if she could ride a unicycle. The topic turned to how many cartwheels in a row Miya could do, and the three took off across the park to demonstrate their gymnastic abilities to each other. By the time Sumi and Wakako had to leave for their piano lessons, Miya had made her first neighborhood friends.

"That's your new kindergarten," Jessie said to Miya, pointing to the building on the other side of the park. "You won't have to take a bus. And your elementary school is right next door. Won't that be fun?"

To her surprise, Miya started to explain the ins and outs of the system. "So, if I can get into the Rose Class, I'll be with Sumi. That's their room over there, next to that big tree. But the other class would be fine, too. In the Cherry Blossom class, the teacher has a mole on her cheek with a really long hair sticking out of it. But that's okay because she's really nice. And Mana is in that class. She's Sumi's best friend. But Sumi told me that in that school, you can have more than one best friend. Isn't that great? And Sumi said Mana can do seven cartwheels in a row without getting dizzy. Seven! And did you know they have squirrels? They have to take turns feeding them and..."

Jessie smiled all the way back to the café. After settling Miya with a notebook and some pencils, she ran upstairs to get the clothes people had ordered before the miscarriage scare. When she returned five minutes later with her arms full, she found Miya huddled with Mrs. Watanabe over the notebook.

"Mommy! Look!" Miya said in Japanese. "This is my address. Obaachan showed me how to write it."

After praising Miya's efforts, Jessie turned to Mrs. Watanabe. "Thank you so much for teaching her."

Mrs. Watanabe grinned and pointed at her nose. "Obaachan. I'm Obaachan."

And that was when she became their unofficial granny.

.   .   .

A week later, Yuya's apprentice crew was hanging wallpaper and installing carpet in what was soon to become Jessie and Miya's new home. Yuya had his head under the kitchen sink on the third floor, studying the pipes, and Jimmy was complaining about the state of the apartment.

"I must have some sort of amnesia. Because I certainly don't remember it being this bad. Didn't you say you got rid of everything?"

"I did," said Jessie. "At least, everything that was obviously garbage, like those empty margarine containers. The broken appliances and the antique electronic equipment. All those 8-track music tapes. But I had to bring the things that I'm selling here so Yuya could fix up the apartment downstairs. That's what all that stuff is over there. But," she added, pointing at the massive wardrobes in one of the rooms, "I'm still trying to figure out what to do with Sachiko's geisha things. Because what if Miya wants it someday?"

"Making plans for her future career?"

"Of course not. But it does belong to her. And, I guess, to the baby as well. It's their heritage, I suppose you could say. I don't really want to keep it, but I definitely don't want it ending up in a used kimono shop in Kyoto where some tourists from Idaho think they've found the ideal Halloween costumes."

"What's the plan, then?" asked Jimmy. "It's going to have to go somewhere. Anywhere but *here*."

"I'm kind of hoping I can find a museum or gallery to take everything."

Jimmy nodded with approval. "That's not a bad idea at all."

"But it's not just the geisha stuff. What about all those books and papers in the boxes? At least, I think that's what's in them. Part of me is tempted to dump everything. But what if there's something important? There must be a reason Sachiko hung on to it."

"Probably the same reason she kept hundreds of old plastic margarine containers." After Jessie laughed, Jimmy added, "But getting back to the problem, maybe you could rent a storage space to keep the stuff."

"And maybe money could grow on trees," retorted Jessie.

"I have an idea," said Yuya, pulling himself out from under the sink, a smudge of dirt streaked across his forehead. "What about fixing the shed on the roof? We could make it stronger and weatherproof. The way it is now, it could fly right off if there's a big typhoon. But we could stabilize it, install some cupboards, and make it more usable. You couldn't keep everything in it, but it'd help. At least a little."

"But aren't there zoning laws or something about that kind of thing?" asked Jessie.

"It's not like we'd build a new structure," said Yuya. "We'd just improve the existing one."

Right then, a young man with a small dragon tattoo on his arm came to ask for advice on how to straighten the wallpaper he was attempting to hang. After Yuya went to deal with that, Jimmy chortled. "Well, you get what you pay for."

"If I had to do the wallpapering myself," Jessie said as they went downstairs, "it'd be far worse than crooked. Maybe all over the windows."

Through the door, Jessie could see Yuya patiently demonstrating the right way of doing things to two young men who looked more like thugs than decorators. They were dropouts, kids who had fallen through the cracks. But Yuya thought people deserved second chances. If any of these guys finished their six-month apprenticeship, he would hire them full-time or recommend them to another company. And most of them did.

It was getting close to noon, so Jessie and Jimmy went to get their lunches ready. Thanks to a tremendous amount of old-fashioned elbow grease, the café could now pass any surprise health inspection should there ever be one. Because of Yuya's guys, fresh white paint was on the walls, and the wooden floors had been stripped down and polished to a high gleam. Jessie had replaced the broken and clawed-up tables and chairs with newer ones she ordered from a used restaurant supply store she had found online. Once the grime was cleaned off the butterfly prints, it was evident that they were nice. Now, displayed in new frames from Ikea, they added a pretty touch to the café. The shelving along one wall, which had also been stripped and polished, no longer housed stacks of moldy newspapers. The decorative butterfly-themed figurines, vases, and teacups scattered all over the building were now sitting on those shelves. Capitalizing on Sachiko's geisha name, the Butterfly Café was going to *be* the Butterfly Café.

"Good morning," Jimmy said pleasantly, flashing his perfect teeth at Mrs. Watanabe, who was moving around behind the counter. "My, don't you look nice today? That color really suits you. You should wear lilac every day, you know?"

Mrs. Watanabe giggled, patted her hair, and said something they couldn't catch. Initially, she wasn't sure what to make of Jimmy or Yuya. But she warmed up to them—especially since

Jimmy never failed to pay her a compliment and since Yuya took his ladder into her shop and changed all her lightbulbs.

"Does she know about the baby?" Jimmy asked when they went into the kitchen.

"Not yet. Just you guys. And my family."

"How'd that go?"

"Well," Jessie said. "My sister was so mad she hung up on me."

"Seriously?"

"You have to remember that this wedding is the most important thing in her life. It's been the only thing she's been thinking about for two years."

"What did you do?"

"I waited and called her back in half an hour. She cried. I cried. She felt guilty. I felt guilty. Typical sister stuff. All's well. Now, my mother—that's a whole different story. I swear, she had me feeling like I should be checking into a home for unwed mothers. She made it sound like I purposely ruined my chances at happiness with," Jessie added with air quotes, "the poor widower Noah and his two poor motherless daughters."

"Your mom never gives up, does she?" Jimmy said as they set their lunches on one of the back tables.

"Disaster mostly averted," Yuya announced, coming down the stairs. He greeted Mrs. Watanabe and picked up a rice ball flavored with salt and black sesame seeds. "But it may not be a good idea to get down on your hands and knees and look too closely at the wallpaper behind the toilet. It's a bit of a patch-up job there."

"I'll try to remember not to do that," said Jessie.

"So, Yuya?" said Jimmy. "Is it a go? Today's the deadline to get the tickets to Bali at the discount price, you know."

Yuya laughed. "It's a go. Book them. We can't do anything upstairs until Jessie finishes selling the family treasures."

"Hey! I'm working as fast as I can," Jessie said with false indignation. "But seriously, you guys go ahead and have your holiday. I'll somehow manage to survive without you. I'm jealous as hell. But I'll survive."

The café door swung open, and in came Mr. Suzuki. "I'm glad you're here," he said. "I've got papers for you to sign. It's an extension for your taxes."

Taxes. Nothing ruined Jessie's day more than that dirty word. But finally, here was something that seemed like borderline good news. "You remember Jimmy. This is Yuya Tamura. He's the person with the remodeling business I was telling you about. He's doing the work for me upstairs." In a loud voice, so Mrs. Watanabe wouldn't have to strain too much to hear, she added, "Yuya, Jimmy, and their daughter will be moving into the third-floor apartment."

The old man was silent for a moment, and the three of them watched him process this information. "But the apartment," he said with a frown, "is too dirty for a family."

.   .   .

Miya turned six years old on January tenth. A week later, it was time for Kiyoshi and Sachiko to leave the picnic table in Jessie's living room and go to their final resting spot in Nagano. Jessie decided to make it a day trip to save time and money. When she and Miya got off the train, pulling a wheeled suitcase with the urns carefully wrapped inside, it was snowing heavily. Seeing the icy roads, Jessie was glad she had decided not to drive.

Taka conducted the brief graveside ceremony because his parents were away at a priest conference at a resort in Thailand. When the ceremony was over, they hurried back to the temple to escape the blizzard-like conditions that were rapidly developing. Jessie downed the post-ceremony refreshments, chitchatted with Taka and the temple staff, and watched the sky from the temple's formal reception room. She apologized for her haste and asked Taka to take them back to the station as soon as possible. The ceremony cost and bullet train tickets were all she had budgeted for, and she couldn't afford to get snowed in. Besides, there was too much work to do before moving to the Butterfly Café later that week.

Taka zipped confidently down the icy roads while explaining that even though Kiyoshi and Sachiko's ashes now resided in the cemetery, their spirits would also live in the family butsudan. The car skidded as he made a left, and Jessie turned to make sure Miya's seatbelt was securely fastened. She said a quick prayer to whatever deity that might be listening, asking for protection so they wouldn't be joining Kiyoshi and Sachiko in the afterlife anytime soon.

When the station came into sight, Taka was saying, "They're just there. Like spirits. You feed them, take care of them, remember them, and they have a happy afterlife. And you can have a happy this life."

"Like ghosts?" piped up Miya from the back seat.

"Oh, no. Not ghosts. Or, at least, not scary ones. Best friend ones. Daddy and Grandma ones. They love you, and you love them. So, it's a happy thing."

With almost no time to spare, they said a hurried goodbye and made it to the platform just as the train was pulling in. The non-reserved car was nearly empty. Jessie bought hot tea for herself and ice cream for Miya from an elderly woman who wheeled the refreshment cart down the aisle as if it were a walker. Miya fell asleep after a little while, and Jessie watched the snowy landscape speed past from the comfort of the quiet, heated train. Oddly enough, she had become accustomed to living with her dead husband and grandmother-in-law's ashes. But even so, giving them their final sendoff this morning and leaving them at the temple was an enormous relief.

CHAPTER TWELVE

One of the first things Jessie did when they moved into the apartment above the Butterfly Café was to place Kiyoshi and Sachiko's formal portraits next to Michiko's in the butsudan. Continuing with an adapted version of this custom would be a way for her children to connect with their father's family. She would skip the daily burning of incense and the lighting of candles. Considering all the times Kiyoshi said he was a complete atheist, she figured he wouldn't mind. But she would keep the altar tidy and feed the Yamada spirits with what she had on hand. Setting a small bowl of mandarin oranges in front of their photos, she said to whoever might be listening, "I hope you're happy here." A second later, she added, more to convince herself, "In my new home."

They settled right into the neighborhood, namely because they already knew many of the locals. And Miya had made friends through Sumi and Wakako, so her first day at the new kindergarten wasn't a big deal. Nobody called her hafu because of having an American mother. Nobody called her a gaijin, either. They were the Yamadas from the Butterfly Café, and that gave them some sort of insider clout.

. . .

One blustery night in late January, Jessie was in the café wearing comfy fleece sweats. She had one of Sachiko's plaid cashmere throws over her lap, and a small ceramic heater was pumping out hot air by her feet. The blinds were drawn in case anyone thought she was open for business, and the door was locked in case Mrs. Watanabe got it in her head to start hanging around at night. Hooked up to Kiyoshi's old speakers, her iPad blasted out Backstreet Boys, Spice Girls, and Destiny's Child, transporting her straight to high school. The baby monitor Jimmy and Yuya had bought as a housewarming present arrived from Amazon earlier that day. For the first time since moving in, she felt comfortable being in the café with Miya asleep upstairs. Jimmy was right. Parents *did* leave their kids in bedrooms upstairs and go down to the living room to watch television or whatever. But leaving an apartment to go downstairs to a shop, even if it was her apartment and her shop, wasn't the same.

Her phone buzzed. *Summer ahead*, Jimmy texted from Haneda Airport, where they were waiting for their flight.

Enjoy Bali, she texted back. *Thanks again for the baby monitor.* She took a selfie with it and made a funny face.

Jimmy replied with a series of smiling-face emojis, adding, *Don't eat too many of those cookies I see on the table. Gotta go. Boarding now!*

Jimmy was also right about the cookies. She put two on a napkin and the rest back into the cookie jar.

Jessie's greatest treasure, her grandmother's cookbooks, recipe cards, and yellowed notebooks, were in front of her. Maybe Grandma Frances did have some sixth sense like she always said she had. Maybe she had known somehow that Jessie would be in the hospitality business someday. Was that why she had left Jessie all the family recipes? She lifted a few cards out of the old, scarred wooden box. Her heart twisted when seeing her grandmother's handwriting describing how to make chicken gravy. The spidery cursive on a different card was her great-grandmother Alice's recipe for biscuits. The cards were splattered with food stains. Remnants of preparation for family dinners long ago. Jessie closed her eyes, brought them to her nose, and inhaled deeply, willing herself to be transported to her childhood.

Now with a great big kitchen and a great big oven, there were no limitations to what she could do. Except, it became obvious after flipping through the cards that some ingredients were unavailable in Japan. Besides, people's taste buds have changed since the 1950s. Salisbury steak, succotash, or chicken à la king probably wouldn't go over big with anyone Jessie would be cooking for, regardless of the country she was in.

But the loaves of bread, the muffins, the cookies! Right here, in her hands, was Grandma Frances's secret recipe for her famous sugar cookies. Her snickerdoodles. And her Russian teacakes. Here, right before her, was the secret to making the perfect pie crust. How to make a German chocolate cake or a strawberry shortcake without any assistance from Betty Crocker whatsoever.

The smell of butter and sugar marrying in a hot oven transported her to her grandmother's kitchen, generous lap, and warm, comforting arms. She had wanted to create the same sort of memories with her own family. But Kiyoshi made a point of never eating any sweets she made, saying that he had no intention of hopping on the fast train to American obesity. Well, that sucked the fun right out of it. It didn't take long for her to learn to bake when he wasn't around to sniff the air and complain that she was setting up Miya for a lifetime of being fat like her. When she had inherited the box of recipes, she packed them away in the back of the cupboard, behind the Christmas decorations and Kiyoshi's out-of-season clothing.

But now, without anyone breathing down her neck, she could bake as often as she wanted. And what better excuse in the world was there than being the owner of a café? Even one without a single paying customer yet!

Jessie looked around her and sighed with contentment.

A rap at the door made Jessie groan. Mrs. Watanabe really needed a talking to about proper visiting hours. A blast of icy air whooshed inside when she opened the door. The foreigner standing there seemed to be just as surprised to see her as she was to see him.

"G-good evening," he said in Japanese.

Jessie responded, also in Japanese.

After staring at each other for a couple of seconds, he switched to English. "Is Mrs. Yamada here?"

"I'm Mrs. Yamada," Jessie replied, looking up at him cautiously.

"I'm sorry. I mean the…um, the older one. Look, I know it's late, but I've been away. I saw the light on and wanted to see if Sachiko could make time for me next week. But if she's busy, I can come back another time."

"Excuse me? What?"

"I'm sorry. I should introduce myself. I'm Mark Peters. I teach at Hanamigawa University. I've been collecting stories from senior citizens in the neighborhood about their war and postwar experiences for my research. And before I went on sabbatical, Sachiko said she'd let me interview her. She said she had some pretty good stories to tell."

"I'm Jessie Yamada. The granddaughter-in-law," she said, wishing that she knew a few of Sachiko's stories herself. "Look, why don't you come in? It's warmer inside." And it certainly wouldn't stay that way if she stood there for much longer with the door wide open.

He shook the rain off his umbrella and put it in the stand by the door. His hair, a dense brown, sprang in waves when he took his knitted hat off. His glasses had fogged up, and when he wiped the mist off with a tissue, Jessie saw his eyes were the color of gingerbread fresh from the oven.

"Things sure do look different," he said after he pushed his glasses back over his nose. "Are you helping her run the business now?"

Well, this is awkward, thought Jessie as she cleared her throat. "I'm afraid I have to tell you that Sachiko passed away in November."

The guy recoiled in shock. "I-I'm so sorry to hear that. My condolences to you and your family."

"Thank you."

"I didn't realize that Sachiko had been sick. She seemed so vibrant for her age. So full of life and really interesting to talk to."

"Um," Jessie said uncomfortably, realizing this was the first time to have this conversation in English. "She wasn't sick. She passed away in a car accident."

"Oh, no! How awful that must have been for you and your husband."

Jessie looked into his face briefly before quietly adding, "My husband was killed in the same accident."

"Oh, my god. That's just..." He stumbled around for words before uttering, "I'm afraid I don't know what to say."

"Thank you," Jessie said again, touched by his sincerity.

"Are you living here now?"

"Yes. I moved in upstairs a few weeks ago. With my daughter." To avoid the awkward silence that always followed when she spoke of her recent bereavement, she began to ramble. "It's been two months now. We're doing okay. They say it gets easier. But I don't know. Anyway, I will probably open the café once we get more settled. And I've been making some changes."

"I can see that," Mark answered, glancing around. "It looks really clean and—oh, I'm so sorry. I didn't mean to imply that before..."

"No offense taken. It *was* a mess in here before."

"What happened to the cats?" he asked.

"Well, I kept two of them, but the rest went to greener pastures."

"What!"

Jessie couldn't help but laugh at the shocked look on his face. "Not *that*! I didn't mean that. What I meant was I found homes for them through a cat shelter. But, believe it or not, some of them did go to a farm in Chiba." She crossed her heart in that childish gesture and added, "Honestly."

He laughed along with Jessie. "Whew. That's a relief." His phone buzzed in his pocket. He took it out and gave it a brief glance. "Anyway, I live on the other side of the park. I come past here every day on my way to the station. Maybe I'll stop in after you open."

"I'm not sure when that'll be," she said, suddenly distracted by a whiff of his citrus-scented aftershave. "But come by anytime. Other than the shopkeepers on the street, we don't know many people around here yet."

"I think you'll like living here. It's a fantastic neighborhood." His phone buzzed again. "Excuse me a sec," he said, turning away to answer.

Jessie didn't mean to eavesdrop, but the conversation *was* in English.

"Don't worry, Kumiko," he said to the person at the other end. "I'll get there before the show starts. Go in and save me a seat, would you? I'll find you." He ended the conversation and turned to Jessie. "Sorry, but I've got to go. There's a midnight showing of *The Godfather* at an art theater in Shinjuku, and I'm running late." With one foot out the door, he turned around and said, "It was nice meeting you."

Jessie shivered in the cold air left behind. She locked the door and sat down to finish her tea, his aftershave still lingering in the café.

.   .   .

Jessie was in the supermarket just before six, along with every other bargain-hunting housewife in the area. Super Thursday was always a madhouse, but every yen saved helped. She had just lost out on getting that last package of pork chops but scored with the forty percent off discounted chicken breasts. She was heading for the bread aisle and saw Mark in the dairy section. His jacket was draped over his arm, and a black backpack hung from the hook on the shopping cart. Nicely filling out his navy slacks and a cream-colored button-down collared shirt, he looked like the type of guy who worked out—but not *all* the time. And judging from the contents of his shopping cart, he looked like a guy who ate pretty well. From that distance, Jessie couldn't tell if he was cooking for one or not.

She walked toward him. "Hey there, doing some shopping?" she asked, slipping a liter of milk into her cart. Well, that sounded stupid. Why hadn't she just said hello? What else would he be doing in the supermarket? The hokey-pokey?

"Jessie! Hi."

"Fancy meeting you here." As soon as those words escaped her mouth, she cringed. That sounded even more idiotic. "Well, I suppose a man has got to eat. Just like the rest of us." Oh, god. She was going from bad to worse.

The corners of Mark's lips turned upward. "What can I say? I do like to eat. Hence, the shopping. Not only that," he said as a supermarket employee moved in front of them to slap ten percent off stickers onto the milk cartons, "I'm a cheapskate at heart and love a bargain." He put the milk that was in his cart back and grabbed one of the discounted ones. He winked at Jessie, and she laughed and did the same.

"It's like a scene from the *Walking Dead*," he said after they moved to make room for the determined shoppers heading toward the discounted dairy as if it were prey. "Need eggs?" He nodded toward the excitement going on in that direction.

"No," she said. "I'm all set."

"Me, too. Not worth risking life and limb."

"Oh," Jessie said, remembering there *was* something she could say and not sound like a total idiot. "How was the movie the other day?"

"Movie? Oh, yeah. *The Godfather*. It was better than I thought it'd be. I saw it once on TV a long time ago but not on the big screen. But my, um…my friend is crazy about it," he added with a laugh. "It must've been her hundredth time. She practically told me what was about to happen in every single scene."

It had been so long since Jessie had talked to a normal kind of guy—someone who wasn't Jimmy or Yuya—and she had pretty much forgotten how to carry on a conversation with one. She was distracted by his eyes, which were the warmest shade of brown. When she realized she had been staring at him while he was talking, she felt a blush crawling up her neck. She ordered herself to say something smart to contribute to this movie conversation, but a tinge of nausea reminded her that she was pregnant, and her mind went blank.

"Well," she said, feeling completely discombobulated, "I'd better let you get on with your shopping. It was nice bumping into you. Have a great evening. See you around." Smiling brightly, she maneuvered her shopping cart in the opposite direction and hurried off.

But back home, later that night, she googled him.

CHAPTER THIRTEEN

The next day, the door opened, and a stylish young woman stepped in wearing a red cashmere coat. By her side was a little girl about Miya's age.

"I'm sorry," Jessie said, looking up from her computer. "I'm not open for business."

"Jessie Yamada?" the woman inquired in English. "May I talk to you for a few minutes?"

Jessie straightened up. The last Japanese English-speaking person knocking on her door, who was this well dressed and had acted this friendly, was a Jehovah's Witness, and she had the damnedest time getting rid of her. She had a lifetime supply of her own religious baggage, and she didn't need anyone else's. "I'm not interested in buying any religion."

The woman looked startled. "I'm not selling religion. I'm not selling anything. But there is something important I'd like to talk to you about. My name is Ayako Nagai. This is my daughter Natsumi."

The woman's glossy shoulder-length black hair, flawless skin, and beautifully cut suit made her look as out of place in the Butterfly Café as if the Empress of Japan had decided to drop in for tea. The little girl, with chin-length hair and practical play clothes, was quite a contrast. From Jessie's experience, Japanese moms who paid that much attention to their appearance usually inflicted the same upon their daughters.

Those thoughts left Jessie's head when the woman leaned forward, took a deep breath, and said, "I have wanted to meet you for a long time. You see, my daughter and your daughter are sisters."

"Wh-what?"

The woman said it again.

Jessie's eyes darted toward the kid. And that was when she saw it. An unmistakable resemblance to Miya. "What do you want?"

"I want nothing—"

"I don't have any money."

"I don't want any money."

Jessie pushed her chair back and stood. "You need to leave. Now."

The woman took a manila envelope from her bag and set it on the table. "Please contact me after you look at this."

The moment they were out the door, Jessie shoved the envelope into the trash, tied the bag shut, and put it outside the back door. She grabbed the spray cleaner and squirted down all the tables and chairs—as if that could erase the fact they had been there. That skinny bitch! Who did she think she was barging in here with a whole pack of lies?

She locked up and went upstairs. She pulled Kiyoshi's mother's photo down from the butsudan and stared at it. There was no mistaking the resemblance between Michiko and that little girl. Or between that little girl and Miya.

Shit, shit, shit. Jessie had thought she was over and done with being furious at Kiyoshi, but now she wanted to take his memorial picture and smash the glass to smithereens and rip the photo to shreds. If he were to appear before her this instant, she would send him right back to the afterlife because she would strangle him with her bare hands.

On top of everything else, he had been screwing around behind her back!

For the first time in several weeks, she vomited into the toilet. The rest of the day, she kept reaching for her phone, but no matter what, she was determined not to bother Jimmy and Yuya in Bali.

Unable to sleep, she went downstairs at midnight in her pajamas and retrieved the envelope. She shook the damp tea leaves off, brought it inside, and dumped the contents onto the table. There were pictures of Kiyoshi and that woman under cherry blossoms. Splashing in waves at a beach. And for fuck's sake, in his and her matching Halloween costumes at some fucking Halloween party.

Jessie inhaled and exhaled, controlling her urge to smash something. Then it hit her that something wasn't quite right, and she examined the photos again. Kiyoshi always had short black hair, but it was long and brown in the photos. She looked at the documents again and read the penciled-in English comments. Because the girl was small, she looked younger than Miya. But it turned out she was born a month before Jessie had even met Kiyoshi.

The woman's family register had listed the girl's father as unknown. But the DNA test, which was clearly marked, said otherwise. Jessie went through everything again. And then a third and a fourth time. After staring at the woman's contact information for what seemed like forever, she sent her a message.

The reply came immediately.

. . .

Jessie peered into the window of a fashionable café near Ebisu Station with the hood of her down parka pulled over her head, not wanting to be the first to arrive. That woman was already there, sitting in the corner, looking all calm, chic, and pretty.

Jessie pushed open the door, clenched her jaw, and strode over to the table. "What do you want from me?"

"I simply want our daughters to get to know each other," the woman replied calmly.

"Cut the crap. Why now? Why did you contact me?"

"I'm alone in this world." The posh way she spoke reminded Jessie of one of the teachers on the JET program who never got tired of bragging about his Oxford background. "And—"

"I don't believe you. I don't have any money, and even if I did, I wouldn't give it to you."

"I do not want your money."

"Were you seeing my husband while we were married?"

The waiter appeared with glasses of water. He looked at the Japanese customer, waiting for her to place the order.

"Coffee?" she asked Jessie pleasantly. "Or perhaps you'd rather have tea?"

"Coffee's fine," Jessie muttered as she sat down. She shrugged off her coat and remembered that she wasn't supposed to have caffeine. But that didn't matter because she wasn't there for a nice chitchat over a nice cup of coffee anyway. She was there to find out what this person really wanted.

"The last time I saw Kiyoshi," the woman said, "was shortly after I became with child. That was nearly eight years ago."

With child? Who the hell says that sort of thing? Jessie picked up the water glass and raised it to her lips. One swallow was all she could manage before setting the glass down on the table. "How did you know about me? How did you find us?"

"I read about Kiyoshi's death in the newspaper. The local news from Nagano."

Jessie narrowed her eyes. "Are you some kind of stalker or something? Because how could you possibly just come across news like that?"

"I admit I was keeping my eyes open for any information concerning my daughter's father. With the internet, that is not difficult to do." Then she changed the subject. "May I ask you something? What was your impression of Sachiko Yamada?"

That took Jessie by surprise, but she wasn't about to admit that she had never met her.

"She gave me a million yen to disappear. To go have an abortion. To go away and never come back."

"What!" That came out much louder than Jessie had intended, and the man at the next table looked up from his comic book and gave her a dirty look. "So, she took a random dislike to you and gave you all that money to go away?"

"She said he had a brilliant career ahead of him. She said I was going to ruin his life, and she called me terrible names. It is true that I was working in a bar then, but everything else she said was a falsehood."

"What did Kiyoshi—"

"He never knew. Not about the bribery. Nor about the baby."

"But how did his grandmother find out about it if he didn't even know?"

"She came to his apartment when I was there alone. She stormed in like a tornado, looking for his bankbooks. To be honest, I found her behavior shocking. When she saw the pregnancy test kit on the table, she forgot about her search and turned on me. You see, I had just confirmed my condition that morning. I was going to take the test home because I needed time to think about what to do."

"So, right then and there," Jessie scoffed. "Kiyoshi's grandmother offered you money, and you—"

"Not at that moment, no. I don't know how she found out where I was working, but she came to the bar with a man. Her lawyer, I later learned. After that, he contacted me with her offer."

"And you took the money."

"Yes, because I had already decided to part ways with Kiyoshi. I was having doubts about our relationship. After meeting his grandmother, I knew I could never become his wife."

"But you went ahead and had his baby."

"I'll be honest with you, Jessie—may I call you that? It would be a falsehood if I said I did not consider the other path. But I thought about it for too long. And by then, it was too late."

The waiter returned with their coffee. Jessie studied hers while adding milk and sugar, even though she never had hers sweet, and she wasn't going to drink it anyway.

"I'm thankful for that delay," the woman said, lifting her cup of black coffee to her mouth. "My daughter is the joy of my life. You understand, don't you? Because I believe you also feel the same way about your daughter."

Jessie pressed her lips together. She wasn't about to get sucked into a 'we're-in-the-same-boat' dialog with this woman.

"My mother passed on when I was in junior high school," she continued, as if Jessie was just dying to hear all about it. "My father—well, he would not have been...how should I put it? Understanding. So, I went to my grandmother. After my daughter was born, I went to an esthetician college. It was the only thing I could think of doing at the time. I became a masseuse. A skincare specialist." Her voice caught a little when she added, "After my grandmother passed on, we moved back to Tokyo. And we managed to survive. My job is good. But it's hard sometimes, being alone."

"Kiyoshi never knew about his...about your daughter?"

"No. Not unless his grandmother told him. I disappeared like she wanted me to. I do not know if he searched for me or not." She turned her gaze to the outside street and added, "It would have been difficult to find me, but certainly not impossible."

Jessie watched her face and wondered if she had been waiting for Kiyoshi to come and find her.

"Because his grandmother said terrible things to me, I had my daughter's DNA tested using Kiyoshi's toothbrush. You have seen the results of that test."

The woman's phone buzzed in her purse. She ignored it, but it buzzed again. Finally, she pulled it out. "I'm terribly sorry. I must return to work." She slid a postcard across the table toward Jessie. "This is a gift coupon. From my salon for a full body massage."

"Excuse me?"

"A luxury treatment. No strings attached. It's a promotion campaign for my shop."

Jessie was thinking that no one in their right mind would want to get a massage from a dead husband's ex-girlfriend when the woman added, "A massage is very good for stress."

"I'm certainly stressed out right now, that's for sure," Jessie said, as if it were a joke.

"Yes, I imagine that is so," she replied seriously, picking up the bill.

"I'll think about it." Jessie put the postcard in her bag.

"Before we say goodbye, may I ask you this? May our daughters meet?"

"Listen, Ayako," Jessie said, saying the woman's name for the first time. "I don't know. I need to be certain that everything you've told me is true. I don't understand exactly what that DNA test says, so I'm going to ask someone to take a look."

"I'd do the same thing if I were you."

"Until I decide what to do, we won't say anything about this to Miya."

"Just like we won't tell Natsumi."

"She doesn't know?"

Ayako shook her head. "I'd rather that my daughter did not know she has a sister than learn she has one with whom she cannot have a relationship."

"But what did you tell her when you brought her to the café?"

Jessie had to give the woman credit because she looked awfully sheepish when she said, "I told her that you might become her English teacher."

CHAPTER FOURTEEN

Jessie called Mr. Suzuki immediately after saying goodbye to Ayako. Without the usual formulaic chit-chat that opened any Japanese telephone conversation, she demanded, "What do you know about Ayako Nagai?"

His hesitation confirmed her suspicions: he knew plenty. "Why do you ask?" he responded cautiously.

"Why? Because she paid me a visit yesterday, that's why. Because I just went to see her. Because she said that—"

"Where are you right now?"

"I'm walking toward Ebisu Station, heading home."

"Can you meet me at Denny's? In twenty minutes?"

"What about your chorus practice?" Jessie was fully aware of his daily schedule thanks to Mrs. Watanabe's running commentary on the guy.

"I will take a rest from that today."

When she got to Denny's, he was in the booth where they conducted much of their business. Jessie ordered the drink bar set and went to get a mug of herb tea and a glass of grapefruit juice.

"I always wondered if she would come back," he said thoughtfully after Jessie sat across from him.

"So, you know what Sachiko did to her."

"She thought she was doing the right thing."

"The right thing!"

"But she never should've interfered. It ruined their already fragile relationship."

"And that's why he married me. Just like that, on the spur of the moment. I guess marrying a gaijin was the ultimate revenge for his grandmother chasing away the love of his life. Kiyoshi was good at that sort of thing. Little ways to get even. But this—"

"I'm not sure I'd go so far as to say marrying you was for revenge," he said. "It's possible he didn't want to give his grandmother the chance to interfere. But the fact is this: you were good for Kiyoshi. And in the end, Sachiko knew that. And she did love Miya in her own way."

Jessie rolled her eyes. "She just liked the idea of Miya. Because if she really—"

"Listen," he said, leaning forward. "Sachiko was a stubborn woman. She made many mistakes, not only with Kiyoshi. She never forgave herself for what happened to her daughter. For not being more aware, more vigilant."

Jessie's anger waned. She couldn't imagine the pain of losing a child to suicide.

"Sachiko did the best she could for her daughter," he said. "But it wasn't easy for Michiko to grow up like that."

"Illegitimate?"

"Not exactly. You should know that Michiko did have a certain amount of legitimacy for that time and that place. She was not the only child whose mother was like Sachiko and whose father was like Saburo. The local elementary school in Akasaka had many children like that back then. But those children rarely went to school beyond junior high. They followed their parents in the family business."

"Michiko worked in Sachiko's bar?"

Mr. Suzuki looked more and more uncomfortable. "No. She got in with some bad people and ended up working in a bad part of town. Dabbling in things that were strictly illegal and in things where police looked the other way."

"Are you saying she did drugs?"

"It's possible." He picked up his coffee cup and held it to his lips for the longest time. "But not only that." From his quiet speech, it was clear that whatever Michiko had been up to was far worse.

"What," Jessie demanded, "was it?"

"She was working in..." Mr. Suzuki's voice faded before he finally added, "a Turkish bath."

"A what?"

"Well, that's what they were called before the Turkish embassy made an official complaint. Then they changed the name to "soapland."

"Soapland?"

"You know. A place where men go to..."

Realization dawned on Jessie. "And Kiyoshi's father?"

He remained silent.

"Who else knows about this? Besides you and me?"

"No one," he whispered.

"Are you sure?" Jessie's voice had turned hard. When he nodded, she said, "Then this information dies right here. I never want my daughter to know her grandmother worked in a whorehouse."

He thrust his chin upward with indignation. "I have kept this secret for thirty-five years," he said quite sternly. "And I can continue to do so."

"I'm sorry," Jessie said, feeling contrite. "But it just seems like every day I wake up with some new crazy thing happening. And now, all this stuff with Kiyoshi's ex-girlfriend. How could Sachiko have been so cold and so—"

"She wasn't always like that, you know. When she was younger, she was different," he said, his eyes softening. "She was special."

"Were you in love with her?" Jessie asked gently.

"When I was a young man, we were close for a number of years. In those days, things were different. But now, my daughters—" He pursed his lips and stared at Jessie. Clearly, that was all he was going to say on that matter.

Jessie nodded to let him know that she would also keep his secret.

"The thing is, Sachiko didn't want to raise her grandson the way she did her daughter. She moved here and lavished him with attention, making sure he went to the best schools and had the best of everything. She wanted him to have every opportunity. To join the best company. To marry the kind of girl who could support the kind of man she hoped he would be."

"And then Ayako happened."

"Yes. Kiyoshi was used to getting his way. But Sachiko never even gave him a chance with her. She took care of things before he knew anything."

"By getting rid of her."

"She believed it was for the best."

"So Kiyoshi never knew?"

"I don't believe he did."

Jessie couldn't help but feel sorry for her husband. And for Ayako. "That's really terrible. I can't even begin to understand how Sachiko thought she had the right to meddle in people's lives like that. But there's nothing I can do about it now. It had nothing to do with me. What she did—it's not my business."

"That's very wise, Mrs. Jessie." He picked up his coffee and took a sip, looking relieved that this conversation was over.

"But what I want to know is this. Does the girl have a claim?"

"Excuse me?"

"Her daughter. Does she have a claim on Sachiko's building?"

"What daughter?"

She handed him Ayako's envelope, and he stared at it before pouring everything onto the table. While studying the copy of the DNA test, he shook his head in disbelief. "We had no idea."

"Does she have a claim? Am I in danger of losing anything?"

"As his wife, you're still entitled to your share—fifty percent. But inheritance laws have recently changed to favor illegitimate children. Miya's share might have to be divided between her and the girl. Half and half. Between the two children."

"Actually," said Jessie. "There's another thing I probably should tell you."

. . .

Jessie went straight from Denny's to the kindergarten, arriving just as the children burst into the garden where mothers and grandmothers were waiting. Miya skipped toward her, and for one brief moment, she forgot that somewhere in Tokyo was her daughter's sister. A child who would not exist if her husband's grandmother had had anything to do with it.

"Mommy, can I go play at Sumi's this afternoon?" Miya begged. "Her grandma said it's okay."

After Mrs. Kikuchi confirmed she didn't have any afternoon appointments and didn't mind the girls hanging around the Hair and Make-Do Salon, Jessie arranged to pick up Miya later in the afternoon

Jessie went home and headed to the third floor to get some work done. She sat cross-legged on a mat and lifted the dry-cleaning plastic off a lined Burberry trench coat, intending to check it for wear and tear. Jessie usually wished that Sachiko had been about eight inches taller and ten kilos heavier when she came across beautiful items like this, even if they were outdated. There was that wine-colored cashmere coat, that 1990s leather jacket with embossed trim and oversized shoulder pads, and that fur coat made from shaggy red foxes. She packed all those things up and sent them to their new owners with a jealous heart. But now, just the thought of putting something on her body that woman had worn made Jessie's skin crawl. She didn't even want to touch any of this stuff to stick on a price tag.

How could Sachiko ever think that it was acceptable to interfere in someone's life like that? To go behind Kiyoshi's back and pay off his pregnant girlfriend—to tell her to just get rid of the baby? What kind of person does that? And then there was the other shocking news of the day: her daughter's unknown grandfather. Had he been a day laborer? A drunken salaryman? A gentle professor? A psychopath? Only one thing was for sure: he was a person who visited prostitutes.

No wonder Kiyoshi had lied about his family. Her own seemed so mild in comparison—just some religious fanatics and a religiously stoned father.

Half an hour passed, and the Burberry coat still sat in her lap, unexamined and unpriced. Giving up the pretense of working, she went downstairs to confront her spirit occupants. But her anger weakened after seeing the grainy black and white memorial portraits of the three generations of Yamadas in the butsudan. Of course, Sachiko would have needed to have developed a tough personality. How could she not after being orphaned in the Tokyo firebombing? It couldn't have been pleasant spending her childhood as a maid. And, when she got a little older, stoking the egos of wealthy men by pouring drinks, singing, and dancing for them. Sure, Taka had called her relationship with Kiyoshi's grandfather an epic love story. For *him*, maybe. Because seriously, what twenty-year-old girl falls in love with a sixty-year-old man unless there's something in it for her? Security. Wealth. Power. Or, as Jessie suspected, an opportunity for escape.

"You were a pregnant widow, too," Jessie said to Sachiko sympathetically. "And you managed somehow, didn't you?"

Then, remembering that Saburo had left Sachiko with economic security, she glared at Kiyoshi, who had done the exact opposite. Had he been a jerk because his grandmother had been too lenient with him, as Mr. Suzuki had suggested? Or had his personality been set in stone the night Michiko's ovulating egg played Russian roulette with a customer?

Jessie's stomach hurt just thinking about all that. Antacids would ease the pain. Wine would take the edge off her nerves. Neither was an option, so she went to the kitchen, poured a glass of milk, and drank it, standing in front of the fridge. While slicing vegetables for a stir-fry, her thoughts returned to Ayako. It was impossible to muster up a good dose of anger toward her for barging in and turning her life upside down. After talking with Mr. Suzuki, Jessie couldn't even bring herself to dislike the woman.

Later that evening, Jessie received a text from Ayako, reminding her about the massage. She pulled the forgotten coupon out of her bag and checked the salon's website. Holy crap! Three hundred bucks for ninety minutes? Clearly, she was in the wrong business.

A moment later, another message came in. *In case you're wondering, someone else would take care of you. Not me.*

Jessie had been wondering about that. Because letting her dead husband's ex-girlfriend, the mother of the child he knew nothing about, touch her—give her beauty treatments—was kind of creepy.

Please do come. We can talk afterward.

How about tomorrow morning? Jessie texted back.

She was beginning to think she had lost her mind.

CHAPTER FIFTEEN

Ayako's salon was several minutes away from Ebisu Station and was larger and more luxurious than Jessie had expected. She almost backed out the door, but the receptionist stood as if she had been expecting her and ushered her to a comfortable armchair under a large abstract painting with dozens of soothing shades of blue. She picked up an international copy of *Vogue* and stole glances at the other customers. There were two Japanese men with skin the color of walnuts and with bodies like musclemen, a slightly overweight blond foreigner, and a well-dressed Japanese woman who could have been anywhere between thirty and sixty. Several minutes later, Ayako, wearing a white smock, came in with a Western woman with a rich-expat-housewife look all over her. They were talking like they were old friends, and Jessie watched them hug goodbye.

No wonder Ayako could afford her fancy clothes. This was quite a fancy place.

Then Ayako turned to Jessie. "I hope you don't mind waiting a few minutes longer." She whispered something to the receptionist, and the girl got up and returned with glasses of barley tea for everyone. A little later, Ayako was back with a man in a dark blue suit. From the somber way he spoke, Jessie wondered if she had gotten in trouble with the boss for giving away free beauty treatments.

"Come with me," Ayako said. She led Jessie to a softly lit dressing room with quiet piano music playing in the background. "Change into this robe and go into Room B across the hall. We'll talk more after you finish."

"Was that your boss?" Jessie asked.

"Who?"

"The man who just left. He looked kind of angry."

"Oh, no. He always looks that way. He's just my accountant."

Jessie took off her clothes, slipped into the heavy white terrycloth robe that looked like it was from a five-star hotel, and padded across the hall in white foamy slippers. For the next hour, she was massaged gently, wrapped in hot towels, and slathered with lotions and oils that smelled faintly of sage and lavender. She tried to take advantage of this once-in-a-lifetime experience by turning her brain off, but it was impossible with all that was going on. And every few minutes, her thoughts returned to what Ayako had said to her right before her treatment began. Surely, the man was *the* accountant and not *her* accountant. She must have heard wrong.

At the end of the hour, the masseuses led Jessie into a large private bath. Feeling like a giant bowl of jelly, she showered, bathed, and sampled all the beauty products on the counter. It was an anticlimax to get into her clothes, but she had to return to reality.

"Ms. Nagai would like you to join her in her office," the receptionist said to Jessie, directing her toward a small room at the end of the corridor. Jessie knocked on the door and opened it. Ayako was on the phone but motioned Jessie to sit across from her. The receptionist came in with a tray of refreshments and set it on the desk.

"I didn't realize that you were the owner," Jessie said after Ayako got off the phone.

"Yes. This is my shop." She poured the tea and passed Jessie a plate with two strawberries, each the size of a small tangerine.

"You're so young to be this successful," Jessie said with a mixture of envy and awe. "How did you do it?"

Ayako took a sip and set the cup down. "I will tell you everything. You see, when I was with Kiyoshi, I was working in a Ginza club. A *nice* one."

Jessie understood her point. Part of the wining and dining companies did for clients included visits to expensive hostess bars. There, intelligent and elegantly dressed girls like Ayako poured drinks, lit cigarettes, and laughed at drunken jokes. Kind of like modern-day geishas.

"One of the customers was an elderly investment broker. He was a kind old man—a grandfather type. Well, he was a lot better than the one I had," she said wryly. "But that's not the point. He learned of my predicament."

"Predicament?"

Ayako gave Jessie a look. "That I was with child and my boyfriend's grandmother was…how should I put it? Bribing me to disappear."

"Oh." Jessie probably would have considered that a lot bigger than a predicament.

"That night, he was very drunk. He said things about the stock market he shouldn't have. I never told anyone about this before because it's not exactly legal, and I didn't want him to get into trouble. But he told us about some companies that were about to go public. It was not common knowledge. It was…"

"Insider trading?" Jessie ventured.

"Yes. Something like that. I'm sure the man forgot because drunken men usually do forget what they say in bars. He was celebrating and ordering champagne and expensive snacks for all the girls. Everyone was having a wonderful time. And naturally, everyone got quite drunk. But because of my situation, I merely drank sparkling water. And when I went home, I investigated those companies on the internet. The next morning, I put Sachiko's money in them."

"All of it?"

"Yes. Plus, my savings. It was a bold move, I know. Perhaps I was young and ignorant. To be perfectly honest, I had no idea what I was doing. For about two weeks, I thought I had made a terrible mistake. That I had lost everything. But it turned out that he was right. Two companies went public, and I made quite a bit of money. And so, like I said yesterday, I went back to Kyushu for a while. I had to think of what to do. How to support myself. And my baby. You see, I never went to school—not beyond junior high school."

Jessie's mouth dropped open in surprise. Ayako was so articulate and well-spoken.

"I'm not formally educated, but I'm smart. I studied much on my own. I liked to read, especially in English. I studied English like a maniac. I loved reading English novels. And in Tokyo, I went to a conversation school for a little while. And I learned a lot during the years I worked in the bar. There were many foreign businessmen, and I was always eager to talk to them."

"It certainly paid off. Your English is fantastic. You sound like you have a degree in literature."

"Yes, I suppose I do sound like that. And in a way, I do have one. An *unofficial* one." She paused for a sip of tea before continuing. "Here is another secret about me. After I came to Tokyo, I pretended to be a college student. I attended classes at Aoyama University in Shibuya. The lectures—as many as possible: literature, history, philosophy. I sat in the back with the sleeping students. No one ever knew I was there. It was wonderful," Ayako said with a nostalgic sigh. "But, returning to the point. While pregnant, I received my high school equivalency diploma. Which," she added with a little chuckle, "was much easier than my university classes. After my daughter was born, I went to an esthetician college. And when I graduated, I opened a tanning salon. When my grandmother passed on, I sold it and returned to Tokyo. And then I started this place."

"Well, it looks like it's doing very well," Jessie said somewhat grudgingly. It was hard not to feel envious of Ayako for her grit and resourcefulness.

"It is, but to be honest, I want my daughter to know that there is more than just work. I want her to know that she has a family—a sister. Don't you think our daughters have the right to know about each other?"

Jessie shifted uncomfortably under Ayako's intense gaze. She didn't disagree with her, but she couldn't entirely agree either.

CHAPTER SIXTEEN

After Miya fell asleep that night, Jessie went downstairs and tried to keep her mind away from all the craziness of the past few days by blasting Back Street Boys on her iPad and sorting through a stack of woolen jackets. She didn't hear Mark knocking on the door until he tapped on the windowpane and waved at her. She turned down the music and went to let him in.

"I don't want to bother you," he said, smiling, "but I was on my way home from the university, and I saw you through the window. I thought I'd say hi, but if you're busy—"

"Not at all. Come on in." Jessie didn't mind him dropping by, but the thought occurred to her she might want to get some better curtains. And that she might want to reconsider her sloppy after-hours leisurewear. Hopefully, on her own turf, she wouldn't act quite as idiotic as she did at the supermarket.

"Are you sure?" Mark asked, glancing over her shoulder toward the boxes stacked on the tables.

"I'm more than ready for a break." Jessie ran her fingers through her hair, trying to remember when it had last seen a brush.

Mark sat down, scooting his chair back a few inches to make room under the table for his long legs. He wiped the fog off his glasses with a tissue and slipped them back on. He pointed toward the piles of clothes and asked, "What's all that?"

"They're my husband's grandmother's things. I hope you don't think it's tacky of me, but I'm selling them online."

"Why would I think it's tacky?"

"Well," she said awkwardly, "some people might think it's a little unfeeling. And, well, maybe a little greedy."

"Why not sell them? It's better than ending up in a landfill. You know what they say? Someone's trash is someone else's treasure?"

"If that's the case, I've got a ton of treasures up for grabs."

"So, what I'm seeing here is the tip of the iceberg?"

Jessie laughed. "You have no idea. And unfortunately, it's not all treasures either."

"I can believe that, considering what it was like in here before." He noticed the butterfly prints on the wall and stood to examine them. "Hey, these are really nice."

Jessie couldn't help but watch him with his back turned to her. Slap a cowboy hat on his head and sling a saddle around his shoulder, she was thinking, and the guy could become the Red, the Brody, the Blade, or the Wilder in one of those cowboy romance novels she devoured as a teenager. Lanky with a slow grin. Wiry but quick to throw a punch to defend someone's honor. Thoughtful speech. All the qualities of the perfect imaginary guy.

Mark's phone rang, and he turned and shot Jessie an apologetic look. Okay, she told herself, maybe cowboys don't usually wear glasses. And they don't have conversations in Japanese with someone about an upcoming curriculum meeting at a university either. Before the fantasy of Cowboy Mark evolved into one called Professor Mark, she went to the cookie jar on the counter and loaded up a plate.

"I made these today," she told him when he got off the phone. "You know, practicing for when I open for business."

Mark bit into one and moaned a little. "If chocolate chip cookies are going to be on your menu, I swear I'll become your number one customer. When's opening day?"

"I'm not sure," said Jessie, relieved to be thinking about the here and now of the café instead of cowboys. "I've got to get things cleared out upstairs first. And that's almost like doing an archeological dig. Sachiko's clothes alone go back for decades. She even had a pair of 1960s patent leather go-go boots."

Mark raised his eyebrows.

"I kid you not."

"Sachiko in go-go boots?" he said with a chuckle. "Now, that would be a sight to see. She was quite a character, wasn't she?"

"I suppose you'd know that better than me," she said before thinking it through. "Because I never met her."

Mark looked surprised. "Really?"

A wave of emotion hit Jessie with a force. Just an hour or so earlier, she had convinced herself that she was fine and ready to move on. But now, she looked down at the floor and stammered, "T-to be perfectly honest, I didn't know a thing about Sachiko. I didn't even know she was alive…until after she was dead. I didn't know anything at all." Her voice shook when she added, "But I had to be the one to identify her body."

"That must've been so awful for you."

Jessie looked up into his brown eyes that were oozing kindness. Everything she had been holding inside rose to the surface. She pressed her palms into her eye sockets and waited to speak until after she had gained some control. "It *was* awful," she said. "And just when I think I've gotten everything under control, something else happens." A single tear escaped, and she brushed it away. She cleared her throat and took on a more casual tone. "Anyway, since you are interested in Sachiko's life story, let me tell you a thing or two about her. Something you may not know. Something to explain the butterflies you see everywhere in here."

But to talk about Sachiko's former career as a geisha, Jessie had to talk about the car accident. And to talk about the car accident, she had to talk about her husband. She groped for the right words, but once she started talking about *him*, she couldn't stop. She found herself telling Mark about how Kiyoshi had lied to her for years. About his nasty temper. About him gambling away their savings. Jessie even got as far as describing her escape plans. A little while later, no longer bothering to brush away the tears streaming down her face, she sobbed, "And to top it all off, my husband's ex-girlfriend came to see me a couple of days ago. It turns out my daughter wasn't his only kid."

Mark fished a tissue packet out of his pocket and pulled one out for Jessie. His voice was quiet and soothing. "That's an awful lot for you to deal with."

She blew her nose loudly, and Mark handed her another tissue. She wiped her eyes and looked down at the table. "Oh, god!" Jessie's hands flew to her face. In the process of telling a complete stranger the intimate details of her life, she had just plowed through most of the cookies on the plate. No wonder her stomach felt queasier than usual. She leaned forward and laid her forehead on the table. She closed her eyes and stayed there. Any sane person would take that as the perfect opportunity to run out the door and escape the crazy woman.

"Jessie. Look at me. Sometimes it's easier to tell a stranger these sorts of things."

Jessie pushed herself up. She tried to smile, but it just came out crooked. At least she hadn't told him she was pregnant on top of everything else.

"Considering everything you've been through, I think you are an incredibly strong woman."

"So, did you know," Jessie said, returning to what sparked the meltdown in the first place, "that Sachiko used to be a geisha?"

The look on his face indicated that he did not.

CHAPTER SEVENTEEN

When Jimmy walked into the café three nights later, Jessie threw her arms around his neck. It felt like he had been gone a year and not two weeks. "I'm so glad you're back."

"Missed me, did you?" he said, returning her hug.

"How was the flight?"

"Hellish. Some kid squawked the whole way. And then, I had to go straight to the university for a complete day of mind-numbingly boring faculty meetings. Let me tell you, that's a surefire way to let a guy know he's no longer in paradise."

"Yeah, I feel sorry for you for having such a hard life," Jessie deadpanned.

Jimmy reached for the Domino's pizza menu that was behind the counter. "I've got a real hankering for some weird Japanese pizza with corn or chicken or curry on it."

"Japanese pizza, eh?" Jessie asked after he called and ordered the sausage combo deluxe.

"Let's just say I missed the idea of one more than the reality."

Jimmy pulled out various souvenirs and set them on a table. "Still hawking the family heirlooms, I see."

"You want a place to live? No wisecracks."

"My, oh my. Give this woman some power and look how she holds it over me!"

"And don't you forget it," she replied with a giggle. "Where's Yuya tonight? Recovering from the trip?"

"He's seeing Hidemi. Something about the legal documents for Kizuna moving in with us."

"You didn't go with him?"

He shook his head and ripped apart a package of spicy peanuts. He popped a handful in his mouth and said, "You know what they say. It's true love when your husband doesn't force you to go with him to see his Queen Bitch of an ex-wife."

"You know what else they say? It's true friendship when your friend eats the souvenir they bring back for you from their fancy vacation in the tropics before they even offer you a bite."

"Oops! Sorry." He held out the package and poured some peanuts into her palm. "Anyway, tell me, Jess. How are you feeling? How did everything go while we were gone? Did you survive without us?"

"Funny you should ask. Because while you two were vacationing in paradise, a major complication walked right through that door. You'd better brace yourself. It's big."

As she spoke, Jimmy's eyes protruded with shock. "Kiyoshi had a *love child*?" he finally managed to get out. "Who imagined the guy had even *more* secrets in his closet?"

"Love child? What century are you in? And it wasn't Kiyoshi's secret. I told you. He never knew about the baby."

"How do you know it's not some elaborate scam?"

"You should see the kid. She looks just like Miya."

"No offense, Jess. But lots of kids look alike."

"The thing is, Mr. Suzuki knew what Sachiko had done to Ayako—that's the woman's name. But he didn't know that she never went through with Sachiko's deal. She had the baby. And there's the DNA test to prove it."

"So, it really is Kiyoshi's kid?"

"Looks that way."

"And this woman shows up, totally out of the blue, and wants to be your friend?" said Jimmy. "It's got to be about money. It's always about money."

"I don't know, Jimmy. You should see the fancy salon she's got. It's a gazillion times better than here."

"Appearances can be deceptive."

"But even if it were about the money, the simple fact of the matter is I don't have any. She'd find out soon enough if that's what she's after."

"Seriously though, what are you going to do?"

"I don't know."

"What are you going to tell Miya?"

"I don't know that either. I haven't even told her about the baby yet." For the briefest instant, Jessie considered telling him what she had also learned about Kiyoshi's mother. But that was one secret that was going to have to die with her. She would never risk Miya finding out her father was the product of a client.

There was a knock on the door. "Finally!" Jimmy said, jumping up and pulling it open. "Pizza's here. I'm absolutely starving and— Oh. Hi."

"Sorry to disappoint you," said a man who was clearly not the pizza guy.

"Mark!" Jessie thought she would never see him again, not after she had dragged him to crazy land and back.

"I didn't see you fighting it out with the other bargain hunters in the supermarket yesterday. So, I thought I'd drop by and say hi."

She turned to Jimmy, whose eyebrows had shot up in surprise. "This is who I was telling you about before. Remember? The person who wanted to interview Sachiko about her life during the war?"

Mark stuck out his hand out in a friendly manner. "Yeah, that's me. Nice to meet you. I live over on the other side of the park."

"Oh, yeah. Jessie did tell me about you. You're at Hanamigawa University, right? Come on in. Stay for pizza if you like," offered Jimmy as if he owned the place.

Mark looked over at Jessie, and she gave a little nod. "That sounds great. How about I go across the way and grab a few beers to go with it?"

"Great minds think alike," Jimmy said approvingly. "But non-alcoholic for her."

After Mark left for the convenience store, Jessie turned on Jimmy. "Well, gee. Thanks a whole bunch."

"What? What'd I do?"

"Now he probably thinks I'm some sort of alcoholic. On the wagon or something. Non-alcoholic beers for her, indeed."

"He doesn't know you're pregnant?"

"Why would a total stranger know that?" She didn't say that particular total stranger knew just about everything else about her, though. Now a drinking problem could be added to her long list of faults.

Mark came back just as the pizza arrived. They popped open their drinks and got acquainted the way foreigners often do when they meet in Japan for the first time—namely, comparing answers to the how-long-have-you-been-here and the what-do-you-do-here questions. When Jessie realized Mark wasn't going to bring up what had happened two nights earlier, she relaxed. It wasn't a secret or anything, but wasn't her finest moment either. Jimmy didn't need to know.

"Your Japanese must be pretty fluent," said Jimmy when Mark mentioned that not only had he lived in Japan as a child for a couple of years, but he also came back as a high school exchange student and again for a semester in college.

"Yeah, I guess it is," said Mark without a hint of bragging. "I'm not completely bilingual, especially with writing. But I suppose I can get by."

It turned out that they all had been English teachers in the JET program, and they rehashed their experiences working with some oddball people.

"And so, like us, you decided to stay in Japan," said Jimmy.

"Yeah," agreed Mark. "I ended up staying."

"I guess you were smart like Jimmy," said Jessie. "You took advantage of all that free time they gave us as JETs and got your MA."

Mark hesitated. "Actually, I already had one when I arrived. I was just starting my doctoral dissertation then."

"Your doctoral dissertation?" said Jimmy, thoroughly impressed. "In language teaching?"

"Not exactly," said Mark. "In history. Mainly pre-war propaganda in Japan."

Jimmy whistled. "You sure were one over-qualified assistant language teacher, that's for sure. I bet that got everyone in a tizzy."

"Considering the Canadian teacher before me had gotten arrested for growing pot on his balcony, I think they were relieved I was just a nerd who sat around most of the time reading."

"What did you do after your JET contract ended? Come straight to Tokyo?" asked Jessie.

"I taught at a junior college for a few years. When I finished my Ph.D., I got the job I have now."

"Teaching history?" asked Jimmy.

Mark snorted a little. "I hate to say this, but you know what it's like. I may have a Ph.D. in history. I may have been hired to teach history classes. But half the people treat me like I'm a glorified English teacher. Or, sometimes, an in-house proofreader for other professors' papers. But that's okay. I like teaching English. And I don't mind helping out my colleagues either."

"Man, I envy you for already finishing your Ph.D.," said Jimmy. "I've got forever to go. I'm doing mine at Temple University and…"

Their conversation turned to stories of dissertation hell. While Mark was saying something about researching archives at the Tokyo University library, a thought occurred to Jessie.

"Hey, Mark," she said, interrupting Jimmy mid-sentence. "You can read Japanese, right? You said you wanted to know more about Sachiko, right? Well, I've got a whole bunch of papers upstairs that might tell you all about her."

Mark shifted his eyes to Jessie. "What kind of papers?" he asked, an intrigued look on his face.

"Old ones. Boxes and boxes of them. I found something interesting the other day that makes me think there could be more." After a pause, Jessie added, "And I can show you her geisha stuff, too, if you like."

"You had me at old papers. But geisha stuff? How could I possibly say no to that?"

"Great. When do you think you'd like to look at them?" Well, that came out a lot pushier than Jessie intended. "I mean—"

"How about now?" said Mark.

"Now?" Jimmy had his eyes on a second beer.

"Sure. At least to give me an idea of what you've got."

"All right. Let's go then." Jessie stood up, and they went outside through the kitchen door.

"Let me just bring my bike around here," said Mark. "I don't want to leave it on the sidewalk."

As soon as Mark was out of sight, Jimmy whispered. "You didn't mention you've been hanging out at the supermarket with such a hunk. Is he—"

"Don't be an idiot. We just—"

"Okay," Mark was saying as he rounded the corner and pushed his bike up against the wall. "Lead me to your treasures."

Jimmy nearly choked. "Treasures? Oh, man, are you in for a surprise." He put on a tour-guide voice as Jessie unlocked the door and waved his arms expansively. "Step right in, folks. Now, underneath all the mountains of clutter is an excellent example of an intact, even if quite shabby, Showa Era apartment. Straight from the time of Emperor Hirohito. With its original tatami mats. Original paper doors on the closets. With ridiculously low counters and ridiculously high cupboards in the kitchen. Enjoy this romp through time while you can, folks. Because the whole thing will be gutted in a few weeks. You'll never see it look like this ever again."

"Oh, quit being so dramatic, Jimmy," Jessie laughed. "Anyway, the geisha stuff is over here." She led them to a massive cedar wardrobe designed explicitly for storing kimonos. She pulled open a drawer and lifted the heavy white paper wrapped around a deep purple kimono decorated with gold and silver cranes. "Isn't it pretty?"

Gently stroking the fabric, Mark said, "It's exquisite. Just look at the gorgeous details on that silk."

"I haven't taken anything out of these wardrobes, so I don't know exactly what's in them," said Jessie. "I'd never be able to get the kimonos folded back the way they're supposed to be. But the kimono sashes are in that wardrobe. The wigs are in those white boxes on the shelf, and hair ornaments and accessories are in these drawers."

"What are you going to do with it?" Mark asked. "Sell it?"

"Fortunately, no," said Jessie. "I found a folk museum in Kanagawa that specializes in Showa Era memorabilia. They sent someone out here last week to check it out. They said it's quite rare to have an entire collection of geisha stuff, so they're happy to take everything for one of their permanent exhibitions. So the end of that story is, worrying about bugs eating away at all that beautiful silk will fall under someone else's watch, not mine."

Jessie offered Mark a tentative smile and returned to business mode. "Now, about all those papers. They're in the boxes over there in the corner. And in the interest of full disclosure, more boxes are in that closet. And in its overhead space. There are more in the bathroom as well. And if that's not enough, the bathtub's filled to the ceiling with boxes, too."

"Get out, man!" Jimmy whispered theatrically in Mark's ear. "Get out while you can."

"But before you decide to make a run for it, take a look at this." Jessie picked up a book on the table and handed it to Mark.

"*Swiss Family Robinson?*"

"I found it in one of the boxes. Look at the inscription inside the front cover. It's also in English."

He opened the front flap and began reading aloud. "When I returned to my native village on account of spring vacation, Mr. K. Endo gave me one yen. So, in memory to this, I bought this book. 14 April. 1914." Mark looked up at Jessie. "That's pretty cool."

"Right?" said Jessie. "And here's another one. It's a 1911 edition of *The Secret Garden*. There's no inscription, but see the notes in the margins? Someone studied English with this book."

"Where do you think the books came from?" asked Jimmy.

"Well, not from Sachiko's side of the family, that's for sure," said Jessie. "They were shopkeepers, remember? I doubt they were reading English classics. And besides, their stuff was destroyed by the firebombs. It has to be from the Okada side, don't you think?"

"Okada?" asked Mark. "Wasn't that Sachiko's benefactor?"

"Yeah," said Jessie. "The people in Nagano told us that they were hotshots back in the day, but they couldn't remember why. But if Sachiko ended up with this, there could be something even more interesting."

"It's possible," agreed Mark.

"But the thing is, everything needs to be cleared out by the end of February. Jimmy's moving in with his partner and his daughter. Unfortunately," sighed Jessie as she held up a 1980s Sony VCR manual, "there's an awful lot like this. But what if I can't tell trash from treasure? Like those 1970s fashion magazines. Do I toss them or try to sell them or what?"

"Well, I do have some free time right now that the semester is over. I could take a look for you."

"Really?" As much as Jessie needed Mark's help, she didn't want to seem too pushy.

"How about Monday? Is that soon enough to start?" He ripped the yellowing tape off one of the boxes, and the smell of old musty papers filled the room. He leaned in and inhaled as if it were the bouquet from a fine red wine.

"Are you for real, man?" Jimmy sneezed and backed away.

Mark grinned. "I guess I should be upfront with the fact that I'm a total geek when it comes to things like this. You know what they say about historians and their thing for old papers?" When Jessie and Jimmy shook their heads, he laughed. "Well, that's probably just an insider joke. Anyway, considering what you told me about Sachiko's background and her connection to the Okada family, it wouldn't hurt to check."

"You think there could be something?" asked Jimmy. "In this junk heap?"

"Maybe." Mark bent down and picked up a 2002 catalog for a meal delivery service. "Or maybe not."

"I guess it would be kind of cool for Miya to find out if her ancestors were famous," said Jimmy.

"Wouldn't that depend on what they were famous for?" Jessie was trying not to think about the DNA donor in the background.

"If any skeletons are hiding in the Okada closet," Mark said while digging deeper into the box, "I'll be sure to let you know."

"Maybe we should have some sort of confidentiality agreement."

Jimmy laughed like that was a joke, but Jessie was actually kind of serious.

CHAPTER EIGHTEEN

Jessie gave Mark a key to the apartment, and he came over early Monday morning. At first, she stayed away, not wanting it to look like she was breathing down his neck. But she needed to focus on her own important task at hand, which was shifting the rest of Sachiko's wardrobe out of her building and into other people's closets. After a few hours of hearing him move things around over her head, she changed into nicer slacks, put on some makeup, and loaded a plate with cookies.

She found a stack of bagged-up garbage near the front door that hadn't been there the day before. A thermos hot pot and a University of Hawaii mug were next to jars of instant coffee and powdered milk on the kitchen counter. The new dish towel and bottle of dishwashing soap by the sink suggested Mark was the kind of guy you could trust not to make your mess worse than it already was. He was bent over a box, looking somewhat like a mad scientist, with his curly hair standing out in every direction and his glasses resting halfway down his nose.

"I thought you might be ready for a break," Jessie said, holding out the plate.

Mark took off his grimy work gloves, tossed them onto the table, and reached for a cookie.

"These are all for you. I promise I won't devour the whole plate again."

"Are you sure? I mean, if you ever feel the need to—um, eat a whole bunch of cookies, that's all right with me."

Jessie smiled. "Maybe not today." And because she couldn't resist, she added, "Nice apron, by the way."

"Why, this old thing?" Mark said in a falsetto, twirling around and letting Jessie get a full view of the pink and green floral print, complete with ruffles. "Thanks to my landlady and her vast collection of aprons, my manly clothes are fully protected." To emphasize his point, he then flexed his muscles.

"Not every guy can pull off that look. But you do it so well," she said seriously.

"I live to please," he said, equally seriously.

Jessie laughed. Mark was so good-looking, but he didn't give the impression of being a vain man at all. Not like Kiyoshi, who took his handsomeness very seriously. But after seeing Mark flounce about in his landlady's apron, it was going to be pretty hard to keep that sexy cowboy image in her head going. Grinning at her own silliness, she gestured toward the table Mark was using. "So, have you found anything interesting yet?"

"If you consider a petrified banana in a box of newspaper advertisements interesting, then maybe."

"Gross. I hope you don't find anything worse. Like a dismembered finger or something."

"At this rate, a dismembered finger would be quite welcome."

. . .

The next afternoon, Jessie was sorting through a dozen pairs of nearly identical size-five black high-heeled pumps. All were in their original boxes, and most looked like they had never been worn. Jessie knew practically nothing about brand names, but she did know from movies that Manolo Blahnik shoes were something fashionistas would go crazy about. She held one next to her size-seven foot and wondered if this was how Cinderella's stepsister felt before she crammed her giant foot into the glass slipper. Jessie made a memo in her notebook to double-check its value and put the shoe back in the box.

On the other side of the paper door, Mark was humming some song that Jessie couldn't identify. Earlier that day, he had come across the papers relinquishing Sachiko from her geisha contract and a box of old appointment books with Sachiko's former client information. Those he had filed away for further scrutiny in one of the plastic boxes he had labeled by decades.

"Jessie, can you come here for a second?"

Welcoming the distraction, she went to the other room. Mark was leaning over a very old photograph of what seemed to be a three-generation Japanese family: grandparents and a younger couple holding a baby. When she reached for it, he stopped her. "There's some writing on the back. Most of it's smudged, but those look like dates. They look like the year the baby was born. And sadly, when he died a year later. It's hard to read, but I think it says Kaiei 2 and 3. Logically, that would make Kaiei 2 the year the photo was taken."

"When was that?"

"That would be the second year of Emperor Kaiei's reign. Sometime in the Edo period. They measured years back then, just like they do now—in terms of the imperial reign. Like how anyone born before 1988 has birthdays in Showa when Hirohito was emperor. After that, Heisei. And now it's Reiwa—"

"I *am* aware of all that," Jessie said with a smile. "I didn't arrive in Japan yesterday, you know. I meant what year was it in the regular calendar?"

Mark hit his head with the palm of his hand. "Sorry. I've got this terrible tendency to over-explain things, especially anything related to Japanese history, whether a person wants to hear it or not. Anyway, I'm not sure what year that would be. I'd have to check."

"But I didn't know Japan had photography back then," Jessie offered.

"To be honest," said Mark, "neither did I."

Jessie leaned into the picture, searching for evidence of her husband or daughter. Other than the kimonos and hairstyles, the unsmiling faces didn't look so different from those she had found in a box of old photos of pioneers in her grandmother's basement.

"I have a feeling this could be important," said Mark. "Maybe not the celebrate-with-champagne kind of important, but somewhere along the lines of a let's-have-a-cup-of-coffee kind."

"Well, I've got brownies in the café. Shall I bring them up?"

"Why don't we go there? I can take some of that stuff down for you."

They entered the café's kitchen via the outdoor staircase, their arms full of shoe boxes.

"Don't worry about that," Jessie said when Mark headed out the door to get another load. "I can bring the rest down later."

"I don't mind." Before Jessie could protest, Mark added, "Besides, it'll give me more space to work."

By the time it took him to make several trips, Jessie had fixed a pot of tea, sliced the brownies, and set a nice table by the window. Mark took off his apron, this one patterned with cute owls, and pulled out his phone. "Let's check out the dates on the photo. Kaiei 2, it seems, is 1849. That means the photo was taken just before the Black Ships arrived. I'm pretty sure the only way a camera could have made its way into Japan then would have been through Nagasaki. That was the only place open to trade. Do you happen to know if your husband's family has any connection to Nagasaki?"

"I have no idea what happened in his family two years ago, let alone almost two hundred." Jessie tried not to sound bitter, but she was failing miserably. "Don't worry," she quickly added. "I'm not about to go all crazy again."

"You know," Mark said, "you weren't the only one in a bad marriage. Mine lasted four years. We got divorced just before I moved to Tokyo."

Jessie had a million questions, but she swallowed them all.

"No kids," he said, as if he could read her mind. "I wanted them at first, but it's a good thing that never happened. That would have complicated everything. But the thing is, I was in a real slump after the divorce, even though we fought the entire time we were married. It was a relief when it was over, but at the same time, I felt like I had failed at something really important. Now, I know what happened to you is different. You didn't get divorced—"

"No," said Jessie. "There wasn't enough time for that to happen."

Mark nodded. "Being in an unhappy marriage is difficult. But being free from one isn't like going through a magic door into a new world of sunshine and rainbows. You can't just forget about the old world. It still exists. At least, it's still inside of us, still a part of who we are. As for me, I felt like I was straddling two worlds for the longest time. One of misery and the other of freedom."

Jessie nodded as Mark spoke. That was exactly how she felt. Miserable, but free.

"And," added Mark, "a good dose of guilt thrown in. For not being able to change the past. I always wondered what I could've done differently." He picked up another brownie and bit into it. After a moment, he said, "But you know how I pulled through? My family back in California was a big help. It turned out that they never liked my wife all that much. They really had my back. Especially my sisters. Let me tell you, there is *nothing* like three big sisters to come to the baby brother's rescue." He folded his arms and leaned across the table. "And then, there were all the new friends I made when I moved to Tokyo. Especially someone from work. Kumiko. She's the person I went to the movies with the other day. I don't know how I would have made it without her. The minute we met," he said with feeling, "we connected. Meeting her was one of the best things that ever happened to me. We're very close, and I can tell her anything."

A period of silence stretched out as Jessie processed all this information.

"Recovering took time. But I don't think I'd be the person I am now if I hadn't gone through all that. A bad marriage, Jessie, can help you discover who your friends are. It can help you let new people into your life and give you room for new relationships. It'll take time, but you'll get there. Trust me."

They finished their tea, gazing out the window at the people passing by. The quiet was shattered when a noisy group of teenage boys gathered in front of the convenience store.

"Believe it or not," Mark said, a nostalgic smile spreading across his face, "I used to go to that high school. Nearly twenty years ago. The uniforms are still exactly the same."

"Were you as geeky as those kids?"

Mark laughed. "Believe me, I was far, far worse."

Their conversation shifted from failed marriages to teenage antics, and the hour disappeared. Unfortunately, Jessie needed to cut the afternoon short to go get Miya.

"If you're free tonight, would you like to have dinner? With me and my daughter?" she hastily added, hoping he wouldn't notice the blush creeping up her neck. "It's the least I can do to say thanks for all your hard work."

"There's no need to thank me for that. But I'd love to come. Shall I bring some wine?"

"Wine? Um—"

"Or," he said as agreeably as if she had just announced to him that she was a teetotaling Mormon, "juice if that's what you'd prefer."

"I guess I should mention the fact that I'm pregnant."

"You're having a baby?"

"I'm twelve weeks along. So, that night I didn't tell you every sordid detail of my life."

"A baby isn't a sordid detail, Jessie."

He said that so kindly her eyes welled up. "I know."

"I guess it's been quite a roller coaster ride for you."

"And that's probably why I told you far more than I should have that night. Hormones."

"I didn't mind. Honestly."

"I had a miscarriage scare around Christmas, and I haven't told anyone except Jimmy and his partner. And my family in America. So, please don't say anything to my daughter. That is if you're still game to come for dinner."

"Why wouldn't I be?"

"You don't mind eating with the pregnant lady and her kid?"

"What can I say? I live for adventure."

She laughed. Maybe they *could* be friends. "Another thing. I haven't told Miya anything about the other sibling. You know. What I was talking about the other day?"

"My lips are sealed. Anything else I should watch out for?"

"Don't say anything about Kizuna moving in, either. That's Jimmy's partner's daughter. The girls don't know because it's not quite a done deal yet. If it falls through, Miya would be very disappointed."

"Even if she tries to torture it out of me, my lips are sealed."

.   .   .

Several hours later, Mark rang the doorbell.

"Mommy! Some man's here!"

"I told you Mark was coming for dinner." Jessie wiped her hands on a kitchen towel and walked to the door, immediately noticing he had changed his clothes and shaved. "He's one of Grandma Sachiko's friends, and he's helping sort things out upstairs."

"Are you Mommy's new boyfriend?" Miya asked before Mark even had his shoes off.

Jessie prayed for the floor to swallow her up instantly.

"No," he replied, a smile threatening the corner of his lips. "We're just friends."

"My Daddy died."

"I heard about that. You must miss him a lot."

"Do you want to see his picture? It's in there. In our family…alternater," Miya said, trying to remember the word in English.

"Well, sure. Lead the way."

And as if things couldn't be any more awkward, Miya gave an update on the who's who of their spirit residents. Her attention then turned to the kittens hiding behind the curtains. While she introduced Mark to Minnie and Mickey, Jessie was thinking of how much worse this could have been had Miya stuck with her original idea to name the cats after her parents.

"Maybe I should've asked if you were vegetarian," Jessie asked when they sat down to a platter of stir-fried pork, cabbage, carrots, and green peppers.

"Nope. Total carnivore. This looks and smells delicious."

Miya leaned forward and squinted at Mark. "So, do you have a girlfriend?"

"Miya! It's not polite to be so nosy. Let Mark enjoy his dinner without all your questions."

"I don't mind," he said with a smile.

"So, what's her name?" Miya insisted. "Is she pretty?"

"Miya," Jessie warned with a stern tone.

Mark laughed. "Well, let's call her Ms. K. And she's pretty, I suppose."

"Pretty like Cinderella or pretty like Snow White?" asked Miya.

"Miya is crazy about Disney princesses," interjected Jessie, hoping to steer the conversation in a different direction.

Having several young nieces, Mark turned out to be fully versed in Disney-speak. While he and Miya discussed the various merits of different princesses, Jessie's brain went into girlfriend-analysis mode. This so-called pretty Ms. K. had to be the Kumiko at work—

the one who's crazy about *The Godfather*. The one who had gotten him through all the rough times after his divorce. The one, he had said, who changed his life and made everything better.

Not that it mattered, Jessie reminded herself, who this Ms. K was, one way or another.

.   .   .

Jimmy didn't waste any time. "So, what's this I hear about you and that gorgeous history professor having dinner together on Tuesday?"

"How in the world did you find out about that?" Jessie poured a latte from a coffee maker she had gotten from a used restaurant supply store and handed it to him across the counter.

"Miya told Kizuna, and Kizuna told Yuya, and Yuya told me. You can't keep anything secret from me, darling. So, spill it. Spill it all."

"Well, it was kind of like this. We ate. It was food."

"Uh-huh. And?"

"Quit looking at me as if I had dragged the poor guy up to the roof for some hot, wild sex."

Jimmy laughed. "Now, there's a thought."

"It was just dinner. To thank him for all the work he's been doing upstairs."

"If you were on the market, you'd totally go for him, wouldn't you?"

"Listen to yourself, Jimmy. I'm not on the market. I'm a widow."

"Are you planning to wear widow's weeds for the rest of your life?"

"Kiyoshi's only been gone three months. That's hardly the rest of my life. Just drop it."

"Alrighty. As you wish. So, what'd you guys talk about during this so-called thank you dinner?"

"We talked about Sachiko's stuff."

"And?"

"And about Miya going into first grade."

"You like the guy. I can tell. And by like, I mean—"

"Oh, shut up," she said, irritated by the condescending way he was nodding his head. "So, what if I do? Do you think a guy like Mark will be interested in someone like me? With a kid and one on the way? He's got everything going for him. Good job, nice personality—"

"Dreamy body."

That did make her laugh. "I'll give you that."

"And Miya said—"

"Why in the world are you quizzing her about Mark?"

"Because I figured you wouldn't spill the beans, and she would."

"There's nothing to spill. He's just a neighbor. A nice guy who's helping me out with a gigantic headache of crap."

"Well, according to Miya—"

"Listen, Jimmy," said Jessie. "You've got to stop grilling her about Mark. If she goes and tells him about it, he's going to think *you* are interested in him."

"He's totally not my type. Although, I suppose in a pinch—"

Jessie reached across the counter and flicked Jimmy on the head. "You're totally insane, you know that?"

Just then, Yuya came in. "Whatcha guys talking about?"

"About how Jimmy would—"

"We were talking about how Jessie should go for the hot history professor she keeps stashed up in her attic when we're not around."

"I do not keep a hot professor stashed in my attic," said Jessie. "Jimmy's lost his already fragile mind. Mark is simply helping me out."

"Can't wait to meet him," said Yuya. He winked at Jessie and then turned to Jimmy. "So, exactly how hot is this guy?"

CHAPTER NINETEEN

Now that Jessie had reached twelve weeks and the chances of miscarriage were slim, she fixed a special breakfast and told Miya that she was going to become a sister.

Miya looked up from her waffle. "A baby? But we don't have a daddy. The book said you need one to make a baby."

"What book?" Jessie reached over and wiped a dab of whipped cream off Miya's chin with her finger.

"The one from the library."

It had been more than a year since they had borrowed that birds and the bees book, so Jessie was surprised it had stuck in Miya's head. "That's right. You do need a mommy and a daddy to make a baby. But it takes a long time for a baby to grow in a mommy's tummy. So, this baby got started when your daddy was still here."

"I miss Daddy sometimes."

"I know you do, sweetie. I'm sure he misses you, too."

"Is he going to be sad if I forget what he looks like? Because sometimes I try to remember, but I can't. I have to go and see his picture to remember."

"Even if you can't see him in your head, you know he's in your heart. And that's the important thing." Jessie felt like she was speaking from a grieving manual for children.

"How did he get in there?" Miya pointed at her chest.

"What I mean is that you'll never forget your daddy. He's a part of you. Inside your heart and inside your head."

"What about the baby?"

"What do you mean?"

"Will Daddy live inside the baby too?"

"Yes. But in a different kind of way. You have memories of Daddy, but the baby won't because the baby will never have a chance to meet him."

"Then how did Daddy get into the baby?"

"Because every person in the world is made up of half their Mommy and half their Daddy. That's how babies get started." Jessie was hoping this conversation wouldn't take a more technical turn. "So, the baby may look like Daddy. Just like you look like your Grandma Michiko. She's in you, too. You never met her either, but you look just like her."

"But the baby won't know what Daddy was really like."

"That'll be your job. To teach your little brother or sister all about him. All the things you remember."

"Like when we went to Disneyland?"

"The baby will love to hear about that."

"And the beach?"

"That too."

"What about when Daddy got mad and was scary?"

Jessie paused. "Daddy *was* grumpy sometimes. Scary sometimes. You can tell the baby about that as long as you never forget the good times. Because there were lots of those."

"I guess I'll be pretty busy teaching it all kinds of stuff."

"Yes," Jessie said, suppressing a smile. "But it'll be fun."

"Babies are kind of cute."

"They sure are."

"But I want a sister," said Miya firmly. "I hate boys."

"Oh, sweetie, we don't get to choose. We get what we get. You'll love a little brother just as much as a little sister."

"Maybe we can give it to Uncle Jimmy if we don't like it."

"What!"

"I heard him and Uncle Yuya talking about how much they wanted to have a happy family. We can give the baby to them, and they can have a family, too. Everyone will be happy that way."

"We're not going to give the baby to anyone. Not even to Uncle Jimmy and Uncle Yuya." And because all the papers had been signed and custody of Kizuna was given to Yuya, Jessie decided to tell Miya that she would be moving in upstairs.

"She's not going to live with her mother anymore?" asked Miya.

"No. Her mother's moving to a different city. You'll go to the same school, and you can play with her whenever you like."

"Kizuna doesn't like her mother's boyfriend." The way Miya said boyfriend almost sounded like a dirty word.

"Why not?"

"It's a secret."

"You can tell me." Jessie kept her voice measured, hiding her alarm. "Why doesn't she like him?"

Luckily, Jessie didn't have to pry it out of her.

"He says mean things about her daddy. And Uncle Jimmy, too."

"Is he mean to her?"

"No. He just pretends she's not there."

"Oh," Jessie said with some relief. "I see."

"But he says mean things about her. He told her mom that something is probably wrong with her because something is wrong with her father. What's wrong with Uncle Yuya? Is he sick?"

"Of course, he's not sick. If anyone is sick, it's that boyfriend. He's sick in the head because he only has half a brain. That's the problem."

"Kizuna told me that her daddy and Jimmy have sex together," said Miya, as if she actually knew what she was talking about. "Is that true? Can they make a baby like you and Daddy made a baby?"

If only Jessie were living back when it was perfectly acceptable for a pregnant woman to drink because a stiff shot or two—even at breakfast—would make this whole conversation go a whole lot easier.

"Sometimes a man and a woman fall in love with each other. But sometimes it's two men, and sometimes it's two women. Love is very mysterious that way." Jessie hoped she wasn't making too much of a mess of this and said, "Only a man and a woman can start a baby. But families are groups of people who love each other."

"Like how Uncle Jimmy and Uncle Yuya are my uncles, but they aren't really my uncles?"

"That's right. And they love each other."

"But who do you love now, Mommy?"

"Right now, I love you! And when the baby comes, we'll both love it. That's enough for me right now."

.   .   .

The following Saturday, Jessie needed to tackle the next issue on the sibling agenda. After several weeks of texting back and forth with Ayako, after consulting with Mr. Suzuki, after a second DNA test, and after giving the matter a gazillion thoughts, Jessie decided to let the girls meet.

Just a playdate. Nothing more.

"Guess what," Jessie said, mustering up as much fake enthusiasm as she could. "We're going to the aquarium today with a new friend. And she has a little girl just a bit older than you. Won't that be fun?"

"Who?" Miya frowned. They didn't have that many friends that they suddenly went off and did things with.

"She was a friend of Daddy's. You haven't met her before."

Despite all the people clustered near the entrance to the aquarium, Jessie spotted Ayako immediately. From a distance, she looked like a fashion model in skinny jeans and a leather jacket.

"Sorry we're so late." Jessie didn't mention she had wasted an hour trying to find pants that could zip up.

"Thanks for texting to let me know," Ayako said pleasantly. "I appreciate that."

With her angled cheekbones, expressive eyes, glossy black hair, and bright smile, Ayako was very pretty. Almost beautiful. No wonder Kiyoshi had been in love with her. When she held up two entry tickets, Jessie pulled out her wallet.

"Oh, no," Ayako said, taking a step back. "This is my treat. I invited you."

Jessie was about to insist on paying their way, but her eyes fell on Miya standing next to her half-sister, and she froze. She glanced at Ayako, and judging from her face, seeing the two girls together for the first time was just as shocking for her. How could they not feel like they were looking in a mirror? Even with the age gap, they looked so much alike. There were *some* superficial differences: Miya's hair hung down her back in a long braid, and Ayako's daughter sported a no-nonsense chin-length haircut. Miya wore a pink down jacket, a pink sweater covered with purple hearts, purple leggings, and glittery black sneakers tied with pink shoelaces. Natsumi wore a simple navy down jacket, a red sweatshirt, and jeans that were becoming a tad too short. Her sneakers were plain white—or under the scuff marks they used to be. But the girls' heart-shaped faces, wide-spaced eyes, slightly pointy noses (which Jessie had always assumed had come from her side of the family), chins with a tiny cleft in them—all of that—they shared.

The mothers managed to pull themselves together and introduce their daughters. They, of course, froze up the way kids do when a parent produces a new friend. Miya stuck by Jessie's side, and Natsumi stuck by her mother's. After an awkward fifteen minutes of filing silently past the schools of sardines, the sea bream, the stingrays, and the turtles, Jessie was beginning to regret this whole thing. Jimmy was right. Just because the two girls shared DNA didn't mean they had to be all best friends about it. Ayako's face looked strained, and Jessie wondered if she was having second thoughts as well.

When they got to Shark Hall, the girls began to change. As the different species of sharks swam inches from their faces, they giggled in delighted terror. They leaped back, away from the glass, but then moved toward it again, just for the sheer thrill of it. Later, at lunch in the aquarium's restaurant, there weren't enough available seats, so the two families sat at different tables.

"What do you think of Natsumi?" Jessie asked over their soba noodles.

"She's going in the second grade." Miya was clearly impressed by her new friend's advanced academic status. "She said first grade's a breeze, and I shouldn't worry."

"Is she nice?"

"Uh-huh. Are we done? Can we go now? We want to get a good seat at the dolphin show."

By good, Miya meant in the splash zone. While the girls lined up with the other kids to compete for the prize seats, Jessie and Ayako sat a dozen rows behind.

"They seem to be getting along well," Ayako said.

"Yes," replied Jessie, wishing she was anywhere but with her dead husband's ex-girlfriend and their kid.

"And Miya is enjoying her new kindergarten? Getting ready to start first grade?"

"Yes."

"Do you think Miya will be happy there?"

She'll have to be, thought Jessie, because it's not like they had any other choice. "Yeah, I think so."

"And the café? When do you think you will open the café?"

Just then, a young woman with an overexcited voice, like an animation character, announced that the dolphin show was about to begin. Jessie turned her attention to the stage, relieved that she no longer had to engage in small talk that was starting to feel like the Spanish Inquisition. An hour later, she was more than ready to head home and hit the box of chocolates she had stashed in the back of the café's fridge. But when the girls insisted on ice cream from a shop just outside the entrance, she put on a smile and sat at a picnic table, watching them lick their cones. A baby at the next table began to cry, and they all turned their heads toward the uproar.

"Babies can be so noisy," announced Miya. Then, with tremendous self-importance, she added, "And my mother's going to have one in the summertime—a sister. And then I'm going to—Oh, look! Turtles! They've got sweaters on!"

Forgetting all about human babies, the girls dashed over to see the half dozen turtles the owners were taking out of a stroller and releasing in the grass, presumably to play.

"Congratulations," said Ayako. "A baby."

"Yep. Lucky me." Jessie's attempt at humor fell flat, and she regretted her tone.

"I envy you."

Jessie looked at Ayako dubiously.

"A baby is a wonderful beginning. I would have loved to have had a second child."

"You're still young. People have babies all the way into their forties."

"Yes, I know. You're absolutely right. But I'm afraid..." Ayako turned toward the girls as her voice faded. "Well, I'm not in a position to even think about that right now." She cleared her throat and asked, "When is your baby due?"

"Middle of August."

"Oh, dear. The worst time of the year to be with child."

"Yeah," Jessie said with a straight face. "I'm really looking forward to that."

When Ayako broke into laughter, Jessie laughed with her. They began talking about pregnancy, birth, and motherhood. Despite their strange connection to each other, an easy conversation began. To her surprise, Jessie found herself beginning to like Ayako even though half the things she said sounded like they came straight from a 19th-century novel.

"Tell me," said Ayako. "Are you happy with your life now?"

Happy? What a question. Widowed, pregnant, broke. Jessie looked at Ayako's face and didn't see anything other than interest. "Yeah, I suppose so. Happy enough, anyway." Feeling strangely at ease, she added honestly, "It's funny. I'm still kind of an outsider in my neighborhood, but it's because I'm new and not because I'm a foreigner. But even though I'm new, I seem to have been given a fast pass ticket like they have at Disneyland. You know, through Kiyoshi's grandmother. I feel like I'm a part of that community more than anywhere else I've lived in Japan."

"It seems like a good place to raise a family."

"Yeah. I think it is." Jimmy's voice in her head was warning Jessie to hold back, that Ayako was *not* her friend. That she shouldn't divulge too much. But it felt good to talk to another woman without worrying it would somehow make its way back to Kiyoshi, where he would twist things around. "But I won't be alone. My best friend Jimmy and his partner and daughter are going to move into the building after it's renovated. In the apartment that's right above mine."

"How wonderful for you to have neighbors who are friends. Or perhaps, it's better to say friends who are neighbors."

"We're going to help each other out."

"That must be an immense relief for you."

Jessie caught a tinge of sadness in Ayako's voice. Maybe she really was just lonely. "What about you?" she asked. "Do you like where you live?"

"It's small but convenient. As a single mother, I have to live close to where I work."

"It must be difficult—"

"My life is my daughter," Ayako said with passion. "And my life is work. I work for her. Everything I do is for her."

Jessie nodded. That was something they did have in common.

After a pause, Ayako added, "And then I had a health scare."

"A health scare?"

"Ten months ago. My blood test came back with an abnormal result."

"Oh, I'm so sorry—"

"It was nothing," Ayako said firmly. "But it made me think about the way we live. I realized I must make our own little world larger. I don't want Natsumi to grow up in…what would you call it? A bubble? With just the two of us? She has a sister. I want her to know that. And maybe it's good for your daughter to have a sister as well."

"Maybe," Jessie said cautiously. She wasn't ready to have this discussion. Not quite yet.

"And work isn't everything. I'm going to start enjoying myself. Take a bit more time off. Spend it with Natsumi. Make friends."

"I'm in the opposite position," said Jessie. "I'm going to have to find a job."

"But I thought the café…"

There was no point in sugarcoating the situation. If Ayako had any interest at all in the financial aspects of Jessie's life, now would be the time to set things straight. "The café," Jessie said, "barely makes enough to cover the utilities. Let alone all the taxes I owe. Sachiko was living on her savings, and what little she had left went to pay off Kiyoshi's gambling debts. I can get by for now, but after the baby comes, I'm going to have to get a real job."

"Teaching English?"

"Probably. But believe it or not, I used to teach English at a high school in California. I'd love to go back to teaching the meaning of *To Kill a Mocking Bird* or Orwell's *1984*."

Ayako's face lit up. "A literature teacher! How wonderful. I had no idea that you were a specialist in books. We have so much to talk about—"

A loud, high-pitched voice came from behind, and they both turned around.

"Yoo-hoo! Mrs. Jessie!"

"Oh, god," muttered Jessie. The one person she had hoped she would never have to see again after moving out of the company apartments was clip-clopping across the sidewalk toward her in high heels and looking all hoity-toity with that Louis Vuitton bag she dragged around everywhere.

"Say hello, Aiko," urged Miki Miyamoto to her daughter, who she had by the hand. "Go on. In English. It's not every day you can practice with a real foreigner."

"Hello, how are you I'm fine too thank you," the girl rattled off, all in one breath.

It wasn't the kid's fault her mother was awful, so Jessie replied with a friendly smile. Then, she turned to the mother and spoke in Japanese with far less warmth. "What a surprise to see you here, Miki-san."

"I thought you went back to America. Well, this is very lucky. I'm delighted to have a chance to say goodbye before you go. Japan is so hard for foreigners," she said, looking over at Ayako with a conspiratorial smile. Miki had lived in New York for one year with her husband ten years ago. And that made her the self-appointed company housing expert on all things foreign, including Jessie.

"Actually, I'm staying in Japan."

"All alone?"

"Well, with Miya, of course." Jessie wasn't about to provide this woman with any specifics.

"Mother, look!" said the daughter. "There's Miya! Can I go say hi?"

"All right," Miki said, releasing her grasp on Aiko's hand. "But just for a few minutes. Don't muss up your dress. And don't touch those nasty turtles." She turned her attention back to Jessie. "We're just extremely busy today. You know how it is before school starts. So many things to do. First, there was a rehearsal for Aiko's piano recital. And we must get back for her calligraphy lesson by five. And we still need to go to Ginza Mitsukoshi and—"

"Looks like you had a pretty full day, all right," Jessie interrupted, knowing that Miki Miyamoto could go on till next week. She glanced over at Ayako and caught the slightest of slight eye rolls. It was all she could do to keep a straight face.

"Honestly," the woman continued. "I'm becoming quite envious of you mothers who are just sending your children to regular public school. That's so much less hassle. You simply can't imagine everything that I have to do to get ready for—"

"Oh. So, Aiko got into…where was it again?"

"Minami Gakuen," Miki answered with a tinge of impatience.

Jessie already knew that because when Miki's daughter got early acceptance back in December, the woman ran around acting as if she had personally won the lottery.

"Well, that's great. I guess you'll be moving closer to the school then." Jessie also knew that Miki couldn't afford to move out of company housing after spending a fortune on cram schools for her kindergarten-aged daughter. She wasn't crazy about how gossip ran rampant among the company housewives, but she certainly paid attention when it came to the number one bitch.

"Well, you know how it is," Miki said smoothly. "My husband works terribly hard for the company. He often stays in the office until late. It's ever so much easier for us to live close by. Especially now that he's up for promotion to section chief and—" Miki stopped short, arranged a horrified expression on her face, and exclaimed, "Oh, my goodness! How thoughtless of me to bring up my husband's success. I mean, with your husband's problems in the company and…"

Jessie caught a ghost of a smirk in Miki's eyes. In her old life, when their husbands had to work together, she would have reassured the bitch that it was okay, that she knew she didn't mean anything by it. But today, Jessie kept silent and coolly watched the woman sweat under her insincerity.

After a long moment, Miki turned toward the girls and took off her sunglasses. "Oh, my. They do look alike. Are they cousins?"

"Not first cousins," said Ayako smoothly, speaking for the first time. Miki turned to her, and Ayako held her gaze without saying anything else.

Miki glanced down at her watch. "Oh! Just look at the time! Come along, Aiko. We must hurry."

After Miki reclaimed her daughter's hand and dragged her away, Ayako and Jessie looked at each other and burst out laughing.

"No friend of yours, I presume," said Ayako.

"Ick, no," Jessie said with an exaggerated shudder.

"Believe me, I do know her type. Smiling on the outside but like a serpent on the inside. Under their smiles, they're bullies." The way Ayako spoke suggested that she had handled one or two Miki Miyamotos in her life, and Jessie suspected that Ayako was the one who had come out ahead.

"Yeah, she's a total bitch, all right. But she was right about one thing. Our girls do look alike."

"They most certainly do."

Right then, Jessie made the decision that would change their lives. "Are you busy next weekend?" she asked Ayako. "Do you want to come over?"

CHAPTER TWENTY

By the time Ayako and Natsumi arrived on Saturday morning, the Butterfly Café smelled heavenly thanks to Jessie's frenzied baking activities that had begun well before dawn.

"I'm practicing for when I open up the café," she said, feeling the need to explain the banana muffins, chocolate chip cookies, oatmeal bars, and angel food cake on the counter.

"It's very impressive," said Ayako. "Your future customers will be delighted. Did you go to cooking school to learn this?"

"No. I learned from my grandmother. She was a really good cook. Me? I guess you could say that I'm still at the beginner stage."

Jessie called up the stairs. "Miya! Natsumi's here."

Miya, who had been excited over Natsumi's visit, came thumping down. The moment the girls were together again, though, the awkward shyness they had experienced at the beginning of their aquarium trip returned.

"Miya," Jessie said in English when they started their tea party. "Use your napkin. Put it in your lap." To her surprise, Natsumi unfolded her napkin and put it in her lap as well. "Do you like cookies?" Jessie asked Natsumi in English. When the girl nodded, Jessie looked over at Ayako. "I'm impressed."

"Last summer, Natsumi went to a ten-day English camp for children in the mountains of Fukushima Prefecture," explained Ayako.

"Ten days!" Jessie was pretty sure she wouldn't have been able to let Miya go away for that long. It was hard enough with the overnight stay at the kindergarten last fall.

"I was somewhat concerned. But she enjoyed it very much and did not become too homesick. Since then, we speak to each other in English sometimes." Ayako turned to her daughter. "Right, Natsumi?"

"Yes, Mama," Natsumi replied, a little distractedly because by then, the girls had begun laughing and whispering to each other as they had the week before at the aquarium.

"Tell Mrs. Jessie what you did at English Camp."

"Basketball!"

"Come on, let's go find the cats," Miya said in Japanese, not paying attention to the parallel conversation concerning Natsumi's linguistic skills.

After the girls went upstairs, Ayako said, "For my daughter, the English learning at the camp was quite incidental. It was basketball she loved. One of the teachers was a coach, and after she came home, that was all she talked about. I have had to learn a thing or two about the game since then."

"Basketball, eh?"

"Natsumi may be short, but she's enthusiastic. And optimistic that she'll grow taller."

After a chuckle, the women fell into silence.

"So," Ayako said finally. "This is where Kiyoshi grew up."

Well, that brought the elephant in the room right out into the open. But before Jessie could respond, Mrs. Watanabe burst through the door.

"Jessie! Did I leave my teeth in here?"

Jessie jumped up, expecting the poor woman to be toothless and gumming it. But there she was, grinning as usual and her white teeth flashing.

"My extra pair," she explained. "I had them in my pocket, but now they're gone."

"Oh," said Jessie. "Sorry, I haven't seen them."

"Keep an eye out for them, would you? They might be in the back of the refrigerator. Oh!" Mrs. Watanabe said, noticing Ayako. "I didn't know you had an English lesson now."

"This is my friend," Jessie said, not wanting to know how a pair of false teeth might have ended up in her fridge.

Patting her hair and smoothing a skirt that probably hadn't come out of the closet in a decade, Mrs. Watanabe scooted a chair next to Jessie and picked up a cookie. "We're going to the movies in Ginza today."

"Oh," Jessie said with a teasing smile. "I see. A date. And here comes the boyfriend now. All spruced up as usual."

Jessie had completely forgotten the thread that tied them all together until she saw the look on Mr. Suzuki's face when Ayako stood and bowed formally. "Good afternoon. Perhaps you remember me. My name is Ayako Nagai."

"Miss Nagai," he said, bowing back. "It's been a long time. I hope you have been well." His composure completely disappeared when the girls came in together, each holding a cat.

A satisfied smile spread across Ayako's face when she saw his jaw visibly drop at the sight of her daughter. "This is Natsumi. She's turning eight next month."

His eyes darted back and forth between the two girls. He opened his mouth a few times as if he was going to say something. But then he turned to Mrs. Watanabe. "Let's go. We don't want to be late."

"There's no need to rush," Mrs. Watanabe said. "We've got plenty of time to—"

"It doesn't hurt to be early." Mr. Suzuki put his hand on his girlfriend's elbow, and with what seemed like an orchestrated dance move, he got her out of her chair and over to the door. Before leaving, he turned around and bowed once again. "Ms. Nagai, I must apologize for my reaction. I need to think for a while. We will talk soon."

Jessie wasn't exactly sure what had just happened. "I'm sorry if that brought back bad memories for you," she said to Ayako in English when they were gone.

"I knew I'd probably have to see him someday," Ayako replied, also in English. "But I didn't expect it to be today. Honestly, though, I was happy he could see my daughter."

"He's been helping me a lot with everything." It would be pretty difficult for Ayako not to have hard feelings over what Sachiko had done, but Jessie's loyalties would have to lie in the Suzuki camp if push came to shove.

"What happened before—well, I suppose that's over and done with," said Ayako. "Besides, he was merely acting on Kiyoshi's grandmother's behalf."

"I owe him an awful lot, you know," said Jessie, somewhat relieved. "He's been like a grandfather to me. And, as you can see, he's got a thing going with Mrs. Watanabe. They're both like family now."

"The kind of family that can leave their teeth in your refrigerator?"

Jessie laughed. "Exactly." Then she changed the subject. "Listen, there's something I want to show you upstairs. Something that might explain Mr. Suzuki's reaction when he saw Natsumi."

At the butsudan, Ayako followed tradition by clasping her hands together, bowing her head, and paying her respects to their daughters' deceased father, grandmother, and great-grandmother. After she straightened up, Jessie reached behind a bowl of apples for Michiko's picture. "This is what I wanted to show you. Kiyoshi's mother."

Ayako brought the photo up close and examined it. Letting out a long exhale, she said, "This is more proof that all those terrible things Kiyoshi's grandmother said about me weren't true. She said the baby probably wasn't Kiyoshi's. She said I was trying to trick him into marrying me. She said she knew all about bargirls like me. She said girls who work in bars usually were…"

Considering Sachiko's daughter's profession, Jessie thought she probably did know a thing or two about shady bargirls. But ignoring that fact, she said, "Did you know that Sachiko actually ran a bar?"

Ayako blinked. "What?"

"In fact, she owned a very fancy one in Akasaka—called Sachiko's. So, I guess you could say she was a bargirl herself. Before that—well, there's a lot more to the story. I'll tell you everything I know. But let's go back downstairs. We can talk there."

Once they were facing each other at the table by the window, Jessie wasn't sure how to start. "This would be easier with wine."

"It would be, indeed."

"Well, you can have some if you like. I think Jimmy's got a bottle stashed in the fridge."

"Actually, I don't drink," said Ayako. "Not anymore. I used to, but now it doesn't agree with me."

Jessie gestured toward the plate of cookies on the counter. "A dose of sugar?"

"Maybe later," Ayako replied.

Jessie, on the other hand, needed extra help to get the conversation rolling, so she reached for a cookie and bit into it. "All right then. Here's the thing. I never met Sachiko. Not even once. I didn't know a thing about her until the accident. Kiyoshi told me that his whole family was dead. And I believed him. Because who would ever lie about that kind of thing if it wasn't true?"

"But Jessie, Kiyoshi lied all the time."

"I know that *now*. But I didn't know then. I was such a fool. The entire time we were married. A fool!"

"It's not your fault for believing your husband."

"It wasn't until after he died that I learned about the lying. The gambling. His grandmother, and…"

"And me."

"And you." Jessie paused before asking her next question. "If you don't want to answer, that's okay. It was a long time ago. But did Kiyoshi ever tell you anything about some missing jewelry?"

"Missing jewelry?"

"Kiyoshi was in terrible debt. Some jewelry went missing, and Sachiko said he had taken it. He said he didn't. But somehow, it's gone. And that's what ruined their relationship."

Ayako shook her head. "Maybe that happened after I went to Kyushu."

"The thing is, I still can't picture Kiyoshi doing that. He'd do mean and impulsive stuff, but he always tried to fix it later. I can't help but think that if he really did steal the jewelry, he would've tried to get it back to her. Or at least he would've apologized. Admitted he was wrong."

"But what if he had done something like borrow money from gangsters?" asked Ayako. "Maybe he had to sell the jewelry. Maybe it was the only way out for him."

"You could be right about that," said Jessie. The scenario of gangsters knocking on her door demanding payment had not been on her radar, and at least she hadn't lost any sleep worrying about *that*. Thank goodness one of the first things that Mr. Suzuki did for her was to take care of Kiyoshi's debts.

"But anyway," Jessie continued, "there's something else I was going to tell you. I don't know the whole story, but here's what I do know. Before Sachiko ran the bar, she was a geisha." The look on Ayako's face made Jessie laugh. "And Kiyoshi's grandfather was her benefactor. He's the one who bought the building where she had her bar. He died when she was pregnant with Kiyoshi's mother, but he left the building to her." After a moment, Jessie asked, "How much did Kiyoshi tell you about his mother?"

"Just that she died of cancer when he was little." Ayako looked out the window and added, "It must have been so hard on him to lose his mother like that."

"I'm sure it was hard on him. But cancer was just another one of Kiyoshi's lies. His mother committed suicide."

"What did you say?"

"She committed suicide."

Ayako's face hardened. "How could a mother ever think of leaving her child like that? On purpose?"

"I-I don't know," said Jessie. "I don't know the details."

"To do that to a child is unforgivable. To leave them behind because you're too much of a coward to stay. It's simply unforgivable."

"It's hard to know what goes on in people's heads," Jessie said gently, wondering if someone close to Ayako had left her like that.

"She had a choice." Ayako's voice was still bitter, but it had lost its sharp, angry tone. "She had a choice to stay with her child. But she decided to leave." She reached for a cookie, took a small bite, and set it down on the saucer. "What about Kiyoshi's father? What do you know about him?"

"Nothing. Nothing at all."

That much was true. Nobody did, not even Kiyoshi's mother.

.   .   .

Jimmy stopped by later to compare wallpaper samples for their future living room and was surprised to hear that Ayako and Natsumi had visited that afternoon. "You said you were going to take things slow," he said disapprovingly.

"I know I did. But she's nice. I like her, and—"

Jimmy snorted. "And what?"

"Well, Natsumi and Miya *are* sisters. That second DNA test proved it. And it wasn't like that would be a big surprise."

"What? So now you're all going to be best friends? Live happily ever after like some kind of schmaltzy sister-wives made-for-TV movie?"

"Yeah, right," Jessie replied sarcastically. "That's exactly what we're going to be doing."

"Or maybe," Jimmy continued, "she's got it in her head that her daughter deserves a piece of the Sachiko action."

"Listen to yourself. You sound like a lunatic. Exactly what kind of Sachiko action are you referring to? The part with all her cats? Her geisha memorabilia? Her wall-to-wall crap?"

"You know what I'm saying."

"It's not like I'm going to give her all my PINs or anything. And even if I did, it's not like that'd do her any good."

"But—"

"Google her salon, Jimmy," she said, exasperated. "It's classier than the Butterfly Café could ever hope to be. But before you say anything else, I'm not an idiot. I promise I'll keep my eyes open. It's not like I'm going to run off and marry her or anything."

Jimmy laughed. "Well, considering your history with people who are practically strangers, I suppose that's good to know. But do you really think she's hanging around here just because she wants the girls to get to know each other?"

"Yeah. Actually, I do. I think she's kind of lonely." After a moment, Jessie added, "Like me. It's nice to have a friend."

Jimmy let out a disapproving sigh. "There are hundreds of potential friends out there with a lot less baggage than Kiyoshi's ex."

"Well, I've got plenty of baggage of my own, in case you haven't noticed. The thing is," Jessie said quietly, "something clicked between us. It's hard to explain."

.   .   .

The next weekend, Jessie and Ayako took the girls to Ueno Zoo, and they had another successful outing. Unfortunately, the following week the weather was too miserable for outdoor activities, so they visited an overpriced animal café and a karaoke box where the girls belted out songs from their favorite cartoons. Miya, it turned out, had inherited Jessie's inability to carry a tune. Natsumi, however, had a sweet voice, just like her mother.

That night as they were getting ready for bed, Miya asked her mother where Natsumi lived.

"Somewhere in Ebisu near where her mother works."

"Did you know she doesn't have a daddy either?"

"What did she tell you?" Jessie asked cautiously.

"Not much. She said her mommy doesn't talk about him. But don't you think it's funny?"

"What's funny?"

"Well, I don't have a daddy. Natsumi doesn't have a daddy. But Kizuna's got two of them. And a mommy. But her mommy's going to get married and go away. Are you going to get married?"

"Wh-what?"

"I don't want you to get married, Mommy. Because where would I go?"

"Oh, sweetie. I'm not planning on getting married. At least not anytime soon. And if I ever did, I'd never leave you. Ever. You don't have to worry about that."

Jessie was about to say she would be there for her daughter forever and ever, but she stopped herself just in time. Promises like that were dangerous.

CHAPTER TWENTY-ONE

The weather had turned unseasonably warm. The sky was crystal clear, and a gentle breeze rustled through the trees. Jessie did not want to squander the day indoors because the weather news warned that winter would return with icy rain tomorrow. The minute they got to the park, Miya ran to the monkey bars where her friends from kindergarten were playing. Jessie didn't see any of the mothers nearby, but there were some older siblings kicking a ball around in the grassy area. What would it be like for the Yamada kids in five or six years? Would Miya be with her gang and her little brother or sister with theirs? What would Jessie be doing when her kids were old enough to play outside on their own? The only thing for sure would be that she would be nearly forty. Forty! Sending her mind right back to where it belonged—her early thirties—she spread a picnic mat out in a sunny spot, leaned against a tree, and pulled *Memoirs of a Geisha* out of her bag.

"Reading up on the family business, I see."

Jessie looked up to see Mark grinning at her from his bike, grocery bags dangling from the handlebars.

"Yes," she replied seriously. "But purely for research purposes."

"I'm glad to bump into you," he said. "I thought I'd tackle the last of the boxes this afternoon."

"The ones in the bathtub?"

"Yeah. If that's all right."

"Of course, it's all right. But have lunch with us first. There's plenty, and it's too nice a day to spend inside."

After Mark rode off to put his groceries away, Jessie checked her face with her iPhone camera. She rummaged through her bag for a comb, lip gloss, mascara, or anything that would make her look less like she had rolled out of bed and straight into the park. She found a tube of lipstick and smeared some on. Dammit! It was too dark! How obvious was that, putting on makeup as soon as the guy was out of sight? She tried to wipe it off with a tissue, but the long-lasting burgundy color was on to stay. At least she hadn't gotten the idea to pretend it was blush and smear some on her cheeks.

"I'm back."

Jessie held up the lipstick as if it were evidence at a crime scene. "Chapped lips."

"Yeah, I always get that in the winter, too. Although, personally, I go for the colorless approach," he said, grinning as he slipped off his shoes and sat down on the mat in front of her, cross-legged. "Here's my contribution to the feast. Strawberries."

Jessie jumped onto that like it was headline news. "Well, that's great! Miya will be thrilled. She loves strawberries. In fact, so do I and—"

"Well, glad to hear that," he said, cutting her off. "Strawberries are good." Then, steering the conversation in another direction, he asked, "So, how are you feeling? No more morning sickness?"

What an idiot she was to have been worried about hair, makeup, lipstick, and all that crap. "I'm starting to feel pretty good, actually."

"My sister had it bad for about six months. But you look so much better than she did. When will you know if it's a boy or a girl?"

"Maybe at the next ultrasound."

There was something weirdly charming about Mark asking her about all that baby stuff, as if it were the most natural thing in the world for a guy to do. Jessie smiled when she realized why. He missed his family. His sisters. No wonder he was comfortable with all this pregnancy talk. When Miya came over a little while later, demanding lunch, she and Mark continued the Disney princess conversation they had started several weeks earlier.

"Can I help you hunt for the treasure?" Miya asked Mark.

"What treasure?"

"I heard Mommy and Uncle Jimmy talk about the treasures in Grandma Sachiko's apartment."

"It's true. I am looking for treasures, but maybe not the kind you're thinking of."

"No gold or diamonds?"

"Nothing that exciting. Just interesting papers that tell some interesting stories."

"Stories? Like with princesses? Genies? Dragons?"

"Who knows? Maybe."

"I tell you what," said Jessie. "Why don't you help me sort the costume jewelry this afternoon? That might be more fun than looking at dusty old papers."

Mark put on an insulted look. "Hey!"

"Oh, Mommy!" Miya exclaimed. "Look! I see—" In her excitement, she knocked over the open thermos, and Mark's pants became soaked.

In a flash, Jessie wasn't sitting in the park with Mark. She was back in the company apartment with Kiyoshi, where such a minor incident would result in either a mild rebuke or a ruined weekend. The outcome often depended on how quickly Jessie would react because always, no matter what, it was her fault. Yanking a hand towel out of her bag, she frantically began wiping up the spill.

"Hey," Mark said, completely unruffled. "It's no big deal." He removed the towel from Jessie's hands and laid it down on the puddle of tea. Winking at Miya, he said, "I hope no one thinks I wet my pants. That would be so embarrassing, don't you think? If people thought I peed myself?"

Miya studied Mark's face before letting out a giggle. "Yeah, especially because you're a grownup."

"So, what do you think I should do?"

Miya frowned. "I don't think you have to do anything. I think your pants will dry pretty fast."

"You know what? You're absolutely right. They *will* dry fast. In fact, I think they're almost dry already. Whew!"

After Miya went to join her friends, Mark said, "Man, you sure have some quick reflexes. I don't think I've ever seen anyone move at the speed of light over a little spill."

Jessie felt her neck turning red. "It's just that—"

"You don't have to explain. I totally get it. Your husband, right?" When Jessie nodded, he said, "I know what it's like to live with someone with a short fuse. I know that any little thing can set them off. Something like a little spill."

Mark turned his attention toward the noisy children by the swings, and Jessie thought the conversation had ended. But after a moment, he started speaking. "I usually don't talk about my marriage or ex-wife, but the truth is, we were doomed right from the start. That time when you—um, ate all those cookies? You said you should've known better than to marry a guy you hardly knew. But you know what? I knew right from the beginning I shouldn't be marrying my wife. I went ahead and did it anyway. So, I guess in a way, that's far worse than what you did."

"But—"

"We dated for about a year. We were very different types of people. But I thought we had an opposites-attract kind of thing going on. I thought that me being a nerdy geek balanced out the party girl in her. And vice versa. It was fun for a while, but it didn't take long for me to turn into Mr. Boring because I didn't want to go out all the time and drink myself silly." He picked up the last strawberry and popped it into his mouth. After a moment, he spoke again. "Jesus, the stupid fights we had in our second year together when I was trying to finish my dissertation. I started sleeping in my office because it had gotten so bad at home. I blamed it on stress and the uncertainty of our future. My contract at the junior college was ending, and I needed to finish the Ph.D."

"It must've been a tough time," said Jessie, resisting the urge to reach out and put her hand on Mark's arm.

"Things completely fell apart when I accepted my job here in Tokyo. In fact, my ex was so upset about that she threw a plate at me. And that," he said, lifting his hair and pointing at his forehead, "is how I got this scar. Six stitches, if you can believe it."

Jessie was shocked. Despite Kiyoshi's temper, he had never laid a hand on her. "I guess some people just want to stay close to home."

Mark's laughter was hard and dry. "That wasn't it at all. She didn't want to stay in Japan. That was when I realized she had married me because she wanted to live abroad. I was the ticket to some sort of international life she had conjured up in her imagination. She couldn't believe I turned down a postdoc position in Hawaii to take a boring job at Hanamigawa University."

"You turned down a job in Hawaii? Hawaii!"

"It sounds great, but it wasn't a real job. It was basically another two years of being a student. After that, I would have had to look for something all over again. But the job at Hanamigawa University was permanent. Tenure. I had just turned thirty, and I wanted to settle down. I wanted to start being a grownup. But living abroad was clearly far more important for Hiroko. Hence the fight that resulted in the plate throwing. I guess I'm lucky she didn't destroy my dissertation like she had threatened."

"Seriously?"

"Seriously. But that wasn't the only problem. Some other things were going on that didn't sit so well with me. Fidelity, for instance. We had completely different attitudes about that."

"Ah."

"But finally, she found someone who could make her dream come true. Someone who would take her out of Japan. And last I heard, she was in some small town in rural South Australia."

"I guess she finally got the exciting cosmopolitan life she dreamed of," said Jessie.

Mark laughed, this time for real. "Probably not quite what she had in mind. All those flies and snakes."

"All that heat and dust," she added.

"The point is this. I know what it's like to be with someone and not know how they'll react from one minute to the next. Living with Hiroko was like navigating through a minefield. I know that's a cliché, but that's the only way I can describe it. And from what I can tell, it was the same with you and your husband. Right?"

Jessie's eyes filled up with tears, and she rummaged in her bag for a tissue. "I don't know why I'm getting emotional."

"Remember, there'll be good days and bad days for you. But I promise you that eventually, the good days will be much more."

Clouds began to gather around the sun, and Jessie reached for her jacket to pull over her knees. Mark didn't seem to notice the sudden drop in temperature. He leaned back on his elbows and looked like he was in no hurry to leave.

CHAPTER TWENTY-TWO

By late February, nearly everything of Sachiko's that could be sold was sold. Yuya had driven twelve huge boxes of miscellaneous items to the Salvation Army. Mark had moved the yellowed diaries, ledgers, and other important documents to his office. All that was left in the third-floor apartment was the trash that Yuya's crew would be taking to the city's garbage center that afternoon. By the end of the day, the apartment would be completely empty. Tomorrow, the transformation would begin.

Jessie was checking the cupboards to make sure nothing had been forgotten when she heard Mark calling from the door. "I thought you were flying to California today," she said, happy to see him.

"I am, but I've got something for you."

Jessie opened the envelope he handed her. "Tickets to Tokyo Disneyland?"

"Kumiko won them at the faculty party last night, and she hates Disneyland. She suggested I give them to you and Miya."

"Kumiko," repeated Jessie, forcing a smile. "Well, that's a nice surprise. But how does she know about us?"

"I guess you could say that I talk about you all the time. Well, about Sachiko, mainly. But I guess that's kind of one and the same," he added with a laugh. "She's really interested in my Sachiko Project. That's what we've been calling it at work. Kumiko's exactly like me in that respect. You know, crazy about digging around for mysteries in a bunch of old papers."

Of course, Mark and Kumiko would be talking about her. Without *her*, there would be no Sachiko Project. "So," Jessie said, putting on an interested expression. "You had a faculty party last night?"

"Yeah. Dull stuff. But Kumiko and I sat in the back and poked fun at some of the professors who take themselves way too seriously. Anyhow," continued Mark, "you and Miya go to Disneyland and have fun. Kumiko may hate the place, but to be honest, I love it. How could any self-respecting Southern Californian not be a Disney fan?"

"If that's the case," ventured Jessie, "we could wait until you come back and go together. That's if Kumiko wouldn't mind. Miya would really love—"

"I wish. The tickets expire in two weeks. It's so typical of my university to give a practically useless prize." Looking at the clock on his phone, he said, "Now I really do have to get going, or I will miss my flight." Mark headed toward the door, but he stopped and turned around. "How do you feel about all this?"

"About what?"

"About accomplishing the impossible. Clearing out this apartment. Getting rid of all the junk."

She couldn't very well tell him that she would miss the time they had spent together *because* of the junk. She couldn't tell him she felt a little sad because he wouldn't need to be coming around much now that the papers were all cleared out. "How do I feel?" she said. "I feel it never could've been done without you." And that was certainly true.

Yuya showed up ten minutes later. "I need to talk to you. Let's go downstairs. It'll be easier there."

At one of the back tables, he laid out some technical drawings that might as well have been written in Arabic for all the sense they made to Jessie. "Sorry to tell you this, but the electrical wiring is shot on the third floor. If you plug in three appliances at once, the entire building could go up in flames."

Jessie felt like she had been kicked in the stomach. "Are you telling me that Miya and I are in danger and that—"

"Your place is fine. The wiring there looks like it was replaced around the same time as the plumbing. The problem is with the third floor. Honestly speaking, it's unlivable."

Jessie's eyes filled with tears of disappointment. "I was really looking forward to you guys living here. It was going to be—"

"Quit panicking, mate. I'm going to get it fixed."

"But Yuya, you can't do that on top of the plumbing. I'd never be able to pay you back."

"Instead of a three-year pay-back plan, it'll just be a five-year one. Yeah, it's longer than we originally worked out, but at least you'll get *some* rental income now. And we'll pay you the going rate at the end of five years. If we ever do move out, you'll have a nice property."

"But Yuya—"

"Don't forget, we need you. Kizuna's a handful, to say the least."

Jessie swallowed her protests. He was right. It was becoming more and more evident that parenting Kizuna was going to require the efforts of more than just two clueless guys.

The next day, a flurry of activity began above Jessie's head. A team of electricians showed up early in the morning, and within three days, the apartment was no longer a fire hazard. She later learned from Jimmy that such speedy work was purely due to Yuya's connections because mere mortals like themselves would have had to wait weeks for the wiring to be replaced.

Yuya's apprentices then got to work, eating their boxed lunches and hanging out in the café on their breaks. She kept them supplied with cookies and coffee and eavesdropped on their conversations.

Having been ordered to stay out until it was finished, that was the only way to get information about what was going on upstairs.

Ten days later, Yuya and Jimmy guided her through the apartment. Jessie gasped at the transformation. "If you guys ever move out, I'm moving in. It's gorgeous."

"It's great, isn't it?" said Jimmy proudly, as if he had done all the work himself. All the rooms had built-in closets and shelves, and the kitchen and the bathroom gleamed with the latest state-of-the-art fixtures and appliances.

"There's another thing," said Yuya. "Tomorrow, someone from the *My Home Sweet Home and Housewife Happiness* magazine will come to take some pictures."

"The what magazine?"

"Don't knock the name. It's really popular, and you never know. Maybe they'll put in a plug for the Butterfly Café. Wouldn't that be great?"

Jessie felt her stomach lurch, but it wasn't stress this time—it was the baby giving her a little kick.

. . .

As soon as Yuya and Jimmy moved in upstairs in mid-March, Hidemi handed Kizuna over to her father and headed off to Osaka to start her new life without so much as a backward glance. The fiancé's family had not been informed about their future daughter-in-law's reproductive past, and the wedding (white dress and all) was to be held at some fancy hotel. Kizuna, unsurprisingly, was not on the guest list.

Yuya stayed close at hand to help his daughter adjust, but there were only so many times you could take a kid to the movies or an amusement park. Eventually, the three adults had to start acting like proper parents. They had to start being a family. The guys went back to work, and the honeymoon period ended when Jessie was put in charge.

Kizuna had been accustomed to a lot more freedom, and she rebelled against all the rules surrounding television, meals, and bedtime. They gave her a lot of leeway at first because, after all, the poor kid had practically been abandoned by her mother. But they couldn't let her go to bed at midnight because she had been playing on the iPad her mother had given her as a parting gift. She would wake up grumpy in the morning, nap in the afternoon, and then be wide awake when even the adults were sleepy.

Everything came to a head ten days into their new lives. Jessie had gone downstairs to mop the café's floor while the girls were watching cartoons on TV. When she returned ten minutes later, she smelled something burning and rushed to the kitchen. The girls were standing in front of a precariously tilting frying pan filled to the brim with smoking hot oil. Kizuna was about to dump in an entire bag of frozen french fries. Jessie yanked both girls away from the stove with such force they all nearly fell over backward.

"What the hell do you think you're doing?" Jessie screamed after she turned off the flame and moved the oil to the back burner. Giving Kizuna a shake, her voice became even louder. "Do you know what could've happened? To you? To Miya? Are you crazy? Do you have any idea how dangerous that was?"

Miya started to cry. Kizuna's eyes flashed with anger, and she tried to squirm out of Jessie's grasp. "I just wanted to make french fries," she said in a hard voice. "I saw it on TV. It's no big deal. I cooked all the time at home."

"In this house, you are to never, never, ever turn on the stove in the kitchen without asking me first. Not without a grownup in the room." Jessie felt dizzy with anger and fear. What if she had been a second later? What if the oil had spilled all over the girls? Her voice softened but was shaky. "You can't do that, ever. It's dangerous. You could've both been seriously hurt."

Kizuna glared at Jessie. "I don't have to listen to you. You aren't my mother."

Jessie wished she could claw her angry words back. After all, nothing did happen. She inhaled and exhaled a few times, hoping her heart rate would slow. "Sweetie, I know I'm not your mother. But you do have to listen to me. I'm an adult, and there are rules. I'll teach you how to cook if you want. Even french fries someday. But if you had dumped in all those frozen potatoes, you could've gotten splattered with the hot oil. You could've gotten burned. Maybe you'd even have to stay in the hospital. I don't want anything bad to happen to either of you."

This time, Kizuna stiffened, but she didn't put up a fight when Jessie pulled them close.

After the oil cooled down, Jessie poured it back into the bottle. Then she showed the girls how to make meat sauce for spaghetti. Over dinner, she extracted promises from both that they would never turn on the stove without adult supervision.

Later, Jessie overheard Kizuna tell Miya she wanted to enter a city-wide drawing contest for third graders. The next day, she went over to Watanabe Stationery and bought a nice set of colored pencils and some fancy sketchbooks and gave them to the girl without much fanfare.

Two weeks passed, and Hidemi still hadn't called her daughter. Eventually, Kizuna stopped asking about her. She became quiet and spent a lot of time hovering over her drawings. Her silence concerned the adults more than when she was up to shenanigans.

"What can we do?" asked Yuya when they were in the café one evening going over their schedules for the upcoming week. "I mean, it's easier now, that's for sure. For us, anyway. But what's it going to mean to her later? Tell me, Jessie. You're the one with the degree in child development."

Jessie shook her head. "I don't know. Hidemi basically abandoned Kizuna, and that's not going to go away. It'll be a part of her life forever, I imagine. Like Miya losing her father."

"That's different," said Jimmy. "It's not like Kiyoshi had any choice in the matter."

"I know that," said Jessie. "But what if things had been different? What if I had left him? What if he took himself out of Miya's life instead of trying to work out something agreeable between us?"

"Sorry, guys, for interrupting," said Yuya. "But you know we *are* talking about Kizuna, right? How can we fix what's going on with her?"

"I don't think there's any easy fix, Yuya. The only thing we can do is help her get through it. Give her time. Make her realize that she's safe here with us." Then Jessie looked over at Jimmy and said pointedly, "It's important that we don't badmouth Hidemi in front of Kizuna. We have to stay neutral. I don't care what she was saying to Kizuna about you guys. We can't go down that road. We're her family now, and we'll show by example. That this is the way to live."

"We're some unusual family," said Jimmy. "That's for sure."

"Yeah, but at least we aren't dysfunctional," said Jessie with a hopeful voice. "Right?"

CHAPTER TWENTY-THREE

"Hurry up, Miya!" yelled Kizuna as she burst into Jessie's kitchen on the first day of school. She was wearing a brand-new outfit that Jessie had helped her pick out during a girls-only shopping trip a few days earlier. "We can't be late."

"You're not going to be late, Kizuna," Jessie said while tying up the ends of Miya's braided hair. "And besides, Miya isn't going to walk with you today. Remember? Today's the entrance ceremony, so she's coming with me." Jessie looked at her daughter with satisfaction. "Now, go wait downstairs. We're going to take some pictures."

Miya grabbed the navy blazer from the hanger and dashed out of the apartment. Ten seconds later, she was back.

Jessie was holding out the outrageously expensive leather backpack that Miya would carry to school every day for the next six years. "Forget something?"

Miya slipped it over her shoulders and looked as if she would topple over once it was filled with books. Jessie followed her down the stairs, wishing she looked as nice as the two girls did. It was a matter of days before her pregnancy became obvious. Now it just looked like she was getting too fat for the suit she had purchased for the kindergarten entrance ceremony three years earlier.

"Okay," said Yuya, his camera perched on the tripod. "Everyone's here. Jessie, you line up over there. Jimmy, there. Miya, you sit in the middle. Natsumi—"

"We forgot Mickey and Minnie!" cried Miya as she ran up the stairs.

"Miya! Forget those crazy cats! Get back here!" Jessie yelled, readjusting the safety pin that was holding her skirt up.

Miya returned with a cat under each arm, a film of fur on her brand-new woolen blazer clearly visible. She handed Minnie to Kizuna, so now there was fur on her new outfit as well. After Mrs. Watanabe arrived, the cats were passed around again, and a new set of photos had to be taken.

The door swung open, and Wakako, Mrs. Kikuchi's oldest granddaughter, called inside, "Are you ready, Kizuna? Let's go find out if we're gonna be in the same class!"

Kizuna's smile was full of relief, making Jessie wonder if she had been a lot more anxious about going to a new school than she had let on. She grabbed her bag and tore off.

Yuya looked dejected. "I kind of hoped that I'd be going with her this morning since it's the first day and all."

"Friends trump parents every time, especially when you're in the third grade," Jessie said, patting him on the shoulder. "But don't be disappointed because that's a good thing."

Jimmy walked with them to the school, and like all the other families, they took pictures together under the blossoming cherry tree. "Be good, kiddo," he said before heading off for his own university's entrance ceremony.

As soon as they entered the school grounds, Miya was whisked away by her new teacher, and Jessie went to sit with the other parents in the gym. The ceremony got underway, and Miya was pretty much like the other first-graders: beside herself with excitement. Most of them were squirming in their seats and turning and waving at their parents. Jessie felt enormously relieved that the kid picking her nose and wiping it in her hair was not hers. Nor was hers the one who wiggled so much his seat fell over right in the middle of one of the bigwig's speeches.

Later, with her knees squeezed under Miya's assigned desk in the classroom, she listened to the teacher. By then, most of the fathers who had attended the ceremony were gone, leaving the nitty-gritty details of elementary school to the mothers. The teacher distributed the textbooks and materials, instructing the women that their child's name needed to be written clearly on everything, including a math set with a gazillion pieces. When it came time to select the PTA class president, everyone stared at their child's desk as if the secret to eternal life had been engraved on it. With no one rushing to volunteer, the teacher drew names.

"Yamada-san," she announced.

Everyone looked at Jessie, their eyes filled with relief.

"Um, thank you for this great honor," Jessie said, pulling herself to her feet, "but I don't think I can accept." This was as good a time as any to announce her widowhood and pregnancy.

After a long, shocked silence, a chubby woman with a pronounced overbite timidly raised her hand, saying she would do the job if no one else could. The other PTA positions filled easily after that.

Later, some of the moms went out for lunch.

"Who was that man with you this morning?" the woman sitting next to Jessie asked somewhat bluntly. "We thought at first he was your husband."

"He's one of my relatives from America. He lives upstairs with his partner and stepdaughter." Jessie had been telling people that Jimmy was her brother for so long that she was almost beginning to believe they were related. "They just moved in, and their daughter is in the third grade here."

"Oh," said the woman across from her. She wore a rose-colored suit and had a brightly colored silk scarf tied skillfully around her neck. "I know who you're talking about. Two men, right?"

"That's right." Jessie sensed the others were paying close attention.

"My older daughter is in the same class." The woman picked up her water and took a dainty sip. "People will talk about them, you know. But not for long. We're a modern-thinking group of mothers. Right, ladies? We're raising our children to be open-minded and intelligent people."

The other mothers' heads bobbed up and down, and Jessie understood that this woman was the leader of the group.

When the waitress came to take their orders, everyone looked at Jessie expectantly. "I'll have the chicken lunch. With rice."

And then, every single other mother ordered the exact same thing. Except for the mom-leader. She ordered the pork lunch. Jessie wasn't sure, but didn't that woman wink at her as she broke the pattern?

Lunch was hurried because they had to be back at the school to pick up the children early. While waiting to pay at the cash register, Jessie said to the mom-leader, "I'm sorry, I didn't catch your name."

To her surprise, the woman replied in English. "I'm Sue Tanaka. Well, Sumiko, actually. I grew up in Singapore because of my dad's job. I went to an international school there and came back when I was fifteen." She turned to the women still sitting at the table and called out in Japanese, "Come on you two. You'd better hurry."

There was no mistake that time. She did wink at Jessie. And then they talked in English all the way back to the elementary school.

"I have to run—I've got to take my father-in-law to the doctor. But let's get together soon," Sue clutched her little boy's hand firmly. He was the kid who had been so full of beans during the opening ceremony he had knocked over his chair. But before she left, she leaned toward Jessie and whispered, "I don't like to make a big deal out of this, but my brother's gay, too."

CHAPTER TWENTY-FOUR

It was time to let Miya and Natsumi know that they were sisters. They had been spending just about every weekend together, and Jessie couldn't see the sense in putting it off any longer. On Saturday morning, she sat across from Miya at the kitchen table. "Can you stop drawing for a second? There's something important I have to tell you. Something that Natsumi's mommy is going to tell her this morning as well."

"You're not going to let me play with her anymore, are you?" said Miya.

"Why would you think that?" asked Jessie.

"Because I heard you talking to Uncle Jimmy about it. You said you didn't know if the sit-sita- station was good for me or not. I don't know about the station, but I like Natsumi, and I don't know why I can't be friends with her."

"Oh, sweetie. That's not it at all. I'm not sure what you heard me say to Uncle Jimmy, but you're right that there is a situation. And that's what I want to talk to you about now." Jessie considered having Miya come and sit on her lap on the sofa but decided to continue at the table. This was, after all, a big girl conversation.

"I want to talk about some things that happened before you were born. Before I ever met your daddy."

"Like when you were a little girl?"

"Not that far back. Like when I was teaching English with Uncle Jimmy. Like when your daddy was in college. Back then, he knew Ayako's mommy. She was his girlfriend."

Miya's face perked up with interest. "Did they kiss?"

"Yes." That was about as good an opening as any. "They kissed, and eventually, they started a baby."

"They did?"

"But Ayako had to go away somewhere, and Daddy never knew about the baby."

"Like how he doesn't know about our baby?"

"Kind of like that, yeah," said Jessie.

"Where's the baby now?"

"The baby grew up. She's eight years old and in second grade."

"But, where is she?"

"Sweetie, that baby is Natsumi. She was born before Daddy and I met and before we made you. You and Natsumi are sisters."

"Natsumi and I are sisters?" Miya repeated in excited disbelief.

"Well, half-sisters, actually."

"What's half a sister?"

"It's like me and Aunt Bethany. We have the same mom but different daddies. For you and Natsumi, it's the other way around. You both have the same daddy but different mommies."

A little later, Jimmy stepped in with the crockpot he had borrowed the day before.

"Uncle Jimmy! Guess what! Natsumi and I have the same daddy! That means we're sisters but not whole sisters, just half ones. But I'm still half-American, and she isn't. Because my mommy is American, but Natsumi's mommy isn't."

"Is that so?" He looked over at Jessie, and she nodded to let him know it was a done deal. "Well, what do you know?"

When Ayako and Natsumi arrived later that morning, Jessie pulled a cake out of the fridge with Happy Sister's Day scrawled across it in chocolate icing.

"Every year, on this day," Jessie said, repeating herself in Japanese to make sure Natsumi could follow. "We'll celebrate the day that you two officially became sisters."

The girls unwrapped presents their moms had given them to find blue and red tee shirts with "Sisters Forever" printed on them. Nothing too fancy or too plain—something that both would enjoy wearing. The girls put them on, and Jessie cut the cake. They toasted each other with sparkling apple juice, took plenty of pictures, and dug in.

"Do we have two mommies now? Like Kizuna has two daddies?" asked Miya, her mouth full of frosting.

"Not exactly," said Jessie. "But we'll both watch out for both of you. Uncle Jimmy and Uncle Yuya are a couple. Natsumi's mom and I are friends."

"How come," asked Natsumi, "I never got to meet my father, but Miya did?"

Jessie and Ayako exchanged glances. They had agreed that while it wasn't ideal to lie if questions like this came up, the girls were too young to understand the nitty-gritty details. They also had agreed that they would keep Sachiko's role in all this quiet.

"We were young," explained Ayako. "And we weren't suited for each other. So, we broke up and went our separate ways. By the time you were born, I was in Kyushu, and we'd lost contact. I didn't know where your father was until I heard he'd passed away. That was when I learned you had a sister, and I came to talk to Jessie."

"The important thing," Jessie added, "is we're here together now."

Later, when the girls went upstairs to play, Jessie raised her glass. "To family."

"Yes," repeated Ayako. "To family."

"I know you said your mother had died and that you lived with your grandmother after Natsumi was born. But what about brothers and sisters?"

Ayako's smile faded. "I don't like to talk about my family. My father passed on earlier this year. He wasn't a nice person. My brothers are like him. Natsumi's better off not knowing them. Can you understand that?"

"It's how kids are raised that's important." Jessie was thinking about their daughters' unknown grandfather—some client.

"I agree. I left my family. I came to Tokyo and reinvented myself. The person I used to be no longer exists. I'm someone else now." Ayako gathered the dirty plates on the table and stood up.

"I totally get it," Jessie said, pushing her chair back. "I'm not the same person I used to be, either. I changed after I left America."

As the two of them washed the dishes in the kitchen, Jessie found herself telling Ayako about her fundamentalist family. She even talked about her pothead father, something she didn't usually do because Japanese people tended to get all freaked out over something like that. "I love my family, but I don't want to live with them. Or even near them. I guess you could say that's one reason I came to Japan. And why I stayed."

"You're fortunate, though," Ayako said, drying the glasses with a tea towel and setting them in the cupboard. "You love your family."

"Yes, I guess I am lucky." Jessie was a little shocked by Ayako's insinuation that she didn't love hers.

"Mommy," said Miya, bursting into the kitchen. "Can we go to the park now?"

"Alone?" said Jessie.

"Yeah! Natsumi's going to show me how to play basketball."

"But do you even have a ball?" asked Jessie.

"I have ball," said Natsumi in English, pointing at her bag by the door.

"Well, all right." Jessie would have to get used to letting Miya go out and about on her own now that she was in first grade.

. . .

Jessie needed to tell her family about Natsumi before they learned it from Miya, so she gave her sister a call. For the first five minutes of their conversation, Bethany gave a rundown on the latest wedding preparations. Then she asked about the baby. Jessie announced that it was going to be another girl. Then Jessie asked how things were going at the church, and Bethany launched into the scandal of the moment involving Cindy Neugent, a deacon's wife. Unknown to just about everybody, including her husband Peter, Cindy had developed quite a penchant for shoplifting. It all came to light when she got caught stealing bras at Walmart. It turned out their garage was full of stuff that had never been paid for.

"It goes to show," Bethany said, sounding an awful lot like their mom, "that you never know what's in people's hearts. But what else can we do but forgive her? Poor Peter. How mortified he must feel."

"I bet you're right about that." Jessie was thinking that it was too bad that her sister had never known their mom before she had become such a stick-in-the-mud fundamentalist. The memories were distant, but there had been a time when they were Presbyterians. Religion was mostly a Sunday thing, an excuse to get dressed up and have brunch with her grandparents afterward. "Anyway, there's something I need to tell you," said Jessie. "It's not a secret, so you can tell Mom. It's about something that happened before Kiyoshi and I were married."

As soon as Jessie finished talking, her sister huffed with indignation. "I tell you, Jessie. So many problems in this world would be solved if people would just wait. Like me and Justin. We believe it's important to come to a marriage pure."

Jessie suppressed the urge to roll her eyes. It was no surprise that Bethany would find a way to work her precious virginity into the conversation. How was her sister ever going to manage after her wedding night was over? One could hardly go through life identifying as a former virgin, could they? Besides, Jessie had plenty of doubts about Justin and his so-called purity. She wouldn't have been surprised one bit if he was out there sowing a few wild oats, just like her equally fundamentalist ex thought it was perfectly within his rights to do. In fact, it was his cheating with a waitress from Appleby's that propelled her to quit her job at West Covina High School and head straight for Japan.

"Listen, Bethany. I'm fine with this. Everything's going to be okay. I just wanted to let you know what's happening here. Miya's quite excited to have an older sister. You should see them together. They really do look alike."

"I guess being full-blooded means that girl looks more Oriental."

Jessie immediately changed the subject. "So, tell me. What did you decide on for the bridesmaids' gifts? The earrings or a pendant?"

Ten minutes after they hung up, Jessie's mom called.

"Oh, sweet Jesus. I just got off the phone with Bethany!"

"I'm all right with this, Mom. It all happened before I even knew Kiyoshi."

"How do you know that woman isn't lying? With that inheritance of yours, all sorts are bound to come out of the woodwork." Since her mom now believed that Jessie had become a great heiress, her criticisms had expanded to include Jessie's inability to fend off gigolos and fortune hunters.

"Natsumi is definitely Miya's sister, Mom. The DNA test proved that. And money isn't an issue. The mother is financially secure."

"So, you just don't know what she wants. Not yet."

Jessie hated to admit it, but those same thoughts were lurking in the back of her mind as well. "So, Mom, tell me what's going on over there."

And then she got another earful about the sticky-fingered deacon's wife.

.   .   .

"There's something I'd like to talk to you about," Jessie said to Mrs. Watanabe later that afternoon when the two of them were alone in the café. As Miya and Kizuna's de facto granny, it was time to tell her that another kid was in the mix. "It's about Miya and Natsumi. You know, Ayako's daughter," she added in case memory needed to be jogged.

"About them being sisters?"

"Mr. Suzuki told you?" Jessie asked in disbelief. Girlfriend or no girlfriend, what the hell ever happened to lawyer-client confidentiality?

"What? Certainly not. I figured it out as soon as I saw Miya and Natsumi together. And then, there was Shige-chan's reaction."

Jessie was momentarily distracted when Mrs. Watanabe called her eighty-something-year-old boyfriend by a childish pet name. "Why didn't you say anything if you knew?"

"I figured you'd tell me if you wanted me to know. And if you didn't, I thought it'd be better to pretend not to."

For once, Mrs. Watanabe was being pretty logical. But if she had been able to put two and two together so easily, she must have been privy to what was happening back then. Jessie leaned forward. "Do you know why Sachiko was so strongly against Kiyoshi and Ayako? Why she—"

"I guess the detective found something out about her."

"Sachiko hired a detective?"

"Back before I was a bride, everyone did that. To find out if people were who they said they were. Do you think parents would leave it up to their children and their love matches?"

"But that wasn't back in the olden days. It wasn't even ten years ago."

"I imagine Sachiko wanted to make sure that Ayako wasn't some kind of gold digger. Or worse, Korean. Or," she added with a whisper, "*Eta*."

Jessie was shocked. Sachiko had been worried Ayako had come from the untouchable class? The *burakumin*? But it made some sort of twisted sense. Maybe that was why Ayako had never gone to high school, why she had left her family, and why she had nothing to do with them. If it hadn't been for an old novel she had stumbled across when she was a JET teacher, she would have never even known there was a caste system in Japan. Intrigued, Jessie asked her supervising teacher if it was true that some people were ostracized and forced to live in ghettos because of their ancestors' occupations. The conservative teacher denied that such a thing ever existed, which of course, made Jessie want to study up on it all the more.

"But would that have been so terrible?" Jessie asked. "If Ayako was Korean? Or—"

"In my parents' time, it would have been. And don't forget, Sachiko was much older than me. Maybe she did care. Now me, I wouldn't have objected if Taro wanted to marry into...well, if he wanted to marry someone like that."

Jessie was thinking that Mrs. Watanabe's son would have been lucky to find a monkey to marry him, the way he just grunted and muttered all day long while watching TV in their shop. But she nodded sympathetically and waited for her to continue.

"I don't know exactly what happened. But Sachiko was ranting and raving about how Kiyoshi's girlfriend would ruin his life. She went on and on and on about it for days. But then she stopped talking about her. She said the floozy—her words, not mine—just left and went back to wherever she was from."

"Did you know what she did to Ayako? Did you know that she gave her money to have an abortion?"

"So, that's what happened." After a moment, Mrs. Watanabe added, "I wonder if that was before or after Sachiko took that fall."

"What fall?"

"She was carrying something down the stairs and tripped. I found her and called an ambulance. It turned out to be nothing serious. All the x-rays came back just fine. But she wouldn't let me call Kiyoshi."

"Because of their fight? Because they weren't talking to each other?"

"Let me think a minute." Mrs. Watanabe closed her eyes and ran through a series of events that had occurred a decade earlier. But she couldn't remember the order they had happened. Was the fight about the jewelry before or after the fight about Ayako? Had Sachiko fallen before or after that? Did that happen before or after Taro got fired from the factory and came home to run the stationery store? The only thing she was sure about was that her husband had passed away before any of that had happened. That, and the fact Sachiko had started behaving oddly. But exactly when, she was unsure.

"Are you saying she was getting senile?"

Mrs. Watanabe recoiled as if Jessie had uttered a dirty word but then, with a resigned sigh, said, "I guess you could say she was beginning to slip. She was fine most of the time. But sometimes she wasn't."

"Well, I guess it's bound to happen when people start getting older. *Some* people. Not all," Jessie added quickly to let Mrs. Watanabe know she didn't consider her in that category at all.

"To be perfectly honest, when Sachiko told me that Kiyoshi had come to see her, I was relieved. I don't know how much longer she could've managed here alone."

"I guess things were getting pretty hard for her."

"That's why I was so relieved that Kiyoshi was planning to move back home."

Jessie must have heard wrong. "He was planning what?"

"To move back home."

"Here?"

"With you and Miya, of course."

All the air in Jessie's lungs was sucked right out of her. What the hell had Kiyoshi been plotting behind her back? She couldn't believe how normal her voice sounded when she directed the conversation away from that alarming subject. "Do you think Kiyoshi had taken Sachiko's jewelry and sold it?"

"He must have," Mrs. Watanabe said, easily switching topics. "Otherwise, where is it?"

Jessie nodded. "You're probably right." It was far more pleasant to think of Kiyoshi as a thieving grandson than to imagine what living above the Butterfly Café with him and his grandmother would have been like. She looked around at her cozy surroundings and felt her heart rate gradually return to normal. That never happened, she told herself. And it never would.

Later that night, Jessie checked Wikipedia. The *burakumin* caste system had been outlawed in 1871, but according to a government survey in 2014, discrimination, especially in employment and marriage, still existed. Jessie stared at the data. Most parents admitted they would object to such a marriage, even though *burakumin* were racially Japanese. That had to be why Sachiko insisted Ayako have an abortion and why she paid for it. It was so logical. The detective must have snooped around and found out. Sachiko simply couldn't stand the thought of her precious blood mingling with the untouchables.

If this was Ayako's big dark secret past, let her have it. Jessie had so many more pressing issues to worry about than if Ayako's great-great-great grandparents had dealt with meat, leather, and the dead.

Who in the world gave a flying fuck about that?

CHAPTER TWENTY-FIVE

"I'm going to Costco today," Jimmy said the following Saturday morning. "I was thinking of picking up some pizzas. Maybe we can all have dinner tonight."

"By we, you mean *all* of us?" asked Jessie as she was packing a lunch to take to the park where she and Miya were meeting Ayako and Natsumi. "You guys, us, and—"

"And Ayako and Natsumi," he said. "Look, I'm sorry I've been so negative. I can't help but think there's something fishy, but like Yuya says, it is what it is."

Jessie looked at him coolly. "What exactly do you mean?"

"As we say in Nebraska, the animals are already out of the barn. There ain't nothin' we can do about it now. No matter how weird the situation is."

"In case you haven't noticed," said Jessie, "just about every single thing to do with the Yamada family is, and always has been, on the weird side."

"The world is full of crazy shit. I'll give you that. And maybe this is just one more example of it."

"So, what're you saying?"

"I guess," Jimmy said, "it's time for us to start acting like a family."

"Really?"

"Really. And that means having dinner together. Tonight. After you ladies get back from whatever sisterhood bonding activities, you have planned for the day. After Yuya and Kizuna get back home from his parents. We'll all have dinner here. Together."

"You're going to cook?" Jessie wasn't prepared to have her kitchen torn apart for one of Jimmy's emotional gourmet ordeals.

"I already told you. I'm going to go get pizza from Costco."

Later that afternoon, the two dads, the two moms, and the three girls were in the Butterfly Café. The adults were having a few awkward moments trying to get their conversation going, but at the back table, the girls were having a lively game of Uno.

"So, it's true. You guys really are sisters." Kizuna was peering closely at Miya and Natsumi from across the table. "Are you sure you aren't twins? There are some boys in my class. Everyone says they're twins, but you guys look a lot more alike than they do. Twins are supposed to look the same. You do. They don't. And that's a simple fact."

"Maybe we're twins!" Miya said to Natsumi, her eyes lighting up with excitement.

"Then how come you're in first grade and I'm in second? And how come we have different mothers?"

Miya looked disappointed.

"And besides," said Natsumi. "We still look different."

"That's because of your hair. If Miya cuts hers, then you'd look the same." Kizuna leaned across the table and picked up Miya's braid. Holding it in her hand, she said with the authority of a third-grader, "I could take care of that for you, you know. Then you both would look the same."

Miya usually couldn't resist Kizuna, but that was one idea she didn't seem keen on at all.

"It wouldn't take long to fix this," Kizuna said, not letting go of the braid. "My dad's got hair-cutting scissors upstairs. I could snip this right off, and you'd look just like Natsumi. Wouldn't your mom be surprised?"

Miya nodded unhappily. Her mom would be surprised. But she was also pretty sure her mom would be upset with her for going along with another one of Kizuna's naughty schemes. "But," said Miya pulling away from Kizuna's grasp, "I don't want—"

"I have a better idea," said Natsumi. "Let's go upstairs."

"Why?" Miya put her hands protectively on her head.

"We'll switch clothes. I'll put on yours, and you can put on mine. We'll fool the grownups."

"But that wouldn't prove you're twins," said Kizuna.

"We aren't going to do that," said Natsumi. "It's impossible. We're not twins. We're just going to play a joke."

"That would be kind of fun, I guess," conceded Kizuna. "But what about Miya's hair? That's a dead giveaway."

"I'm not letting you cut my hair." With emphasis, Miya added, "And that's a fact."

Kizuna shrugged like it was no big deal. "Whatever."

"We'll put on hats," said Natsumi. "If you tuck your hair in, it'll look like it's short."

The girls abandoned their game and headed toward the staircase.

"Where're you going?" called Jessie. "We're about to eat."

"We'll be right back," said Kizuna.

Jessie shot a worried look at Yuya.

"Let's give them a few minutes," he said.

A short while later, the girls were back to their game and giggling wildly. They had definitely been up to something, and Jessie wondered if she should go upstairs and check for damage.

"Pizza's ready," said Jimmy, placing it on the counter.

The girls were still giggling as they made their way across the room.

"What in the world is wrong with you, Miya?" Jessie asked. "You're acting like you've got ants in your pants. You—" She blinked at the person wearing Miya's clothes. "Natsumi?"

When Natsumi and Miya took off their caps and exposed their hair, everyone howled with laughter.

Ayako grabbed Natsumi and hugged her. "You're wearing pink! You hate pink."

"You didn't know it was me, did you?" she said to her mom.

"See," said Miya to Kizuna. "You didn't have to cut off my hair to fool my mommy."

"What!" exclaimed Jessie when she heard that. With a dangerous tone, she asked Kizuna, "You were going to cut Miya's hair?"

"It was just an idea."

"I wasn't going to let her do it," Miya announced proudly. "I said no."

Jessie forced a smile back on her face. "Well, you sure tricked us."

"So, are they twins or not?" asked Kizuna.

"Twins?" said Jessie. "Don't be silly. They're sisters. Sisters who look an awful lot alike."

After dinner, the girls changed back into their own clothes, and Yuya went to get his old Monopoly set. Kizuna had played the game before, but Natsumi and Miya hadn't. He got the girls situated with their cash and showed them how to acquire enough property to take over the world.

"I can't believe Kizuna wanted to cut Miya's hair," said Jessie, watching them from the other end of the café. "Just to pull off their joke."

"Do you think she would've done that?" asked Ayako.

"It's possible," said Jimmy. "She's what you'd call rather high-spirited."

"High-spirited! I guess that's one way of putting it." Jessie turned to Ayako, and as she described the chain of events that permanently brought Kizuna into their lives, Ayako's face clouded with anger.

"But that's far worse than what Kiyoshi's mother did! To leave your child just to go and have a new life! Because it's inconvenient! That's inexcusable!"

"Yeah." Jimmy looked at Ayako with new approval. "I couldn't agree with you more."

"The poor thing," she said, looking over at the girls. "No wonder she acts so tough. She must be broken inside."

"We make allowances for her," said Jimmy. "But because she's a smart kid, she knows how to take advantage. Unfortunately, that bi—" he stopped when Jessie kicked him under the table. "Unfortunately, Kizuna's upbringing was not—"

"It's not too late," interjected Ayako. "People are brought up in all sorts of ways. But they can change. Living with decent people will make all the difference in the world."

Jessie nodded, thinking that if Ayako could put whatever was in her past behind her, so could Kizuna. And so could Miya, for that matter.

CHAPTER TWENTY-SIX

In the middle of April, Jessie decided to hold a party to announce the opening of her business. That Saturday morning, five-dozen butterfly-shaped sugar cookies were cooling on the counter. Jessie sipped a cup of decaf, wishing her body would be fooled into thinking it was caffeinated. She had only gotten six hours of sleep between cooking, cleaning, and making cookie dough.

"But Mommy," Miya asked for the umpteenth time, "how do you know for sure Hanako doesn't exist? That there isn't a toilet ghost?"

"Oh, Miya," Jessie said, sliding the rejected cookies into a plastic container to eat later. "That's just a story the big girls tell to scare the little girls." Since two sixth-graders had gotten caught breaking into the school at midnight to check if a ghost named Hanako really did live in the girls' bathroom, Miya talked about little else.

"I'm not afraid of ghosts," said Miya. "Because Daddy's a ghost, and I'm not afraid of him."

That discussion on the supernatural was halted when Mrs. Watanabe marched into her kitchen. "For the party," she said, hoisting a two-liter bottle of whiskey—the kind favored by day laborers—up on the counter. "From Mr. Suzuki."

"Well, that was nice of him," Jessie said, wondering how much alcohol he thought people would be drinking today. "Is he having a nice time at his elementary school reunion?"

"Sure," she replied cheerfully. "Most of his classmates are dead or senile now anyway, so it's just a small group going to the hot springs this year." Then she opened the fridge and started nosing around.

"That's potato salad. American style. And that's a ham. From Costco." From the way Mrs. Watanabe was sniffing at it all, Jessie might as well have said it had come from Mars.

Miya rounded up the kittens to take upstairs, and Jessie followed her to change for the party. While they were gone, Mrs. Watanabe had taken the three dozen hard-boiled eggs from the fridge and mashed them into egg salad, effectively removing deviled eggs from the party menu.

Even though Jessie had told people it wouldn't be necessary to bring food or drinks, no one listened. The people from Piggy Piggy Donburi arrived at two on the dot with a platter of potato croquettes. Right behind them were the people from the ramen shop with fried rice and gyoza. Then came Rahul and Rama from Delhi Palace with samosas and tandoori chicken. Everyone brought drinks. By three o'clock, there were so many people in the café that Jessie was afraid it was a greater safety violation than when it was simply filled with cats.

"Hi, Jessie," said Mark, setting two bottles of wine on the counter with the rest of the booze.

"Welcome back from California. And welcome to total chaos." She leaned closer to him because the noise level was so high but nearly swooned when she got a faint whiff of his citrus-scented shaving cream. Damn, that man was sexy in his skinny jeans and corduroy jacket. Jimmy had that one right—Mark *was* one hot professor. She stepped back to a safer distance and looked over his shoulder. "Where's Kumiko? I wanted to thank her for the Disneyland tickets. We had a wonderful time there last week."

"I hate to tell you this, but Kumiko's not much of a partygoer."

"That's too bad." Jessie figured she would have to meet this Kumiko at some point, but at least it wouldn't have to be today.

Just then, Sue and her husband arrived. Jessie introduced them to Mark, and when he learned that Sue's husband was a science teacher at the high school he had gone to, they began talking about the teachers from Mark's time who were still there. Jessie moved from table to table, topping up everyone's glasses and stealing glances at Mark. But when his eyes met hers, and he grinned and waved, she felt as if she had been caught spying on him through his bathroom window. Turning away, she saw Ayako and Natsumi over by the door and hurried toward them.

Natsumi headed into the kitchen to help finish decorating the cookies, and Jessie poured barley tea for herself and Ayako. They had just clinked their glasses together in a toast when someone at a back table knocked over a liter bottle of Kirin beer. Jessie rushed to mop it up, and while she was back there, she checked the condition of the unisex bathroom. The way the old geezers were guzzling beer, it would need careful surveillance. Then Jessie went around to all the tables, thanking her guests for coming and for their future support, just as Yuya had suggested.

The girls passed their platters of butterfly cookies around to all the guests. Everyone, even the drinkers, sampled them and said they were better than what could be found in any department store bakery. When the platters were empty, they headed upstairs to play.

Mrs. Watanabe and her pals were having a wild case of the giggles, thanks to the nearly empty carton of sweet plum wine on their table. Jessie grabbed a bottle of oolong tea from the counter and set it between them as a hint to slow down a little.

The afternoon passed, and when she had a moment, she gathered a stack of dirty plates and carried them to the kitchen. Fumes from the smoking area she had set up behind the café were wafting in, and she was about to shut the window when she overheard Ayako speaking to someone on the phone. Jessie didn't intend to listen, but she could hear the distress in Ayako's voice. It sounded as if she was trying to appease someone about something but not doing a very good job of it. Before Jessie could check if she was okay, Mr. Iwao opened the kitchen door and yelled for her to come because a platter of spaghetti had fallen on the floor.

As the afternoon progressed, the noise level increased. People passing by the café were looking into the windows with curiosity. Jessie stood behind the counter and watched all the activity in front of her, marveling at the laughter, the rapidly disappearing platters of food, and the friendly faces. She had never envisioned this life for herself, not in a million years.

"Where's Mrs. Watanabe going?" Jessie asked Jimmy, watching the woman wobble out the door.

"She said something about going home to cook for her son."

"Oh, god. She's not in any condition to do that." Jessie fixed a plate, covered it with wrap, and slipped out the back. Taro, in his usual spot by the window, was so engrossed in a variety show he didn't notice her going straight through the shop and into their tiny living room in the back. Mrs. Watanabe was already sound asleep in her chair, a dribble of drool running down her chin. Jessie set the plate of food on the table and hurried out. Her lazy son was a regular idiot, and she didn't care if he starved. But she did love Mrs. Watanabe. This tray was for her, even though she knew it was Taro who would be eating it.

"I bet you anything," Jessie said to Jimmy when she got back, "she's going to have a doozy of a hangover in the morning."

"It's time for us to be leaving," said Ayako, tapping Jessie on the shoulder. "I wanted to say goodbye. I had a great time, and so did Natsumi."

"Can't you stay any longer?" Jessie had been looking forward to rehashing the party with her friend when it was over. Girlfriend style.

A tired smile spread across Ayako's face. "That would be wonderful, but I'm catching a cold. I'd better have an early night."

"Oh, that's too bad. I was too busy to talk much today. Things were a little crazy, as you may have noticed."

"It was a wonderful party. Congratulations on its success." Ayako's phone started to buzz, and she looked down at it. She shoved it in her bag and gave Jessie a hug. Before going out the door, she turned around and said, "I think you'll have a *wonderful* business."

When Jessie stepped outside to say goodbye to Mrs. Tamura a few minutes later, she saw Ayako talking to a muscular man over on the next block. From the way he was gesturing, he seemed pretty angry. Ayako's head was moving up and down, but she had Natsumi pulled close to her in a protective manner. Remembering what she had overheard earlier, Jessie was about to get Yuya. But then, the man burst into laughter. Ayako seemed to offer a bow to the guy, and the three of them turned toward the station. Jessie shook her head at her imagination running wild. The guy was obviously one of the bodybuilders who tanned at her salon. Maybe one who didn't quite like the shade he got.

Finally, the very last stragglers from the party, Mr. Noguchi from the hardware store and Mr. Ikeda from the teashop, hoisted themselves up, shook Jessie's hand, and informed her that this was the best international party they had ever been to. They helped each other out the door, and despite having consumed an entire bottle of strong shochu, they headed to the yakitori bar down the street to continue the party.

"Holy moly, am I tired. Also starving," Jessie reached for the platter of leftover food and bit into a stone-cold samosa, finding it delicious. "What do you guys think? Was the party a success?"

"Judging from all the empty booze bottles in the kitchen, I'd say so," said Jimmy. "Even that big bottle of cheapo whiskey Mrs. Watanabe brought has quite a serious dent in it."

"If the party is anything to go by," added Mark. "I'd say it's a pretty good indicator for the new and improved version of the Butterfly Café. Although I bet you'll never have as many people in here all at once again."

"I certainly hope not. What a nightmare that'd be." She stretched out her legs and propped her feet on the chair across her. "I'm pretty sure I can sleep for twelve hours straight tonight."

Then Yuya came out of the bathroom, a frown on his face. The toilet was overflowing, and he couldn't figure out why.

CHAPTER TWENTY–SEVEN

May passed with a series of perfect sunny days, only slightly marred by various glitches while the Yamada-Maeda-Johnson family was trying to get itself up and running. One day while Yuya was out in Hachioji on a job, Jessie was called by the principal because Kizuna had given Satoshi Sakuma a bloody nose. She rushed to the school, praying that Kizuna wasn't going to get expelled on her watch, but the meeting with the principal, the teacher, and Kizuna went smoothly. They didn't come right out and say it in so many words, but what Kizuna had done was stand up to the class bully.

"I don't think his parents will file a complaint," said the principal, "but we can't condone violence in school, Kizuna. Do you understand?"

The girl nodded, and Jessie took her home. She knew she was supposed to enact some sort of punishment, but instead, she offered her butterscotch cookies straight from the oven and a tall glass of milk.

"You won't be punching that boy again, right?" asked Jessie.

"Nope," said Kizuna, reaching for another cookie. "Unless he deserves it."

Jessie turned away so Kizuna couldn't see her smile. It was unlikely that nasty kid would be making any more wisecracks about her two fathers.

Later that same week, some money went missing from Jessie's wallet on the kitchen counter. She wondered how she was supposed to handle that sort of problem. No one had been in the kitchen except her and the girls. She couldn't see Miya taking it. But then again, she couldn't see Kizuna doing that either. While she was trying to figure out how to approach the topic with them, a text came in from Jimmy. *Really sorry,* he wrote, *but I was in a terrible rush, and I borrowed ¥5000. I thought I left you a note, but just now found it in my pocket. Hope you didn't get freaked out about it.*

Jessie sighed in relief as she tapped out a white lie: *I didn't even realize it was missing.*

The rainy season arrived in mid-June, and Jessie was now well into her third trimester. Just getting around was becoming a struggle, and the humidity was enough to kill a horse. As she hurried back from the station, black clouds darkened the sky, and the misty drizzle of the past day transformed into a deluge. By the time she opened the door, she was soaked. Shaking the rain off her umbrella and leaving it by the door, she called out thanks to Mrs. Watanabe for taking care of things. She put on the more comfortable sneakers she wore in the café, carried her wet shoes into the kitchen, and set them on a newspaper by the back door. Hopefully, they would dry before the great enemy known as mold sets in. What an idiot she had been for leaving the house in the only nice pair she had left.

She stepped into the cooler café and breathed in the heady mix of coffee and the lingering aroma from her early morning baking. Daisuke, who had started coming in every afternoon to work on his samurai time-travel fantasy novel, was at his regular table. Concentration was etched on his face as his fingers flew over his laptop's keyboard. Haruka, the college-aged granddaughter of the Iwaos from the real estate company, was at a different table. Her

English textbooks were open, but judging from the attention she was giving her phone, another afternoon had slipped by without much progress on the language learning front. Haruka's family was under the impression that she came in nearly every afternoon to practice her English, but Jessie was pretty sure the real reason was to kill time until her boyfriend got off work at the Yoshinoya beef bowl restaurant near the station.

"Hi, Haruka," Jessie asked in English, speaking slowly and enunciating clearly. "How is everything going today?"

The girl blinked at her as if this conversation had never happened before. "Oh, hello!"

"Do you need help with your homework?" Jessie asked in English.

A pristine grammar workbook was next to a Japanese translation of *Moby Dick*. Haruka was an English literature major at some university even Yuya had never heard of, but the girl couldn't even string three words together. She shook her head and said she still had a few days before her assignment was due. She then returned to her phone, which clearly seemed to be a much more pleasurable activity than translating passages from Melville.

"So, what did they say about your weight gain?" Mrs. Watanabe asked when Jessie passed by her table.

Jessie pretended she hadn't heard. She wished she had never told Mrs. Watanabe how a forty-five-kilo nurse had tried to bully her into going on a diet to slow down her pregnancy weight gain. No matter how many times she tried to convince the woman that she was perfectly average for an American of her height and age, she had begun to eye her every mouthful. Jessie moved behind the counter, eased into the chair she kept there, and opened her laptop. She secretly nibbled at a cookie and studied the figures in her new accounting software. It wasn't rocket science. She needed to earn more and spend less. How long would it take to move from moderately in the red to dangerously so? Mr. Suzuki had said the government probably wouldn't confiscate her property if she couldn't pay the taxes. But the "probably" part of his assurance wasn't all that reassuring. All the money from Kiyoshi's last paycheck and bonus—the money she had planned to live on after the baby was born—had been used to replace the water pipes in the café after the toilet broke. Yuya said she wouldn't have any more plumbing problems for decades to come, but that wouldn't do her much good if she and Miya were tossed out on the streets. Yay for the next owner because all their pipes would be in perfect condition.

Jessie opened her email to see if there had been any more inquiries for her two English classes since the last time she checked that morning. None. At least with the four students signed up on Wednesdays and three on Thursdays, she could buy groceries. If she stuck to the bare necessities. She had been sure that the Wednesday afternoon English Tea Time, where anyone could drop in for an hour and chat in English for the price of a drink and a cookie, would attract people. But considering that two of the five regulars were Mr. Suzuki and Mrs. Watanabe (and she could hardly charge them), that scheme wouldn't make her rich anytime soon.

Her phone buzzed, and Jessie perked up when she saw it was Ayako.

Sorry. Can't make dinner on Friday. Have doctor's appt.

Everything okay?

Just a check-up, Ayako replied.

Jessie swallowed her disappointment. It was funny how quickly Ayako had become such a good friend. Her best friend, if truth be told. Outside of Jimmy, of course. But he's a guy, and guys are different. *See you Sunday.* Jessie texted. *Jimmy's got a new card game.*

Ayako followed that with a smiling emoji.

Jessie glanced at the clock and got the brownies out of the fridge. Every afternoon Mrs. Watanabe's cronies gathered here for an hour of freedom from their newly retired husbands. After decades of doing zilch around the house, the men had decided that their wives had somehow been doing it wrong all those years. Now, with nothing better to do, the bored husbands felt it was up to them to rectify the situation.

Mrs. Noguchi came in first and went straight to the large table by the window. Mrs. Watanabe left her puzzle to join her. Then Mrs. Aoki, Mrs. Hamano, and Mrs. Yamamoto arrived. At first, Jessie had been shocked when they had practically come right out and congratulated Mrs. Watanabe for having the good sense to be a widow. But that was before she understood it was their way of including her in the husband discussion. At the end of the hour, they would head out to hunt for late afternoon bargains, having learned the hard way not to let the husbands anywhere near the supermarkets.

Jessie listened in as she brought the coffee to the table. Mrs. Hamano was rehashing the time she had sent her husband out with five thousand yen to buy milk. He came back with packages of salmon roe and raw sea urchin. And no milk. No change, either.

"And then they wonder why we aren't managing on their meager pensions," grumbled Mrs. Aoki.

The other women agreed enthusiastically.

Haruka packed up her study materials and went to pay. "See you tomorrow," Jessie said as she dropped her money into the cash register.

Jessie's phone was buzzing in her pocket, so she pulled it out. A text from Sue. *The kids have to bring a box of tissues tomorrow. And three garbage bags and five new cleaning rags.*

Thanks! It really was Jessie's lucky day when she met Sue because she always let her know whatever was important in the never-ending barrage of messages from the teacher and other mothers. *Anything for Kizuna?*

Signed permission slip for the field trip.

I'll remind Yuya, Jessie wrote back. He didn't have trouble keeping up with school communication, but Sue, whose older daughter was in Kizuna's class, kept Jessie in the loop, anyway. Because, as she liked to say, men are men.

After the women left, Jessie carried their cups into the kitchen and washed them. She topped up Daisuke's coffee, figuring he would appreciate the extra caffeine to help him get through his night shift at the nearby convenience store. Then she wiped the tables, straightened the chairs, and checked the bathroom for soap and toilet paper. With nothing else to do, she went back to her computer and scanned the want ads. She found an employment website looking for freelance proofreaders and editors. Thinking that was something she could do from home, she filled out an application and sent in her resume.

Yuya texted. *Eating out tonight. Sorry for the late notice.*

No worries. Jessie was in charge of Tuesdays because Jimmy had night classes, and Yuya's schedule was unpredictable. She usually had an early dinner with the girls, and the guys ate whenever they came in.

And don't forget. Three of my men are coming at 9:00 tomorrow for the roof, he wrote.

Thanks. Another thing to be grateful for. If it weren't for Yuya and his ragtag band of apprentices taking care of things, she would either be bankrupt or the building would be condemned. *Oh, and Kizuna will need that permission slip signed by tomorrow.*

Right. Are the girls back yet?

Soon.

Several minutes later, Miya and Kizuna burst through the door, their faces gleaming with sweat.

"I'm hungry!" shouted Miya as she tossed her umbrella into the stand and her school backpack onto a table.

"Me, too!" echoed Kizuna in Japanese.

"I've got some fruit in the fridge for you," Jessie said in English and in Japanese, trying to follow a bilingual principle at home. "And cookies." She snapped a few pictures of Kizuna and sent them to Yuya, who replied immediately with a series of hearts.

"Next weekend, there's going to be a PTA volleyball game," announced Kizuna. "All the parents are going to play."

"Not me." Jessie was relieved to have the best excuse in the world for not having to subject herself to *that* particular humiliation. "But I bet your dads will be great in it."

"Yeah," said Kizuna. "Because they're so tall." Jessie watched for a hint of embarrassment for having two fathers participate in something so public, but Kizuna added, "I'm glad it's next weekend and not this weekend. I've got to go see my grandparents, and I'd sure hate to miss the game."

Kizuna's maternal grandparents had known nothing about her new living arrangements until they arrived at their daughter's second wedding. Not only did they find no trace of their granddaughter, but they were also forbidden even to mention her name. The following week they contacted Yuya, saying they wanted to see Kizuna. Mrs. Watanabe, as if it were any of her business, thought that they were all making a huge mistake. She felt that the sooner the girl forgot about her mother, the better. But, they all had argued that just because something looks like it's forgotten doesn't mean it is. They felt the more people who were in Kizuna's life and who loved her, the better. Even, it was turning out, Mrs. Watanabe.

"What are you going to do with your grandparents?" Jessie asked.

Kizuna shrugged. "They're too old to do anything fun. My grandpa always wants me to plant some vegetables or something with him. That's all right, but it's kind of— Oh, look! It stopped raining!"

Miya ran to the window to peer out. "Can we go to the park?"

"All right. But be back by five." Jessie spoke in Japanese, so Kizuna couldn't claim to misunderstand this time.

After the girls tore out the door, Daisuke shut down his computer and went to the cash register.

"How's the writing going today?"

"So-so." His grin, however, suggested the opposite.

Jessie went back online to search for food ideas for the café—something she could add to the menu that would require little or no culinary skill. Something that wouldn't require a degree in hospitality management but could squeak out some sort of profit. Something that a one-woman show—the cook, the waiter, the cashier, the dishwasher, and the English teacher could pull off. So far, her only lunch items, in addition to the sweets she was making, were melted cheese toast and melted cheese and ham toast. Grandma Frances would be horrified by such a meager menu, but that was about all Jessie could manage. A six-hundred-yen meal when a cup of coffee was thrown in. After the baby was born, she would have to serve more than that if the plan of turning the Butterfly Café into an English school didn't pan out.

While studying the spreadsheet again, she saw Mr. Hamano peering into the window, probably checking to see if his wife was still there. Jessie waved at him, thinking that if alcohol were served in addition to coffee, the men would also be in the café every afternoon. But the downside of that would be they would probably never go home.

When her daughter's foot jabbed her in the ribs, she heaved herself up to stretch. She had crossed over from the I-feel-great pregnant stage into the I'm-a-waddling-elephant-and-can't-wait-to-give-birth one. Since she was standing, she might as well go measure out the dry ingredients for tomorrow's brownies. Maybe she could make muffins, too, since no one wanted to eat the bananas going black upstairs. The bell on the door jingled, and she turned around. "Hello!" she said, genuinely glad to see Mr. Suzuki. "Come on in. Have a seat."

"Are you busy right now?"

Jessie laughed. Did she look busy? "Would you like some coffee?"

"No, thank you. I'm on my way to my Bee Gees fan club meeting. I just stopped by to tell you about the house in Chiba. There's a buyer."

"Really!"

"Well, it's a little less than your asking price, but it's your first and only offer in six months. In fact, it's the only offer we've ever had."

"Will it cover the inheritance taxes?"

"I'm hoping that it will."

If Jessie hadn't felt so bloated, she would have jumped up to do a little jig. Instead, she gave him a hug. "Oh! That's fantastic news!"

"There is just one thing," he said, taking a step back to be safely out of arm's reach. "It seems that Sachiko had been storing things at that house. You must go and clean out the shed in the backyard."

She blinked at him. "Are you kidding me?"

Later that evening, a little before ten, Jessie was dishing up curry in her apartment kitchen for Jimmy, who had gotten back after the girls were asleep. "And there I was, thinking I'd finally gotten rid of all of Sachiko's stuff. Now I find out there's a whole bunch of who-knows-what out in a storage shed in Chiba."

"Did Mr. Suzuki say what's in it?" Jimmy asked.

"He didn't know a thing about it. According to the tenants, it's mostly boxes and shopping bags. Probably more trash. Anyway, I'm going to have to go see what it is and make arrangements to ship it here if anything's important."

"This weekend? Sorry, Jess, but I've got a conference in Tsukuba, and Yuya's taking Kizuna to see her grandparents. Otherwise, we'd help."

"Well, I was thinking to see if Mark wanted to come with me."

"Mark? Well, that's an interesting idea. You and Mark can—"

"God, Jimmy! Quit leering at me as if I had just told you I'm dragging Mark off for an illicit rendezvous. It's just because there might be some more old papers or something out there. And you know how he gets over old papers."

"Listen to yourself, darling. The only leering going on is in your pretty little head. I personally think it's a good idea that he goes with you. You shouldn't go all the way out there in your condition.

Let me check with Yuya to see if you guys can take the van. Mark could do the driving."

"Fine," Jessie snapped as if she needed any reminding that she was pregnant. "And by the way, I'm tired of you making all these wisecracks about me and the hot professor. I need you to stop it right now."

"But—"

"I mean it. No more teasing me about him. Mark's with someone. Some woman he works with."

"But Jessie—"

"I mean it. No more. Got it?"

"All right, all right," Jimmy said, throwing his hands up in the air dramatically. "Don't bite my head off. No words on this particular subject shall ever escape from my lips again."

CHAPTER TWENTY-EIGHT

Mark's cheerful mood when he came over on that rainy Saturday morning made Jessie feel less guilty for having asked him to go out to Chiba with her. "I'm sorry to take you away from your weekend plans," she said as they buckled up their seatbelts in Yuya's van.

"Yeah, right. It's real difficult to tear myself away from all those fascinating freshmen essays sitting on my desk."

Jessie laughed. "Thank you for your sacrifice. I really appreciate it. I just hope it's not another secret stash of old warranties and broken-down washing machines."

"Who knows?" Mark said as they set off. "Maybe this isn't the end of it. Maybe Sachiko has secret hiding places all up and down the coast."

"Don't say that!" Jessie said in mock horror. "What if just saying it makes it come true?

"I guess we'd somehow deal with it, wouldn't we?"

Delight tingled in Jessie's toes from the way he said *we.*

"So, how much longer do you have?"

Well, that brought Jessie right back to reality. Pregnant reality. "A month." Clasping her hands across her belly where the baby's bottom seemed to be lodged, she ventured, "So, how's your...um, how's Kumiko these days?"

"Kumiko? Oh, she's great, I guess. She's in Hong Kong right now, presenting at a conference. It's not even in our field. But some people will do anything to get out of attending faculty meetings." Mark chuckled and added, "But that's just your typical Kumiko."

Jessie laughed along with him but wasn't sure what was so funny.

By the time Mark exited the expressway and drove through the more rural part of Chiba, the rain had completely stopped. The clouds had parted, and beams of sunshine sparkled across the rice fields. The landscape teemed with countless shades of green, and they rolled down their windows and inhaled deeply the country air. Ten minutes later, the van hitched over train tracks in an area that once had the promise of development. But that dream for the community died after a train station was built in the next town, creating a commuter hub and a housing boom over there. They took a few wrong turns on dead-end streets before pulling up in front of the house. Mark parked next to a bush exploding with the most gorgeous lavender-blue hydrangeas Jessie had ever seen.

Mr. Suzuki had told the tenants they were coming, but he had forgotten to mention that they were foreigners. The old man, certain that Jessie and Mark had gotten lost on their way to Disneyland, the airport, or anywhere else but there, rushed out to give directions so they could get on their way. Being quite hard of hearing, he responded to what they were saying by shouting, "No English! No English!" at them in English.

It took a few minutes before they could make him believe they were in the right place, that Jessie was his new landlord, and that they were speaking to him in Japanese. When that was finally settled, he grinned and called his wife out to join in the excitement. The couple then showed them the house from top to bottom as if they were the proud owners themselves. The Tanakas had taken such good care of everything it was kind of sad that the person who had bought it was planning to tear it down. But at least Jessie wasn't selling the house out from under them—they had been wanting to move in with their son's family further down the Chiba peninsula for quite some time.

Mrs. Tanaka served cups of green tea and sticky rice cakes filled with sweet beans in a Japanese-style room where the tatami mats were old but not tattered. The paper doors on the closets were discolored with age but not full of holes. They kneeled at a black lacquered table gleaming from decades of polish, and while looking out at the tiny but well-tended garden, they nibbled at the refreshments as if they were in a Kyoto temple's tearoom.

After twenty minutes of polite chitchat, Mr. Tanaka led them to the storage shed, a prefabricated unit the size of a small bedroom. When he unlocked the door, they reentered Sachiko's cluttered world.

"I'm terribly sorry," he said as he lit two coils of incense to ward off the mosquitos already buzzing around their ears. "Maybe I should've cleaned this up before you arrived. I came in here from time to time, but only when Mrs. Yamada sent me things to store."

"Do you know what's in here?" asked Mark.

The old man shook his head.

"I guess it doesn't matter. We'll soon find out," said Mark cheerfully before he headed back to the van to get aprons, work gloves, and garbage bags.

Mr. Tanaka reappeared with an old electric fan connected to power in the main house by three extension cords. Mrs. Tanaka brought out a sturdy folding chair for Jessie to sit on. After thanking them for their thoughtfulness, they got to work.

"I can't sell any of this," Jessie said a little while later, wiping the sweat off her brow with a small hand towel she had in her pocket. "These clothes look like they've been used to mop the floor. What in the world was Sachiko thinking? Why would she want to save such crap?"

"Toss them in that corner. Let's make that the garbage area."

Next to that, Mark dumped a box of papers that must have gotten wet and solidified into an unidentifiable cube. More papers.

Some moldy magazines from the 1990s. Behind the stack of flimsy and damaged cardboard boxes was another wall, but this one was made up of well-packed and well-preserved plastic containers. They moved those to the look-at-later side of the shed.

Jessie came to a faded Mitsukoshi Department Store shopping bag filled with silky party clothes and some beaded and sequined bags. The dress on top had a red wine stain, and she was about to toss it into the throwaway pile before it occurred to her that the girls might enjoy that stuff for dress-up. She took the bag out to the van, giving her legs a stretch.

A little while later, Mrs. Tanaka called them into the air-conditioned house for a lunch of cold noodles and watermelon. Later in the afternoon, Mr. Tanaka kept checking up on them, eyeing the garbage piles with growing agitation and sucking air through his teeth. The reason for this agitation became evident when he wheeled out a steel barrel that was nearly his size. Scooping up as much trash as he could hold, he dumped it in. He lit a rolled-up newspaper with a lighter, adding it to the barrel when the fire got going. As stuff went up in flames, his eyes glowed with excitement.

Just ten minutes earlier, Jessie had been wishing she could torch it all, and apparently, Mr. Tanaka had the same idea all along. After the fire died down, he burned another batch. And another. Over and over again. When all that could be burned was burned, they had coffee and grapes back inside the house while waiting for the Black Cat delivery company to pick up the boxes that couldn't fit in the van.

On the way home, Jessie said, "Since we're going to go right by Costco, would you mind stopping? I can pick up our pizza for tomorrow night, and that'd save me a trip tomorrow."

"Something going on?"

"Not really. Ayako and Natsumi come over on Sundays. We have pizza, and then we all play silly games. You're welcome to come if you want."

The next night, the café's shades were lowered, and the closed sign was up. Miya, Kizuna, and Natsumi were having a lively Monopoly game with Yuya at the back table. Jimmy and Ayako were putting the finishing touches on salads in the kitchen. Pink Floyd, Jimmy's favorite, was playing in the background. Jessie, refreshed from a three-hour nap that afternoon, was sitting with her legs propped up and poking at her swollen ankles with her finger, watching the indent slowly return to normal.

"Are you sure you don't have anything else to do?" Jessie asked Mark when he slid across from her with a Corona.

"I suppose I could be home going through Sachiko's papers if that was some sort of hint to get rid of me."

"That's not what I meant," she said with a laugh. "Don't you have a date or a party or something more exciting than this?"

"Nope," said Mark. "I lead a completely boring life."

"You think our little dinner is boring, do you?"

"I fell right into that trap, didn't I?"

"Don't mind me," she said, feeling ridiculously happy. "I'm just the grumpy pregnant lady."

"Well, I'm glad to report that all the boxes arrived this morning, and I've got them stashed away until I can get to them. Which, by the way," Mark said, taking a swig of his beer, "won't be tonight."

Ayako and Jimmy came out of the kitchen, placed the salads on the counter, and sat down. Yuya escaped the game by randomly distributing his cash and properties. "Anyone else up for another cold one?" He headed toward the small fridge behind the counter. "Say, Jessie. Before I forget, you left a bag of stuff in the van, so I set it in the pantry in the kitchen."

While waiting for the Costco pizzas to finish baking, Jessie and Mark described their day in Chiba and how Mrs. Tanaka had dashed out of the house just in time to stop her husband from setting a bag of clothes on fire that was destined for the dry cleaners.

"It was no wonder their house was so well organized," said Mark. "Because—"

"Anything out of place," Jessie said, jumping in, "would get torched, pronto."

"Aren't there any laws about that kind of thing?" asked Jimmy. "Aren't people supposed to be careful about what they set on fire?"

"You'd be surprised what country people do," said Yuya. "One of my clients decided to burn his sofa because he was too cheap to pay for the recycling costs. It was made from some kind of synthetic material, and the smoke was so toxic the neighbors called the fire department. He got hit with a fine that was much more than if he had just paid to have the thing taken away."

They continued talking like this over the pizza—the adults at one table and the girls at another. Afterward, they played charades and a rip-roaring game of musical chairs. Mark and Jimmy were the last two standing, and when Jessie stopped the music, they both dove for the chair, causing it to bounce across the floor.

"That's it. I call a tie," said Jessie. "Before someone breaks an arm or a leg. Or one of my chairs."

"Come on, Natsumi," Ayako called. "It's almost eight, and tomorrow's school. We'd better get going."

"Are we going by taxi again?" The girl asked, speaking half in English and half in Japanese.

Jessie raised her eyebrows. "Taxi?"

Ayako gave an embarrassed laugh. "If Natsumi falls asleep on the way, it's easier. And besides, it's a tax write-off."

"So, if I start taking taxis," said Jessie, "can I write it off, too?"

Yuya snorted into his beer. "Technically, yes. But that only works when your income is greater than your expenses."

"Then I guess it's good that I don't have to go anywhere. I'm saving a fortune on transportation."

After Ayako left, Jimmy and Yuya washed up and put things away. "Why don't you close up down here?" Jimmy said. "We'll do bedtime."

"I won't argue with that," Jessie replied, avoiding Jimmy's eyes as he gathered up the girls. She would be in charge for the next three nights, so she certainly was entitled to an evening off, even if Mark was still around.

In the quiet left behind, Jessie rubbed her giant belly and said wistfully, "This heat is really getting to me. I'd kill for a beer."

"You know, I could go get you some of that nonalcoholic beer," Mark said. "And you could pretend."

"That might just do the trick."

She watched him from the window as he went to the convenience store, and as always, she wished things were different.

CHAPTER TWENTY-NINE

"Jesus. Aren't you hot in here?" Jimmy reached for the AC remote control and lowered the temperature in Jessie's apartment. "Haven't you heard? It's August, not May."

"Yeah, I'm hot, Jimmy. I'm always hot," Jessie said waspishly, her face shiny with sweat. "I'm thirty-eight weeks pregnant, just in case you haven't noticed."

"Then why don't you turn the AC—"

"Because unlike you, with unlimited amounts of money, I can't afford to run it at arctic temperatures." Jessie grimaced. "Sorry. I don't mean to snap at you. The humidity is really getting to me."

"Nah, don't worry about it. So, what did the doctor say today? They're okay with me being there for the birth when it's time?"

"Everyone feels so sorry for me. I think they'd let me bring in a trained monkey."

"Well, gee. Thanks a bunch. Just see what kind of souvenir from Guam you'll get." Jimmy put his arm around Jessie. "But seriously, you'll be okay while we're gone, right?"

"What if I said no?"

"I'd stay, obviously."

"Liar," she grumbled. "You'd go right ahead on your fancy holiday and leave me behind."

"Yeah, you're probably right about that."

Jessie laughed. "But seriously, it's just a few days. I'll be fine. Miya's spending the weekend with Natsumi. The whole weekend! I can't believe how grown up she's getting. Do you know what she called me the other day? Mom! That's my mother, not me."

Jimmy laughed. "I guess it's a good thing that Natalie will be here soon. She'll call you Mommy."

"Oh, wait. What do you think of Emma? Or maybe Anna?"

"Personally, I'm partial to Gertrude. Or maybe Gladys."

Jessie rolled her eyes and made a face.

"Anyway," Jimmy said as he headed toward the door. "Send me a message if you can think of anything else you need from Kmart."

"Have fun, and don't get eaten by sharks."

"And don't you go and have that baby while I'm gone."

"I wish. I'm sick to death of being pregnant."

The following morning, Jessie dropped Miya off at Natsumi's apartment for their big sleepover. Having the café to herself in the late afternoon, she sat at the back table reading a paperback mystery with the AC running full blast. Customers or no customers, she told herself, it was a business expense.

"Hi, Jessie."

She jumped, and so did the baby. "Mark! Sorry, I didn't hear you come in."

"I didn't mean to startle you. Are you open? Can I still get a cup of coffee and maybe a brownie?"

"Yes to the coffee, but no to the brownie. Mrs. Watanabe and her gang devoured every last one. Do you want hot or iced coffee? You'd better say iced because I don't feel like making hot."

"And you call this a café," Mark said, laughing. "Iced is fine."

Jessie went to the kitchen to get it, and when she returned with the coffee, he asked where Miya was.

"She's spending the night at Natsumi's because Kizuna and the guys are off on their trip to Guam. So, I'm here all by my lonesome."

"Got any big plans for your wild night of freedom?"

"Well, there is that hot date I've got lined up with Netflix."

"How about I take you somewhere for dinner?"

Jessie's neck heated up. "I hope you don't think I was fishing for an invite."

"I know you weren't. But you might not have an opportunity to go out much after the baby comes. I'll be taking students to LA for a couple of weeks, and I want to try this new Thai place near Shinagawa Station before I go." Jessie was frowning at him, and after a long pause, Mark said, "I guess I didn't realize that having dinner with me would be such torture."

"What?"

"I honestly didn't think having dinner with me would be *that* bad. You should see the scowl on your face."

Jessie laughed. "I'm sorry. That's not it at all. I was just thinking about my clothing crisis. I'd love to go out for dinner—as long as there's air conditioning and as long as I don't have to wear anything fancy. Or walk too far. Because ditto for the shoe problem."

"Okay. It's a date, then." Mark finished his coffee and stood. "I'll come and get you around six. I'll bring my car, so you won't have to walk too much."

Jessie locked up and went to get ready. *It's a date* is just an expression, she reminded herself. People say it all the time, and it doesn't mean a damn thing. She took a shower, and while drying herself, she stared at her protruding stomach in the mirror. "Yeah, right. Date," she muttered while selecting her least hideous maternity outfit. "A date with a whale is more like it."

The next issue was makeup. Should she, or shouldn't she? She wanted to look nice but didn't want to look like she was trying to look nice. Because what exactly did *it's a date* mean, anyway? The last thing she needed was for him to think she thought it was one. When, of course, it wasn't.

She went to retrieve a cotton shawl from the chest in the tatami room and jumped when she saw two pairs of spooky eyes staring down at her from the butsudan. Stupid cats giving her a fright like that! "It's just dinner," she told them as if it were any of their business in the first place.

An hour later, Jessie was with Mark in a restaurant a few notches above what she had been expecting in terms of decor and price. Before she had a chance to consider what she could afford, Mark ordered one of the dinner sets. Not the most expensive one, but not the cheapest one either. Nonalcoholic beer for the pregnant lady and the driver.

"Mmm. This is great," Jessie said, dipping a spring roll appetizer into chili sauce. It was too late now to worry about the price, and she decided to enjoy every mouthful. "I haven't eaten Thai in forever. It's too spicy for Miya."

The waiter set down bowls of tom yon kung, and after her first taste, her mouth was on fire. She drank some water and then had more soup. If it weren't for all that activity that started going on in her belly under the table, she might have been able to convince herself that this thing with Mark *was* a date. Because it was almost beginning to feel like one. They talked about their families back home and their college days. Their favorite TV shows as kids. The books that changed their lives. For Jessie, it was a tattered copy of Pearl Buck's *The Good Earth* that she had found on her grandmother's bookshelf that set her interest in Asia in motion. "Don't laugh," she said. "I know that book is problematic from all sorts of viewpoints, but I was thirteen, and it had a huge impact on me."

"For me," said Mark, "and don't *you* dare laugh—it was, if I remember correctly, a book called *Uncle Monty's Book of Magic Tricks*. I swear, for a couple of years, I thought I was David Copperfield. My poor family. I subjected them to terrible abuse. I retired my magician cloak when I was about twelve, so don't be asking me to perform at any birthday parties."

Jessie did laugh, and two hours sped by. The waiter brought the check after they finished their small scoops of coconut ice cream, and Mark produced a credit card before Jessie could protest. "My treat," he said casually.

"Thank you," she said, too poor to argue.

"And besides," he added, "there's something important I want to talk to you about."

There it was—the reason for the dinner. Jessie had seen enough movies and had read enough books to know that business matters were usually discussed at the end of a meal. Date indeed! She put on an appropriate expression and settled back into her chair. "What's up?"

"Do you feel up to coming over to my place?"

That wasn't what she had expected to hear at all.

"You don't have to get back home right away, do you? Because I found something that I really want to show you. Something in one of the boxes from Chiba."

"Really? Something important?"

Mark broke out in a grin. "Well, maybe not in a discovering-a-cure-for-cancer kind of importance. But I have a feeling it could be important in a historian kind of way. At least, I hope so. It's technically yours, so I wanted you to be the first to see it."

"All right," she said, pushing back her chair. "You've got my curiosity up. But before we go, I've got to use the bathroom."

In the car, the conversation returned to lighter topics. He was so funny and easy to talk to that once again, she imagined what it would be like if she were on a date with Mark. When he parked in front of a solidly built home—not one of those flimsy prefabricated things designed to self-destruct after twenty-five years—he warned her to be quiet. They didn't want to be waking Poo-Poo, his landlady's yappy chihuahua. "And before you make any wisecracks," he whispered, "I didn't pick the name."

Mark unhooked the latch on the gate. He took her arm and led her around the side of the house, past the laundry poles, and into the back, where there was a Japanese garden. To the tiny pond's left was a small, freestanding wooden structure. Mark opened the door, and they slipped off their shoes and stepped inside.

Jessie gasped. "This is amazing! It should be on one of those tiny house TV shows! How on earth did you ever find this place?"

"Confession time. I lived here when I was a high school student. Well, not *here*, but in the big house. My host father designed this little house for an architectural contest. Which, by the way, he won."

"I can certainly believe that," said Jessie. "I love how the wooden floors blend in with the built-in bookcases and cabinets."

"Yeah. The kitchen area is tiny, but I can do pretty much anything but cook a turkey. Now, over there," he said, pointing at the sofa and wall-mounted TV, "is the relaxation zone. That cupboard on the other wall is a Murphy bed. And that cubby hole back there is my office."

"So, you're like one of those minimalists."

Mark looked slightly embarrassed. "Well, I also have two rooms inside the house. One for my books and another for my out-of-season clothes."

"Ah. Cheating, are you?"

"Hey! Don't knock it. That's how I can keep all of Sachiko's stuff."

"Then far be it for me to judge."

"I admit it, though. I've got it pretty good here. My host father got transferred to New York. The family knew I'd just gone through a nasty divorce, so they asked me to live here and keep an eye on the grandmother. They said they'd feel better if someone they trusted was around. Anyway," he said as he offered Jessie a chair. "Something to drink?"

"No. I'm good. But I do need the bathroom."

It was damned embarrassing to have to poop right at that particular moment, but the spicy food was shooting through Jessie's body at a breakneck speed. She found a deodorizer, cracked the window, and prayed that Mark wouldn't need to go in there for a long time. Good thing for sure that this wasn't a date. It would be too mortifying.

Not saying a thing about her five-minute absence, Mark motioned her over to his desk, where he had pulled up another chair. "Okay, the simple stuff first. I found pictures—quite a few. I put them away for safekeeping. I don't want to handle them until I figure out the best way to do that. But take a look."

Jessie leaned over Mark's iPad while he scrolled through dozens of pictures. "Why didn't you say anything about this at dinner?"

"Honestly? I knew that if I got started, I wouldn't be able to talk about anything else. Kumiko's always complaining that I get carried away on something and bore people silly. And besides, I didn't want to ruin your one night out with shoptalk."

"Well," Jessie said, putting on a smile as if she was simply dying to hear all about Kumiko's opinions. "Go ahead. Let loose. Bore me silly with shoptalk."

Once Mark got going, his voice took on a serious tone. He pushed his iPad closer to Jessie and swiped through portraits, scenery, and street scenes. Jessie glanced sideways at him while his eyes were on the iPad, and she had the strongest urge to brush his hair off his forehead.

"Most of them aren't labeled," he was saying. "But some, like this one, are. Can you see the date? 1859. And the name in the corner? That's Ukai Gyokusen. He was the first Japanese professional photographer in Japan." Mark scrolled to another one. "See that one by Orrin Freeman? It turns out he opened the first photography studio in Japan. All these pictures kind of tell a narrative—a story, so to speak—about the history of Japanese photography. But anyway," Mark said, "there are a couple of photos that I want you to see with your own eyes."

Before opening the box, he put on white gloves and laid out several in front of Jessie, who grunted a little and shifted in the chair. "Are you uncomfortable?" Mark asked. "Would you rather sit on the sofa?"

"I'm fine. I've just got a bit of indigestion. The baby takes up so much space. And I'm sorry, but I've got to go to the bathroom again." Jessie heaved herself out of the chair. "Now you know what it's like to spend a Friday night with a pregnant lady."

In the bathroom, her stomach tightened again. She breathed through the Braxton Hicks contraction, which was completely normal this late in pregnancy.

"Now," Mark said, after she returned. "Take a look at this photo I found online. It was taken by Admiral Perry's official photographer. You know, Perry was the guy who persuaded the Japanese government to open up the country. Well, compare that picture to the one here."

Jessie looked at it carefully. "It kind of looks the same."

"That's what I thought," Mark said, his voice growing with excitement. "Eliphalet Brown took hundreds of pictures of Japan. But only six are accounted for today. So, if my hunch is true and this picture is his, it's very rare."

"Oh, my god," Jessie exclaimed when the baby gave her a hard kick in the ribs.

Misinterpreting her reaction, Mark said, "Don't get too excited, though. Unless there's a collector for this kind of stuff, it's probably not worth a fortune. Historical value," he added with a happy grin, "could be an entirely different story."

"Can I have some water, after all? I don't think the baby liked all that spicy food. She's doing the tango."

"Sure, but can you drink it over there? No food or drink allowed near the photos."

"Yes, sir!" she said with a salute and pretended to march after Mark to the dining area. The water helped, and she felt much better when she sat back at the desk.

"Now I've saved the best for last. Remember that very first picture I found? The one with the baby?"

"Yeah."

"Well, going by the baby's birthday, that's the oldest photo of the bunch. Look at the man next to the baby and compare him with the man here." He placed a group photo with fifteen serious-looking young men on the desk and handed her a magnifying glass. "That one right there. Now, tell me. Isn't that the same man in the picture with the baby? Look at what he's wearing."

"Maybe. The kimono looks the same. And isn't that a scar on his cheek?"

"Correct!" Mark exclaimed as if Jessie had gotten the correct answer for *Jeopardy*'s Daily Double. Mark enlarged the photo of the man on his iPad and pointed at the scar. "Same guy, right? So, logically speaking, this photo could have been taken in 1849, the same time as the family portrait."

Jessie was nodding along, but she was barely listening. The Braxton Hicks contractions had become too distracting.

"Now then, we've pretty much established that this picture with these men was probably taken in 1849. Look at it carefully. What else do you see?" When Jessie was slow to answer, he prompted her. "Look at the guy in the middle. What's he wearing?"

She leaned in close. "A suit?"

"Exactly! A suit! Everyone else is wearing a kimono. Now, does that guy look like a foreigner to you?"

She looked through the magnifying glass again. "I don't know. He kind of looks Asian."

"Well, he'd look Asian if he was part American Indian, don't you think?"

Jessie was thinking Mark was pretty cute, getting all excited over these old pictures.

"I could be wrong, but I have a hunch that he's Ranald MacDonald."

Jessie laughed.

"Not the clown! This is Ranald with an "a" MacDonald. He was shipwrecked off the coast of Hokkaido in 1848. They say he was the first native English-speaking teacher in Japan."

"I don't know why I think that's funny," she said, laughing some more. "But it is. The first English teacher."

Mark launched right back into professor mode. "Japan had closed its doors to everyone but a handful of Dutch, right? All the information of the world was coming into Japan via the Dutch and translated into Japanese by generational translators."

"Generational translators?"

"Yeah. The job was handed down from father to son. Anyway, after a shipload of Brits rioted in Nagasaki in the early 1800s, the Shogun ordered the translators to learn English. He didn't want anything like that to happen again, so they found a Dutchman to teach them English. But apparently, he didn't know much, and he guessed the pronunciation. But based on those lessons, the translators made grammar manuals and dictionaries and used them for decades. They were basically all wrong, but—"

"And that MacDonald guy?" Jessie wanted Mark to get to the point.

"Well, when Ranald MacDonald got arrested for entering Japan, he was sent to Nagasaki. Most people who ended up in Japan were shipwrecked sailors. Illiterate sorts. But he was different. He even had his books with him."

"His books! How did he manage to do that?"

"The story is he bribed the captain of the ship he was on to let him go ashore in a rowboat. For some reason," Mark said with a laugh, "he was really keen to go to Japan."

"That's crazy," said Jessie.

"Crazy, right?" Mark agreed happily. "But before they deported him, they got him to teach the interpreters English. So, when Admiral Perry's crew came back the second time, they were there to meet him. And because of Ranald MacDonald, they could negotiate in English."

"I guess he wasn't just the first English teacher in Japan—he was the first *successful* one." Jessie peered at the photo again. "Do you really think it's him?"

"It might just be wishful thinking, but if the date on the picture with the baby is anything to go by, the timing certainly fits. And another thing, Ranald MacDonald had fourteen students. Look again. Fifteen people. Fourteen students and one teacher."

"So, if you're right about this—"

"If I'm right about this, it could be a pretty significant historical find. Because as far as I know, there aren't any photos of Ranald MacDonald taken when he was in Japan. You know, I can't wait to see the look on Kumiko's face when I tell her about this, too."

The moment she heard Kumiko's name, Jessie knew it was time for her to get going. "I hate being a party pooper," she said, "but I'm exhausted." When Mark stood, she added, "You don't have to come with me. I'm perfectly capable of going a block and a half on my own."

"I'm sure you are," he replied. "But my mama always said that if you take a girl out on a date, you've got to see her to her door."

There he went with that date word again.

The minute they moved outside into the sultry night, Jessie felt better. She wasn't sure if her heart was beating too fast because of the Braxton Hicks that had just ended moments earlier or because Mark had his hand on her elbow. They cut through the park, where a full moon was hanging above the trees. Teenagers, drinking beer and setting off firecrackers, got their attention by calling out friendly drunken hellos in English as they walked past. Except for the yakitori restaurant on the corner, all the shops on her street were closed for the night. While Jessie fumbled for her keys at the back entrance, she felt her belly tighten up again. This time something popped, and water gushed down her legs.

Jessie stared down at the ground in horror.

"Is that—"

"I- I think so."

"The baby's coming *now*?"

"Shh. I don't want to wake up Mrs. Watanabe." They hurried inside, and Jessie locked the door behind them. "I guess all those contractions I had been having were the real deal."

Mark gaped at her. "You were in labor, and you didn't say anything?"

"I thought it was false labor. The baby isn't due for another two weeks."

"I'll go get my car. I'll be right back."

Jessie grabbed his sleeve. "We can take mine. I need to change my clothes and get my bag first."

"I can't believe how calm you are," Mark said as he followed Jessie up to her apartment.

"It's not like in the movies, you know. Make coffee, if you want. I'm going to take a quick shower." She closed the bathroom door behind her just as another contraction hit.

Several minutes later, Jessie stepped into the living room wearing stretchy yoga pants and an oversized t-shirt. Her face was free of makeup, and her hair was pulled back into a ponytail. "Miya is with Ayako tonight, but tomorrow I don't—" The next contraction took her breath away. When it subsided, she said, "Please stop staring at me like that. It's embarrassing enough as it is. Everything's fine. I'm fine."

The next contraction came while Mark was backing the car out onto the road. "I'm no expert, but aren't they coming kind of close together?"

"Maybe we should hurry."

Two contractions later, Jessie began to yell. And with the one after that, she unbuckled her seatbelt and pulled down her pants. "The baby's head's coming out!"

Mark managed to get to the hospital without being stopped by the police, despite making some illegal left turns at the red lights. As he pulled in front of the emergency entrance, he blasted the horn and jumped out of the car. "Help! Help! She's having a baby right *now*!"

A security guard ran over with a wheelchair, but Jessie was having none of that. A white-coated woman with a stethoscope dangling around her neck hurried toward them, pulling on a pair of latex gloves just as Jessie started to lie down on the pavement.

"When did the contractions start?" the doctor asked Mark as he was trying to hold Jessie up.

"I- I don't know!"

When the doctor glared at him, he was about to point out that he was just a friend. He snapped his mouth shut when he realized a friend might be told to go home. "They came on quite suddenly. Before her waters broke, she thought it was false labor. I'm not sure when the…"

By then, the doctor had already turned her attention toward the gurney someone had brought outside.

Jessie grabbed Mark's hand. "Don't leave me!"

"I'm right here!"

"Don't push! Wait!" shouted the doctor when Jessie bore down.

"You the fuck, wait!" Jessie shrieked as they burst through the door to the emergency room, silencing the dozen people waiting for their own emergencies to be dealt with.

"The baby's head is crowning," shouted the doctor to the emergency room staff.

A nurse hurried over with wheeled partitions, creating a makeshift delivery room two feet from the entrance.

"Breathe! One, two! One, two!" said one of the nurses.

"Aagh!" came out of Jessie, her eyes wild with pain.

"Look at me! Breathe it with me!" Mark put his face up to hers. "Breathe! One, two! One, two!"

"Wait!" shouted the doctor. "Don't push yet!"

"Pant!" Mark ordered, just like they do in the movies.

Jessie responded by clutching his fingers with the strength of an industrial crane, and she groaned, grunted, and made primal sounds. Then the baby slipped out: bloody, shiny, and covered with muck. The silence of several seconds lasted forever, but when the baby finally cried, a palpable sense of relief spread throughout the entire waiting room. People began whispering to each other about the miracle they had just witnessed.

"Congratulations," said the doctor to Jessie. "It's a boy."

"No," she corrected weakly. "That's wrong. She's a girl."

"He's a boy, all right," said Mark. "No question about it."

"But everything's pink and—" Another contraction stopped Jessie mid-sentence.

"Oh, my god!" Mark exclaimed. "Twins?"

The doctor gave him another look. "It's the afterbirth."

The nurses wheeled Jessie and the baby off.

"How are you feeling?" Jessie asked Mark half an hour later when the nurses finally let him into her room.

"Shouldn't I be the one asking you that?" He leaned over and kissed her on the forehead.

"I guess this wasn't exactly how you imagined you'd be spending your Friday night."

"It was, without a doubt, the most terrifying and most exciting experience of my entire life."

Jessie nuzzled the baby, who still had some dried muck on his head. Beaming with pride, she said, "The little devil must've had his legs crossed during every single one of those ultrasounds. Because we thought for sure he was a girl."

"Do you want me to call anyone?"

"I'll talk to my family tomorrow. I've already sent a message to Ayako. But can you take some pictures for me? Jimmy and Yuya will have heart attacks when they wake up and see him."

After taking a few photos on Jessie's phone, Mark collapsed into the chair next to Jessie's bed and dozed until she was moved to the maternity floor a few hours later. In the afternoon, Ayako brought Miya to meet her new brother.

"I didn't know it was going to be purple," Miya said, peering closely at the baby. "And how come you changed your mind, Mom? How come she's not a girl?"

"Oh, Miya, I didn't change my mind. The doctor just made a mistake."

"Are you sure it's a boy?"

Jessie lifted the baby's nightgown and slipped off the diaper. "Take a look."

"Is that his *chin-chin*?"

"Yes," said Jessie.

"What's his name?"

"What about Yoshio Daniel? The Yoshi part sounds like Daddy's name. And Daniel is my father's name. It's Jimmy's middle name, too."

"Not that it matters," added Mark, who had stuck by her side most of the day. "But that's also my middle name."

CHAPTER THIRTY

They called the baby Danny.

The day he turned two weeks old, Jessie got up early to get ready for her sister's wedding ceremony in California. With the time difference, it was going to start at four a.m. Japan time. That hour didn't make a bit of difference to Jessie—her nights and days were one long blur of feeding, burping, and changing poopy diapers. On the other hand, getting fully dressed and slapping on some makeup to be a presentable virtual guest was a completely different matter.

The sky was beginning to brighten when she took the baby downstairs and brewed herself a pot of Earl Grey tea. As previously arranged, she called her cousin's iPad. While waiting for the service to begin, she chatted with old friends from church. A wave of homesickness washed over her, and she really did wish that she could have been where it was all happening.

Everyone stood when the "Wedding March" started, and Jessie's heart lurched at the sight of her baby sister in her white gown. With Danny in her arms, she recalled the day her mother had brought Bethany home from the hospital. Her stepfather went utterly gaga over his newborn daughter, and that was when she finally warmed up to him. He became more human—less scary.

There was an unmistakable look of pride on Tom's face as he escorted Bethany down the aisle toward Justin Washington, newly released marine (presumably trained to kill) and evangelical Christian. Even though Jessie still thought Bethany was too young to be getting married, she reminded herself that this was what her sister had always wanted, ever since she was fifteen.

"I'm really happy for you, Bethany." The ceremony was over, and everyone had moved to the VFW hall down the street for the reception. "Everything was beautiful. *You* were beautiful."

They chatted for a few seconds before her mom took charge of the iPad. "Jessie," she said, "you haven't met Rachel Woodward, have you? She's new to the church."

Rachel, a pretty blond with shiny shoulder-length hair, leaned toward the screen, smiled, and said hi. Jessie smiled and said hi back.

"Rachel just moved here six months ago." Her mom zoomed out a little bit so she could see the man sitting next to Rachel. "You remember Noah Stevens, don't you, Jessie?"

Sure, she did. The widower with two daughters. "Hey, Noah. How are things going?"

"He's engaged!" interjected Jessie's mom. "To Rachel! Isn't that simply wonderful news?"

Rachel and Noah leaned closer together, and Rachel waved her engagement ring happily at the camera.

"That's wonderful news indeed!" Jessie said. "Congratulations to the two of you."

Before her mom had a chance to give Jessie a you've-missed-the-boat kind of look, her other cousin grabbed the iPad. From the way Katie was giggling, Jessie figured she must have smuggled in vodka to spike her fruit punch, just like she did back when they were teenagers. "Jessie!" she squealed. "I want to show you how big my babies are now!"

Jessie admired the two-year-old twins who were sleeping in a stroller with their thumbs in their mouths in an identical manner.

Katie reciprocated by equally oohing and aahing over Danny. Waiters began serving, and the iPad was set down somewhere, offering Jessie a perfect view of the ceiling. She stayed by her iPad, listening to the sounds of people chatting, eating, and laughing. After a while, the batteries on their end ran down, and her screen went blank.

The summer sun was already high in the sky, but Miya was still sleeping. Jessie climbed the stairs to make breakfast, feeling relaxed, content, and happy. As she nursed Danny, she nuzzled his head. His peach fuzz feathered her lips, and she gathered in his baby scent. It was almost as if a switch in her brain had been turned off—the switch that sent her straight to self-defense mode whenever she talked to her mother. The switch that raised her blood pressure and made her feel like an incompetent child.

It wasn't clear what had happened, but Jessie knew that she wasn't going to let her mother get to her any longer.

.   .   .

Japanese folk wisdom has it that a new mother should do nothing but recover and nurse a baby for thirty days after giving birth. While Jessie was all on board with that notion when it came to cooking, cleaning, or teaching English, she wasn't crazy about being held an indoor hostage. Sure, she could sit in the café or go up to the roof, but she was getting cabin fever. That evening, there was the neighborhood's annual summer festival to celebrate the ancestral spirits' return. Miya and Kizuna, wearing new summer cotton kimonos, had left for it an hour earlier with their friends. Miya's yukata was pink with yellow flowers, and Kizuna's was indigo with colorful bursts of fireworks.

Jessie could hear the drums and recorded flute music, and it was simply too much to resist. When she finished nursing Danny, she changed into something without breast milk stains, strapped him to her chest, and stepped outside into the sultry evening.

Twenty-six days stuck in the house were more than enough. She was done with this cloistered existence. She would walk down, get some fresh air, watch the dancing, and then come back.

The park had been transformed into a summer wonderland. The lanterns strung throughout the trees shone brightly, and dancers of all ages—most in yukata—surrounded the stage and moved rhythmically in a circle. Jessie spotted Mrs. Watanabe and Mr. Suzuki with the dancers and moved back into the shadows before they noticed her.

She saw the girls at a booth giving away baby chickens as prizes and hurried over to inform them in no uncertain terms that they were not to come home with one. Festival goldfish was one thing, but live poultry was entirely another. The girls watched with envy as a second grader carried off her new fuzzy pet.

"But Mom—" whined Miya.

"Don't even think about it."

"Hey there," said a voice behind her after the girls had moved on to the cotton candy booth.

"Mark! When did you get back?"

"Yesterday. Tired as anything. Three weeks with the students in Los Angeles was quite a challenge. But at least no one got arrested, and no one got into an accident. We all returned in one piece. But I'm pretty sure I've added quite a few gray hairs to my poor aging head."

Jessie laughed. "Did you get to see your family?"

"I did. Kumiko took charge of the students for a couple of days, so I snuck off and spent some time with them."

"Oh," said Jessie. "I didn't realize she went on the trip with you."

"Yeah, they like to send two teachers along—especially a woman. Just in case. You know, if something happens with any of the female students."

"I suppose it would be handy to go in pairs like that," Jessie said, feeling rather awkward and stupid. She blamed it on post-natal baby brain. "In case something happens."

"Right," said Mark, wiping the sweat off his forehead with a handkerchief. "Anyway, how's my little namesake doing?"

Now, this was an easier topic of conversation. "That's funny," she said. "Jimmy always says the same thing. He's fine. Pooping, peeing, and eating. Right on schedule."

"A regular genius, I see."

"Listen," Jessie said, "I never got a chance to tell you how much I appreciated—"

"I wouldn't have missed that experience for all the world," said Mark. "Let me tell you, my family was thoroughly impressed by my heroic feats when I told them about the night Danny was born."

"Is that so? I seem to remember someone in major panic mode the whole way in the car."

"Well, I might've embellished things for my family a bit."

"What? The part where you single-handedly delivered the baby while wearing a tuxedo and drinking champagne?"

"Something like that. So, if you ever do meet any of them, please go along with the story."

Jessie wanted to laugh, but she felt choked up with emotion. "Seriously, you were great. I don't know what I would've done without you. You're going to be a great dad someday. I mean, when it's your turn to do that for your own kid." Jessie laughed off her shaky voice and blinked back tears. "Don't mind me. Hormones. You didn't get into an accident on the way to the hospital, and you didn't pass out during the birth. Definitely award-winning behavior in my book."

"You're the one who should win the award. Seriously. And look at you now. You look great."

"Liar," she said, grinning happily.

They sat on a bench, watching the festival activities around them, and Jessie felt like she could've stayed there all night. But Danny had other ideas. He raised his head, turned purple, and let out an explosive sound. "Well, this was fun while it lasted." Jessie sighed as she pulled herself up.

"I can go back with you if you want. Pick up a few beers and keep you company."

"Sounds great, but I'd better have a fake one. I'm nursing."

They stopped by the convenience store for drinks and snacks. When they stepped into the café, Mark stopped short and whistled. "No offense, but it looks like a colony of babies has taken over in here."

Jessie laughed. "It does, doesn't it? You'd be surprised by all the baby stuff the neighbors had stashed away in their closets. I haven't had to buy a single thing. Mind you, almost everything is at least thirty years old. Relax," she said, switching on the air conditioner and heading up the stairs. "I'll be down after I get this little monkey cleaned up."

Even though she had given birth right under Mark's nose, she felt shy about nursing in front of him. Luckily, the baby was quick and soon fell asleep. She carried him back downstairs, laid him in a wicker bassinet behind the counter, and sat across from Mark.

"If I close my eyes," she said after they clinked their cans together in a toast, "maybe I can imagine this is the real deal." She took a swig and laughed. "Nope. But close enough. It still hits the spot."

"Before I forget," Mark said, "while I was in California, I went to see a professor at UCLA to ask about the photos."

"What photos?"

"The photos in Sachiko's stuff."

"Oh, those. I forgot all about them."

"You forgot? I can't believe it. And here I am, hardly thinking about anything else."

"In case you haven't noticed, I've had other things on my mind."

"Touché."

"I'm interested, though. What'd you find?"

"You remember that I was hoping that one of the photos was taken by Admiral Perry's photographer? Well, it turns out it wasn't. It was taken about ten years later. Same shot, but a different type of camera."

"So, it isn't valuable?"

"I wouldn't exactly say it's worthless, but it's not a rare find. Not to a collector, anyway."

"I'd better not quit my day job then," Jessie said.

"No, you'd better not do that. But I'm still waiting to have the other picture authenticated."

"What other picture? Oh, yeah. The one with old Ronald McDonald Whatshisface."

"That's the one. Old Mr. Whatshisface. Well, the guy who could possibly verify it is on sabbatical and refuses to correspond with anyone until he finishes the book he's writing."

"So, I guess you just have to wait."

"Yeah, but when I told the head of my department about all this, he suggested I apply for an internal grant. Maybe I can get a research assistant to help transcribe Sachiko's papers. The handwritten ones are pretty hard for me to read."

"Do you really think you'll find something in her papers?"

"Shall I say I'm cautiously optimistic?"

A squawk came from behind the counter, and Jessie went to get the baby.

. . .

The roof was the perfect spot to watch the August fireworks display over the Shinagawa River. Everyone had gathered for what Jessie hoped would be the first of many parties. Mark and Jimmy were carrying up some tables and chairs, and Yuya was fiddling with their new Costco grill. Danny was sleeping peacefully in the roof's storage shed, under a fan and out of the way. Mr. Suzuki was leaning against the railing, catching his breath after lugging a giant watermelon up the four flights of stairs. And, of course, Jimmy's attention was on the two bottles of French merlot that Mrs. Watanabe had produced from a Hello Kitty shopping bag.

Earlier, there had been a violent thunderstorm, but now the sky was clear. Cicadas on top of the roof's shed, with their high-pitched cry, announced summer would soon come to an end.

Jessie went downstairs to get the steaks out of the fridge.

"Are you finished with the salad?" she asked Ayako, who had been washing and cutting vegetables. "Let's go up."

Jessie switched off the kitchen lights, and they went out the back door to the outside stairwell. "I can't believe we're finally having a party up there. And—" Jessie turned around, surprised that Ayako wasn't right behind her. "Did you forget something?" she called down.

"No," Ayako called back. "I had to take off my shoe. There was a pebble in it. I'll be right up."

By the time Ayako emerged from the stairwell, Jimmy had lit mosquito coils in strategic places, and Yuya had hooked his iPhone to speakers.

Mr. Suzuki asked Yuya to play Latin music, and when Cuban salsa came on, he tried to pull Mrs. Watanabe up from her chair. "Come on, let's dance," he said to her playfully.

But just the idea of dancing cheek-to-cheek, as she kept saying, gave her the giggles, and she refused to stand up.

"Miss Ayako?" Mr. Suzuki offered a bow and held out his hand.

After a fast-paced song, Ayako gasped for breath and pulled away. "I really must go to the gym more often," she said, reaching for a soda and sitting down.

Mr. Suzuki wiggled his eyebrows at Jessie.

"Why not?" Thanks to his expertise, her two left feet barely got in the way, and he whirled her around the roof. She was just getting the hang of it when Danny cried, putting an end to her new Latin maneuvering.

Mr. Suzuki showed everyone the basic steps, and after a few minutes, the three men and the three girls were dancing. Jessie moved along to the music with Danny in her arms. A few songs later, everyone was hot, sweaty, and in need of drinks. Hungry, too. They got the meat and vegetables on the grill, and soon they were loading up their plates.

"Is that all you're having?" Jimmy asked Ayako. "Are you on some kind of diet?"

"It's too hot," Ayako said. "I don't have much of an appetite."

"Heat or no heat," said Jessie, taking a bite of potato salad, "I'm starving. But eventually, I'll have to put on the brakes, or I'll never be able to lose the baby weight."

"I guess today's not the day," remarked Jimmy, pointing at the ear of corn on her plate that was dripping with butter.

"Damn right, it's not," said Jessie. "And he who makes any wisecracks about my weight may end up with a fork in his eye."

"Well, I think you have nothing to worry about," said Mark. "You look great, considering Danny's only a little over a month old.

"And that," announced Yuya, "is how you appease a hormonal woman. He stood and gave Mark an exaggerated bow, making everyone laugh. "Now, some people can obviously eat whatever they want without getting fat. Jimmy, for example. He's a natural string bean."

"Hey, who are you calling natural? I work at my string beaniness!"

"Or others," Jessie added, looking over at Ayako, "save room so they can dig into half a cake later. Genetics," she said with an envious sigh. "It's just not fair."

"It's true," said Ayako. "I'm saving room for dessert. There is such a thing as priorities, you know."

"And I'm," said Jessie, "saving up for the famine. Because when it hits, I'll be ready. You guys will be the first to go, but I'll survive for months and months. Just wait and see."

The fireworks started, and while everyone focused on the bursts of color exploding in the sky, Jessie was thinking that she felt happier than she could ever remember.

CHAPTER THIRTY-ONE

As soon as the girls returned to school in September, Jessie resumed her English classes in the morning with eight more students. Danny wasn't too distracting, and no one seemed to mind if she shoved him under a shawl to give him a snack during the class. In the afternoon, she opened the café for her regular customers. Money was tight, but for now and the immediate future, things were about as ideal as they could be with a six-week-old baby in the house. At some point, she would have to find more paid work, but the pressure was off since the sale of the Chiba house had taken care of the inheritance taxes. Property tax wasn't due for a year, and the goal was to put aside a bit every month for that. If nothing major happened to the building, things were set.

One afternoon while Danny was napping, Jessie was mustering up the energy to do some prep for the next day's baking. The bell on the door jingled, and a man strode in like he owned the place. At first, Jessie mistook him for one of Yuya's apprentices, but he sat at a table and asked for a menu.

"I'm sorry. All I have right now is coffee and tea. Some brownies. That's American-style chocolate cake."

"No spaghetti?" he asked. "Curry rice?"

"Not at the moment. Just drinks and desserts."

He didn't seem like the brownie-eating type, but he ordered one.

The guy looked familiar, and Jessie tried to place him. Having gotten a better look, it was obvious he wasn't one of Yuya's crew. Despite a smattering of acne across his cheeks and forehead, he was too old—nearly forty. His tattoos suggested more than youthful transgressions—full-body tattoos like that usually meant affiliation with a gang.

The man finished his coffee and got up to pay. "You haven't been here very long, have you?"

"Not really. I've been open since May. Took a break in the summer, though."

"I heard the old lady who owned this place died."

"Oh," said Jessie with some surprise. "Did you know her?

"No. But I heard you were the one who inherited it."

Jessie clamped her mouth shut and stonily handed him his change.

"Was that one of Yuya's boys?" asked Mrs. Watanabe, breezing in just as he was leaving. "Because I've got a leaky faucet, and if he's got time, maybe he could—"

"He was a customer," Jessie said.

"Here?"

Jessie understood her surprise. Because of its location, the Butterfly Café wasn't a place people accidentally stumbled into. Jessie felt uneasy for a while, but as the afternoon wore on, she forgot about him.

"Shall I watch the baby?" Mrs. Watanabe asked as Jessie was setting out to run some errands. She was always pleased to take charge of the café but even more delighted if Danny was a part of the deal.

"No, that's okay. The fresh air will do him good."

Jessie went to the bank and then the post office before picking up a few things at the supermarket next to the station. As she was heading toward home, she saw the same man who had been in the café earlier leaning against the wall and smoking a cigarette. A plume of smoke swirled over his head as he flicked ashes onto the sidewalk. She turned to go back in the other direction, but then she saw Ayako walk straight up to him.

That made Jessie recall where she had seen him before. He was the man Ayako had been arguing with on the street the day of her party. She watched them from behind a pachinko parlor sign, and it wasn't until her feet marched her over that her brain caught up to ask what the hell she was doing.

The guy muttered a few words, threw his cigarette on the ground, and walked off.

Jessie turned to Ayako and said coldly, "What nice friends you seem to have. Although, I admit I was surprised to have him as a customer this afternoon. I was even more surprised that he seemed to know all about Sachiko. All about me inheriting the café. Gee Ayako, how could he possibly know any of that? Unless *you* told him?"

Ayako's cheeks flushed, and she stared at the ground like a high school student being scolded by the teacher for smoking in the bathroom.

"Are you involved in some kind of scam?" Jessie demanded.

Ayako shook her head vigorously. "What? No! Certainly not."

"Then what's going on?"

"There are some things I must talk to you about."

"Like about that guy?"

"Shall we go to the café?" asked Ayako. "I don't want to talk about this here."

Jessie's voice was steely, and a hardness gripped her features. She wasn't about to budge without an explanation. "I'm not going anywhere until you tell me. Who was that man?"

"He's my cousin."

They walked back to the café in silence. Mrs. Watanabe was playing solitaire and waiting for her friends to arrive for their afternoon gossip session. Daisuke was at his usual spot, hunched over his computer and typing furiously. Jessie and Ayako moved to the back table where they could have some privacy.

Taking Danny out of the sling and jostling him in her lap, Jessie said, "You told me you didn't have anything to do with your family."

"I don't. I hadn't seen them in years. Not until recently. Not until my father's funeral in January."

Jessie fixed her eyes on Ayako, her jaws clamped together. She wasn't about to make this easier for the woman she thought was her friend. Just what had she been cooking up with that cousin of hers? Had Jimmy been right about Ayako all along?

"Maybe it's best to start at the beginning," said Ayako.

"Yes," said Jessie. "Why don't you do just that?"

Ayako raised her chin and spoke as if she had prepared her words in advance. "Well, the beginning is like this. My mother's family was a typical middle-class family. Normal. Well, normal for Kyushu, anyway. My grandfather was a high school math teacher— one of those typical old-fashioned Japanese men. Powerful. My grandmother was a typical old-fashioned Japanese wife. Sweet as can be, but also obedient and subservient. My mother was an only child. A wild one. She rebelled. She got in with the wrong crowd. And then she met my father. My father's family couldn't have been more different. They were—well, it's obvious, right? Yakuza."

Ayako waited for Jessie to nod before continuing. "It's not like in the movies. That's all mostly made up. But they were involved in stuff you find in every city. Prostitution, gambling, and drugs. Maybe other things as well. I don't know..." Ayako's voice had begun to quiver. "I'm sorry. May I have some water?"

Still holding Danny, Jessie went to the sink behind the counter, and while filling a glass, it dawned on her that she had been wrong about Ayako's background. Her family weren't *burakumin*. They weren't untouchables—they were from a completely different sort of undesirable class: gangsters. Jessie set the water down and watched Ayako pick up the glass and carry it to her lips with shaky hands.

"Anyway, my mother became with child when she was seventeen. My grandfather disowned her. Because what would it look like if he, a high school teacher responsible for the moral welfare of his students, couldn't control his own daughter's morality?" Ayako stared at the table, and the following words came out in a rush, almost as if everything needed to be said in one breath. "By the time my mother was twenty-one, she had three children. My older brothers and me. When I was twelve, she got uterine cancer. She passed on within nine months. Just nine months. And she was gone. I was alone."

Ayako looked up at Jessie and blinked back tears. "It was hard. Not just losing my mother. But growing up like that. You can't imagine what it was like. When I was in elementary school, everything was okay. I was a normal girl. But junior high was awful. My teachers were awful. They treated me terribly. And there was no reason for such treatment. My brothers were indeed troublemakers, but I wasn't like that at all. I was a good student. I was smart. I didn't have to study much to get perfect test scores," she said without a hint of pride. "But the teachers' cruelty wore me down. Their determination to put me in my place because of my family was just too much to bear. By the time I was in ninth grade, I'd given up. The only thing I was interested in was English. And reading. In both English and Japanese. I read everything I could get my hands on. But now you can see why I didn't attend high school."

"Surely you could've found one where the teachers would've been better," said Jessie.

"You have to pay for high school," said Ayako. "It's not compulsory. And it certainly wasn't a priority in my family. We were expected to start earning. And whenever I talked about getting an education, my brothers would smack me on the head and tell me not to get bigger than my boots. I ended up joining the family business. In a noodle shop."

That surprised Jessie. She would have thought it to be something far more sinister.

"It wasn't an ordinary noodle shop, mind you," said Ayako. "It was a front. You know, a legitimate business to hide the other stuff. My uncle owned it. He was smarter and more ambitious than my father. But a lot meaner. I'm pretty sure he was working for a bigger boss, who was working for an even bigger one. I guess," Ayako added with a humorless laugh, "you could say it was a kind of elaborate pyramid scheme for criminals. Well, I worked there for a couple of years. One day, I overheard my uncle telling someone that he had a niece who would make a good wife. That was me. You see, my father had gotten into some difficulties with an associate. And my uncle thought that doing a bit of matchmaking to bring the families together would be a win-win situation for everyone. I was eighteen. A perfectly good age to get married, as far as he was concerned."

"Could he have forced you to marry someone you didn't want to?" asked Jessie.

"At the time, I believed that he could. I ended up stealing money from the cash register, and I came to Tokyo. I admit it," Ayako said, jutting her chin out. "I was a thief."

"But—"

"Stealing is bad enough, but I embarrassed my uncle. I returned the money within a year, but I still had to pay for what I did. That's why my cousin was here to see me. To work out a deal. To wipe the slate clean, so to speak."

"But—"

"I know what you must be thinking. If I had stolen my uncle's money, I must have stolen Sachiko's jewelry as well. You probably think that was how I got the money to start my business."

That hadn't occurred to Jessie, but after Ayako pointed it out, it seemed quite obvious.

"I can prove I didn't take it. When I was pregnant with Natsumi, I found a picture of Sachiko in the society section of an online newspaper. I printed it out, thinking that maybe someday my baby would want to know about her family. I forgot all about it until I came across it the other day when I was cleaning. She's wearing a big diamond pin. And diamond earrings. That picture was taken months after Sachiko told me to disappear. *After* I bought the stocks. You can check. I told you the truth about the jewelry."

"But why didn't you say anything about that picture before?"

"I'm telling you now. I only found it last week. To be honest, I had completely forgotten about it."

"Is that why Sachiko paid you to go away? She found out about your family being—"

Ayako looked surprised. "How could she know that?"

"Um, I don't know. Maybe she hired a detective? People did that all the time before." Jessie remembered Mrs. Watanabe's words and added, "To make sure no one was from an undesirable background."

"I suppose that could explain—"

Just then, four of Jessie's afternoon regulars burst through the door, eager for their hour of freedom from their husbands. "Oh dear," Jessie muttered.

"Do you want me to hold Danny?"

Thirty minutes ago, she would have preferred handing him over to Cruella de Vil. "Sure."

Jessie put on a smile and went to get the women's orders. By the time she was back, Danny had fallen asleep. She extracted him from Ayako's arms, put him in his bassinet, and sat down.

"I need to tell you the rest," said Ayako. "While I still have courage. You already know that I went to my grandmother after I became pregnant. She was a widow then. I never loved anyone else in my life as much as her. Outside of Natsumi, of course. We were a family. I thought she'd be with me for a long, long time. She wasn't old like my grandfather. She was fit and healthy. But she was hit by a taxi when she was crossing the road. It was an accident. The driver took his eyes off the road for a second, and it happened. Just like that." She reached into her bag, pulled out a floral handkerchief, and dabbed at the tears forming at the corners of her eyes. "I can't blame him. Or hate him. It could've happened to anyone."

"Oh, Ayako," Jessie murmured.

"By then, I had my esthetician license and had started a small business. But I couldn't bear to stay there any longer. I sold it and moved back to Tokyo. And there was the money from the taxi driver's insurance company. As if that could compensate for our loss," Ayako said bitterly.

"Mrs. Jessie?" Mrs. Iwao was calling loudly. "We have a question for you!"

"Wait a sec," Jessie said with a groan. "I've got to go see what they want."

Jessie returned after refilling the women's water glasses and offering a quick opinion on whether it would be better for them to take a trip to Hawaii or Guam.

"And there you have it. The background," continued Ayako, as if Jessie hadn't left the table.

"Background?"

Ayako nodded. "There's more. Last year, my father got sick. Liver failure. It's common for men like that."

"He was an alcoholic?"

"Well, he was a heavy drinker. That is true. It's also likely that his tattoos contributed to his disease. That's something most people don't know. If you cover your body with tattoos—your skin can't breathe, and your body can't rid itself of toxins. And then the liver could get damaged. Anyway, when my father passed on, I went to his funeral. There was a truce between my uncle and me those two days."

"Truce? But I thought you said you'd paid the money back."

"I did. But not the interest."

"Interest?"

"Maybe interest isn't the best word. Maybe a fine? A kind of punishment fine? Wait. I know. Restitution. That's it. Restitution." Ayako smiled wryly when she came to the right word. "Anyway, in the end, I got off rather easy. Probably because I was family and probably because I was nothing more than a young, foolish girl when I acted so impulsively. But I told my uncle I'd do whatever it'd take to be right with the family again. Not because I want to reunite with them or anything. I want to be free from them. But I don't want to have any of what I did fall back on Natsumi someday. Maybe you can't understand, but criminals tend to have a long memory. Anyway, it was decided that I'm to give my uncle two million yen. That was what I'd been negotiating with my cousin about. They investigated and found out about my salon. And, I admit, about the Butterfly Café. But they also learned I had no stake in it. Just my own salon. I'll pay what I owe and close the door on my youthful transgression."

"Mrs. Jessie," called Mrs. Iwao from the cash register. "We're leaving."

Jessie rang up their order. Daisuke was packing up his computer and papers, so she waited for him to pay as well.

"There's more," Ayako whispered when Jessie returned. Her eyes were glued to the table.

For the first time that afternoon, Jessie felt fear rather than anger. "What is it?"

Ayako swallowed hard, and her whisper was almost inaudible. "I have cancer. Cancer," she repeated, her voice a little stronger. "Just like my mother." Ayako took a deep breath and looked out the window. Her voice grew stronger and took on a practical tone. "I was diagnosed last year. I had a hysterectomy, but it didn't help."

"Cancer." Jessie felt her lips move, but no other words came out.

"Now they tell me it's back. Stage 4. They tell me that chemo or radiation would only prolong my life for a just little while. They said I'd feel sick and that it would ruin the time I have left."

"So, that was the health scare you told me about," Jessie said softly. "The one that you said made you want to change your life. It was a lot more than just a scare, wasn't it?"

"You have to know that after the surgery, there *was* hope. At least, I was hopeful. I wanted to believe things would be better. I thought I was strong enough to overcome it. But now…"

"I- I don't know what to say."

"I need to go into the hospital for a few days," Ayako whispered. "And I can't leave Natsumi alone."

"Natsumi can come and stay with us," Jessie said immediately. And then it dawned on her that Ayako was actually asking for much, much more.

. . .

That night, Jessie couldn't even begin to think about sleeping. For once, she didn't mind Danny's fussiness. Trying to calm him down provided a good excuse to pace the apartment and think about that afternoon. She hadn't noticed Ayako's transformation from slender to skinny to downright bony until her gauzy scarf had slipped off her shoulder today, revealing an ultra-thin neck and a deeply chiseled clavicle. Jessie now saw the dark circles under Ayako's made-up eyes. She remembered all those times Ayako had joked about being out of shape and needing to get to the gym more.

Danny let out a shrill cry, and Jessie was tempted to do the same. Life was so unfair. So fucking unfair! So fucking unpredictable! It was now crystal clear why Ayako had been so eager to become friends—she was working on her exit strategy. Jessie couldn't blame her for that, though. What would she have done if she needed to find a total stranger to look after Miya?

But Jessie and Ayako weren't exactly strangers. Not anymore. And Natsumi wasn't just any kid, either. She was her children's sister.

Jessie went downstairs after Danny finally fell asleep. The peanut butter bars in the cookie jar were tempting, but overdosing on sugar would just make her feel worse. Instead, she measured flour and water and yeast and slapped around a hunk of dough, pretending that it was the sole thing responsible for turning everyone's lives upside down. Waiting for it to rise, she made a pan of coconut bars. And then she put together a triple batch of chocolate chip cookie dough to keep in the freezer. She could have continued indefinitely, but running out of flour halted the baking activities.

Before going to bed, she sent a message to Jimmy and Yuya. *Are you guys around after the girls leave for school and before my English lessons at 10:30? It's really important.*

After a bit of consideration, she messaged Mark, too.

.   .   .

The next morning the blinds were drawn, the banana muffins on the table were untouched, and everyone's coffee had turned lukewarm.

"Bloody hell," Yuya finally said.

"I always figured something was going on with Ayako," said Jimmy. "But I never imagined anything like this."

"She didn't come right out and ask me to take Natsumi. But I know that's what she wants." Jessie picked up her coffee and took a sip. "But I don't see how I can. I can barely manage as it is. I'd help out. I'd definitely do that. But I can't be Ayako's permanent solution. There's no way, right? Natsumi will have to go to Ayako's family. That's all there is to it. They're her blood." As soon as those words were out of her mouth, she cringed. "I sound just like my mother."

"Ayako's family raised her. She survived," said Yuya. "And I guess so would Natsumi."

Jessie turned on him. "Survive! Is that going to be Natsumi's fate? To just survive?"

"There's also foster care," he ventured.

"Strangers?"

"Maybe that would be better than her family."

"But what would Miya and Danny think when they grow up and learn that I sent their sister off to be raised by strangers? Or, I don't know which is worse, thugs?"

Mark cleared his throat. "Jessie, what would you do if you were in the same position as Ayako?"

Jessie exchanged glances with Jimmy and Yuya. "We made arrangements. After Kiyoshi died. After Yuya got custody of Kizuna and after I knew I was pregnant." A moment later, she added, "I guess I'm a bit like Ayako. I don't want my kids to go to my family. They aren't criminals or anything like that, but I wouldn't want them to be brought up the way I was, either."

"So, you're lucky then," Mark said. "You guys have each other."

"Yes. We're lucky," Jessie replied.

CHAPTER THIRTY-TWO

"I-I brought chocolate chip cookies," stammered Jessie when she and Danny went to see Ayako at her salon a week after she got out of the hospital. What a difference. Ayako's face had become gaunt, her complexion gray, and her hair lank. "Are you sure you have time to go out for lunch, or are you too busy with your clients?"

"Oh, Jessie," Ayako said with a sad smile. "I'm not dealing with clients anymore. I'm not a good spokesperson for beauty treatments. I'm just doing the paperwork in the back room."

At a nearby restaurant, they ordered the ladies' lunch set. Ayako took only a few bites of the salad and left her quiche mostly untouched. Jessie wolfed hers down because Danny could wake at any minute, destroying any opportunity for eating in peace.

"Thanks for keeping Natsumi when I was in the hospital. I hope she wasn't any trouble."

Jessie didn't tell her that Natsumi had spent most of the weekend on Miya's bed surrounded by a pile of unread comic books, acting as lethargic as if she had caught a nasty cold. In the evening, they watched *The Sound of Music*. Jessie, sitting between the girls, put her arms around them. Miya snuggled into her mother, her eyes on the von Trapp children as they climbed trees in their new outfits made from curtains. Natsumi quietly moved to the floor and sprawled out on a cushion. Jessie was pretty sure the girl was aware that something terrible was happening.

Jessie wanted to tell Ayako that Natsumi was welcome to come and stay any time and that she didn't have to worry about her daughter. And that was true. At least partially. For short-term stays, Jessie was more than happy to have her.

The waiter came to collect Jessie's empty plates, and Ayako slid hers across the table. "Please take mine away as well."

Jessie began to speak. "Um, Ayako—" But just then, Danny woke up. She reached into the stroller, pulled him out, and kissed his head. She felt tremendously relieved because she had no idea what she was about to say.

Several weeks later, Ayako collapsed at Ebisu Station and was taken to the hospital in an ambulance. When it was uncertain how long she would have to stay this time, Ayako asked if Jessie could arrange for a temporary school transfer for Natsumi. Jessie agreed. That was the least she could do until something more permanent could be decided. When she went to Ayako's apartment to get Natsumi's things, she found boxes neatly packed and labeled: photos, keepsakes, books, and clothes. It was as if Ayako knew she wouldn't be coming home.

That night, Jessie listened to the girls talking while making dinner.

"Where's your mother?" Kizuna asked with her characteristic bluntness.

"In the hospital. I think she's going to die soon."

Jessie pushed aside the cucumber she had been slicing and set down the knife. She went into the living room, sat on the sofa, and put her arm around Natsumi. The girl stiffened, but after a moment, she rested her head on Jessie's shoulder.

Miya and Kizuna watched Natsumi with sad faces, and Jessie's heart ached. Both had experienced the loss of a parent, one way or another, and she felt a surge of protective love for all three of them.

When Jessie's dad called a few days later, she found herself pouring her heart out. He was never one for practical advice, but he was always a good listener.

"So, she has no family," he said.

"She does. But they don't seem to be good people."

"She chose you because she thinks you are a good person."

"She chose me because there's no one else."

"It would be a lot of responsibility for you, honey. Not just for a day or a week, or a month. It would be for years and years."

Jessie sighed. "Years and years."

"So why haven't you told her yet that you can't do it?"

Jessie stopped to think. Why hadn't she?

"Have you thought about the rewards you might get out of it?"

"What do you mean? Good karma and all that crap?" she said with more of a bite than intended.

"Well, that, too," he said thoughtfully. "But what benefits would you have from having a third child? The joy? The happiness?"

"I don't know," said Jessie.

"Or, maybe you can think of it another way. What sadness would you have if you raised your two children, knowing that you might've had three? How would you feel if that little girl ends up unhappy somewhere else when you know she could've been happy with you?" After a long silent moment, he added, "I guess you don't have to decide right now, do you?"

Jessie nodded into the phone. But she would have to decide soon.

. . .

The next day, Ayako took a turn for the worse, and she messaged Jessie to come without Natsumi. Just before going into her room, Jessie was stopped by the doctor.

"May I ask, what is your relationship with Miss Nagai?"

"Um, it's kind of hard to explain…"

The doctor repeated his question in English when Jessie's voice faded.

"My husband was the father of her child."

"Then, I suggest," he said, scraping his finger through a dandruffy scalp, "that he make arrangements to come and see her as soon as possible. She has an infection. She may not have much time if we can't stop it."

Jessie was quite shocked by his abrupt manner. "Not much time?"

His bulbous eyes studied the chart in his hand. "So, where is he?"

"Who?"

"Mrs. Nagai's, um…Miss Nagai's…her daughter's father."

"Oh. He's dead."

The doctor looked up, putting on a humanlike expression for the first time.

"I've been looking after her daughter."

"I see. Who'll take care of the paperwork?"

"I'm sorry," Jessie said, shaking her head. "I don't know."

As if on cue, a man in a dark gray suit materialized right in front of Ayako's door. He had fierce eyebrows, which were contradicted by a rather warm smile. "Are you Mrs. Yamada?" he asked in slow Japanese while pulling out a business card. "I'm Hiroshi Fujita, Ms. Nagai's lawyer. I'm here to make the arrangements. I want to speak to you. But first, I'd like to talk to the doctor alone, if I may."

The doctor led him to one of the small meeting rooms near the nurses' station. Jessie went into Ayako's room and sat down. After a moment, Ayako whispered Jessie's name.

"I'm here." Jessie took Ayako's hand.

Ayako could barely talk. "I…"

Jessie was shocked by the sour smell venting from her friend's mouth. "Shush. Don't talk. This is just a little infection. The antibiotics will get you back on your feet. You'll be fine."

Ayako closed her eyes and drifted into a drug-induced sleep. The lawyer came in, and when it was evident that Ayako wouldn't be waking up soon, he suggested they go to the hospital's coffee shop.

"Mrs. Yamada," he said before the waitress even brought their drinks. "The situation is not good. Ms. Nagai is very concerned about her daughter." Jessie swallowed her guilt like it was a giant nasty pill and let the man continue. "But there is one thing. She wants her daughter's name placed on the Yamada family register."

"Does that mean adoption?" asked Jessie.

"No. But it gives her a family name—a recognized father. As a foreigner," he said without judgment, "it might not seem so important. But it could be of great value to Natsumi later when she looks for a job or wants to get married. This country still has many conservative people, and the family register is an important document."

"I'll need to check with my lawyer," Jessie whispered. "But I don't have any objections to that."

.   .   .

The infection cleared up, and Jessie brought Natsumi to see her mother. Ayako was sitting up in bed and wearing makeup. After an hour, her face became pinched with pain, and she didn't protest when Jessie suggested it was time to leave.

Natsumi barely spoke for the rest of the day.

A week later, Jessie slipped out of Ayako's room to buy sandwiches at the hospital's convenience store. When she returned, two men were standing over Ayako's bed. From their tattoos, she figured they were her brothers.

"Thank you…for coming…all this way." Each of Ayako's breaths was labored.

"When did you get sick?" the shorter one was asking in the kind of rough language Japanese men use when speaking to an inferior.

"Last year."

"You look just like Mama," said the taller one, "right before she died."

"Why did you call?" asked the shorter one, a frown on his face. "Is it money?"

Jessie stood by the door and watched Ayako struggle to speak. She seemed to have shrunk even more with her brothers looming over her. The shorter one pulled out a cigarette and flipped it around in his fingers before tucking it behind his ear.

"How are your families?" Ayako managed to ask. "The children?"

"Fine," said the taller one. "The kids are troublemakers at school, but what can you expect when the teachers are a damned bunch of—"

The shorter one interrupted impatiently, making it clear that he was the boss in this family. "So, where's the kid?"

"At school," said Jessie, still standing by the door. "Natsumi's at school."

He spun around. "Who're you?"

"I'm Jessie."

He gave her a dismissive nod and turned back to his sister. "How old is she?"

"Eight."

"How long do the doctors think you have?

Ayako shook her head, her eyes full of sorrow.

"And the kid?"

"I—"

"What is it you expect us to do?" he demanded.

Ayako sank back into the pillow and closed her eyes. She inhaled a ragged breath and tried to speak again, but that seemed too much of an effort.

The brothers exchanged rapid words in a dialect Jessie couldn't follow. The shorter one shook Ayako's shoulder, and when she opened her eyes, Jessie caught a glimpse of fear in them. That sick and still afraid of her brothers. In a flash, Jessie saw what Natsumi's life would be like if she went to live with those people.

"What about a government home?" said the taller one, not unkindly. "We've already got enough kids as it is and—"

Jessie felt her spine stiffen as her temper simmered to a boil. She marched over to the bed, elbowed the brothers out of the way, and took Ayako's hand. "The only home Natsumi is going into is mine." She glared at the men, thinking she could punch their lights out if need be. She was *that* angry. "Natsumi's coming with me."

"Who are you again?" asked the shorter one.

"I'm the one who takes Natsumi." There was a fierceness in her voice she had never heard before.

Ayako's eyes bore into hers, and Jessie nodded. She was a hundred percent certain. She was going to adopt Natsumi. She was going to have three children, and hell would freeze over, as her grandmother always liked to say, before letting these people get their hands on Ayako's daughter. She wouldn't go into foster care either. She would stay with her brother and sister.

They would be a family.

. . .

A few days later, Jessie sat beside Ayako's bed while her lawyer and Ayako's lawyer hashed out many details.

"We will sign these papers now," Ayako said to Jessie while the men were talking. "But they take effect when I die."

Jessie nodded, unable to speak. Ayako sounded much better than she did a few days back, possibly because the weight of worrying about Natsumi had been lifted off her fragile shoulders.

Ayako's lawyer handed Jessie a pen and pointed at every spot she needed to fill. Jessie's hand shook so badly when writing out her address in Japanese that she had to start over again on a new document. Three times, in fact, because just like when she filled out the death certificates for Kiyoshi and Sachiko, no mistakes were allowed.

Twenty minutes later, the adoption papers were packed away. Mr. Fujita pulled out a different file. "The next issue for us to discuss is money."

Ayako closed her eyes and let him do the talking. He explained that Ayako had sold the salon three months ago. Even though it was a profitable business, it involved hands-on management, and the running costs were high. There were employees to deal with, up-to-date equipment to buy, and bank loans to negotiate.

"I had no choice," murmured Ayako, her eyes still closed. "I needed to sell. For Natsumi."

Jessie reached for her hand and leaned in so Ayako wouldn't have to speak up. "That's okay. I understand."

"Ms. Nagai," explained Mr. Fujita, "used the money from the sale to buy the apartment she and her daughter had been living in. The owners went bankrupt, and there was a foreclosure. Ms. Nagai now owns the apartment outright, but I will manage it as a rental property and hold it in trust until Natsumi is twenty-two. After that, she could live there or sell it."

Ayako coughed weakly, and Jessie held a cup of water to her lips. After taking a sip, she sank back and closed her eyes. "Use the rent money," she whispered. "To pay for—"

Jessie put her finger on Ayako's lips and squeezed her hand. She vowed never to touch Natsumi's money. They would survive without it.

. . .

Three days later, the hospital rang at four in the morning, urging Jessie to bring Natsumi right away. Because Jessie had been expecting this call, she was prepared. She called Jimmy to come stay with Miya and get her off to school in the morning, and she sent a hasty message to Natsumi's teacher. She got Danny fed, dressed, and set the bag she had packed the day before next to the door.

The moment Jessie shook Natsumi's shoulder, her eyes flew open. "Is it Mama?"

"Yes. We have to go to the hospital now."

She strapped Danny into the car seat, buckled Natsumi up, and drove off in the chilly dark, arriving at the hospice ward a little before five. On their way to Ayako's room, she passed a young couple in the waiting lounge with a small dog in a carrier, their faces ashen. They were at the hospital at that ungodly hour for the same reason: to say goodbye to someone they loved.

Ayako, looking like a ghostly caricature of herself, was barely conscious when they quietly entered her room. She opened her glassy eyes and gave a weak smile. Natsumi looked frightened and moved behind Jessie. But after her mother motioned for her to come, Natsumi forgot to be afraid. She kicked off her shoes and climbed up next to her. Jessie settled in the chair by the window, thankful that Danny was still sleeping soundly in his stroller. A little while later, she heard Ayako whisper that she loved Natsumi.

Those were the last words Ayako would ever say.

After a long period of silence, Natsumi got out of the bed.

"Are you hungry?" asked Jessie.

"Uh-huh." Natsumi bit into a sandwich that Jessie had handed her. While chewing thoughtfully, she said, "Mama told me to call you Mommy. Or Mom. But never Mama."

Jessie didn't trust her voice, so she just nodded.

The morning passed, and Jimmy and Yuya arrived after lunch to take Danny out for fresh air.

"We'll be close by," Jimmy said as they slipped out of the room.

Fifteen minutes later, Natsumi became her daughter.

CHAPTER THIRTY-THREE

Jessie had assumed that Ayako's funeral would be small since she said she didn't have any close friends. But there were plenty of people: her staff from the salon, suppliers, and clients. A few mothers from Natsumi's former school.

And Ayako's brothers. They wore somber clothes covering most of their tattoos. Jessie was surprised that the wives looked as ordinary as they did and not more like mobster molls. In black funeral wear, the two middle-aged women offered standardized condolences to Natsumi as if she were an adult stranger and not the grieving child of their sister-in-law. But Jessie also saw them eyeing the line of mourners waiting to sign the guest book and to leave a monetary envelope at the reception desk. They whispered together, and Jessie imagined they were talking about how their sister-in-law must have been a much bigger person than they had thought.

Jessie had left Danny with Mrs. Kikuchi and Mrs. Iwao, and she stayed right next to Natsumi in the front row during the Buddhist service. Yuya, Jimmy, and Mark sat with Miya and Kizuna in the row behind. And next to them were their de facto grandparents: Mr. Suzuki and Mrs. Watanabe. When the service was over, Jessie's arm wound around the little girl as she stood sobbing by her mother's casket. The mourners filed past, bowing to the uncles and aunts and then to Natsumi. One by one, lilies were laid across Ayako's body as each person said a final goodbye. A small shuttle bus then took the brothers, the wives and Natsumi and her new family to the crematorium.

A year earlier, Jessie had no idea what to expect at a Japanese funeral. She had stumbled around her husband's and his grandmother's in utter shock. Knowing what was to come this time didn't make it any easier. She placed a photo of Ayako and her daughter, taken last spring under the cherry blossoms, into her friend's hands. The priest chanted some more, and the funeral parlor worker shut the casket and bowed deeply before the conveyer belt took Ayako away. Jessie felt as if cracks were forming under her ribs. Her heart was breaking, not just for herself, but also for Natsumi.

It would take some time before Ayako would be returned in the entirely altered physical state of ashes, so they were led to a lounge next to a room filled with rowdy old men from a different funeral making good use of the provided beer and whiskey. Ayako's brothers and their wives also drank up, but Natsumi's team stuck with soft drinks.

A while later, Jessie went to the bathroom. Just as she was about to flush, a tipsy woman who had come in after her began talking. "You know what?" she said to the person with her. "To be honest, I never knew that Kenji's sister had done so well for herself."

Jessie's hand froze on the handle.

The woman continued. "He never said anything other than the fact she got herself knocked up and had a baby and worked as a hairdresser or in a massage parlor or something. I always wondered if it was a soapland."

"It'd have to be a pretty high-class soapland," cackled the other, "judging by all the stylish people there today. Did you see the diamond on that one gaijin's hand?"

"Goes to show men never know what's going on."

"Ain't that the truth? I told Shinji there was no way I'd take in another brat when it's bad enough with the ones we already have. But that gaijin said she'd take the kid. Can you believe that? No skin off my nose as far as I'm concerned."

"But you'll never guess what Kenji just told me. There's a will. He and Shinji are supposed to go talk to the lawyer about it tomorrow."

"A will?" The woman's voice grew with excitement. "Maybe we'll get the money, and the gaijin will get the kid."

The other woman exploded with laughter. "Maybe fairy tales do come true."

Jessie flushed the toilet, stepped out of the stall, and washed her hands. Before leaving the bathroom, she turned around and said in Japanese. "You'd better hurry. The final ceremony is about to begin, and it wouldn't be right for you to be late."

The look of embarrassment on their faces for being caught talking like greedy bitches was priceless.

That evening, after everything was over and done with and the kids were asleep, Jessie went downstairs. The guys were slumped at a table in the back. They had already finished one bottle of wine and were working their way through a second.

"How's Natsumi doing?" asked Yuya.

Jessie shook her head and set Danny's baby monitor on the table between them. "She won't leave the tatami room. She wants to stay next to her mother's urn. I got a futon out and told her she could sleep there, but she could get in with me later if she wanted. Or with Miya."

"Poor kid," said Mark. "I can't imagine what's going through her head right now."

"Thanks," Jessie said to Jimmy after he poured her a glass of cold barley tea. She raised it. "To Ayako." They drank in silence, and Jimmy asked if she wanted more when her glass was empty. She shook her head and said with a sob, "I can't help but think where Natsumi would be if I hadn't—"

"She's safe," said Mark. "She's *here*. With you."

Jessie remembered what had happened in the bathroom at the crematorium, and as she recounted the story, everyone laughed long and hard—as if it was the funniest thing they had ever heard.

"I wish I could see the look on their faces when they find out what's in the will," Jessie said, wiping tears out of her eyes. "Mr. Fujita said Ayako needed to give them *something*, so they can't contest the will. It's just twenty thousand yen for each brother. Everything else goes to Natsumi."

"Brilliant," roared Jimmy.

Their laughter faded away when they remembered that Ayako was gone, and after a moment, Jessie pushed back her chair. "I'd better get back upstairs in case she needs me."

.   .   .

The next night, Natsumi insisted on sleeping in the tatami room again. Toward midnight, Jessie went to check and found the girl sobbing quietly under the quilts.

"Do you want to come and sleep with me?" Jessie whispered, kneeling beside her.

Natsumi grunted a no.

"Do you want me to get in with you?"

There was no reaction, so Jessie eased herself under the quilts. Natsumi didn't pull away, and they lay side by side until Natsumi's breathing slowed and became a soft snore.

Jessie woke up to find the girl's legs tangled with hers.

On Monday morning, Miya and Kizuna left the house as usual, but Jessie kept Natsumi home. She hesitantly asked Natsumi if she wanted to go get the rest of her things, and from the way the girl's face lit up, that was clearly a yes.

Jessie closed the café, and they spent the entire day in Natsumi's previous home. Not because anything needed sorting—Ayako had taken care of pretty much all that. But that day, while Danny crawled about, Natsumi talked and Jessie listened. Natsumi described how she and her mother would go to the bakery down the road on Sunday morning to get bread for breakfast while it was still warm. About the word games they played while cooking dinner. About how the toilet got plugged up after Natsumi tried to flush a small stuffed rabbit down it when she was still in kindergarten. Some of her stories were bigger. Like when she realized that her mother was not merely sick but was going to die. Jessie planned to write everything down as soon as they got home, knowing that these memories would fade with time. Someday, Jessie wanted to be able to tell Natsumi about her childhood with her mother. Her *first* mother.

On the way home from the station, Natsumi slipped her hand into Jessie's, wrapping it around her heart.

The next day Jessie opened the café, but with few customers, the two of them spent most of the time in the kitchen. She taught Natsumi how to roll out a pie crust, and when Miya and Kizuna came home from school, they sat down together and ate apple pie. When they wanted to play in the park that afternoon, Natsumi went with them. And that night, Natsumi slept with Miya.

On Saturday, they all went to Ikea. For the second time in less than a year, new furniture was picked out for Miya's room. This time, bunk beds.

CHAPTER THIRTY-FOUR

A wistful expression crossed Jessie's face when she looked out the window and saw Mark approaching. Since Ayako's funeral several weeks back, he had been checking in every day to see if she was okay. A couple of times, he served coffee to customers and washed a cup or two when the café was busy. He helped the girls with their homework and even took Danny out in the stroller once so Jessie could get some messy chores done.

She found herself leaning more and more on him and asking his advice for this and that. Unlike Jimmy, who liked to tell her what to do and how to do it, Mark generally let her go on until she talked herself into the decision. And she knew by the look on his face when it was a good one. He had a different sort of look for when something might need a bit more consideration. He was the best listener *ever*. Except, she thought, smiling to herself, when he got going in professor mode. Then the best thing to do was to just sit back and watch him move his lips. She wished she could attend one of his university lectures and stare at him for an entire hour without worrying about being creepy. She always had to watch out for that—no sense in scaring the poor guy away because of her silly crush.

"Come on in," she called out as he opened the door. "I was just getting ready to close up. Come in and keep me company."

"Hey, big feller!" he said to Danny, pulling him out of the playpen and onto his lap. He laughed when the baby tried to grab his nose and suck on it. Turning to Jessie, he said, "I know it's a big weekend for you with the memorial services and all. Are you going to be all right?"

Jessie nodded. "Yeah, I think so. It's hard to believe that it's been a year. The girls are excited about going on a road trip, but they don't really understand what it's all about. Not even Miya. She barely remembers her father from when he was alive, let alone the accident."

Jessie wanted to change the subject because there was something she was dying to tell—something that had only been finalized that morning. "But listen," she said. "I've got some good news for a change. Do you remember my friend Sue? From the girls' elementary school?"

"The one whose husband teaches at West Omori High School?"

"Yeah, her. Well, guess what? She told me the English teacher at the high school is leaving at the end of the school year. Guess who went to an interview there this morning? And guess who scored a job starting in January?"

"Hey, that's great!"

"It's not full time or anything. Just two mornings a week. But because I have a California teaching credential, they said they might hire me full time if they expand their program. Benefits and all!"

"Wow! And at my alma mater, too!"

"It wouldn't be right away. There's quite a bit of red tape, so if they do expand their international program, it wouldn't be for a couple of years. But that's perfect. I don't want to work full time while Danny is so small. But from April, it'll be six hours a week. Mrs. Watanabe can watch Danny for me. It's so close that I can be home in five minutes if there's an emergency."

"That's really great," said Mark. "Well done!"

"I'm so relieved to get some regular income. I mean, it's great to have English classes here, but private students are so fickle. All gung ho about learning English one minute, and then the next, it's all about tap dancing. And— Oh, shit!" Jessie grabbed a towel behind the counter as Danny projectile vomited all over Mark.

"It'll wash," he said, gingerly handing Danny back.

Jessie, watching the stain spreading across his cream-colored cashmere sweater, wasn't so sure about that. "I guess it could've been a lot worse. It could've been—"

"That'd wash, too." He dabbed at his sweater with the towel Jessie had given him. He handed it back, and she tossed it into the laundry basket that was behind the counter. After she cleaned the baby up, she put him in the playpen with his toys.

"Anyway," Mark said, as if getting puked all over was no big deal. "I have some news of my own. I got that grant from my university, so I'll be able to hire a research assistant to transcribe Sachiko's letters and diaries. Why don't we have dinner together to celebrate your new job and my new grant? Maybe next week or the week after?"

"That's rather brave of you, considering what happened last time."

"Are you planning on giving birth before the evening is over again?"

Jessie laughed. "I can offer a personal guarantee that won't be happening again. Ever. The thing is, I can leave Miya with Jimmy and Yuya. But it's harder to leave the baby. And it's even harder to take him to a restaurant now."

"Well, how about I fix dinner at my place and you bring him? You've seen it. It's not much bigger than the playpen, so he could crawl around to his heart's content. And you may not know this about me, but I make a pretty mean enchilada."

"Enchilada! How can I say no to that? But are you sure? I mean, Danny just ruined your sweater."

Mark chuckled. "I'm sure."

. . .

The following morning, Jessie, Jimmy, Yuya, the three girls, and the baby piled up in one of Yuya's larger company vans while it was still dark. The girls fell back asleep, and they had two hours behind them by the time they stopped for breakfast. Despite their trip's solemn purpose, it became a holiday. They sang songs, played I-Spy, and told funny stories. When they reached the mountainous area, Yuya stopped to put chains on the tires. Early snow had transformed the landscape into a winter wonderland.

Mr. Kanemitsu rushed out of the inn to meet them as they piled out of the van. Even though Jessie had reserved rooms for six people and a baby, he still seemed surprised by how much Jessie's family had expanded. He wouldn't have known the reference, but they had turned into a modern version of that 1970s TV show, *The Brady Bunch*. Miya, with a somewhat sketchy memory of exactly what had happened a year ago, recalled there had been puppies. Before Jessie could tell her they wouldn't be puppies any longer, she ran to check. The mother had a new litter, so things were pretty much the same, after all.

The girls and Yuya changed into warmer clothes, borrowed sleds from the inn, and went to play on the hill behind the main building. Jimmy, Jessie, and the baby went to the temple to finalize the arrangements for the service. Taka's mother, who probably thought she made a regular habit of turning up for funeral ceremonies in inappropriate attire, had all of her dead mother-in-law's funeral outfits laid out for Jessie to pick from. But this time, Jessie was fully prepared, right down to the black tights, black pumps, and black handbag. When everything was over and done with, she planned to put them in the back of the closet, where she hoped they would remain for a long time.

The next day, they visited the graves when the ceremony was over. Jessie had Miya and Natsumi lay flowers at the Yamada headstones. Then she introduced the newest members of the clan to the resident ancestors, even the Okadas. They may have been a bunch of bigwigs in their day, but from the dilapidated look of things, it seemed like it had been quite a while since any of their direct descendants had paid a visit. Jessie took one of the floral bouquets and laid it down by their headstone. As her mom liked to say: blood was blood. The family may have hated it when Kiyoshi's grandfather bought a grave for his mistress right next door, but at this point, it seemed like the gaijin and her kids were about all they had.

"Ready to go back?" Jimmy asked, shivering in the wind.

"You guys go ahead. Just give me a few minutes."

Jimmy took Danny from her arms and headed toward the temple where tea, cakes, and a warm room were waiting.

Jessie straightened the flowers at the Yamada grave. When the others were out of earshot, she whispered, "Thank you, Sachiko. For everything. Not just the café and place to live but also the neighborhood. The community."

Jessie hoped that Sachiko knew how grateful she was. If it hadn't been for her, Jessie would probably be back in California, living with her parents, working to pay off Kiyoshi's debts, and trying to prevent Miya from becoming thoroughly indoctrinated by the church school. Jessie couldn't even begin to imagine what Natsumi would be doing now if it weren't for Sachiko. She would probably be in foster care. Or worse, with those bitchy sisters-in-law of Ayako's.

Feeling Kiyoshi's presence much more here than she did at their butsudan at home, she spoke as if he were sitting right on top of the headstone. "Maybe I'll never know why you did what you did. All your lies. Your secrets. Your gambling. Maybe it was your mother's death. Maybe it was like Mr. Suzuki says—Sachiko spoiled you. And maybe it was your unknown DNA. I don't know. And to be honest, I don't care. Not any more."

The anger that Jessie had been harboring toward him since the day he died lifted from her heart. True, she would be financially secure if it weren't for his gambling debts. She wouldn't have to worry about every crack and leak in the building. About taxes, her kids' schooling, or, far down the line, her old age.

But none of that money stuff mattered. Not really.

"Kiyoshi," she said. "You'd be surprised at how well we're doing. And you know what else? I've decided to be happy." She started toward the temple, but after a few steps, she turned around. "And I won't feel guilty for being happy, either." With a wavering voice, she added, "I love our children. Even your other daughter. She's my daughter now. I promise I won't let the kids forget you."

When she caught up with Jimmy, he asked, "Are you okay?"

She just nodded and linked her arm with his.

That evening, Taka and his father came to the inn for dinner, this time with his mother as the designated driver. The priest robes had been discarded, and like last year, Mr. Kanemitsu had a heavy hand when it came to pouring booze for himself and his drinking buddies. Jessie turned on her phone to record them when they started reminiscing about the Okadas, thinking they might spill something useful for Mark. It didn't take long for them to become incoherent, so she soon switched it off. Mr. Kanemitsu stumbled off to bed close to midnight. Yuya and Jimmy carried Taka, who had passed out, to the car. Taka's father was belting out a Barry Manilow song at the top of his lungs as his wife got him in and buckled up.

Jessie said goodnight to the guys as they headed off for a midnight soak in the outdoor hot springs. Mr. Kanemitsu's teenage daughter, who had been keeping an eye on the kids, was asleep on the tatami floor of their room. Jessie switched off the TV and gently shook the girl awake. She protested half-heartedly when Jessie pressed a couple of thousand yen into her hands but left the room with a big smile on her face. The kids were dead to the world after all the day's excitement, so she sat by the window and watched the twinkling stars over the darkened mountains until she felt drowsy. Before crawling into her own futon, she straightened the girls' twisted covers. Natsumi muttered something and rolled onto her stomach, filling Jessie's heart with quiet joy.

When she woke up the next morning, she saw Mark had sent a text. *When do you think you'll be back?*

Depends on traffic. Maybe 5 or 6, replied Jessie.

Can I come by? I want to talk to you.

Jessie frowned as she typed. *Anything wrong?*

I found something in Sachiko's stuff.

What is it? I'm curious!

Mark sent some funny emojis and wrote, *You have to wait and see.*

CHAPTER THIRTY-FIVE

The drive back from Nagano took forever because of heavy traffic. It was nearly ten-thirty when Jessie got the girls settled into bed. *Sorry, we got back so late*, she texted Mark. *If it's too late, we can meet tomorrow.*

His response came immediately. *Are you too tired for company?* *Not really.*

I'll be there in five minutes.

"Did you run here?" she said when he flung open the door, gasping for air.

"Kind of." He headed straight for Danny and pulled him out of the playpen. "Hey there, champ. This time I'm ready for you. I've got on a puke-proof tee shirt today." Danny squealed with delight when Mark tossed him up in the air.

"You think you may be as prepared as a Boy Scout," warned Jessie. "But here's a spit cloth just in case."

Mark's eyes glittered as he sat down with Danny on his knee. "Remember that picture we found in the storage unit? The one I thought might be Ranald MacDonald with some young samurai? You know, the guy who shipwrecked himself off the coast of Japan and—"

"Yeah, I remember. Did you get it checked out by that guy who was on sabbatical or something?" Jessie felt proud of herself for remembering that detail.

"It's even better. I'm now certain that the guy in the pictures *is* Ranald MacDonald. And 'how,' you may be asking yourself, do I know that without getting it authenticated? Because there are letters!"

"Letters?"

"Letters! I didn't see them because they were tucked away inside some other papers. I took those papers out last night, and there they were. Three hand-written letters. All signed by Ranald MacDonald."

"But how do you know for sure they're from him?" asked Jessie. "Isn't MacDonald a pretty common name?"

Mark handed Danny back to Jessie, pulled his iPad out of his backpack, and showed her an enlarged image of the letter. "MacDonald *is* a common name, but just look at who they're addressed to."

Jessie read the name aloud, no recognition in her voice at all.

"I guess the name Tatsuichiro doesn't ring a bell. He's not famous like Einoske Moriyama."

"Who?"

"He was the Chief Dutch Interpreter," Mark said, launching straight into professor mode. "MacDonald's most famous student. Moriyama was involved in the negotiations between Commodore Perry and the Shogunate. That was one of the most significant moments in Japanese history because—" Mark cut himself off and gave a guilty laugh. "Anyway, it looks like MacDonald wrote letters to his *other* student, Tatsuichiro Shizuki." He pushed his iPad across the table, pointing at the youngest samurai in that picture that had been in one of the boxes they had found in Chiba. "I think that's him. He was just seventeen when MacDonald was his teacher."

By then, Danny had drifted off to sleep and was weighing heavy in Jessie's arms. She laid him in his bassinet behind the counter and squinted at the letters again.

"That fancy penmanship is pretty hard to decipher," Mark said. "There's stuff about the Bible. About doing good. About walking in the light. Salvation through social work. Typical Christian missionary discourse from that era." Mark zoomed in and enlarged the print. "But here's what I think you'll find interesting. Look at this part here. He's writing about someone named Ujitada Hoshina."

"Who?"

"I've no idea. Nothing came up on Google. But it looks like that Hoshina guy was arranging for a group of men from Nagano to study at some Christian college in Illinois. I can't make it out because that part of the letter is smudged. But don't you see? That might be the connection with the Okada family. I might find the link if I go backward with what we know about the Okadas and forward with what's written about Tatsuichiro."

"So," said Jessie, trying to interpret what Mark had just told her. "There're two things here. The biggest, for you anyway, is finding hand-written letters from Ranald MacDonald. Right?" Mark nodded, and she continued. "And the other is the possibility of finding something about Kiyoshi's ancestors. And that could be a big deal for my kids."

"That pretty much sums it up," said Mark.

"You know what?" said Jessie. "I believe that this calls for a celebration. I'm sure Jimmy's got some good wine stashed somewhere."

"Well, I'm certainly in the mood to raise a glass to good old Ranald MacDonald and his students," said Mark.

Jessie found a bottle of Merlot under the counter and poured two glasses. They sipped the wine in silence, which felt amicable and comfortable. They smiled at each other over their glasses.

Later, Jessie couldn't remember exactly how the kiss had happened. One minute, they were both sitting on their sides of the table. The next, they were leaning toward each other. It was as if a magnet was in charge of her head, and it wasn't until her lips were fastened to Mark's that she was jolted back to reality.

She pulled back and saw the disbelief on Mark's face. Oh, crap! What had she done? "Oh, Mark. I'm so—"

Before she could apologize, blame the wine, or try to make light of what had just happened, Mark tossed his glasses onto a table. He pulled her to the back of the room, away from the windows, and enveloped her in his arms. His mouth came down on hers, hard and unrelenting. After what might have been a few minutes—or possibly an hour, Jessie's chest was heaving, and her knees were wobbling. Mark nudged a chair out from a table with his leg and tugged her into his lap. Once again, the two were entwined. Jessie felt his heart beating nearly as fast as hers through his shirt. Somewhere at heart attack level.

Mark pulled back and looked into her eyes. "I've been wanting to do that for the longest time."

"The longest time?" Jessie repeated, her lips struggling to function after the workout they had just had.

He looked like he was about to get started again, but Jessie needed to stop things before they went any further. "We can't do this, Mark," she said with a determination she didn't feel. "What about Kumiko?"

Mark pulled back. "What does she have to do with anything?"

"I can't do this to her," Jessie whispered. "I'm sorry. I'm not that kind of person."

"What in the world are you talking about?"

"You know. You and Kumiko."

"Me and Kumiko?" It took a couple of seconds before he realized what Jessie was getting at. "Me and *Kumiko*! Why would you ever think *that*?"

If Jessie's face was going to turn any hotter, it ran the risk of bursting into flames. "Because she's Ms. K?"

"Who?"

"Your g-girlfriend?" Jessie's voice sounded like coarse sandpaper.

"What girlfriend?"

"You told Miya about Ms. K that night you came over for dinner. And I thought…" If Mark hadn't been holding onto her so tightly, Jessie might have escaped out the door and never returned, kids or no kids upstairs.

After a couple of seconds, Mark began to laugh. "Oh. That Ms. K. You thought Kumiko was Ms. K?"

Jessie gave the slightest nod.

"Kumiko's my colleague. And friend."

"Friend?" Jessie repeated, streaks of crimson painting her cheeks.

"She's American. Japanese-American, actually. We're the only two Americans in the department, so of course, we became friends." Mark was still laughing and shaking his head when he reached into his pocket and pulled out his phone. "Here. This is me and Kumiko in California."

Jessie stared at the picture of Mark standing next to a stout, gray-haired woman in her fifties.

"We're friendly, I'll admit it. But not *that* friendly."

"You never said…" Jessie didn't know how to finish the sentence and still sound halfway intelligent.

"I guess I do talk about Kumiko a lot. I wanted to bring her over to meet you, but she's not that sociable. And to be honest, she doesn't like kids. But somehow, I thought you *knew* that Kumiko was just Kumiko. I had no idea," he added, laughing even harder, "that you mixed up Kumiko with the infamous Ms. K. Who, I believe, I mentioned only *one* time. And that," he said in a way to let Jessie know it was a joke, "was just to answer your snoopy daughter's question."

"So, Ms. K—"

"She was a woman I was seeing for a little while. Only about three months. And that was a couple of years ago. I haven't heard from Kaori since she started teaching in Kyoto right after we broke up."

"You aren't with anyone?"

Mark snorted. "Now, when would I have the time for that? I've been spending all my time *here*. In the Butterfly Café. With *you*. Haven't you noticed?"

"I—"

Mark put his finger over Jessie's lips. "It's *you* I've been wanting. It's *you* I've been waiting for. Don't you know that?" He stroked her hair and looked at her with his delicious brown eyes. "I wanted to tell you how I felt, but how could I? Not when you were going through such difficult times. I almost said something the night of the festival. But Danny was just a newborn. It was too soon. And then, after that, there was all that stuff with Ayako. Besides," Mark added, "I wasn't sure if you liked me. Like *that*. I thought that maybe I was just another Jimmy or Yuya for you. A friend."

"I was afraid you'd stop coming around if you found out I had a crush on you."

"You had a crush on me?"

Now, the whole thing seemed funny. "You have no idea," said Jessie. "It was something terrible."

"The thing is, I decided that I was going to tell you how I felt in January. It would have been more than a year after your husband died. A decent amount of time in the traditional sense. And if I was wrong and you didn't have feelings for me, it wouldn't have ruined your holiday. But," Mark added with a teasing voice, "there you were tonight, leaning across the table with your lips all puckered up. So, what's a fella to do but go with the flow?"

"My lips were not all puckered up!"

"Yes, they were. Totally puckered and totally irresistible." Mark lifted her chin and kissed her again. And again.

Jessie wanted nothing more than to drown herself in his kisses, arms, and body. But there was that other thing. "Mark," she whispered between kisses. "What about my kids?"

"What about them?" he said distractedly, concentrating now on her neck.

"Well, to start with, I've got three."

He pulled back. "I can count, you know."

"What if things don't work out between us? What if my kids get used to you being around, and then you leave?"

"Ah, Jessie," he said, her name sliding softly from his lips. "I'm not planning on doing that."

"Maybe not now. But there's no guarantee—"

"There's no guarantee with anything. You know that. Does that mean you don't even want to give us a try?"

"The thing is, my kids need stability. You know what they've been through. What's going to happen when you decide you want to have kids of your own? Because there's no way I'd go for number four or five—" Jessie stopped. What was she thinking, fast-forwarding from a couple of kisses to having babies together?

"I do want kids."

"So, you can see—"

"But it's you I want. *You.* You've got kids. I want kids." Before Jessie could respond, Mark pulled back and drank in Jessie's eyes. "You know, the night Danny was born was the most profound experience of my life. That night, I wished that he was my son. That I was his father. And," he whispered. "I still do, to be perfectly honest."

Jessie's heart completely and irreversibly melted. "Can we take it slow?" she whispered.

"I've waited this long—I can wait longer. Until you're absolutely sure."

"What I mean by waiting," Jessie said carefully, "is not telling anyone. The kids. Jimmy and Yuya."

"You mean you want to keep our relationship secret?"

She paused to savor the word relationship. "For now. I need to get used to the idea of—well, the idea of us."

"Us," Mark repeated.

Jessie looked at the floor and took a breath. "It's late. I need to put Danny to bed. Upstairs. You can come with me if you like."

"Does that mean—"

"Yes. But you can't stay all night. Is that okay?"

CHAPTER THIRTY–SIX

Three afternoons later, everyone was in the café putting up the six-foot Christmas tree they had gotten at Costco back in September when the thermostat was still pushing ninety. After the lights were strung, the adults sat at one of the tables with mugs of tea and watched the girls hanging the ornaments.

Jessie hadn't said anything, but it was exactly a year since she had discovered she was pregnant. She could vividly recall the roller coaster of feelings that day. Alone, pregnant, and certain she would never be able to survive with a baby on top of everything else. Now, she couldn't imagine life without Danny. Suddenly, she had two kids. And then three. Four, if you counted Kizuna, which she did.

A year ago, she had never dreamed a man like Mark would come into her life. Just thinking about last night made her feel weak in the knees. She had confessed that when they first met, she fantasized about him being one of those sexy cowboys from the romance novels she read as a teenager. Then, he confessed that he actually had a cowboy hat he had bought on a whim when he was in Arizona. Boy, did they have fun with that little scenario last night. Her eyes met his, and she could tell he was thinking about the same thing. She cleared her throat and gathered an armful of plates to take to the kitchen. Mark followed a few seconds later with a tray of glasses. They set everything into the sink and slipped outside the backdoor into the wintry night.

"I feel like I'm having a clandestine affair with the neighbor's wife," Mark whispered as he pulled Jessie close, as much for warmth as for passion.

"But we said—"

"I know. I promised to keep us a secret. How will I survive when I want to shout out to the world: This woman's mine!"

"Hey, Jessie!" Jimmy was calling from the kitchen. "Where's the long extension cord?"

They sprung apart.

"It's in the pantry," Jessie called back. "Next to the box of light bulbs."

"You'd better go in first," Mark whispered. "I need a minute to recover."

After the Christmas tree was up in all its splendor and the adults were chatting at one of the tables, Mark put a friendly arm around Jessie's shoulder and said, "Hey guys! We've been waiting to tell you this, but we've got some exciting news." Before Jessie had time to shoot him a look, he added, "Guess what we found in Sachiko's stuff!"

"Oh, yeah! Guess what?" said Jessie, catching on. Mark gave her a hint of a wink, and she almost burst out laughing. The sneaky devil would pay for this later!

"Exactly what kind of stuff are we talking about here?" said Yuya.

Mark told them about the letters, which were almost certainly from Ranald MacDonald, and gave his theories on how all that might be connected to the Okada family. "Everyone in my department is talking about my discovery—"

"Even Kumiko?" interrupted Jessie coyly.

"Yes, even Kumiko," Mark replied in all seriousness. "And I spoke with a publisher who said they were interested in getting a proposal from me. If all goes well, maybe I can turn it into a book. So, take that old sourpuss Yamamoto Sensei!"

"The guy who tried to block your promotion last year?" asked Jimmy. "The one who wanted to take away your seminar classes and make you teach freshmen English?"

"That's the one. The idiot who's been publishing the same paper over and over again in a different form for ten years. You should've seen his face when I announced my finding to the department."

"I guess you showed him a thing or two," said Jessie, beaming with pride.

Jimmy laughed. "You're acting like you made the discovery."

"I guess," Jessie retorted, "in a way, I feel I did. After all, whose idea was it to have Mark look through the stuff in the first place? Huh? And good thing I did too because otherwise, the place would still be a mess, and you never would've been able to move in."

"True, true," said Yuya, laughing.

After dinner, the topic shifted back to planning their first Christmas together in the Butterfly Café.

Jessie lowered her voice so the kids wouldn't hear. "You know, when I invited Mrs. Watanabe for Christmas dinner, she was horrified."

"Horrified?" asked Jimmy. "Why in the world would she be horrified?"

"Since we're still in mourning for Ayako," said Jessie, "we're not supposed to be celebrating anything."

"Well, technically, she's right," said Yuya. "No New Year's cards. No New Year's food. No saying 'Happy New Year' on January 1."

"Christmas isn't something you just cancel," said Jessie. "But Mrs. Watanabe seemed to think that Natsumi would feel we had forgotten her mother if we went ahead with our holiday plans. So, I brought up the subject with Natsumi to see how she felt."

"And?" asked Jimmy.

"The poor kid didn't have a clue what I was going on about," said Jessie, laughing.

"I'm not surprised," said Yuya. "What child knows about any of that funeral stuff, anyway?"

"Right? I just changed the subject, and now it's full speed ahead with Christmas."

"Look. Don't worry about it too much," said Jimmy. "She'll survive. Mrs. Watanabe, that is."

"It's important to make your own family traditions," said Mark. "New beginnings and all that."

"That's right," said Jessie absentmindedly. Suddenly, all she could think about was climbing onto Mark's lap and kissing him until neither of them could think straight. She pushed those dangerous ideas out of her mind before she did precisely that.

"And besides, didn't Ayako buy all those presents for Natsumi?" asked Jimmy. "And write the letters?"

"Yes. One for each birthday," said Jessie. "And Christmas. Until Natsumi turns twenty-two. Mr. Fujita is keeping them all for her."

They fell into a gloomy silence that ended when Danny started to cry. But before Jessie needed to get up to calm him, Kizuna shook a rattle in front of his face. With a look of surprise, he grabbed it and shoved it into his mouth.

The adults laughed, and the easy conversation returned.

The next afternoon, Mark was sitting across from Jessie in the café. His hands were where they belonged but not where either of them wished them to be. "How long before we can tell anyone?" he asked.

"It's only been a week," she said in a neutral voice, glancing over at her afternoon regulars, who were happily arguing over who had the worst husband. Today Mrs. Uchida seemed to be the winner because hers had decided that dry cleaning was too expensive, so he shrunk her favorite cashmere sweater by washing it with the towels.

"I'll have you know, it's been one week and two days." Mark held up his iPad and pretended to show her something.

"Let's give it six weeks." Jessie leaned in, pretending to take a look but actually to inhale his aftershave.

"Six weeks," he said, nodding. "Okay. But six weeks from today? Or six weeks from…you know."

"Six weeks from…you know," Jessie replied with a giggle. "If you decide you can still stand me after that much time, we'll tell people."

"What if you decide you can't stand me?"

"I'll take that into consideration."

The women were finished for the day and eager to get home before their husbands created more domestic mischief. She rang up their bill and escorted them to the door.

"Are you leaving, too?" Jessie asked Mrs. Watanabe, who usually lingered until the girls got home from school.

"It's Taro's birthday. I'm making him a special dinner."

"Well, that's nice," Jessie said. "I'm sure he'll be pleased about that."

Danny was sleeping soundly behind the counter, and Jessie called to Mark. "I've got some heavy things to move around in the back. Would you mind giving me a hand?" She flicked her hair behind her shoulder and sauntered toward the kitchen.

"I suppose I could do that." He scooted the chair back slowly and followed. As soon as the door closed behind them, they were in each other's arms. When Mark lifted Jessie's skirt, she pulled back. "What if someone comes in?"

He left her skirt alone but kissed her mouth, neck, and breasts.

Oh, what the hell! They had already christened the stairwell between the café and the apartment and the storage shed on the roof. Why not the pantry? She pulled him in and shut the door.

The next five minutes in cramped darkness were intense, and after, she couldn't find her panties. She stumbled out and peeked into the café. Danny was still sleeping, unaware of the gymnastics his mother had just been up to. No customers had wandered in either, thank goodness. She went back to hunt for her underwear, which she found behind a giant bottle of vinegar.

"Does that mean we aren't on for tonight?" Mark had a satisfied grin plastered across his face.

"It certainly does not," she said, wagging her finger at him.

Jessie had no idea how much fun secrets could be.

When the girls burst in ten minutes later, Mark was supposedly working on his laptop at one of the tables. Jessie was behind the counter on her laptop, also supposedly working. But what they were really doing was sending sexy messages back and forth. Jessie closed her computer and went to hug each girl. Danny woke up and squealed for attention, knowing how much fun it was when his sisters were around.

Jessie sliced the persimmons Mrs. Watanabe had brought over that morning and cubed some cheese. She set everything out and suggested the girls get their homework out of the way. "We'll be eating down here tonight since your dads will be late. And maybe we can watch a movie if there's time." She turned to Mark. "You're welcome to stay if you like. If you don't have anything better to do. It's just curry. And a Disney movie."

"Let me check," he said, looking at the calendar on his computer. "Well, it turns out I'm totally free. But is your curry spicy? Because that's how I like mine, you know."

Jessie glanced over at the girls, who weren't paying attention, and then laughed.

The next morning, Jessie was straightening out the pantry—another place in the Butterfly Café she would never again see in the same light—when she spotted a shopping bag. She pulled it out to take a better look. It was filled with those party dresses of Sachiko's that she had brought back from the storage unit in Chiba last summer. They smelled musty, and she was about to throw them away. But the frilly dress on top caught her eye. She carried it all up to the roof and hung the clothes and beaded and sequined bags in the sun to air out. She would bring all that out on Christmas Eve morning to help take the girls' minds off Santa and the presents they would be getting.

What a ridiculous notion that was! They would be beside themselves with excitement. Honestly, Jessie could hardly wait.

CHAPTER THIRTY-SEVEN

Christmas Eve arrived, and the café had been abuzz since morning. Jimmy took over the kitchen and booted everyone else out. He barked out instructions, expecting whoever was closest to comply like a marine recruit would to a drill sergeant. Jessie had already been to Mt. Fuji Fruit and Vegetable Parade twice that afternoon— once to buy a lemon and the other time for carrots. No complaints on her part, though. Both times Mark tagged along, and they put the baby in the stroller and took the long way home.

Upstairs, the girls were playing dress-up with the clothes Jessie had given them earlier. They had decided to provide the after-dinner entertainment by putting on a play. From what Jessie could tell from the elaborate scenes Kizuna was making on poster paper, it would be a hybrid of a dozen Disney movies.

Unlike Jimmy's previous Christmas dinners that continued for hours, with each course paired with exquisite wine, this year would be different. They would start eating at five. Instead of searching the internet for culinary masterpieces involving dozens of steps, he spent several weeks poring over Jessie's grandmother's recipe collection. This year it was going to be a good old-fashioned Christmas fare. Of course, no one said a peep about last year's fiasco when Miya and Kizuna turned their noses up at the brandied figs, the smoked salmon mousse, the oyster stuffing, and the honey-glazed Brussels sprouts.

Mark and Yuya pushed the tables together to make one long seating arrangement and covered them with a red tablecloth. The green and white candles and the white plates provided a festive atmosphere. Mrs. Watanabe and Mr. Suzuki were excited yet slightly apprehensive about having Christmas without a whipped creamed-covered sponge cake and Kentucky Fried Chicken. The girls wore matching black velvet dresses Jimmy's mom made from a Simplicity pattern she had used for her daughters when they were little. With leftover material, she even made a tiny jacket for Danny.

Wine flowed for the adults, and there was sparkling grape juice for the kids. The turkey, roasted to perfection, was brought out. The mashed potatoes, dressing, gravy, candied carrots, beets, spinach salad, and fluffy homemade dinner rolls were passed around the table at least twice. Everyone ate until they could hold no more.

The girls went upstairs to prepare for their performance. Even though the adults groaned over how much they had eaten, they were eyeing the desserts on the counter. Everyone, including Mr. Suzuki, who had probably never done such a thing in his entire life, carried their plates to the kitchen, scraped the leftovers into the garbage, and dropped them into a sink full of sudsy water.

It was showtime. Wine glasses were filled again, and the chairs were moved back. The audience sang along when requested to do so. They cheered for the swashbuckling hero. They booed the villain, and they hurrahed the rescue of the princess. After sword fights, a combination of dragon/magic carpet flight, and a near-deathbed scene, the princess finally reached her quest. She found the pirate's treasure: a golden ring containing all the world's magical powers.

When the performance was over, the girls received a standing ovation. Then everyone dug into dessert: pumpkin pie, minced meat pie, and slices of the heavy homemade fruit cake Jimmy's mother had also sent. When Christmas dinner was over, it was uniformly agreed that no one would eat for a week.

After Mr. Suzuki and Mrs. Watanabe left, Jessie turned to the girls. "Well, kiddos. It's time for you to get to bed. Otherwise, Santa won't be able to come, and we can't have that, can we?"

They no longer believed in Santa, but they certainly believed in presents. Without any argument, they headed up the stairs with Jessie on their heels. She knew they would giggle together far into the night, especially with Kizuna sleeping over. But if you couldn't get overexcited at Christmas, when exactly could you?

While rocking Danny to sleep, Jessie texted messages and sent some pictures to her mom and Tom, her dad, and her sister. She would call everyone tomorrow when it was Christmas Eve in California. She sent photos of the evening—not just of their biological grandkids but of the whole family. Her dad, she knew, was okay with her communal living. No surprise there. But her mom was still adjusting to Jessie's new lifestyle. The gifts they sent to Miya and Danny arrived in early November but had probably been purchased in August. It wasn't their fault for leaving Natsumi out, especially since they didn't know they had a new granddaughter until after Ayako's funeral and Natsumi's adoption was a done deal. Jessie went out and bought a present for Natsumi, writing her mom and Tom's names on the gift tag. Her dad's gifts would arrive in January or February, judging by previous years. It wouldn't matter much because they were always a random jumble of stuff, anyway.

Jessie scrolled through all the other pictures she had taken. There were some nice shots of Mrs. Watanabe and Mr. Suzuki with the kids, but they made her feel a little sad. Maybe she could put aside enough money to take the kids to see their real grandparents next year. As crazy as they were, they were still her family.

She studied the photos of her and Mark standing next to each other and wondered if anyone else would be able to see the happiness in her eyes. Her parents would definitely approve of him even though his Episcopal background may not be as churchy as Tom would like. But still, that would be a whole lot better than having an avowed atheist like Kiyoshi in the family. Anything, even being Episcopalian, would be better than that.

Jessie laid Danny in his crib, slipped the baby monitor into her pocket, and went to check on the girls. They were shivering in their underwear and huddled over a comic book.

"What on earth are you doing? Why aren't you in the bath?" Jessie scolded in a fake, angry tone. "Do you think Santa will come if you act like this?"

"Sorry," said Natsumi in English.

Jessie smiled. In just a few months, the girl would be bilingual. "Hurry up now! You don't want to catch a cold and miss the fun tomorrow." Then she noticed the necklace around the girl's neck. "What's that?"

"It was in Grandma Sachiko's bag of stuff." Natsumi spoke in Japanese this time.

"Let me have a look." Jessie undid the clasp and held the necklace in her hand. She turned to Kizuna. "Wh-what about the magic ring? Can you show it to me?"

Kizuna dug around in the pencil container on Miya's desk and pulled out an intricately carved man's ring. It was so ornate it looked fake during the play. Looking closely at it now, Jessie could see that it was anything but.

"Is there any more like this?"

Miya picked up a large black and gold sequined bag on the floor next to the bottom bunk bed. She removed a velvet pouch from the side pocket and handed it to her mother. Jessie poured its contents onto the desk, and her eyes nearly popped out of her head. In front of her lay a brooch with a sapphire the size of a quail's egg. Another one was quite similar, but this one held a huge emerald. There was a diamond ring that must have been at least four carats. Heavy gold chains. Diamond earrings—the screw-on type. A heavy gold bracelet. A double strand of pearls—each the size of a marble. A watch with at least a hundred diamonds in the band. Among other things, there was a gold Charles and Diana commemorative coin from their wedding.

Jessie stared at it, speechless. The girls must have thought this was costume jewelry, just like what she and Miya had sorted through last winter. That had to be why they hadn't said anything about it. Besides, they knew nothing about Sachiko's missing jewelry.

"Okay." Jessie scooped everything back into the bag. She mustered up a normal voice and announced, "Bath time. And come say goodnight to everyone when you're done."

Downstairs, the guys were sipping cognac and dipping into the box of Godiva chocolates Mr. Suzuki had brought.

"Um, guys?" Jessie clutched the handrail of the staircase. She could barely operate her voice, let alone her feet. In danger of toppling down the stairs, she took them one at a time.

Mark looked alarmed and jumped up. "What's wrong?"

"Bloody hell, mate. You look like you've seen a ghost," slurred Yuya, who was slightly to the left of tipsy. "You okay?"

Jessie moved her mouth, but no sounds came out.

"Are you having some sort of heart attack?" asked Jimmy.

Jessie shook her head and stumbled to the table. "Th-this was in the b-bag of play clothes," she managed to say while pouring everything out. "That bag we brought back from Chiba. It must've been sitting in that storage shed in Chiba for years. And then it was in my pantry. For months! I almost threw it out! Can you imagine? Two days ago. I almost threw it all away! Oh my god, you guys—"

"You're hyperventilating." Mark pressed Jessie into a chair. "Put your head down between your knees. Breathe in. Out. Again."

Jessie wanted to say that she wasn't the fainting type, but that did make her feel better. "Tonight's play," she said, still gasping. "No wonder it was all about pirate treasure."

Jimmy scooped up a handful of the jewelry and let it fall through his fingers. "This is a treasure, all right. No other words for it."

"Bloody hell," said Yuya, who had immediately sobered up. "So, Sachiko had it all along."

"But why," said Jessie, "would she ever send such valuable jewelry out to Chiba in a bag of old clothes?"

"Do you have the bag it was in?" asked Mark. "Those people out in Chiba said Sachiko never visited them, but maybe the delivery receipt is still in it. Maybe you could find out when it got sent."

"I threw it away. But I don't remember seeing any delivery receipt in it."

"But it had to be after Sachiko paid off Ayako," said Jimmy. "Remember that society page photo Ayako had in her stuff? The one where Sachiko was wearing the jewelry?"

"That's right," said Jessie. "I've got that picture somewhere. But if I remember correctly, she was wearing dangly diamond earrings. Probably those right there. And that looks like the broach that was pinned on her dress."

"This stuff has to be worth a fortune," said Mark. "Every diamond in that watchband must be a quarter carat each."

"I guess this explains that great big safe in the closet," said Yuya.

"But if Sachiko had the jewelry all along, why would she accuse Kiyoshi of taking it?" Jimmy asked.

"Mrs. Watanabe said Sachiko had changed after having a fall. Maybe that made her forget what she had done with it." Jessie stared at the pile of glittering gems and shook her head in disbelief. "I suppose we'll never know what really happened."

"But does it matter?" said Mark. "At least now you know your husband didn't take it."

"You're right," said Jessie. "It doesn't matter. And I *am* glad to know that."

"Try some on," suggested Jimmy. "Let's see how it looks."

Jessie picked up the four-carat diamond solitaire ring. It would look impressive on her hand, but something was holding her back. "You know what, guys? I'm not the superstitious type, but Sachiko's jewelry has already caused enough trouble." She put everything back into the bag and pulled the drawstring tight. Then a thought occurred to her. "This will complicate my tax problems, won't it?"

Yuya nodded. "It probably will."

"Maybe I should just hide it," she said, panic rising in her voice. "No one has to know. I don't have to tell the tax people anything. And if I don't tell them, they won't know. I can keep it secret."

"You could do that," said Yuya. "But think about this. You could declare it. Sell it. And take the proceeds from a ring or two to pay the taxes. The rest of the money you could put in the bank.

"Even if you had to pay half its value on taxes," said Mark, "there should be plenty left. Maybe enough for the kids' college. For your future."

"For your new roof," added Yuya.

The grownups were interrupted when the girls came thumping down the stairs with their cheeks flushed from the bath. Jessie hugged them and informed them that they were true heroes for discovering a treasure that had been lost. She took the jewelry upstairs to keep with the property-related documents, birth and death certificates, passports, and Natsumi's adoption papers. For the first time ever, she locked the safe.

Downstairs, the celebrations had already started. Jimmy had cranked up the stereo and put on Abba, the girls' current favorite from watching *Mama Mia* a dozen times that month alone. All pretense of getting them into bed at any reasonable hour had gone straight out the window.

"Come on, Jessie," Jimmy said. "Time to dance! This is your song!"

"Idiot!" Jessie laughed, her eyes glistening while she sang "Money, Money, Money" along with everyone at the top of her lungs. When the song ended, drunk with happiness, she threw her arms around Mark and kissed him hard.

Everyone froze.

"Well, I guess that secret's finally out of the bag," Jimmy whispered theatrically to the entire room.

"Are you my mom's boyfriend now?" asked Miya.

Mark looked down at Jessie. "To hell with six weeks," he whispered. To the others, he said, "You bet I am."

And they kissed again.

ACKNOWLEDGMENTS

I'd like to thank the members of the Tokyo Writers Workshop (TWW) for giving me invaluable support, advice, and inspiration. In particular, thanks go to: John Gribble, Tracy Sherman, Sue Brennan, Sean Donovan, Peter Marsh, Elaine Lies, Sarah K. Ellis, Yoshibumi Takahashi, Brandon Lindsey, Nora Ueda, Travis Sullivan, Ryan Davis, Julz Riddle, Jam Kay, Ileana Aponte, Susannah Howard, Melissa McIvor, Bethany Park, Rosemary Kavanagh, Mike Grist, Phillip Johnson, Arvin Yamauchi, David Eves, Ian Priestly, Tom Baker, Greg Strong, Johnny A., and Mars.

I am also particularly grateful to TWW members Karen McGee and Amy Vickers for reading and providing feedback on an early draft of the entire novel. Thank you to other readers of early drafts: Catherine Oshima, Debbie Stone, Patricia Hawley, Melissa Senga, Loretta Hyland, Toni Johnson-Woods, and Necef Yuksel. Your words of encouragement always kept me going. And thanks must also go to Wendy Jones Nakanishi, Rebecca Otowa, and Muriel Ellis Prichett, and Patti Liszkay.

To Suzanne Kamata: Thank you for being such an inspiration over the years! I am tremendously grateful for your encouragement and support.

To Melissa Noguchi: Thank you for not only reading an early draft of the novel, but also for running your eagle eyes over its final version.

I also want to say thank you to Alicia Guercio for providing some extra ideas to add to the story, to Adam Jenkins for technical support and advice, and to Laura Kawaguchi for providing ideas for the book's cover.

To the members of AFWJ (Association of Foreign Wives of Japanese): Thank you support, friendship, and inspiration during the four decades I have lived in Japan. I couldn't have survived without all of you.

Finally, I want to say thank you to my entire family. You have always supported my dreams!

ABOUT THE AUTHOR

Diane Hawley Nagatomo was born in the UK and lived in Nebraska, Spain, Massachusetts, New Mexico, and California before coming to Japan in 1979. She is a retired professor from Ochanomizu University and has written extensively on issues concerning English language education, culture, and gender. While not teaching or writing, she and her Japanese husband of more than 40 years spend time with their six grandchildren. *The Butterfly Café* is her first work of fiction.

NOTE FROM THE AUTHOR

Word-of-mouth is crucial for any author to succeed. If you enjoyed *The Butterfly Café*, please leave a review online—anywhere you are able. Even if it's just a sentence or two. It would make all the difference and would be very much appreciated.

Thanks!
Diane Hawley Nagatomo

We hope you enjoyed reading this title from:

www.blackrosewriting.com

Subscribe to our mailing list – *The Rosevine* – and receive **FREE** books, daily deals, and stay current with news about upcoming releases and our hottest authors.
Scan the QR code below to sign up.

Already a subscriber? Please accept a sincere thank you for being a fan of Black Rose Writing authors.

View other Black Rose Writing titles at
www.blackrosewriting.com/books and use promo code
PRINT to receive a **20% discount** when purchasing.

www.ingramcontent.com/pod-product-compliance
Lightning Source LLC
Chambersburg PA
CBHW050138120726
47903CB00002B/398